PRAISE FOR ST[

THE RESCUE

"Steven Konkoly's new Ryan Decker series is a triumph—an action-thriller master class in spy craft, tension, and suspense. An absolute must-read for fans of Tom Clancy, Vince Flynn, and Brad Thor."

—Blake Crouch, *New York Times* bestselling author

"*The Rescue* by Steven Konkoly has everything I love in a thriller—betrayal, murder, a badass investigator, and a man fueled by revenge."

—T.R. Ragan, *New York Times* bestselling author

"*The Rescue* grabs you like a bear trap and never lets go. No one writes action sequences any better than Steve Konkoly—he drops his heroes into impossible situations and leaves you no option but to keep your head down, follow where they lead, and hope you make it out alive."

—Matthew Fitzsimmons, *Wall Street Journal* bestselling author

"Breakneck twists, political conspiracy, bristling action—*The Rescue* has it all! Steven Konkoly has created a dynamic and powerful character in Ryan Decker."

—Joe Hart, *Wall Street Journal* bestselling author

"If you are a fan of characters like Scot Harvath and Mitch Rapp, this new series is a must-read. Steven Konkoly delivers a refreshingly unique blend of action, espionage, and well-researched realism."

—Andrew Watts, *USA Today* bestselling author

"An excellent source for your daily dose of action, conspiracy, and intrigue."

—Tim Tigner, author of *Betrayal*

"Fans of Mark Greaney and Brad Taylor, take notice: *The Rescue* has kicked off a stunning new series that deserves a place on your reading list. Ryan Decker is a must-read character."

—Jason Kasper, author of *Greatest Enemy*

"*The Rescue* immediately drops the reader into a well-drawn world of betrayal, revenge, and redemption. Ryan Decker is a flawed, relatable hero, unstoppable in his quest for justice."

—Tom Abrahams, author of *Sedition*

"From the very first page, *The Rescue* comes at you like the literary equivalent of a laser-guided missile. Impossible to put down, with explosive action, a great hero, and political intrigue. This one will grab you."

—Joseph Souza, award-winning author of *The Neighbor*

SKYSTORM

Also by Steven Konkoly

Ryan Decker Series

The Rescue
The Raid
The Mountain

The Fractured State Series

Fractured State
Rogue State

The Perseid Collapse Series

The Jakarta Pandemic
The Perseid Collapse
Event Horizon
Point of Crisis
Dispatches

The Black Flagged Series

Alpha
Redux
Apex
Vektor
Omega

The Zulu Virus Chronicles

Hot Zone
Kill Box
Fire Storm

SKYSTORM

STEVEN KONKOLY

THOMAS & MERCER

Text copyright © 2021 by Steven Konkoly
All rights reserved.

No part of this book may be reproduced, or stored in a retrieval system, or transmitted in any form or by any means, electronic, mechanical, photocopying, recording, or otherwise, without express written permission of the publisher.

Published by Thomas & Mercer, Seattle

www.apub.com

Amazon, the Amazon logo, and Thomas & Mercer are trademarks of Amazon.com, Inc., or its affiliates.

ISBN-13: 9781542022644
ISBN-10: 1542022649

Cover design by Rex Bonomelli

Printed in the United States of America

To Kosia, Matthew, and Sophia—the heart and soul of my writing.

CLEAN SWEEP

M/V Aurora Sky
Port of Houston

Ryan Decker emerged from the darkness underneath the cargo container platform and planted his waterlogged boots on the ship's rough metal deck. He scanned for sentries before heading aft toward the looming superstructure. Security lights mounted high on the five-story structure blazed down on the stacked containers, leaving Decker little more than a sliver of shadow for concealment.

A quick look beyond the bright lights confirmed that the sentries on the bridge were not in a position to spot their approach. He set off at a quick but quiet pace, rapidly alternating his attention between the bridge and the deck ahead of him. He was far more concerned about the sentries up high. They'd spot Decker and Pierce the moment they looked down.

Two dark, fast-moving forms would be pretty hard to miss. Especially tonight. Tensions would be high on board the ship after last night's mission. The APEX Institute had gambled nearly everything on the cargo hidden inside these containers and would no doubt defend it to the last man—a scenario Decker was more than happy to facilitate.

But not here on the exposed cargo deck. He continued aft, his boots squishing every time he took a step. They hadn't bothered to change after the swim, opting to save the time and hassle by donning their dry tactical gear directly over the wet suits. Now he started to wonder if the few minutes' delay might have been worth it.

The suits turned out to be more constrictive and awkward out of the water than he had expected. To make matters worse, the tight neoprene layers trapped his body heat, intensifying the effects of this oppressively hot and humid Houston night. Too late to do anything about it now—and they wouldn't be here long enough to get really uncomfortable. He hoped.

Decker glanced over his shoulder to check on Pierce, who trailed him by several feet, rifle covering their six. With Pierce in position, he turned all his attention back to what lay ahead and above him, closing the distance to the superstructure, where they'd take the exterior stairs as far up as possible before entering and making their way to the bridge.

They had almost no information about the size of the security garrison assigned to the ship, which made him want to spend as little time inside the superstructure as possible. The last thing Decker or Pierce wanted was to engage in a close-quarters battle within the tight confines of a ship—against an unknown number of hostile, well-trained operators. The quicker they got to the bridge the better. The bridge had one point of access, which the two of them could control until the helicopter arrived for the extraction.

A body armor–clad man cradling a rifle materialized from about thirty feet in front of him, walking casually toward the guardrail. Decker stopped and tracked the sentry through the holographic sight attached to his suppressed HK416 rifle. The man grasped the top rail with both hands and scanned the water. Decker fired twice, both shots connecting with the man's unprotected head and collapsing him against the guardrail.

A few moments later, a pair of suppressed shots echoed off the containers—Pierce's rifle dispatching someone, somewhere. Decker took off without giving the situation a second thought. Pierce would follow. He was certain of that. The four suppressed shots had been far from silent—and guaranteed to attract the wrong kind of attention from the professionals patrolling the ship.

Decker skidded to a halt next to the dead sentry near the super-structure, grabbing the man's tactical vest and muscling him onto the top rail before he pushed the body over the side. The man splashed into the water, creating an unmistakable sound that was guaranteed to turn heads.

Without speaking, they made their way to the foot of the exterior stairwell, where Pierce turned to watch the deck while Decker ascended the first flight of stairs. He took the metallic steps as quietly as possible with his squishy boots, reaching the first platform seconds later. After checking the circular window on the closed hatch leading into the superstructure and seeing nobody inside, he called to Pierce.

"Clear."

While Decker pointed his rifle up the next flight of stairs, Pierce made his way to the platform, tapping Decker's shoulder when he was in position to guard the hatch. The two of them repeated this process, reaching the second platform as frantic voices called out from below. Decker took a quick look over the guardrail, immediately spotting the body he'd dumped over the side. Two sentries stood where he'd heaved the man overboard, talking excitedly into their radios. Time to speed things up.

He tapped Pierce on the shoulder before bolting for the stairs. Decker skipped checking the hatch when he reached the third platform, immediately mounting the adjacent stairs instead. The quicker they got to the fourth and final platform the better. The bridge lay only one level above that, and they'd need every second they could gain to stay ahead of the security detachment's inevitable response.

"Clear," he said, and Pierce started his ascent.

Decker was halfway up the next flight when he heard the hatch on the platform he'd just departed suddenly swing wide open. He looked back and saw a heavily armed mercenary unexpectedly emerging to block Pierce's path.

Shit!

Part One

Three Days Earlier . . .

CHAPTER ONE

Ryan Decker opened the glass slider and stepped out of the bedroom onto the slate patio, ready to take in a deep breath of the crisp canyon air.

"Your mercenary is here to pick up Riley," said his dad, Steven, startling him.

His dad sat at the table next to the pool, facing the expansive canyon view behind the house. A lone coffee mug in front of him. Decker headed in his direction.

"She's your granddaughter's personal protection detail right now, and we're lucky to have her," said Decker, sitting down next to him. "Where's Mom?"

Steven regarded him with a playful smirk and a raised eyebrow. "Her new yoga class started today. She was out the door before six. We're grabbing some breakfast when she gets back."

"I thought she was going to try kickboxing," said Decker.

"That was the mercenary's idea," said his dad. "Luckily, Harlow talked some sense into her."

"I think Mom would have enjoyed it."

"The last thing I need is your mom hobbling around on crutches from a kickboxing accident."

"Or you laid up in bed from a well-placed and well-deserved punch. Yoga is probably safer for both of you."

"Funny," said his dad, before taking a sip of coffee. "But true."

"I better see why Brooklyn showed up twenty minutes early," said Decker, patting him on the shoulder.

"She's probably sick of chauffeur duty. Nobody to shoot."

Decker glanced through the open slider, catching a glimpse of Brooklyn seated at one of the kitchen island stools—hopefully out of earshot. His parents had a somewhat annoying way of talking about people a little too loudly. Particularly when they hoped to be overheard.

"You really don't like her, do you?" he said quietly.

"It's not that I dislike her. She's not bad or anything," said his dad. "I just don't like her spending so much time with Riley."

"What are you talking about? The two of them hit it off from day one," said Decker.

"That's what I'm worried about," said Steven. "She's not the best influence in my opinion."

"She's a highly decorated former Israeli commando," said Decker. "I'd struggle to find a better role model for Riley right now—or a better bodyguard."

"I'll give you the bodyguard part."

"And the arrangement is temporary," said Decker. "I guarantee you this isn't what Brooklyn had in mind when Harlow offered her the job. I'm guessing she's here to request a reassignment."

Bringing Brooklyn on board had actually been his idea. The bullet that had shattered her knee during the Nevada raid had effectively killed her career as a soldier of fortune. The moment he'd seen the wound, he'd known her days of negotiating brutal terrain and trekking long distances with sixty pounds of gear had come to an unceremonious end.

Giving her a purpose while she recovered from multiple complicated surgeries felt like the right thing to do under the circumstances. And if she decided to stick around and work for the firm, they could do a lot worse than a combat-proven Shayetet 13 commando—with a slight limp.

"Speaking of Harlow, she hasn't been around much since we moved in," said his dad. "Is everything okay? I hope your mom didn't piss her off."

Brooklyn caught his attention with a quick nod. He flashed her a discreet hand signal that indicated he needed a few minutes. His dad's question couldn't wait. Admittedly, the situation in the new house had been a little awkward since Riley and his parents had moved in about a month ago.

They'd bought a house big enough to give everyone space and privacy when they needed it, but Decker had drastically underestimated the amount of time they'd all be in contact—and how it would affect Harlow. She hadn't grown up in the kind of close-knit, supportive family environment that had instantly materialized here with everyone present. Her home life experience had been the exact opposite, which made the Decker family reunion a little suffocating. Especially under a single roof.

"Everything's fine. Harlow's just a little overwhelmed by the close company," said Decker, deciding to go with the short version of the backstory. "She didn't have a tight family like ours. Between you and me, her family situation growing up was tough. She's been on her own since she was in high school. It'll take her a little time to come around."

"I honestly couldn't tell. She's about as warm and friendly as they come," said Steven. "That's why I thought something might have gone sideways."

"No," said Decker, stifling a laugh. "She really likes you guys and Riley. Always has. What you're seeing is a concentrated effort by someone that doesn't want to give the wrong impression. Give her some time to adjust. It won't take her long to figure out she doesn't have to be *on* all the time."

"Good. This isn't a tough crowd to please—by any stretch."

"I keep telling her that," said Decker, patting his back. "I better see what Brooklyn wants."

"Be careful."

"Funny," said Decker, before heading inside.

Brooklyn nodded toward his father. "I don't think he likes me."

"Nobody likes you," said Decker, pretending to be serious.

She cocked her head and gave him a quizzical look.

"Just kidding. About the rest of us," said Decker. "Don't worry about my dad. He's very protective of Riley. They've been inseparable since . . ."

A few moments passed before Brooklyn let him off the hook.

"I get it," she said.

Decker still couldn't bring himself to say what had happened to his wife and son. To his family. He could barely think about it without screaming *STOP*—on the inside.

"Espresso?" said Decker.

"Sure," she said.

Decker slid two porcelain espresso cups under the automated coffee machine and pressed a button. The JURA GIGA 6 did the rest. He presented Brooklyn with a perfect double espresso less than a minute later, keeping one for himself.

"Getting a little tired of sitting in a car all day?" asked Decker. "I wouldn't blame you if that's the case."

"No," she said, shaking her head. "It's not that. I actually use the time to study for my classes. It's not a leather club chair at Starbucks, but it works."

She took a sip of her espresso and nodded her approval before continuing.

"I was hoping to pick up a few hours of PI work after I bring Riley back in the afternoon. Even with this associate degree, I'll need five thousand hours of certified experience to get a PI license. Figured I'd get started."

"You plan on sticking around LA that long?" asked Decker.

"I couldn't think of a better gig," said Brooklyn. "Or a nicer group of people to work with."

"I can't tell if that last part was sarcastic," said Decker, before downing the rest of his espresso.

"I spent two months recovering with Pam, under the same roof," said Brooklyn. "If the two of us can survive each other for that long, I think this is a good fit for me."

"Truer words have never been spoken," said Decker.

Harlow emerged from a hallway adjacent to the kitchen.

"What did Pam do now?" she asked, heading for the coffee machine.

"Nothing. We were just talking about Brooklyn spending some quality after-hours time with the team. She's trying to get a leg up on the million hours it takes to get a private investigator's license," said Decker. "Cappuccino?"

"Yes. Please," she said, before giving Decker a quick kiss. "We can definitely work something out. It's not like we have a shortage of work. We outsource a good portion of the surveillance and tracking as it is. Good to hear you're hanging around. I was telling Decker it might be time to find Riley a new friend."

"Other than getting my knee blown apart at the very start of this, everything has worked out surprisingly well," said Brooklyn. "And I truly enjoy Riley's company. No need to change that up anytime soon."

"I get the strong sense that the feeling is mutual," said Harlow.

"It is," said Decker.

"I'll talk to Pam about getting you started," said Harlow. "She's running that schedule."

"Thank you," said Brooklyn. "Tell Riley I'll be in the car. I didn't mean to impose."

"You're not imposing. She should be out any minute," said Decker.

On cue, Riley wandered into the kitchen and set her backpack on the island. Decker raised his eyebrows and stared at the pack long enough for Riley to get the hint.

"Not sure what the big deal is," said his daughter, moving it to the floor by her feet. "But whatever."

She wore that always slightly annoyed teenager look he'd come to know all too well over the past month.

"You take that into the bathroom with you, right?" said Decker.

"I hang it up on a hook."

Harlow shook her head—at Decker. Message received.

"Fair enough. Just humor me and keep it off the countertops," said Decker. "Can I make you something quick before you take off?"

"That's okay, Dad," said Riley. "We're grabbing bagels on the way to school."

For a moment Brooklyn looked a little surprised by the statement—but she recovered quickly. "I did promise to take her this week. We wanted to check out the new place in Westwood."

"If the bagels are good, can you grab a dozen sesame? We're running a little low," said Decker.

"I'll make it happen," said Brooklyn.

"I appreciate the effort," he said, before giving his daughter a hug. "See you after school. Still up for lap swimming?"

"Definitely. Can we go before dinner?"

He turned to Harlow. "What time do you think we'll be back?"

"Your mom said dinner would be ready around seven thirty. That won't give you much time for a swim," said Harlow. "You can take an Uber back if it looks like things are running late at the office."

"Sounds like a plan," said Decker, hugging Riley one more time. "See you around six? Maybe a little earlier."

"Perfect," said Riley.

"Take care of my baby," said Decker.

"Seriously, Dad?" said his daughter, shaking her head.

"I got this," said Brooklyn. "She's in good hands."

"Oh my God, all of you are so embarrassing. Except Harlow," said Riley.

"I'm working on him," said Harlow.

"Please work harder, Harlow. He needs the help," said Brooklyn.

"Why do the women always gang up on me?" asked Decker.

"Easy target," replied Brooklyn, before glancing at Riley. "We need to go."

"Be right out. I need to say goodbye to Grandpa."

Once Riley stepped outside, Brooklyn turned to Decker. "She's a really good kid. Tough as nails."

"Thank you," said Decker, following up with a statement he felt oddly compelled to say out loud. "She's been through a lot."

"She takes after someone else I know," said Harlow, winking at him. "I better go say goodbye to your dad, too. I feel like I've been a little unavailable lately."

"He understands."

"Understands what?" said Harlow, eyeing him critically.

"Nothing. No big deal. Trust me. Go make the old man feel good about himself," said Decker. "I'll tell you on the way to work."

"Sounds like something," she said as she headed to the terrace.

"It really isn't," muttered Decker, a little too loudly.

"I'll be the judge of that," said Harlow.

"Judge of what?" asked Riley, who had just passed Harlow.

"Nothing," said Decker. "See you after school. Love you."

"Love you, too, Dad," she said, grabbing her backpack.

Decker swallowed hard as she walked away. Those four words always got to him.

Chapter Two

Quincy Rohm eased the Bombardier Challenger jet out of a wide turn onto the next leg of her surveillance run. The sleek twin-engine aircraft effortlessly settled on its new course—due west across the base of the Texas Panhandle. They'd be on this heading for roughly twenty minutes before she nudged the jet south several miles and brought them back over the search area.

With close to eight thousand square miles to digitally catalog, they'd be at this for the rest of the day, crisscrossing these sparsely inhabited plains in search of an undocumented, active airfield. That's all Rohm knew, and she suspected it was all anybody knew. Bernie had given her the search area coordinates, the same vague description of their surveillance target—and nothing more.

Not that she required more to accomplish the mission. At nearly six thousand feet above the ground, they had little chance of spotting the airfield from the jet. Her job was to run a tight surveillance pattern over the colossal patch of land identified by their client, Senator Margaret Steele. The extensive digital and thermal imagery captured by the aircraft's sensor suite would be downloaded and analyzed later.

"Roll the cameras," she said.

"Rolling," said Jake, the surveillance technician, over her headset.

"Fun day," said Geoff Hopkins, her copilot and the newest addition to Bernie's team. "Back and forth, and back again."

She smirked. "Ninety-five percent of this job is mind-numbing. You get used to it."

"And the other five percent?" he asked, glancing across the cockpit at her.

"You don't want to know," she said.

"My guess is that the other five percent doesn't involve this baby."

"Solid guess," she said. "Bernie's Vietnam-era bird is a shit magnet."

"Good to know," said Hopkins. "I start training on that next—"

A string of bright-orange flashes zipped skyward, just ahead of the Challenger's nose. A fraction of a second later, before Rohm could fully process what she was seeing, the aircraft shuddered—and the cockpit exploded in a maelstrom of plastic and metal fragments.

Rohm raised both arms at the same time—an instinctive move that saved her eyes from the shrapnel that peppered her elbows and forearms. When she lowered them a few moments later, a vast, uninterrupted sea of brown filled the window. The jet was headed straight for the ground. She immediately seized the yoke and started to pull the thirty-ton beast out of its terminal dive.

"Could use some help here!" she said, struggling with the barely responsive controls. "Dammit, Hopkins! I need—"

She took her eyes off the rapidly approaching ground long enough to confirm that she was on her own. Her copilot's head hung forward, vacant eyes staring at the gaping hole in his abdomen. Bright-red blood and dark chunks of gore covered his side of the cockpit.

"Shit. Shit. Shit."

Rohm wrestled with the controls until she could see the horizon again, her narrow focus expanding as she came to grips with the situation. Altitude roughly two thousand feet—*not as bad as I thought.* Airspeed nearly cut in half—*need to fix that pronto to get out of here.* Dozens of audible cockpit alarms told her the Challenger was in bad shape—*no shit.*

"Jake. Are you still with me?"

Nothing from the back of the aircraft.

"Jake!"

"Still here. Barely," he said. "I'm bleeding out."

"Hold on. I'm headed back," she said, starting to unbuckle her five-point harness.

"Don't bother," he said, sounding even weaker than before. "Seriously. I'm done."

She scanned the sky through the blood-splattered windows, hoping to catch a glimpse of whatever had attacked them. Nothing but empty blue sky. She needed to know what they were up against right away. Whatever had hit them would be back, and the likelihood of surviving another attack hovered around zero. She had to do something.

If they'd been hit by a propeller-driven aircraft, she'd hit the throttle and open the distance. Problem solved. Even at half speed, she could outrun anything spinning blades. Another jet changed things significantly. She'd be forced to climb to a higher altitude, where she would have more room to maneuver—if the Challenger could handle it. And that was a big *if* under the circumstances.

"Any idea what hit us?" she said, flipping switches to silence the alarms.

"Negative. All I can say for sure is that it came from below," said Jake. "Heavy caliber. At least a twenty-millimeter gun. A dozen rounds tore through the cabin."

"Ground fire?"

Rohm knew the answer before Jake responded. A twenty-millimeter antiaircraft gun would have little chance of accurately tearing into them moving this fast at six thousand feet. Had to be another aircraft.

"Never mind. Dumb question," she said. "What's the status of our sensors?"

"Screwed," he said. "Everything is off-line."

"Can you get a message out to Bernie?"

"I already tried. No joy," said Jake.

"Emergency beacon?"

"I flipped the switch, but I can't tell if it's transmitting," said Jake. "One way or the other, it should activate when we hit the ground."

He grunted a laugh over the headset.

"Hang in there," she said. "I'm getting us out of here."

She increased the Challenger's speed, feeling for a problem with the jet's airframe. That was all Rohm had to go on at this point. She had no idea what kind of damage the aircraft had sustained. A quick look at the instrument panel gave her more bad news. They were dumping fuel at an alarming rate, and the jet was losing altitude. She pulled back on the yoke, and the aircraft slowly leveled, but it fought her the entire time. Something was definitely wrong with at least one of the jet's flaps.

"Jake. You still with me?"

No answer. Rohm flipped the autopilot switch and was rewarded with a little good news. The system appeared operational. She locked in the Challenger's present flight profile and engaged the system, hoping for the best. The aircraft held its course and altitude while she disentangled from the seat harness. Satisfied that the jet wouldn't dive while on autopilot, she slid between the cockpit seats and opened the door leading into the main cabin.

Wind from several jagged holes buffeted the compartment, creating a vortex of loose papers that swirled around Jake's wilted, motionless body. Still seated at the shattered electronics console, Jake was either already dead or most of the way there. Eyes closed, he lay with his left leg beneath him, detached just above the knee. The last of his blood pumped weakly onto the deck.

"Jake?"

No response. *Definitely gone.* She reached inside the cabin for her flight bag, finding the shredded nylon satchel flapping against the bulkhead separating the cabin from the cockpit. Her Sig Sauer pistol lay on the buckled deck below the bag, next to a smashed hunk of plastic she barely recognized as a satellite phone. *Wonderful.* She zipped the weapon into one of her cargo pockets, along with three spare magazines, before heading aft to retrieve one of the parachute rigs.

With the free-fall rig strapped snugly to her torso, Rohm returned to the cockpit. Reaching between the seats, she disengaged the autopilot and pulled the blood-splattered throttle levers back gradually until the speed indicator read one hundred knots per hour. Any slower and the aircraft could stall. Any faster and her ill-advised jump from the cabin door could get ugly. The Challenger wasn't designed for what she had in mind.

Rohm engaged the autopilot and made her way back into the main cabin. She yanked the exit door lever to the "Open" position and kicked the staircase hatch out of the aircraft. Air rushed in, pushing her away from the door.

The gust died down a few seconds later, allowing her to approach the opening and grip its edges. She peered through the hatch at the wing, making a quick calculation. She'd be lucky to clear that wing. Before she could process another thought, the cabin erupted in a deafening fury of shredded metal and shattered plastic. A tracer flashed past the door—close enough to touch.

Rohm didn't hesitate. She dived headfirst toward the ground, one hundred knots of air striking her like a bus the moment she cleared the hatch. Nothing was in her control right now. She'd either slip past the immovable aluminum wing or strike it at breakneck speed.

Rohm bounced along the underside of the wing, suffering a few painful, glancing blows before streaking clear of the aircraft. Free as a bird—sort of. A few seconds later, after streamlining her body in a head-down position for maximum free-fall speed, a boxy-looking, single-propeller plane dived parallel with her, about a half mile away to the west. The flaming wreckage of the Challenger seemed to follow it down.

"Shit," she muttered, hoping the pilot hadn't noticed her.

There was nothing she could do about that right now. She needed to focus all her attention on the rapidly approaching ground. Free-falling from two thousand feet didn't give her much time to play around. Maybe fifteen seconds. Half of which had already expired.

She counted to five in her head, the rapidly approaching ground no doubt accelerating the pace. When Rohm reached five, she extended her arms and quickly achieved a neutral arched position. With her descent slowed enough to safely deploy the main parachute, she reached back with her right hand and threw the drogue chute away from her body. A moment later, the harness pulled excruciatingly tight across her torso, suspending her under the ram-air canopy, a mere few hundred feet above the flat, hardscrabble landscape.

Rohm pulled the toggles to bleed as much air as possible from the rectangular canopy. She was still looking at close to thirty to forty seconds of extremely exposed descent time. If the pilot had somehow observed her parachute, she might not make it down in one piece. The aircraft dived toward a pillar of black smoke that she assumed to be the Challenger's crash site. Hopefully, the pilot was too preoccupied with their handiwork to notice her dark-green parachute.

Rohm executed a perfect flare landing, her feet lightly skimming the ground until she could walk under the canopy. After taking a few steps, she detached the risers from the harness and let the billowing parachute collapse to the ground behind her. A quick glance around identified a few hiding places within easy scramble distance. A craggy arroyo with signs of dry scrub and several jagged rock formations.

She dragged the parachute into the shallow gulch and compacted it until she had a beachball-size jumble of dark-green nylon. Rohm jammed the silky material under a thick stand of dry brush, anchoring the canopy with several rocks to prevent a gust of wind from unfurling it and giving away her position. She scanned the western sky for the aircraft, finding it south of the crash site—flying away from the area.

Rohm sat against the side of the riverbed and started taking deep breaths to calm herself. *What the hell just happened?* Less than three minutes ago, she had been flying carefree at six thousand feet. Now she was sitting on her bruised-up ass at sea level, shaking from an adrenaline overload—miles from the nearest town. Not exactly how she had expected the morning to go down.

Now for the really fun part. An hours-long hike through this Texas wasteland to reach a phone. She absolutely had to get in touch with Bernie as soon as possible so he could warn Senator Steele.

Her surveillance flight had obviously touched a very raw nerve somewhere.

CHAPTER THREE

Harlow took her eyes off the road long enough to gauge whether now was a good time to ask Decker what he had meant about his father "understanding." Elbow out the car window. Contented, easygoing look on his face. No sign of stress at all, so she didn't see any reason to hold back.

"What was that little comment about your dad back at the house?"

"It really was nothing," said Decker. "He had asked me a little earlier if maybe they—specifically my mother—had said anything that might have bothered you."

"Because I've been sort of avoiding everyone lately?"

"Pretty much," he said. "But I dispelled that notion immediately. I told him you had just been pretending to be nice in the beginning so they'd accept you."

"You what?"

"Just kidding," said Decker. "I gave him a very abbreviated version of your family history."

"Great. Now they'll really wonder what you've gotten yourself into with me."

"Abbreviated and devoid of unsavory details," said Decker. "I just let him know that you more or less grew up in the opposite of our kind of family environment and that it's going to take a little time for you to adjust to your new surroundings."

"You said it like that?" said Harlow. "Sounds like something a psychiatrist would say."

"No. I'm paraphrasing," said Decker.

"That was the short version of what you said?" said Harlow, knowing what he meant but wanting to push his buttons a little.

"What? No," said Decker, shifting in his seat to face her. "I told him you needed some time to adjust to the warm-and-huggy Decker family dynamic."

"Because I'm cold and distant?"

"That's not what—"

"I'm messing with you," said Harlow. "We're cool. Your dad is going to put a good word in for me with your mother."

"Everyone is making a much bigger deal of this than necessary," said Decker.

"Joking again. Whatever you said to him obviously put him at ease. Thank you," she said. "And for the record, I'd be worried if they weren't concerned."

"Me too," said Decker. "I think they were more worried that they did something wrong than anything else. They really like you. Not sure why."

"Well, they think the world of you," said Harlow. "So. Maybe bad judges of character?"

They both laughed for a few seconds.

"Touché," said Decker, before checking his phone. "Did you move me off the Chang interview?"

"Yeah. I didn't want to say anything in the house, but I don't think that interview will be over in time for you to get back to join Riley for lap swimming," she said. "I put you on the equipment inventory with Garza."

"That's like a one-hour job. For one person," said Decker.

"I expanded it to all of our storage units. Three hours tops," said Harlow. "I want you to spend as much time with Riley as possible. The work will always be there. Your daughter won't."

She instantly regretted her choice of words. Nobody was more agonizingly aware of the value of time lost than Decker. Or of having that time ripped away unexpectedly—never to be returned.

"Sorry. That didn't come out right," said Harlow.

"I didn't take it the wrong way," said Decker. "You don't have to keep tiptoeing around me. I know your head and heart are always in the right place. Damn. That sounded like a line from a Hallmark card."

"I hear a second career calling," said Harlow.

"Might keep me out of trouble," said Decker. "I don't think the drug cartels or Russian mafia would dare try to break into the cutthroat holiday gift card industry."

"Sounds like a safe bet," said Harlow. "By the way, Garza said he's running late."

"What else is new," said Decker. "I'll talk to him about it during the inventory."

"It's getting a little old," said Harlow.

"I know."

"And he's starting to grate on people's nerves during stakeouts," said Harlow. "I think he's getting bored."

"He definitely doesn't like to sit still for long, unless he's behind a rifle scope," said Decker. "I'll put him on notice."

"Don't shit on him too hard. I'd like to keep him around. His contributions are solid—when his head is in the game. If he needs to shift into something a little more part-time, that's fine. Maybe that'll give him a chance to work on a few jobs outside of the agency. Let him burn off some steam."

"We'd need to be really careful with that," said Decker. "The merc world is small. The last thing we need is for him to bring trouble back from a job. If he needs to take other work to keep the ants out of his pants, I'd prefer that he go back to contractor status with the firm. We hire him as needed. That keeps us insulated from what I know to be a very chaotically opportunistic world. We have enough to worry about as it is."

Decker was right. The fewer solid links back to any of these dark underbellies of the world right now the better. The very nature of the firm's work undoubtedly drew the attention of some dreadful organizations. More than just attention in some cases. The risk came with the territory, and they all accepted it. Harlow saw no reason to open up another avenue of risk, especially after living with the APEX Institute's thinly veiled threat for several months.

Within a week of the Nevada warehouse raid that had no doubt deprived one of the Institute's closest proxies of a fortune in recently harvested marijuana, every member of their firm had come under intense twenty-four-hour surveillance. Teams had made no effort to remain hidden and followed them to and from work.

They had parked overnight on the streets in front of firm members' apartments or homes. They had bribed restaurant hostesses to be seated at adjacent tables. No outing had been off-limits. Their presence, while never directly confrontational, had felt increasingly oppressive and threatening. The harassment had abruptly lifted around the six-month mark, with a brief escalation meant to drive home the Institute's message.

Brad Pierce and his family, who previously had been spared APEX's wrath, had woken up to a spray-painted house. Police investigators called to the scene had classified the repeated strings of hastily sprayed pyramids and eyes as gang tagging, but the message had been clear. *We're watching—and we're everywhere.*

Decker hadn't waited for the same message to reach his parents' house in Idaho. He had immediately moved Riley and his parents to Los Angeles, where he could watch over them. Where the firm could watch over them. So far, Harlow's extensive network hadn't caught a whiff of APEX in LA, but that didn't mean they were in the clear. The hammer could drop at any moment. And it was obvious that Senator

Steele's money and influence couldn't shield them from the threat—no matter how hard she tried.

"On second thought, just read Garza the riot act," said Harlow. "He's been invaluable in the field, particularly with the higher-risk jobs. And it can't hurt to keep someone with his skill set close, given the circumstances."

"It certainly can't," said Decker. "I'll talk to him."

If the hammer dropped, she fully intended to hit back with every tool in her arsenal.

Chapter Four

The smoky aroma of freshly brewed coffee had built a strong presence in the room. Overbrewed as always, but who was he to complain? The new smell meant one thing. His shift had come to an end. Finally. Another twelve hours in front of these screens, doing jack shit and making bank, had almost expired. And just in time. After nearly three months trapped in this brownstone, hours now felt like days, and the days passed with little more fanfare than the rising and setting of the sun—observed through thin curtains.

Timothy Graves took a long, unhurried drink from a well-worn plastic mug, finishing the last of the coffee he'd made a few hours earlier to help him stay awake through the morning. Not that anything had ever transpired requiring his detailed attention. Like clockwork, Ezra Dalton's armored town car had picked her up at 7:25 a.m. and turned south onto Wisconsin Avenue, headed for the APEX Institute's headquarters building in Tyson's Corner.

Over two hours had elapsed, her town house now completely quiet and still. Except for one little thing that he couldn't stop thinking about. His eyes darted to image number eleven, nestled in the bottom center of the expansive screen. A beautifully unobstructed, top-down view of Ezra Dalton's office desk. He'd placed the microcamera in the bookcase flanking the desk, expecting it to be the most productive of the twenty cameras hidden throughout her Georgetown flat. Of course, Murphy's Law had something else to say about his camera placement.

While the desk camera's feed had produced their only actionable intelligence to date, the past few days had painfully demonstrated that he may have overlooked a more productive location.

"Tim! Tim! Wakey wakey, eggs and bakey!"

Tim glanced over his shoulder. Anish Gupta, his agonizingly cheerful and comically challenged partner of more than a decade, strode into the room holding a carafe of coffee.

"Refill, bitch?"

"How old are you?" asked Tim.

"Old enough to know you're one out-of-touch mother-effing fool," said Anish, before taking a seat next to him.

"Let me know when you're done with the Snoop Dogg routine for the day," said Tim.

"I'm done," said Anish. "More coffee?"

"Maybe a little later," said Tim, turning his attention back to the screens. "I'm thinking about changing the angle of the camera in Dalton's study. She's taken a recent liking to that club chair."

"She's taken the good shit to that club chair," said Anish. "Who the hell reads classified papers all curled up with a pot of tea?"

"Someone who sits behind a desk at an office all day," said Tim, before pointing at image number eleven. "If I move the book housing our camera from the bookshelf next to her desk to the bookshelf adjacent to the french doors, we'll have a bird's-eye view of the club chair and a good enough chance of catching anything she lays flat on the desk."

Anish examined the screen and nodded. "Agree."

"Glad you're on board," said Tim.

"Who's on board with what?" said Jared Hoffman, suddenly standing in the doorway.

"Timbo is thinking about going all *Mission: Impossible* and moving the camera in her study," said Anish.

"Right now?" said Jared, stepping into the room.

"I figured we'd give it thirty minutes or so to make sure she didn't forget anything," said Tim.

"Her schedule is clean?" asked Jared.

Tim spun his chair to face the veteran operator, who stood at the window, peering through a crack between the curtains. Jared sported the same outfit he'd arrived in a few months ago. Hiking boots, a pair of slightly wrinkled khaki pants, and an untucked gray T-shirt—a black pistol grip pressed against his right hip. The T-shirt changed occasionally from gray to black, but the rest remained the same.

Jared had been with the team as long as Tim could remember. Before Argentina. They were considered plank owners by General Sanderson. Only a few members of the team went further back than that. The scarce few who had somehow managed to survive close to two decades of this kind of work.

"Housecleaning came through yesterday," said Tim. "Clean as it gets. No pun intended."

Jared chuckled before going stone-cold serious.

"I don't know about swapping between bookcases. Dalton strikes me as the attention-to-detail type. I'd feel more comfortable adding a new camera. Give us a view of both locations. How long would that take?"

Tim clicked on a file, which displayed an image of the bookcase in question. He zoomed in on the top two shelves, which mostly housed red-and-brown clothbound classics. The kind of books Tim, and most high school graduates, had been forced to read at some point. A number of more contemporary titles spoiled that highbrow selection. They could easily find one of those in a used bookstore.

"We could have a book ready by tomorrow morning," said Tim. "But I really don't think she'll notice if we swap one of the Penguin

Classics for another. Seriously. She hasn't touched a single book on those shelves since we started watching her."

"Is there any downside to waiting until tomorrow?" asked Jared.

"Reading files in that chair is a new behavior. Something might be up over at the Institute," said Tim.

"SKYSTORM?" asked Jared.

"Unknown. We can only pan the camera for a partial view of the chair. Not that it would make a difference. The way she holds the files upright has prevented us from viewing the material. We need to get a camera in the bookshelf above her," said Tim.

Jared rubbed the thick stubble on his face. "She's never done this before?"

"Not in the ninety-three days we've had her under direct surveillance," said Tim. "On top of that, it's pretty rare for her to bring files home."

Anish pressed his finger against the screen. "We could swap the current book for this one. Same color. Same size. Nobody is going to notice *Moby-Dick* swapped for *The Count of Monte Cristo*."

"You really think this can't wait?" said a gruff voice.

Richard Farrington stood next to the door, arms crossed under a dour face. He'd somehow slipped into the room undetected. Again. Tim had known him longer than Jared and still found his presence somewhat unnerving—in a "slit your throat before you knew what happened" kind of way. A good thing if he was on your side.

"Damn. How long you been ghosting us, dog?" asked Anish.

"Can it wait for a replacement book or not?"

Brass tacks. That was Rich in a nutshell.

"No," said Tim.

"I'm with him," said Anish.

"You're always with him," said Jared.

Rich shook his head almost imperceptibly. "Jared?"

"Ideally, we'd wait, but I'd really hate to miss an opportunity," said Jared. "And we're looking at a simple run. Door to door, this won't take me more than twenty minutes."

Rich locked eyes with Tim, as though the operative had been reading his mind.

"Anish will move the camera," said Rich.

"Uh. I don't know if that's—" started Jared.

"You don't think I can swap two books?" asked Anish.

"Do you really want me to answer that?" said Jared, rolling his eyes.

"We need two operators covering the streets. Front and back of the house. And one here," said Rich. "That leaves Anish and Tim. Whoever we send will need to perform a minor Cirque du Soleil act to reach the top shelves. Tim walks with a noticeable limp and can barely raise his right arm above his shoulder—thanks to his previous willingness to absorb bullets on the team's behalf. Anish?"

"I was born for this shit."

"Please don't make me reconsider," said Rich.

"Sorry. I can handle it," said Anish in a rare moment of seriousness.

Rich checked his watch. "We should do this before lunch. Before all of the baby strollers and yoga-mat hustlers come out of hibernation. Twenty minutes. Door to door. No messing around. There's no margin for error with APEX."

Chapter Five

Bernie strode through the massive, sweltering hangar, barely glancing in the direction of the mayhem his in-house team of aviation mechanics had unleashed on his beloved C-123. Normally, he'd be all over that crew, micromanaging them with the same obscenity-laced, insult-heavy dialogue everyone had come to expect when working on his "baby." But not this morning. His mind was fifteen hundred miles away from this dusty Nicaraguan airstrip. Somewhere over Texas.

The GPS tracker on Rohm's aircraft had stopped transmitting—nearly an hour ago. On top of that, she wasn't answering her personal satellite phone. He could envision a system-wide satellite communications problem. They'd experienced a number of issues with the electronics suite on board the overpriced jet since he'd added it to his fleet. But Bernie couldn't rationalize why Rohm wasn't monitoring her satellite phone. That had been the whole point of it.

He stepped into the blazing sun just outside the hangar and checked his phone. It had locked onto three satellites. Bernie gave the phone a minute to download any messages before looking again. Nothing. He tried to place a call to her phone, yielding the same result. Something had gone disastrously wrong. He was sure of it now.

Bernie stormed back into the shade, a full flop sweat having enveloped him in the two minutes he had been standing outside. Sean Fitzgerald (a.k.a. Fitz) intercepted him on the trip back to the air-conditioned office.

At six foot five, the security officer's two-hundred-fifty-pound frame towered over Bernie. Probably enough to shade him from the ghastly midday sun. He'd keep that in mind the next time he left the hangar.

"Still nothing?" asked Fitz.

He shook his head and kept walking.

"I'll increase our security posture," said Fitz.

Bernie nodded absently. He hadn't thought of that. The surveillance flight may have finally kicked the proverbial hornet's nest. The dense jungle surrounding this airstrip suddenly felt more like a liability than an asset. *Shit.* He highly doubted APEX had traced his operations to the remote jungles of Nicaragua, but stranger things had happened in his lengthy career. He couldn't discount any scenario. Even the very remote possibility that Rohm had been shot down over Texas.

When he got back into his air-conditioned oasis, Bernie shut the door and quickly went to work on his laptop. His first step would be to call the Air Force Rescue Coordination Center. The aircraft had been equipped with an emergency locator transmitter, which transmitted a 403 MHz signal to the NOAA Search and Rescue Satellite Aided Tracking (SARSAT) system orbiting high above the United States. The beacon automatically activated if the aircraft crashed, or it could be triggered midflight by one of the crew members. Either way, SARSAT would mark the last known position for search-and-rescue efforts.

If the rescue coordination center strategy didn't yield results, he'd contact air traffic control towers in the vicinity of Rohm's mission area to see if they had received a distress call from her aircraft, starting with the international airports in Amarillo and Lubbock and expanding to smaller airports. Someone somewhere would have heard or seen something. The Texas Panhandle was a vast, sparsely populated region of the country, but an aircraft that size couldn't disappear without a trace—unless it was somehow blown to pieces in midair. And Bernie didn't even want to think about the wide-reaching ramifications of that scenario right now.

CHAPTER SIX

Senator Margaret Steele's phone buzzed somewhere behind her, momentarily distracting her from the tariff briefing. She glanced back at Julie Ragan, who mouthed, "I got it" and started digging through her leather satchel. Right about now was one of those times she wished Ragan weren't such an efficient chief of staff. Steele needed an excuse to mentally check out of this agonizing regurgitation by her fellow senators of the same PowerPoint presentation she'd received late yesterday afternoon and could have digested on her own in a fraction of the time—sipping a glass of wine on her deck. She turned her attention back to the droning.

A few seconds later, Ragan tapped her shoulder before whispering in her ear. "This can't wait. SKYSTORM."

Steele tensed. A combination of excitement and distress instantly elevated her heartbeat. She'd taken an awful risk over the past few months. A high-stakes shadow investigation with one purpose—to bury the APEX Institute once and for all. To make them pay dearly for their complicity, no matter how indirect, in her daughter's murder.

She didn't care how far removed they claimed to be from Jacob Harcourt. Their bloodstained business model of Beltway power broking enabled the worst our broken military-industrial complex had to offer. The kinds of murderous, greedy rogues who steamrolled the competition and anyone caught in the cross fire—all to secure more power and money. She would soon expose this shadow industry to the sunlight, turning these vampires to dust.

Without saying a word, she stood and took the phone, leaving Ragan to represent her at the briefing. Once outside the conference room, Steele put the phone to her ear and sought an empty corner or alcove to keep the ensuing conversation private.

"That was quick," she said.

"We have a problem," said Bernie. "My surveillance bird is down. SARSAT registered a distress signal at eleven-oh-five Eastern Standard Time. The signal lasted two-point-two seconds. Crash site confirmed from the air. Nothing but pieces left."

She stopped in the middle of the brightly lit hallway, trying to process what she had just heard. It took her a few seconds to come back online.

"The crew?"

"No word on that yet. Rescue crews haven't reached the site, but I'm not very hopeful," said Bernie.

"I'm so sorry," she said, pausing for a few moments. "Is there any way this was an accident?"

"This wasn't an accident. We're talking about a perfectly maintained aircraft and my best pilot," said Bernie. "Someone shot it out of the sky, which changes the game significantly."

"Yes. It does," she said, suddenly thinking about the surveillance operation in Georgetown. "I need to make a call right away."

"I figured you might," said Bernie. "Let me know what I can do. I have no intention of letting this go unanswered."

"You don't have to—"

"You know how to reach me," said Bernie, before disconnecting the call.

Steele glanced up and down the hallway, no longer feeling safe deep inside the Hart Senate Office Building.

"Calm down. Think," she muttered, moving herself into a small alcove outside another meeting room.

Steele gave the news some time to settle in before making her next move. One thing was clear: Bernie's surveillance flight had seriously rattled someone's cage. She was onto something with SKYSTORM, and that something was located in the Texas Panhandle and connected to APEX. What she didn't know was exactly how far and wide APEX would take their response.

They'd more than likely dig a little deeper before taking any further action. She fully expected an afternoon visit from Ezra Dalton, who would deliver a "final" cease-and-desist warning from the Institute while probing for information. Steele would deny any involvement, agree to stay out of APEX's business—and immediately modify her strategy to unmask SKYSTORM.

One way or the other, she'd get to the bottom of whatever had necessitated blowing a jet out of the sky. Until then, she'd ease up on the other side of her intelligence-gathering operation.

CHAPTER SEVEN

Rich held a finger up while absorbing Senator Steele's words. The team had been moments from walking out the back door and moving on Ezra Dalton's brownstone.

"Ma'am. If it's all right with you, I'd like to put this on speakerphone so we're all on the same page," he said.

"I'm fine with that," said Steele.

"Our client has just learned that a separate surveillance asset assigned to investigate one of the leads we developed . . . has been terminated. As in a very expensive jet has been shot out of the sky over the area we identified."

"Shit," muttered Jared, who was joined by a similar chorus from the rest of the team.

Tim asked the first and most logical question. "Did the surveillance bird send any pictures before it went down?"

"No," said Steele. "For reference, the incident occurred less than forty minutes into their mission. They had only covered a sixth of the designated surveillance zone before they went down."

"Someone moved on them fast," said Anish.

"Right. Which is why I think you should reconsider the visit you have planned," said Steele.

A few seconds of heavy silence fell over the crew. Steele was the client, and if she wanted them to pull back, so be it. But she hadn't ordered them to cancel the trip. She left it open for discussion, which meant she didn't want to close that door for good.

"Without overstating the obvious, we're clearly onto something with SKYSTORM," said Rich. "Moving the camera to take advantage of Dalton's new reading habit might provide the insight needed to further your investigation. We've been at this for close to three months and haven't detected a trace of focused counterintelligence. They do regular visual and electronic sweeps of the neighborhood and Dalton's brownstone, but our efforts have remained undetected. We're confident of that."

"My concern is that she will link her new habit to the flight and suspect she's under surveillance," said Steele.

"Then we have nothing to lose by moving the camera," said Tim. "If they swoop in and tear the place apart later, that's that. They'll find the gear. If not, we might get another chance to glean some actionable intelligence. Either way, they can't trace this back to you or us."

"I'm mostly concerned with your safety at this point," said Steele. "If we need to rethink this entire operation, I'm fine with that."

"Our stakeout location is secure," said Rich. "Let's see how this plays out at the target's brownstone. If the mission there gets burned, we'll come up with another approach."

Steele took several moments before she responded. While they waited, Jared shrugged in a show of noncommittal solidarity. He was good with whatever she decided. They all were. That was the way this worked. It didn't matter how much they believed in the job or wanted to see it through to the end. The client had the final say.

"Just be careful. Any sign of trouble and you pull your team back," said Steele.

"Understood," said Rich. "I'll call you when it's done. I estimate thirty minutes at most."

"Talk to you then," said Steele.

Rich stuffed the encrypted phone into his sport coat pocket and turned to Tim, who was making a final adjustment to Anish's earpiece.

"Watch everything with an eagle's eye," said Rich. "If anything feels off, you pull the plug. You have the absolute authority to make that call."

"Got it," said Tim, patting Anish's shoulder. "I have a nifty program that has analyzed neighborhood vehicle and pedestrian traffic since we arrived. License plates. Facial recognition. Dozens of metrics."

"Don't overly rely on the technology. Look and listen," said Rich. "Nothing will ever replace a set of seasoned eyes and ears. That goes for everyone."

He locked eyes with each member of the team long enough to gauge their nonverbal reaction. So far, so good.

"Anish. How are you feeling?"

"Nervous," he said, pausing for a moment. "But ready to roll like a motha-effin' gangsta!"

"Maybe a little amped," said Tim.

"I can live with nervous and amped," said Rich. "All of you. Remember. If anything goes sideways, Tim will coordinate your exfil and extract. Do what you have to do to get clear of trouble, but listen to Tim. We have a team standing by for pickups—just in case. Any last questions or comments?"

"Can I have a gun?" asked Anish.

Rich just stared at him. Anish had proved untrainable with a firearm, making no progress after hours of patient instruction on several different occasions. It was like something on a deep DNA level prevented him from competently handling and using any kind of weapon.

"Thought I'd try," said Anish.

"I'd expect nothing less," said Rich. "Tim?"

"On it. Give me a minute or two to double-check the streets and target house," said Tim, before heading for the stairs.

While they waited, Rich made everyone check their equipment one last time before stepping off. He and Jared carried the same gear: Sig Sauer MPX submachine gun with several spare magazines, detached suppressor for the MPX, two flash bang grenades, and two smoke grenades. Everything quickly accessible. Rich's gear fit snugly in a leather satchel that matched his business casual attire. Jared's was hidden inside a roomier, custom-designed backpack that blended in with more of a young, hipster look.

"Final comms check," said Tim through his earpiece.

They answered one at a time.

"Everyone sounds good," said Tim. "You have a green light."

"Let's do this," said Rich, opening the back door to a brick courtyard.

CHAPTER EIGHT

Anish started to seriously regret his overly enthusiastic support of the camera-swap idea the moment he turned down the cramped alley behind the target house. He was truly on his own from now until he reemerged onto Thirty-Third Street. Jared was somewhere nearby, but he couldn't hover too closely without drawing attention if APEX was somehow watching the streets. That mentally jarring logic, unexpectedly proclaimed by Rich a few minutes earlier, had entirely undermined Anish's confidence. If APEX was watching the street, wouldn't they also be watching the house?

Just keep moving and get the job done, Anish told himself. Jared would take care of any problem that arose. Hopefully. He really didn't want to be here right now.

"Everything okay?" asked Tim through his earpiece. "You've slowed down."

"Fine. Just taking in the sights," said Anish, his voice automatically activating his headset microphone.

"Pick up the pace, please," said Rich. "You can sightsee later."

"Yes, sir," said Anish, forcing his unsteady legs to move faster.

Good thing he wasn't hooked up to a remote heart-rate monitor. They might think he was having a myocardial infarction. He'd feel a lot better if they'd given him a pistol. Actually, that wasn't true. That would probably make things worse.

"You're almost there, buddy," said Tim. "Everything looks clear on the streets. The house is clear. This is a walk in the park. Nothing to it."

Anish could sense the snide remarks forming in Rich's and Jared's minds. When they didn't materialize over the radio net, he settled into a solid stride. The thick, dark-green ivy along the six-foot-tall redbrick wall cleared to reveal a black metal door. He took a few deep breaths and reached for the inset keypad, punching in the six-digit code they had observed Dalton's security team use to admit the housecleaning crew yesterday. The door clicked, and he paused to take another deep, cleansing breath before pushing the heavy door inward and stepping inside.

"I'm through the first door," said Anish, closing the door behind him.

"Told you. Nothing to it," said Tim.

Anish took a moment to observe the compact courtyard between the brick wall and the three-story brownstone. A pergola-covered slate patio took up most of the space, furnished with expensive-looking all-weather seating for up to four. Overall, a comfortable outdoor refuge in the middle of the capital. He walked past the furniture and approached the back door with a set of keys.

"Ready to breach," said Anish, regretting his choice of words.

The peanut gallery would no doubt lambaste him later for equating what he was about to do with a tactical breach.

"The alarm is disabled. Proceed," said Tim. "Carefully."

No shit, Sherlock.

"Take the time to look, listen, and smell once you step inside," said Rich. "Trust your senses and your gut. If something feels off, that may be the only warning we get."

Wow. This is not helping.

"Got it," said Anish, before inserting the key marked with black electrical tape into the dead bolt lock.

A few seconds later, after pocketing the keys, he turned the doorknob and slowly opened the door. The faint aroma of a cooked meal froze him in place. As Rich had suggested, he took a few moments to analyze the odor. Definitely nothing too recent. Anish proceeded inside and shut the door behind him, reengaging the locks as Rich had suggested. If an unexpected visitor showed up, the time they spent on the locks could spell the difference between a quick escape through the front door or a less-than-optimal scenario.

He walked slowly and softly through a short hallway to reach a spacious and modern kitchen. Anish stopped next to the black granite island and engaged all his senses. The countertops looked immaculate, as always. Nothing left out after breakfast. Not an item out of place. If their three-month-long surveillance had proved anything, it was that Ezra Dalton was meticulous about keeping the place organized and clean. *Obsessive* might be a better word.

Several more seconds of absolute stillness pretty much convinced him he was alone in the brownstone. Not one hundred percent, but as close as he'd get under the circumstances. Anish started walking toward the front foyer, where he knew the stairs were located.

"All quiet inside. Headed for the study."

He had reached the hallway leading out of the kitchen when Rich spoke a single word that stopped him in his tracks.

"Tim?"

A long pause ensued, which was entirely unlike his colleague of many years.

"Tim?" said Anish.

"Get the hell out of there. Right now," said Tim. "Go back the way you came."

"Okay. Okay. I'm going," said Anish, taking off for the back door.

"Talk to me, Tim," said Rich.

"Vehicle and pedestrian patterns just went haywire on North Street, moving in from Thirty-Third and Potomac."

They were converging on the street in front of the house. Not good, but it would give him a solid chance of slipping away. Maybe this was some kind of false alarm. Anish threw the dead bolt and opened the door, only to find a murderous-looking, body armor–clad man pointing a pistol at him from across the patio.

"Down on your knees!" yelled the man, before moving deliberately toward Anish.

No longer in control of his body, Anish started to back up. His brain told him to get back inside and lock the door. Let Jared and Rich figure this out.

"You move another inch, and I'll blow your brains right out of your fucking head!"

That stopped him.

"On your knees!" the man repeated, before taking one hand off the pistol to trigger his radio. "I have him on the patio."

A second man rushed onto the patio through the open alleyway door. He raised a compact submachine gun from under his unbuttoned gray blazer.

"We need to ready him for transport," said the new arrival. "Shit's about to get noisy across the street."

Two distinct, muted snaps drew the shooters' attention toward the alley behind them. A figure crumpled to the cement just beyond the doorway as Jared slipped inside the courtyard, the business end of his weapon leading the way. He fired twice, shifting from one hostile target to the other faster than Anish, and apparently the two operatives, could register. The men dropped to the slate as though their breakers had been tripped.

Anish just stood there, staring at their sprawled bodies. He would never get used to the sudden and often unpredictable finality in this business, where even under the most controlled circumstances, the margin for error was minimal. And almost always lethal.

"Let's go," said Jared, motioning for him to follow.

He couldn't move.

"We need to get moving—right now," hissed Jared. "Tim. How are we looking?"

"Head east to Potomac. Then north. Rich should be able to cover you when you reach Potomac," said Tim.

Tires screeched somewhere on the street in front of Dalton's house, jolting Anish out of his paralysis. He sprinted toward Jared, who nodded at him before disappearing into the alley.

"How far out is our extraction?" asked Jared.

"Just do what I told you," said Tim.

He'd never heard Tim talk like that to anyone on the team before. The situation was worse than the dead men lying on the ground behind Dalton's house indicated—which was hard to imagine.

CHAPTER NINE

James Guthrie put both hands on the dashboard to brace himself for the sudden stop. In three. Two. One.

"Here," he said to the driver.

The fast-moving SUV screeched to a halt in front of the target house, skidding into place to block oncoming eastbound traffic, as his assault teams stacked up on the front porch. The men and women wore bulky olive-drab ballistic vests over civilian clothes, giving them the option of quickly ditching their gear and melting away if things somehow went completely sideways.

"Alpha in position," squawked his headset.

"Bravo. Status," said Guthrie.

He needed the team watching the back door in place before initiating the breach. Dalton had been clear. She wanted the entire surveillance crew that had been working her brownstone dead or captured. No exceptions. Donnelly's team had grabbed the cat burglar presumably sent to adjust the camera in her study. The lure of gleaning sensitive information from her new favorite reading location had worked almost too predictably.

Now to clean up the rest of this infestation. APEX countersurveillance technicians had identified the town house across the street as the source of the stakeout after detecting a distinctly out-of-place pattern of radio frequency emissions.

"Bravo ready," said another voice.

Time to wrap this up.

"Alpha. Breach," he said, before getting out of the SUV.

From a covered position behind the hood, he watched the assault teams work their magic. To minimize their noise and hopefully delay the inevitable police response to their obtrusive presence, they had opted to use an unorthodox method to quickly defeat the front door. Two team members pressed handheld thermal torches to the lock points along the door and ignited them.

A brilliant shower of bright-yellow sparks erupted along the door-frame, each TEC torch's five-thousand-degree-Fahrenheit metal vapor jet cutting through the locks and extinguishing in two seconds. When the sparks stopped, a third operative shouldered the door open and disappeared inside. The entire team followed.

"Donnelly. What's your status?" he said over the radio net, checking on the bag-and-tag job behind Dalton's place.

No response. This wasn't the time for even the slightest misstep.

"Donnelly. I need—"

A sharp, earsplitting crunch cut off his transmission, followed almost instantly by an explosion of debris from the very recently breached target house doorway. Guthrie instinctively ducked behind the SUV as fragments of wood and metal clanged across the hood and peppered the windows. He stayed low for several long moments, until only two sounds could be heard at the scene: agonized screams for help from inside the house and car alarms throughout the neighborhood. Neither the surviving members of the team inside the house nor their adversaries had engaged in a gunfight—yet.

"Alpha. Report," he said over the net.

Nothing.

"Bravo. Report."

"Holding in position. What the fuck just happened?"

"The house is a decoy. Get out of there immediately," said Guthrie. "E and E package Zulu."

"Shit. Copy that," said the team leader. "Moving out."

Escape and evasion package Zulu was the catastrophic plan. They'd change vehicles in predetermined locations twice as they executed separate surveillance-detection routes to clear the DC metro area. Several hours later, they would converge on a yet-to-be-determined location hundreds of miles from here for a headquarters-level debriefing. If APEX didn't decide that Guthrie's entire group was too much of a liability moving forward. In that case, they would all be driving to their deaths.

"Donnelly. I need a status report."

No response. He glanced over his shoulder at Dalton's brownstone a few houses down. *What the hell was going on over there?*

Guthrie backtracked along the side of the SUV, grabbing the submachine gun in the front passenger footwell along the way. He knelt beside Davitts, who had crouched next to the rear bumper. Guthrie had to get everyone off these streets and driving away in a minute or less. A bombing this close to the seat of government, combined with neighborhood reports of gunmen running amok, was guaranteed to draw a swift tactical response. The situation would go from screwed to beyond screwed if he didn't get his mercenaries out of there ASAP.

"I'm headed inside to make an assessment," said Guthrie. "If I'm not back out in ten seconds, get everyone back inside the vehicles and out of here. You got that?"

The visibly shaken operator nodded, inspiring little confidence in such an important job. He glanced up at the next closest team member, Laura Bachmann, who had her compact rifle pointed at the house. She had always been entirely focused and reliable, which was exactly what he needed right now.

"Bachmann. Make sure that gets done," said Guthrie. "And reassign Davitts to cover the approach from Dalton's place. I can't reach Donnelly."

"Got it. Ten seconds or we're gone," she said, scooting over next to Davitts.

"Get the backs of the SUVs open," said Guthrie, yelling over his shoulder as he approached the blasted door. "We'll pile everyone in. Dead or alive."

A figure appeared through the thick haze obscuring the doorway. Guthrie raised his MP7 and placed the green holographic reticle center mass. The shape staggered forward, resting against the doorframe. The desperate pleas for help coming from inside the house had settled down into a discordance of resigned moans.

"Anyone in ALPHA. Respond," said Guthrie, holding the figure in his sights.

"It's me," gasped the man in the doorway.

"Moreno?"

"Everyone is down," he said, taking a knee.

Guthrie rushed forward to help him, immediately determining that Moreno wasn't going to make it. His arms, legs, and lower abdomen had been shredded. And he was bleeding profusely from the right side of his neck. He could drop the team leader at a nearby emergency room—maybe. But that wasn't a viable option. He signaled for the teams on the street to start the cleanup.

"What happened?" asked Guthrie, moving him clear of the doorway.

"We got inside the front hallway and fanned out into the adjacent rooms," said Moreno. "Grenades fell from the ceilings. Short fused. No time to react."

"We're gonna get you out of here. Get you some help," said Guthrie, before turning to Bachmann, who was on her way up the long brick stoop. "Should be safe to proceed. Medical treatment in the vehicles. I want to be rolling in forty-five seconds."

"Copy that," she said, raising her rifle and stepping into the house. Moreno grabbed his arm. "If they got us here . . ."

They got us there, too. He couldn't afford to think about Dalton's brownstone right now. Getting out of here without tangling with the police would take every bit of focus he could muster. And they didn't have the time to investigate anyway. The best he could do was hope that the mess was contained inside Dalton's property—and that it would escape police attention until APEX could get a team in to straighten up the mess. He just hoped APEX didn't consider him to be a mess that needed cleaning.

CHAPTER TEN

Tim sat in front of the screens, simultaneously stunned by what he had just witnessed and thankful he did not have a second round of improvised explosives at his disposal. Rich would have undoubtedly ordered him to unleash it on the rescuers. A classic guerilla warfare tactic. Enough was enough. Rich had made his point—and likely stirred up a hornet's nest that would not be easy to shake.

"What are you seeing inside the decoy house?" asked Rich.

"Not much. Most of the cameras went off-line," said Tim, not wanting to go into a description of what had happened in there.

He'd seen the grenades fall from the cylinders mounted to the ceiling and hit the floor. Watched the operatives' panicked responses—before three of the camera views flashed No Signal. His only remaining view of the mayhem originated from a camera mounted in the kitchen and facing the front hallway. Three bodies lay crumpled in a fairly compact pile in the center of the passage. They had been moving in a tight formation toward the kitchen when they'd been bracketed by grenades. One in front of them. One behind. The opposing blasts had dropped them in place—on top of each other. The operative in the middle had survived, the men in front and behind him absorbing most of the fragments.

"Cut the shit, Tim," said Rich, seeing right through him. "What's happening in there? Do I bail or do I need to drive home the message a little further?"

Tim wasn't sure how the message could be made clearer. A quick glance at the screen displaying police response codes and locations helped him with the answer.

"I have three police units headed toward the scene from the east," said Tim. "You need to clear the area. Head north on Potomac and link up with the others. They should have emerged from the alley."

"You still didn't answer my first question."

"Their entire breach team went down hard," said Tim. "The backup team is carrying out the casualties and tossing them in the back of the SUVs. Looks like they're trying to get out of there before the police arrive. I strongly advise you do the same."

"I thought I saw one get out."

Rich could be ghoulish when it came to this part of the job.

"He didn't look like he had much fight left in him," said Tim.

"Fair enough. I'm headed north," said Rich. "Wait until our new friends depart so we can get as much video as possible; then execute a soft scrub. Head south on foot for Rosslyn Station, take the subway west past Falls Church and grab an Uber. Rally point is the safe house in Rockville."

It was interesting that Rich didn't want any of them traveling in their own cars but not at all surprising. They'd misjudged APEX's countersurveillance capabilities, and he wasn't taking any chances that their vehicles had somehow already been compromised or could be tracked by traffic cameras. More accurately, he and Anish had underestimated APEX. The attack had hit them without any advance warning. Fortunately, APEX's underestimation proved to be far worse, giving Tim what he assumed would be a one-time pass. APEX wouldn't make the same mistake again, and neither would he.

"Do you want me to cancel your pickup?"

"Already canceled," said Rich.

"And our client?"

"Calling her as soon as I hang up with you."

"I'll be out the door in ten," said Tim, ending the call.

He set the alarm and walked through the back door seven minutes later, carrying the server hard drives and laptops in an obviously strained backpack. Tim wasn't looking forward to the long walk across the Key Bridge with this beast on his back, but the extra weight would be worth the discomfort. He could have taken a few extra minutes to remove the laptop hard drives and memory cards, but that would leave them temporarily cut off at the safe house, especially if Rich intended to sequester the team for a few days to ensure they'd made a clean break.

Police sirens echoed off the buildings that surrounded the small courtyard, coming at him from every direction. The sound didn't give him pause. He was four blocks northwest of the explosion, which may as well be four miles in the city, and there wasn't a single physical or digital trace connecting this location with either house on N Street. Georgetown's more exclusive and privacy-cherishing clientele made sure that DC's extensive public camera network didn't take root on these streets.

The stakeout house would remain undiscovered, providing safe refuge again once the dust settled from this little mess. If it ever settled. APEX was a powerhouse inside and outside the Beltway, with a nearly unlimited reach. Anish and Jared would be identified by their intelligence apparatuses within the hour. General Sanderson would be implicated shortly after that—along with anyone ever connected to his notorious black ops enterprise.

By midafternoon, Tim would have a price on his head that would make his own mother think twice about not turning him in.

PART TWO

CHAPTER ELEVEN

Decker checked his phone and sighed. A little too loudly. Harlow glared at him.

"The pressure's on," she said.

"Five minutes," he said, holding up his phone—as though Garza's text would help the situation.

"It was five minutes twenty minutes ago," said Pam. "And he was already thirty minutes late at that point. That's fifty minutes we've wasted."

"Why are we even waiting for him, Harlow?" said Katie. "I thought you already reassigned him to some bullshit admin job this morning."

"Careful, Katie," said Pam, smirking. "Decker is babysitting him today. Or maybe it's the other way around."

"I'm going to have a long talk with Garza," said Decker, "while we count shit."

"I really want to keep him on board. For a number of solid reasons that directly benefit the firm," said Harlow. "But he has to change his tune."

"If by *tune* you mean attitude and work ethic," said Sandra, "I agree."

"He could also play a little nicer with our contract crews," said Sophie.

"I think that falls under attitude," said Pam. "But point well taken. You have your work cut out for you, Decker."

His phone vibrated on the table.

"Let me guess. Ten minutes," said Sandra.

Decker got up and checked the screen. Senator Steele. He hadn't heard from her in a few months, which had been a good thing. They all needed a long break after dealing with APEX's twenty-four-seven harassment campaign. He hoped this was just a friendly check-in. Wishful thinking.

"It's our favorite senator," said Decker, answering the call. "Good timing. Everyone is—"

"Ryan. I need you to listen carefully," said Steele.

Decker sat back down. She hadn't called him Ryan since they'd met at St. Mary's Cemetery in Annapolis. Harlow mouthed, "What?" He shook his head and focused on the call.

"I'm listening."

"You're all in grave, immediate danger," she said.

"Hold on—"

"Stop talking. You need to pull the trigger on your worst-case scenario APEX plan right now. Assume that everyone is being targeted at this very moment."

"Wait. What happened?"

"I screwed up," she said. "I'm very sorry. I'll explain later. Remember, you have unlimited access to the bank account we arranged. Use it. And call me when you're safe."

The call ended before Decker could form another word. He glanced around the table, locked in a momentary daze.

"You okay?" said Harlow.

He shook his head. "No. Steele said we need to activate BROKEN ARROW."

Pam got up from her seat. "Right now?"

"Right now," said Decker, before calling up a never-before-used number on his phone's contact list.

The team scrambled out of the conference room, Pam barking orders.

On her way out, Harlow put a hand on his shoulder. "You're sounding the alarm?"

"Yeah. And calling in our favor with the Sinaloans," said Decker.

"You really think it's that bad?"

"Steele sounded scared," said Decker. "Really scared."

She nodded solemnly, a worried look breaking through her normally stoic mien. Decker knew what she was thinking. It was the same thought that had flashed in neon lights the moment Steele had said to assume everyone was being targeted—Riley and his parents.

"They'll be fine. Riley's in good hands, and your parents know what they need to do," she said, squeezing his shoulder. "We'll head over to the school first thing."

He pressed "Send" and put the phone to his ear. The call connected to a custom-designed, automated phone-tree system. He entered his six-digit access code and spoke. "BROKEN ARROW." The system sent him a text displaying what he had spoken, plus a code, which he promptly repeated for final confirmation. Outside the conference room, several cell phones rang simultaneously. Brooklyn, Riley, his parents, Garza, and Jessica Arnay would receive the same warning.

"Where's Jessica today?" asked Decker.

Jessica Arnay, the firm's in-house attorney, spent the bulk of her time in court. Decker could count on one hand the number of times he'd run into her at the firm over the past few years.

Harlow paused. "She had a hearing this morning. Los Angeles County Superior Court building. Very secure. I'm not worried about her."

Before Decker could respond, his phone buzzed with a text.

DAD: Real deal?

DECKER: Yes. U in a safe place?

DAD: Was headed home from breakfast. Turning around. On way to Riley.

DECKER: Head to the nearest police station.

DAD: No can do. Riley top concern.

DECKER: Then keep a safe distance until I get there. Ten minutes.

DAD: I'll coordinate with Brooklyn. Stay safe.

DECKER: U 2.

"Pain in the ass," he mumbled, before another text rolled in.

RILEY: What's happening?

DECKER: Not sure yet. Do exactly as Brooklyn says. I'm on my way. Love U.

RILEY: Love U 2.

BROKEN ARROW was in motion. Decker just hoped Steele had been overreacting. Not because he didn't want to upend everything and go into hiding. Or burn a once-in-a-lifetime, potentially fate-altering favor the firm could use to make a difference on the streets. Because if Steele was right, they would soon be in the fight of their lives—and nothing would ever be the same once that fight started.

Decker considered calling his Sinaloa Cartel contact to get that ball rolling but decided it could wait until they were in the car and on the way to meet Riley. The clock was ticking, and his number one priority right now was safeguarding his daughter and parents.

"Let's gear up and head out," he said, stepping into the hallway. "Brooklyn is good, but she'll need backup."

"Brooklyn will have to do for now. We have our own problems."

A few doors down, Joshua Keller, their electronic surveillance guru, bolted out of the firm's Sensitive Compartmented Information Facility enclave.

"We have suspicious vehicles on Sunset and Holloway," he yelled. "The inside of the building and the critical approaches look clear, but Mazzie is running through the recorded feed to see if anyone entered earlier. Someone may have stowed away out of sight."

Joshua and the firm's electronics support team had hacked into the building's security system when the firm first moved into the third-floor office space, coopting all its interior and exterior cameras. They had also installed additional hidden cameras, which better covered the streets in front and in back of the building and gave them a view of the stairwell. The secretive installations had been designed to augment what they could access through the building's system.

"Let's see what we're up against on the street," said Decker, starting toward Joshua.

"I have a team inside the building!" said Mazzie, her voice bellowing from inside the SCIF. "Nine subjects entered three minutes ago through the ground-floor lobby and disappeared."

"Scratch that. I'm headed to the armory," said Decker. "Get with Mazzie and map the known location of every hostile, plus all of the blind spots. I need that data available to us in real time, while we're on the move. Joshua can make that happen. We need to get out of here now."

"Why don't we just call the police and the FBI," said Harlow. "Hunker down in here and wait for the cavalry to arrive."

"Because we need to go *poof*," said Decker. "As in vanish. We can't do that if we drag law enforcement into this."

"Are you sure about this?" asked Harlow. "We can't walk out of the lobby. The vehicles in the parking garage are our best chance of going *poof*, as you say, but APEX will have anticipated that."

"They don't know about the tank. And even if they do, it won't matter. They'd need a grenade launcher to stop us. Get everyone to the reception area," said Decker. "We'll distribute equipment there and move out together."

The "tank" was the Toyota Land Cruiser the firm had purchased last winter for high-risk rescues and stakeouts. The fact that APEX had been hounding them day and night for a number of months at that point had also contributed to the decision. Along with Senator Steele's pocketbook. Capable of stopping seven-point-six-two-by-fifty-one-millimeter NATO bullets and deflecting up to thirteen pounds of TNT planted underneath the vehicle, the "tank" had set the senator back close to a half million dollars.

"How are we going to safely move eight people through a dynamic active-shooter situation against APEX operatives?" said Harlow. "Half of us are useless in a gunfight."

"The plan is coming together," said Decker, suddenly thinking of something else that would help immensely. "And tell Mazzie we're going to need one of her drones."

"You just came up with that, didn't you?" said Harlow. "Must be one hell of a plan."

"It should be enough to get us out of here."

What he didn't tell her was that his plan was more of a loose collection of ideas than anything concrete. He took out his phone and put one of those ideas into motion.

CHAPTER TWELVE

Brooklyn's cell phone buzzed once in the center console cup holder, immediately followed by a distinctive chime assigned to a number that meant one thing. Trouble. She checked the message: BROKEN ARROW.

"Shit," she mumbled, before moving a thick criminal justice textbook off her lap and onto the seat next to her.

She stuffed the phone in her pants pocket and scanned the school parking lot without making it too obvious. Nothing had changed. Nobody looked out of place, from what she could tell. A few dozen oversize SUVs and luxury sedans sat in the parking lot, each sheltering an armed personal protective detail for one of the "high value" students inside Crossmount High School. The exclusive all-girls school drew students from obscenely wealthy families in Beverly Hills and the hillside neighborhoods overlooking northwest Los Angeles. Protective families.

If anything, Brooklyn was the black sheep among the sharply dressed, crew-cut muscle-heads crammed into these vehicles. She had shown up for her first day at work in a stylish black suit, which had been recommended by her professional contacts in the business. Athletic and wiry, Brooklyn now sported the same kind of California-casual attire Riley usually wore to school.

Riley had been polite at the house, but as soon as they'd gotten in the Range Rover Decker had leased for the job, the sixteen-year-old had told her the suit wasn't going to work. Brooklyn hadn't argued. She'd returned the *Men in Black* costume a few days later, spending the refunded amount at the same Santa Monica discount clothing store Riley had taken her to after school.

From day one she'd known the job was right for her. That her "principal" wasn't like the rest of the nose-upturned face-lifts parading in and out of the school. Brooklyn had finally gotten a break after a long string of setbacks, and she had no intention of screwing this up. After another casual glance around the parking lot, she grabbed her leather cross-body bag from the passenger footwell and started for the school's main entrance.

Upon reaching the locked doors, she pressed the intercom button, buzzing the main office.

"Ms. Cohen. What can we do for you?"

"I need to pick up Riley Decker. Family emergency," she said.

"I understand. Is it all right to have her escorted by security from class to the waiting area? Or would you prefer she remain in place? Keep in mind the protocols required for you to retrieve her from class."

She'd have to surrender the pistol in her bag to proceed beyond the secure waiting room. Better to let the school's heavily armed and well-trained security team bring her most of the way. If anything went wrong, they'd lock down the school. Brooklyn wondered if Riley might be safer staying inside this VIP fortress than taking her chances on the road.

APEX would need a small army to get at Riley here, not to mention the platoon-size group of bodyguards that would help defend the place. No. She'd gone over this with Decker. Keeping her in place would only delay the inevitable. They needed to disappear. That was the only way to truly buy time against an organization like APEX.

"You can escort her to the waiting area. Thank you," said Brooklyn.

"Our pleasure," said the security officer.

The door buzzed a moment later, admitting her to a glass-enclosed space with two entrances. One led into the school for students, faculty, and approved—presumably unarmed—guests, the other into a well-appointed, recessed waiting room. She took a seat on one of the couches facing the glass interior, since the school had obviously designed the waiting room for the privacy of its students' parents—obstructing any view from the parking lot or public spaces outside of the school. Brooklyn had never asked what it cost for Decker to send Riley here, though she got the impression that Senator Steele had made this happen.

Riley appeared at the school-side door to the waiting room shortly after Brooklyn sat down. The suit-and-tie-clad, iron-jaw security guard who had escorted Riley nodded absently at Brooklyn before turning away. Riley looked appropriately worried under the circumstances.

"What's going on?" asked Riley, rushing over to Brooklyn.

"I have no idea. I didn't get a follow-up text," said Brooklyn, checking her phone again. "Did you?"

"He said he wasn't sure what was happening and that I was to follow your instructions to the letter," said Riley. "So. Are we going?"

"Hold on. I'm going to send your dad a quick text to let him know we're leaving the school," she said. "You should do the same. He's probably worried out of his mind right now."

While she tapped her message, a call came through from "Avi." Not good. Avi Stern, a former Israeli Army officer, was one of the few bodyguards in the entire parking lot she considered a friend. The timing of his call meant one thing.

"I need to take this," she said.

"Is that my dad?" asked Riley, looking up from her phone.

"No," she said. "But get your dad on the phone. I need to talk to him immediately."

"Okay."

Brooklyn answered the call from Avi. "I assume this isn't an invitation to coffee?"

"Ha. Like you'd accept," said Avi. "No. No. I'm just jealous of your new admirers out here."

"How many?"

"Four. In the black Suburban," said Avi.

"That really narrows it down," she said.

"Does it even matter?" said Avi. "Your Range Rover is no longer an option."

"Good point," she said. "Do they look antsy?"

"Antsy? I'm not familiar with that term," he said. "They look like cobras ready to strike. Three of them must have hidden in the back. They materialized as soon as you stepped inside the school. Shall I call the police?"

"And tell them what?"

"I'll think of something good. If the police block the gate on Sunset, that could buy you some time."

"I need to get out of here without drawing that kind of attention," said Brooklyn, her mind scrambling for a solution.

"Dinner and drinks," said Avi.

"Now's not the time," said Brooklyn.

"That's my very low price for potentially losing this job," said Avi. "I have an idea."

"Agreed. Dinner and drinks—if I survive the day," she said, before listening to his simple but effective plan to buy her some time.

Riley shoved her phone in Brooklyn's face. "My dad is on, but he's in a hurry."

She grabbed Riley's phone, putting it to her other ear. "I need a pickup. The parking area is hot. We can't use the Range Rover."

"Brooklyn. I can't help you right now. I really wish I could, but we're outnumbered and outgunned at the office. It's gonna be the fight of our lives to get clear of this place. You're on your own."

"Shit. The parking lot team is probably just the tip of the iceberg here," said Brooklyn. "Maybe we should sit tight. This place is like Fort Knox."

"Listen to me, Brooklyn. Think about how they got a team into the Fort Knox parking lot."

Jesus. How had she missed that? APEX had someone inside the school.

"I'll get her out of here," said Brooklyn. "Walk in the park."

"'Walk in the park,' my ass," said Decker. "But I know you'll pull it off. Can you put Riley back on?"

She handed the phone back to Decker's daughter and returned to her conversation with Avi.

"You still there?" asked Brooklyn.

"Still here. With all of your new friends," said Avi. "I like your boss."

"Well, if you lose your job in the next ten minutes, I'm sure he'll hire you," said Brooklyn.

"I'll keep that in mind."

"Text you when we're ready," she said, ending the call.

Riley lowered her phone. "This is real, isn't it?"

She looked terrified. Pale and about to go catatonic. Brooklyn gripped the sides of her shoulders and forced eye contact before cracking a thin smile.

"Riley. We're going to be fine. Trust me," she said. "I have a few tricks up my sleeve."

Riley nodded, but her expression didn't change. She looked even more disconnected than before. As though she was checking out.

"Hey. Your dad will be fine, too. Trust me. I've seen him in action," said Brooklyn. "I actually feel sorry for whoever is messing with us right now."

She let that statement sink in for a few moments, until Riley took the bait.

"Why would you feel sorry for them?"

"Because your dad would claw his way through hell to get back to you," said Brooklyn. "I'm not worried about him. Not worried about us, either, because he'd claw through hell to get to me if I let anything happen to you."

Riley squinted, her focus returning. "How are we getting out of here without the Range Rover?"

"Uber. Lyft. Hot-wire a car?" said Brooklyn. "I'm still working on that part."

"I think I can help."

"Don't tell me you somehow snuck a car into the student parking lot under my nose," said Brooklyn. "Even though I'd be pretty happy right now if you had."

Riley chuckled. "No. No. Nothing like that. My grandparents. They're less than a mile from here having breakfast. They could pick us up at one of the exits on the other side of the school."

Brooklyn's faith in Riley's true assessment of the situation faltered. She understood they were in danger, but she clearly didn't have a good handle on the scale of their current peril. The chances of escaping without a gunfight were slim to none. Dragging her grandparents into this might complicate matters. Then again, she couldn't think of two more dedicated allies than Audrey and Steven Decker.

"We'll call them," said Brooklyn. "But first I need you to buzz security and tell them you forgot something in your locker."

Riley nodded and winked, the confident young woman Brooklyn had come to know over the past few months back in action.

CHAPTER THIRTEEN

Decker stuffed the phone in his pocket and closed his eyes—resisting the urge to scream. He'd give anything to be four and a half miles west down Sunset Boulevard, at his daughter's school. Brooklyn was shit-hot resourceful, but she represented little more than a speed bump against an organized, concentrated attempt to grab Riley. And Decker had no doubt APEX would throw the works into the effort. Riley's capture was leverage if Decker escaped his current predicament.

"We'll get to Riley soon enough," said Harlow. "Brooklyn will buy us that time."

"I guess," he said.

"She will. One way or the other," said Harlow. "You ready?"

"I guess," he repeated, cracking a smile.

Decker briefly inspected the group, making a few cosmetic adjustments to their body armor and communications sets. Combined with shoulder slaps and banter, his final check amounted to little more than motivational theater. He was pumping them up. Falsely boosting their confidence in the borderline suicidal plan he'd concocted to safely get them clear of this building and through the small army of assassins surrounding it.

Suicidal wasn't the right word, and he immediately regretted thinking it. *Long shot* fit better under the circumstances. Decker was accustomed to working against long-shot odds. Plus they had a few cards up their sleeves. High-tech cards. He singled out Mazzie.

"You sure you can work that thing inside the building?" said Decker, nodding at the paperback-size drone in her hand.

"You're kidding, right?" said Mazzie.

"Not really," said Decker.

"Hold this," she said, giving him the drone.

Mazzie lowered a pair of helmet-mounted goggles over her face and pressed a button on the controller she held in her other hand. The drone buzzed, its four encased propellers instantly activating. Before he could react, the drone rose above him and raced off—circling the group twice in a dizzying display of aero agility. Several seconds later, it eased into a hover a few feet above Mazzie's head.

"She races drones semiprofessionally," said Joshua.

"Okay. I didn't know that," said Decker. "And you're sure you can walk with those on?"

She patted his shoulder. "Pass-through mode, Grandpa. I can control the drone and still see my real surroundings."

"I'll shut up now," said Decker. "Joshua? Anything new?"

"Nothing."

By the time they had finally assembled at the front door, geared up and ready to go, Joshua had figured out that APEX had hit the building's security office soon after infiltrating through the lobby. The building's security cameras now played a continuously looped feed showing all the hallways and common areas to be clear. Fortunately, APEX hadn't discovered Joshua's independently installed network. But Decker's crew still faced a serious dilemma. They were blind right outside the firm's entrance—a frosted-glass door that opened into a hallway shared by an insurance company.

Joshua had assumed uninterrupted access to the building's security cameras, which covered the entire hallway with a three-hundred-sixty-degree dome camera in front of the elevator door. A mistake in hindsight but not necessarily fatal.

The hidden stairwell camera system told them that four operatives had stopped on their floor, two entering the elevator lobby, where they disappeared from camera view. The other two remained on the landing, crouched next to the door—ready to enter at a moment's notice.

Less than a minute later, a separate two-person team entered the stairwell from the first floor and diverted through the door one floor below them. He'd keep that in mind if he made it off this floor alive.

"It's time," said Decker.

He rejoined Pam, who stood at the corner of the hallway that emptied into the firm's tiny lobby, her shotgun pointed at the entrance.

"Any movement out there?" said Decker.

"Not that I can tell," said Pam. "How are we going through the door? There's only room for one at a time."

"Rock, Paper, Scissors?" said Decker.

"Loser goes first?" said Pam.

"The drone is going first," said Decker. "We'll clear the corners by the door from inside the office before moving into the hallway."

"Crisscross?" she asked.

"Fast. No time to aim. Just blast away at your corner if Mazzie screams 'Fire,'" said Decker. "Then down to the floor, weapons pointed at the stairwell door—ready to engage the two yahoos that pile through."

He glanced back at Harlow, who nestled a nine-millimeter CZ Scorpion EVO 3 onto her shoulder. This semiautomatic, civilian version of one of the newer submachine guns on the market was a far better option in her hands than a pistol or compact rifle. With almost no recoil.

Crouched next to Harlow, Katie gave him a quick nod before flipping the selector switch on her EVO 3. She carried a cross-body satchel stuffed with flash bangs and smoke grenades in case they needed a little extra help. Her job was to feed those to Pam and him when requested.

The four of them—Decker, Pam, Harlow, and Katie—would methodically engage any emerging threats, while the rest of the team served as their digital eyes and ears. Mazzie working the drones and Joshua scanning the camera feeds—with Sophie and Sandra serving as their bodyguards and shepherds while they stayed glued to their screens.

"All right. Let's get this over with," said Decker, before moving quietly toward the door.

Pam followed closely behind, the rest of the team remaining out of sight until they cleared any hostiles from the area outside the firm's entrance. The drone buzzed into place several feet back from the door and hovered. Decker took a deep breath and exhaled slowly before nodding at Pam. She scooted in front of the door, staying in a low crouch, and gave a thumbs-up to the drone. The door clicked, its locking mechanism remotely disengaged by Joshua.

"Do it," whispered Decker, rising out of his crouch to a standing ready position.

Pam yanked the door open and quickly shifted to the side opposite Decker as the drone zipped between them and disappeared into the hallway.

"Fire! Fire!" came a moment later from Mazzie, followed by the distinct snap of a suppressed weapon outside the office. Moving simultaneously, they extended their weapons through the doorway—Decker's compact HK416 high, Pam's Mossberg 930 SPX low. Three rapid, ear-splitting explosions from the semiautomatic shotgun drowned out the six five-point-five-six-millimeter bullets fired from his rifle.

They both dropped flat on their stomachs after shooting.

"Two targets down!" said Mazzie.

Decker immediately shifted his rifle's aim to the stairwell entrance. Just as the red holographic reticle settled on the opening, two hostiles charged through, firing suppressed weapons on automatic. As bullets snapped through the air above him and pounded the doorframe, Decker pressed his trigger repeatedly until both targets crumpled to the floor.

"Mazzie! I need you to check the two in the middle of the hallway," said Decker.

Her drone zipped across the lobby and hovered directly over the bodies.

"The one closest to the elevator! He's still—"

Before Mazzie could finish, Decker adjusted his aim and fired twice at the man's exposed head, splattering the wall next to him with blood. Pam was up and through the door in a flash, forcing him to scramble after her. He peeled left to check his first target, finding a very dead man slumped against the wall next to the door. *Not bad for six blind shots.*

At least three of the six bullets he'd fired had struck home. One of them had punched through the bridge of the guy's nose. A quick glance over his shoulder revealed an even more gruesome scene. Pam's target had taken a blast directly to the face, erasing most of it.

He could hardly believe their luck. Four down in the first engagement. Only five to go inside the building, assuming APEX didn't bring in more people once they took over the cameras. It was probably better to keep that thought to himself right now. Speaking of the cameras—he snapped off a quick shot at the small black reflective dome in the ceiling by the elevator door, instantly shattering it.

"Good call," said Pam.

"Make sure we hit the building-controlled cameras in the stairwell," said Decker, before motioning for Harlow to bring everyone else forward.

He stopped them at the door.

"Keep a tight formation without falling over each other. And don't look to your left or right when stepping through this door. It's not a pretty sight," said Decker. "Josh. Any movement on the stairs?"

"No. But I located a team in the parking garage. Two, possibly three, hostiles hiding inside a vehicle with clear lines of fire to the elevator and stairwell doors."

"Not a problem," said Decker.

"Plus the team on the second floor somewhere," said Harlow.

"I have a plan for that, too."

"I'm starting to think that's your new answer to everything," said Harlow.

"Me too," said Pam.

"Me three," mumbled Katie.

"That's part of the plan, too," said Decker, stepping off. "Stay close."

They didn't get far before someone started retching. Dry heaves from the sound of it.

"Someone looked," said Harlow.

Through a sputtering cough, Sophie responded. "Most of his head was missing."

"Do I need to say it?" said Decker.

"No," said Harlow.

"What?" asked Katie, taking the bait.

"Decker—" started Harlow.

"I gave her the heads-up," he said.

Pam stifled a laugh, followed by Katie.

"That was a good one," said Sandra.

"I'll be performing here all week," said Decker, focused on the stairwell door as they walked across the elevator lobby.

He halted them next to the door.

"Mazzie. You're up," said Decker. "Full stairwell sweep."

"Got it," she said.

Decker opened the door far enough to let the drone through before pulling it shut. Several seconds later, Mazzie confirmed what Joshua's camera network told him. The stairwell was clear on all levels. So far, so good.

"I want two weapons covering the stairwell doors at all times," said Decker. "Talk to each other."

After they murmured agreement, he led them into the fluorescent-lit stairwell, shooting out the camera on the third-floor landing the moment he stepped through the door. Two reciprocal sets of concrete stairs led to the second-floor landing. Decker paused the group on the first set, just out of sight of the landing, before firing a single bullet through the camera above the door. He waited for a response, not at all surprised when no attack materialized.

"Katie. Can you hand Pam one of the flash bangs?"

"Sure thing," she said, digging into her satchel.

Once the flash bang was in Pam's hand, he let everyone in on the plan.

"Did you just make that up?" asked Pam.

"Pretty much," he said, before slipping around the corner.

Decker and Pam pressed against the stairwell's outside wall and quietly made their way to the landing, where he knelt about six inches back from the door. A quick nod to Pam set things into action. Pam pulled the pin on the flash bang grenade and released the spoon.

When the plastic handle clattered to the concrete, Decker jerked the door open far enough for Pam to toss the flash bang through. When the grenade vanished, he slammed it shut and lay flat on the polished concrete floor, his body jammed against the door. He was instantly rewarded with several repeated attempts to push the door inward. Panic.

Decker held firm—his one-hundred-eighty-pound, body armor–encased frame keeping the door in place—even as a burst of several bullets punched through the metal a few feet above him. A second round of bullets immediately followed the first, striking much lower, the closest hole just inches from his head. He'd just started to rethink his plan when the flash bang detonated, putting a sudden end to the struggle coming from the other side.

"Open. Open!" yelled Pam, already on her feet.

Decker pulled the heavy door inward, clearing the way for Pam, who crouched in the opening and fired her shotgun twice in rapid succession.

"They're done," she said, starting down the stairs.

"Hold up," said Decker. "Mazzie. I need the drone."

"We need to speed this up, Decker," said Pam, taking the moment to reload her shotgun. "The police will be here any minute—complicating matters."

"Not to mention more APEX reinforcements," said Harlow.

"I haven't forgotten that we're on a timeline. It's just that we know this floor is most likely clear of hostiles," said Decker. "And my plan kind of involves the elevator."

"The elevator?" said Pam. "Are you kidding me?"

"I'm not getting cornered in an elevator," said Katie.

Harlow just gave him that look—and slowly shook her head.

"Just hear me out," said Decker.

Pam aimed her shotgun down the stairs. "Please make this quick."

"We catch them in a cross fire—split their attention and firepower. It's the only way this works," said Decker. "I'll ride the elevator down from this floor when everyone is in position on the parking garage level. Josh. Do you still have eyes on the three hostiles waiting for us?"

"Yes. Same vehicle. A black Mercedes SUV. G-Class. Eleven o'clock position, if twelve is looking straight out of the elevator. Can't miss it."

"The same could be said of the elevator," said Harlow. "Are you sure about this?"

"I don't see another way to do this," said Decker. "We can't walk out the front door. We need to be in vehicles, racing away from here in the next few minutes. They'll pick us off one by one if we try to leave on foot."

"Then let's get this over with," said Pam, starting down the stairs. "I'll text you when we're in position."

Decker nodded. "Don't open the stairwell door until I've emptied at least half of my first magazine. Then let 'em have it with the shotgun and the two Scorpions. Empty your weapons. I'll be back up and shooting before you finish. Watch for my hand signals after that."

Harlow gave him a quick kiss on her way past. "Don't do anything stupid."

"I'm not making any promises," said Decker.

CHAPTER FOURTEEN

Brooklyn kept Riley close as they dashed through the last stretch of hallway toward the bank of doors at the opposite end of the school. Thanks to a series of creative shortcuts identified by Riley from the very start of their unauthorized journey, they'd managed to bypass any Crossmount security officers. The last thing Brooklyn needed right now was a pointless confrontation that would cost her precious time and—more importantly—her pistol.

"How far away are your grandparents?" she asked.

Riley relayed the question over her phone, coming back with an answer right away. "Three minutes. They're halfway through the UCLA campus, on Gayley Avenue."

"Remind them of the pickup location," said Brooklyn.

"They know where to go," said Riley.

"Please remind them," she said. "We'll only get one shot at this."

"The pickup is on Charles E. Young, somewhere just past the Westwood Plaza intersection. After the athletic fields," said Riley. "We'll flag you down."

The door loomed dead ahead. Brooklyn placed her shooting hand inside her bag and gripped the Sig Sauer P320 XCompact—just in case APEX had already figured out they had made a run for it.

"Ms. Cohen! Ms. Decker!"

The familiar Scottish accent originated behind them. Riley slowed, but Brooklyn pressed forward without looking back. Murray McDonald, the school's head of security, would undoubtedly hold them up.

"Ms. Cohen!"

"Keep going," she said. "We're almost out of here."

She pulled Riley along, entirely absorbed with the job Decker had entrusted her to execute. Less than twenty feet to go and she could focus on the next obstacle.

"Ms. Cohen! The least you could do is afford me the courtesy of your attention for a moment!"

Dammit. The accent made his request sound infinitely more reasonable than she knew it to be. Brooklyn stopped just short of the door to face McDonald.

"Quickly. Please," said Brooklyn. "I'm dealing with a time-sensitive matter."

"I figured that to be the case, which is why I arranged for you and Ms. Decker to arrive here unmolested," he said. "So that I could have a word with you."

"I'm walking through that door in five seconds," said Brooklyn.

"Right. I need to know if the threat to which you've responded extends to any other students. In other words—"

"The threat is limited to Ms. Decker," said Brooklyn. "Though I'd strongly suggest you take a very close look at anyone on your staff or the school's who could grant vehicle access to the secure parking lot. My intelligence strongly indicates that they are not working in the best interests of the students you are charged to protect. Ergo—my unauthorized transit through the school."

"Understood," said McDonald. "Shall I summon the police?"

Brooklyn removed the pistol from her bag. "That'll only complicate matters."

McDonald raised an eyebrow. "Godspeed to the both of you."

"You might want to move the students and staff away from any windows facing Sunset Boulevard," said Brooklyn. "Just in case."

"How long do I have?" said McDonald.

Brooklyn raised the phone in her other hand and pressed "Send" on a text she had already composed.

"Not long," she said, before bolting through the door marked EXIT, with Riley in tow.

CHAPTER FIFTEEN

Avi Stern studied the hostile black Suburban from his new position closer to the school guard's shack. The four operatives appeared to be caught up in an animated argument. No doubt debating what to make of Brooklyn's conspicuously long absence. If they made any attempt to leave the parking lot before she contacted him, he'd put his plan into motion.

Given the elapsed time, he wondered if she'd managed to sneak away unobserved. For her sake, he hoped that was the case, even if a part of him wished the bastards in the Suburban would give him the opportunity to do something more than sit on his ever-expanding ass and collect a so-so paycheck.

Crossmount parents paved their prodigies' paths forward with gold bricks but tended to skimp on the less cosmetic aspects of the "keeping up with the Joneses" stuff. He was underpaid and generally treated like shit by his principal. Avi couldn't say the same about the kids' parents. He'd never met any of them, which spoke volumes about the value they placed on his job. Not that they were wrong. Until just a few minutes ago, he'd felt the same way. He'd been convinced that not a single kid at the school required a bodyguard and that his job was entirely pointless—reflecting the harsh reality of his newly formed life in America. Now he wasn't so sure.

His dashboard LCD screen displayed the text he'd been waiting for.

On the move. U better make this worth dinner.

"It'll be worth it," he muttered, shifting the SUV into drive.

Stern's armored Lincoln Navigator lurched forward, closing the distance to the parking lot control point within seconds. A quick glance in the rearview mirror confirmed that he'd made the right decision to change positions in the parking lot. The black Suburban quickly closed the distance, headlights flashing to urge him out of the way.

He drove past the guard shack, nodding at the retired police officer who checked his ID every day, and immediately turned left—effectively blocking both the inbound and outbound lanes. Avi briefly considered abandoning the vehicle and clearing the area but decided he would be safer inside the Navigator. As soon as he screeched to a stop, the guard rushed out of the shack.

Avi opened his window. "Get in the back seat or the men in that Suburban will kill you!"

Incredibly, the guard didn't hesitate. He bolted for the rear driver's-side door and piled inside. With the window on its way back up, Avi drew the pistol from his shoulder holster and discreetly aimed it through the front seats—just in case the man was allied with the Suburban's occupants.

"Friends of yours?"

"Are you shitting me? McDonald told me to wave that truck through. I didn't know it was carrying a Marine fire team," said the guard. "Is this thing armored?"

"It can withstand a fifty-caliber hit or two," said Avi.

He sent a quick text to Brooklyn, using the SUV's touch screen. Block in place. MCDONALD DIRTY. You owe me dinner. Movement to the left, in the outbound lane, drew his immediate attention.

"Hang on," said Avi, shifting into park.

"What do you—"

The SUV shuddered, knocked a few feet sideways by the Suburban, which had picked up speed passing the guard shack—but not enough to dislodge his vehicle from its blocking position. Nothing short of a bulldozer could get through this choke point with Avi's Navigator locked into place. Bullets cracked against the driver's-side windows a few seconds later, the volume and caliber posing no immediate threat.

"We need to get moving!" said the guard.

"They're not after us," said Avi, dialing 911 against Brooklyn's wishes.

By the time police units responded, she would either be long gone—or dead. Regardless of the outcome, he had every intention of making this as complicated as possible for the people who had perpetrated this mess. Including the school's head of security. With that thought in mind, he added to his previous text.

And a new job.

CHAPTER SIXTEEN

The words *MCDONALD DIRTY* sent a jolt of adrenaline through Brooklyn's already-overamped sympathetic nervous system.

"Shit," she muttered, scanning the street.

She had no idea how Avi had come to that conclusion, but if McDonald was APEX's insider at Crossmount, the odds against them surviving the next few minutes had just skyrocketed. She kept them moving down the concrete stairs toward Sunset Boulevard.

"What?" said Riley.

A gray sedan pulled out of a parallel parking space about seventy-five yards away and slowly cruised in their direction.

"Nothing. Stay right on my ass," said Brooklyn.

"Doesn't sound like—"

The screech of metal crunching metal reached her next, focusing all her attention on the sedan. Full house—all four seats occupied. *Here we go.* Brooklyn pulled Riley down behind an SUV parked on Sunset Boulevard and drew the microcompact Sig Sauer P365 from her ankle holster. She handed it to Riley.

"Just in case. There's a round in the chamber. All you have to do is pull the trigger," said Brooklyn.

Distant gunfire erupted, and Riley took the pistol without hesitation, immediately settling into the grip they'd practiced at the firing range. Brooklyn slid the spare magazine out of the holster and handed it to her.

"Stay here. I'll be right back."

"Where are you going?" said Riley.

"To buy us some time," said Brooklyn, before sliding between the parked SUV and the sedan behind it.

Staying low, she leaned a few inches past the front bumper to catch a glimpse of the sedan. Automatic gunfire slammed into the side of the car by her head and peppered the liftgate of the SUV behind her. She dropped to the pavement and inched past the front tire, quickly acquiring the target that had unleashed the unexpected fusillade as pieces of safety glass rained down on her.

A bearded man wearing yellow shooting glasses leaned out of the front passenger side, his face mostly concealed behind a suppressed rifle. He registered her new position a fraction of a second too late, his head hammered back from the two tightly spaced bullets she'd fired before he could press his trigger. She shifted her aim to the driver's seat, but the sedan swerved sharply left before she could fire, exposing her to one of the gunmen seated in the back of the sedan.

A long volley of gunfire from the rear passenger window ricocheted off the street next to her face and exploded the tire she'd chosen for cover—forcing her to scramble back out of sight. A car door slammed, followed by another long burst. A quick peek confirmed the three surviving gunmen had gotten out of the sedan, taking various positions behind it. They'd be on the move soon enough. Three against one. Car tires screeched farther down Sunset Boulevard. Seven against one. Time to even those odds.

Brooklyn backed up onto the curb, her pistol aimed down the line of vehicles parked on Sunset Boulevard, waiting for a target to appear.

"I'm gonna move forward and mix it up with these assholes," she said. "You make a run for the other side of the street once the shooting starts. Don't hesitate. Don't stop. I'll make sure you're the last thing they're worried about. Got it?"

No response. She glanced over her shoulder.

"Riley. I need you—"

Riley was gone. Nowhere to be found. *Shit.* Brooklyn expertly divided her attention between the three men ducking and weaving between the vehicles in front of her and a desperate search to locate Decker's daughter. Seconds later, she determined that Riley had done the right thing and vanished—taking her fate into her own hands. *Smart kid. Decker would be proud.*

Brooklyn bolted forward, leading with her pistol. A figure leaned around the back of an SUV and fired a rifle on full automatic—the bullets snapping past her head. She snapped off two rounds and ducked between the next two cars, staying below the hood.

Bullets shattered the windshield and sprayed glass fragments across the hood as she scrambled toward the street. Brooklyn fired two rounds at a figure mostly hidden behind the sedan stopped in the middle of Sunset Boulevard. She ducked back down without knowing if her bullets connected. This fight wasn't going in her favor. Not even remotely.

She returned to the curb and searched for targets, finding one aiming a rifle in her direction. Bullets cracked past Brooklyn's face, the pressure differential tickling her cheeks. Definitely outgunned. A quick look confirmed the end. Two operatives had slightly fanned out along the grassy strip, driving her back with short bursts of suppressed rifle fire. The third operative was no doubt sliding along the outside of the vehicles, moving into position to take a shot at her from the street.

Brooklyn reloaded her pistol amid a blizzard of bullets and glass fragments. She'd give anything to know that Riley was safe. Her own death was certain at this point, a fact she didn't dispute. She just hoped that Riley had backtracked to the school, seeking refuge somewhere. McDonald may have cut a deal with APEX, but there had to be a limit to how far he was willing to go to make good on that deal. Sending them off and notifying APEX was one thing. Doing the deed himself was another. If Riley made her way back inside the school, Brooklyn could die with a modicum of honor.

A series of pistol shots rang out, odd against the background of suppressed rifle-caliber bullets. Brooklyn risked a look down the curb. The same two operatives who had been firing mercilessly at her a moment ago had stopped. One of them fell sideways onto the grassy strip. The other clutched his throat. She fired a single bullet through his forehead, dropping him between two vehicles. Riley sat crouched behind him, two cars back, her pistol smoking. While Brooklyn was pinned down she'd managed to sneak down the line of cars and take a position where they would never have expected her to be.

Brooklyn gave her a quick thumbs-up before sliding between the two cars next to her. She leaned a few inches beyond the bumper with her pistol, catching the last operative off guard. His head had been turned toward the sidewalk when a single bullet from her pistol punched through his left temple, dropping him to the street. She rushed forward and grabbed his compact assault rifle—some kind of suppressed M4 variant—and sprinted for the sedan several yards away.

When she reached the front of the sedan, Brooklyn leveled the rifle at the approaching Suburban and applied the maximum amount of pressure to the trigger without sending a round downrange. The SUV kept coming, its windows tinted to the point where she couldn't see inside. Brooklyn tracked the vehicle's approach through the rifle's magnified sight, begging for any indication that it was friend or foe. A mere twenty yards away, automatic gunfire erupted from a position to the right of her.

A quick glance to her right confirmed what she had suspected. Riley had gone full-on Ryan Decker—moving beyond the unexpected P365 marksmanship and graduating to full close-quarters combat. Decker's daughter fired one short burst after another from one of the dead operatives' rifles into the approaching SUV.

For a moment, Brooklyn questioned Riley's judgment. Aside from being in the wrong place at the wrong time, the SUV demonstrated no hostile intent as bullet holes dotted the windshield. Until it did. Like the sedan, the Suburban lurched left to expose a broadside of guns, the occupants firing from open windows.

Brooklyn ducked below the hood and slid back—along the side of the sedan—until she reached the trunk, where she popped up and emptied the rifle's magazine into the front windshield. Her rounds punched through the glass, rocking the driver's and front passenger's heads back and forth, until the rifle's slide locked back, begging for another magazine.

Riley's fire methodically punched deep into the rear seats, one bullet at a time, until nothing stirred inside the SUV. Yep—full-on Ryan Decker. Incredible. Brooklyn searched for viable targets, finding none. The past few seconds had proved entirely lethal for the occupants of the hostile vehicle. She started to move toward Riley, who remained locked into place, empty rifle still aimed at the crippled SUV, when a bullet cracked past Brooklyn's head.

Riley sprinted between the cars next to her, joining Brooklyn behind the sedan.

"I don't remember going over assault rifles with you," said Brooklyn, opening the car's door to search for ammunition.

"Recent weekends with my dad!" she said over the growing volume of gunfire.

Four hostiles moved from tree to tree along Sunset Boulevard, seeming to have originated from the secure parking lot. She checked her phone. Avi had confirmed that they had originated from the Suburban he'd blocked. Brooklyn chuckled at his request for a new job. He was a saint. She'd help him with that if she survived the next few minutes.

"Riley. I'm going to unleash hell on earth here in a few seconds," she said, freeing a fresh magazine from one of the dead men's tactical vests.

"When I start firing, you get across the street and push through those bushes. Your grandparents should be on the other side."

Decker's daughter nodded absently, her hands wrapped tightly around the rifle she'd just emptied on the curb. Brooklyn grabbed the rifle and eased it out of her grip, jarring Riley out of her trance. She pointed at the thick row of bushes on the other side of Sunset Boulevard.

"Go now! Your grandparents will be there any second!"

"We'll wait for you."

"No. You get the hell out of here right away," said Brooklyn, slapping a fresh magazine into the rifle. "These people will kill you and your grandparents without any hesitation. I'll be fine."

"My dad wouldn't leave you," said Riley.

"He would if I insisted," said Brooklyn, locking eyes with her. "And I truly insist. Do not wait for me. Are we clear?"

Several bullets popped into the other side of the sedan, underscoring her point.

"We're clear," said Riley, drawing the compact pistol Brooklyn had given her just minutes ago.

"I'll be fine," said Brooklyn. "Ready?"

"Ready."

"Go!" she said, and Riley took off.

Brooklyn rose far enough above the trunk to fire a short burst at a hostile that had chosen the absolute wrong moment to change positions. The man fell face-first on the sidewalk, as though he'd slipped on a patch of ice. Brooklyn shifted fire between the three remaining targets, sending two bullets at a time downrange, until her thirty-round rifle magazine ran dry. From what she could tell, none of her bullets had connected—but that hadn't been the point of her shooting rampage.

She glanced across the street, catching a last glimpse of Riley's tie-dyed shirt before she vanished inside the thick hedgerow. Mission accomplished. Riley's fate was in her grandparents' hands at this point.

Tires squealed in the distance. A bad omen unless accompanied by police sirens, which were still conspicuously absent. Brooklyn considered scavenging for another rifle magazine but decided she'd spent far too long in one place. Instead of following Riley, she bolted for the concrete staircase leading back to the school, hoping to distract their attackers.

She'd gotten about halfway up the steps before the first bullet struck home, punching through her left leg. The hit stopped her in place, but she didn't fall. The second bullet knocked her off the stairs, striking the top edge of the ballistic plate hidden underneath her shirt and ricocheting through her shoulder. Brooklyn hit the grass and started to roll toward the sidewalk.

Bullets sliced past as she careened down the short hill. When she finally came to rest on the sidewalk, she straightened her body, feet toward the threat axis, and started firing. If she was cashing out this morning, she was going out right—"Guns of Brixton" style.

Chapter Seventeen

Steven Decker slowed his decade-old Honda Pilot after passing through the intersection, coming to a stop right around where Riley had indicated.

"I don't see her," said Audrey, leaning forward in her seat to scan the street. "Did we miss them?"

"We got here as soon as we could," said Steven. "Did she leave a message?"

His wife checked her phone and shook her head. "No. Roll down your window. Maybe she's yelling for us."

That doesn't make any sense. He pressed the button to lower his window. The moment it cracked open, the sound of gunfire filled the SUV. He was really glad he'd kept that comment to himself. Without giving it a second thought, he popped open the center console compartment and removed the Lightweight Colt Commander his son had given him as a gift several years ago.

"There she is!" said Audrey, pointing toward the bushes separating Charles E. Young Drive from Sunset Boulevard.

About twenty yards down the street, Riley broke through the bushes and stumbled into the street—holding a pistol. Steven pulled up next to her a few seconds later. Automatic gunfire, punctuated by sporadic smaller-caliber shots, raged back and forth beyond the dense hedgerow.

"Get in!" he yelled through the open window. "Where's Brooklyn?"

Riley opened the door behind him and jumped inside. "She's back there. Buying time. I don't know. Just drive. She insisted."

Steven hit the accelerator, propelling them along the northern edge of the campus. Part of him wanted to stop the SUV and get out to help Brooklyn, but given the volume of automatic fire and the fact that he wasn't half the shot he used to be, he acknowledged the futility of the gesture. Still, leaving Brooklyn to fend for herself didn't sit right with him. He'd been wrong about her. Whether she was dead or alive right now didn't matter. She'd saved their granddaughter. An act of valor and personal fortitude he'd repay if given the chance.

"Turn up here," said Audrey, studying her phone. "There's a parking garage we can hide in."

He eased right onto Royce Drive and followed the signs for the garage. A few minutes later, they had settled into a space on the exposed roof. The gunfire had stopped by that point, replaced by a discordance of police sirens. He glanced between the seats at his granddaughter, recognizing her vacant stare. He'd seen far worse during his back-to-back tours in Vietnam.

"You okay, Riles?"

She took a long time to respond, prompting Audrey to cast him a worrisome glance.

"I don't know," she said. "Everything just kind of went crazy. Where's Dad?"

"He's at the office, dealing with his own stuff right now," said Steven. "We're going to sit tight and wait for instructions."

The gunfire started up again. Its intensity suggested a pitched battle between responding police units and the APEX mercenaries. Even though it took place a few hundred yards and several streets away, Steven didn't feel entirely comfortable with the refuge they'd sought in the parking garage.

"I'm going to take a seat by the ramp," he said. "Just in case."

"I think I should join you," said Riley, locking her pistol's slide back.

She replaced the magazine and slid the lock back into place, chambering a round and readying the pistol like it was second nature. His son had taught her well—or maybe that had been Brooklyn's work. Either way. Impressive to say the least.

"I want you to stay with your grandma," said Steven.

Audrey laughed softly, opening her purse and removing a pistol that looked identical to Riley's.

"I'll be fine," she said.

Riley poked her head through the seats. "Did Dad take you shooting with that?"

Steven cocked his head. "That would be news to me."

Audrey chambered a round without hesitation and laid the pistol in her lap. "Your son left no stone unturned, given what this family has been through."

A furious exchange of gunfire echoed outside the parking garage, coming from the direction of Crossmount High School.

"Can you send a text to Brooklyn?" asked Steven.

"I don't think we should distract her," said his wife.

"From the sound of the gunfire," said Steven, "my guess is she's no longer the focus of APEX's attention. They have the LAPD to worry about."

"Hold on," said Riley, digging for her phone.

While Riley composed a text, he showed Audrey his phone. No message from their son.

"Same," she said quietly, after checking her own phone.

Steven glanced over his shoulder. "Anything?"

Riley shook her head, and the gunfire outside intensified. Nobody said a word. They were on their own for now.

CHAPTER EIGHTEEN

Harlow crouched next to Pam in the stairwell, her CZ Scorpion EVO 3 aimed at a point on the door where she guessed her first shots would strike the Mercedes SUV sheltering the APEX team sent to kill them. Katie edged into position to her immediate right, the barrel of her Scorpion just a few inches from Harlow's shoulder. The initial fusillade of gunfire was going to render her momentarily deaf. She glanced at the shrouded barrel, then at Katie.

"Too close?" asked Katie.

"No," said Harlow, stifling a laugh. "Just wish I had some hearing protection."

"It's gonna get crazy," said Pam, her shotgun pointed at the same point on the door.

"Any word from Decker?" asked Sandra.

"The elevator is on the way," said Joshua.

"Anything unusual in the garage?" asked Harlow.

"The garage level looks clear except for the Mercedes," said Joshua.

"What about Holloway Drive or Hancock Avenue?" said Harlow, referencing the streets behind the building complex.

"Four SUVs for certain. Three on Holloway parked close to the exit. One on Hancock facing the exit. Three to four hostiles in each, except for the closest vehicle, which just has a driver. I have three guys on foot congregated near the parking garage exit, so I'm guessing they belong to that vehicle."

"Can you tell what kind of weapons they're carrying?" asked Harlow.

"Not really. Definitely hiding some serious hardware under their jackets, but that's all I can determine," said Joshua.

"Jackets?" asked Harlow.

"More like cheap windbreakers," said Joshua. "Dark blue. No stenciling."

"Feds?" asked Pam.

Harlow scooted back to take a look. Long hair and beards. They appeared more like APEX contractors than feds, but it was hard to tell these days with so many former Special Forces types running around with law enforcement. At any given time, more than half of the high-risk federal task force operators looked as though they'd just returned from back-to-back overseas combat deployments.

"They look the same as the guys inside the building," said Harlow. "I think they're using the jackets to try to conceal their weapons. I definitely saw a rifle muzzle. Probably some kind of compact rifle like Decker's."

"How the hell are we getting past all of that? Did Decker share his master plan with anyone?" asked Pam, turning her attention to Harlow.

"Don't look at me," said Harlow. "I got the impression he was mostly winging it."

"Elevator door opening!" said Joshua.

"Shit," said Pam.

Harlow applied the maximum amount of pressure to her trigger without discharging the weapon. Automatic gunfire erupted, somewhat muted by the thick metal door, in front of them. Pam scooted forward, gripping the door's handle.

"Ready?"

"Do it," said Harlow, focusing down the sight of her weapon.

Pam yanked the door inward, and Harlow focused her attention on the black Mercedes SUV in her weapon's sight. She repeatedly pressed her trigger—sending dozens of nine-millimeter bullets toward the SUV's occupants. Every gun in the stairwell followed suit, mercilessly pounding the side of the Mercedes until nothing moved inside the squat vehicle. The brief explosion of gunfire inside the cramped stairwell had left her ears ringing.

Harlow noticed movement in the SUV's back seat. She pressed her trigger—and nothing happened. *Shit.* She'd expended her entire magazine. A single gunshot fired from an unknown location slammed the man's head backward against the rear driver's-side headrest. She reloaded the Scorpion with a spare magazine from her vest, dropping the empty plastic magazine to the concrete floor.

"Mazzie!" yelled Decker from the elevator. "I need some BDA."

"BDA?" asked Mazzie, pushing forward to get closer to the open doorway. "I can't really hear what he's saying."

"BDA. Battle damage assessment," said Joshua. "Your drone."

"Oh yeah," said Mazzie, activating the drone in her hand.

The quadcopter zipped through the door and took a circuitous route to the Mercedes SUV, where it hovered next to the shattered passenger-side windows for a few seconds. The ringing in Harlow's ears slowly let up, replaced by distant police sirens.

"How are we looking, Mazzie?" asked Harlow. "I think we're running out of time with the police."

"Everyone looks pretty dead," she said. "I really don't like doing this BDA thing."

Harlow squeezed her shoulder. "We'll be done with this soon."

"God, I hope so," said Mazzie.

Pam's voice boomed through the ringing. "All clear, Decker!"

"Taking out the camera!" he said, followed by a single gunshot that startled all of them. "On the move! Headed for the tank!"

"Right behind you!" said Pam through the door, before turning to the rest of them. "Katie. Harlow. Watch our left side. We'll make our way to Decker."

"Let's go," said Pam, leading them into the garage.

Harlow swept her sector with Katie as they converged on Decker, who had slowed down so the group could catch up.

"Who has the keys to the tank?" asked Decker.

"I do," said Harlow.

"It'll be a tight fit, but we won't last thirty seconds in one of the unarmored SUVs."

Police sirens echoed through the open parking structure, but the sound felt distant, as though the responding units had focused entirely on the Sunset Boulevard side of the building. Something about the police response didn't feel right.

"Josh. Are you seeing any police units on Holloway Drive?" she asked.

Joshua scrolled through the feeds with his tablet while they walked briskly toward the tank, which sat among their personal vehicles in a section of assigned parking spaces.

"No response yet," he said. "Just our new friends."

"There's something wrong with that," said Harlow, stopping the group in its tracks.

"What do you mean?" said Decker.

"I mean the police would seal off all of the exits in an active-shooter situation. Especially one with the amount of gunfire the office across from ours would have reported," said Harlow. "Something doesn't add up."

"I need more than that to work with," said Decker, before continuing toward the armored Land Cruiser. "The parking garage is our only real way out at this point."

"I know. I'm just saying there's more than meets the eye with this," said Harlow. "It's almost like they're coordinating with the police."

"How would that even be possible?" asked Sandra.

"Remember when Gunther Ross and Harcourt tracked us down using the city's camera network?" asked Harlow, fishing for the tank's keys in her pockets.

"Reeves tracked us down at the same time," said Joshua. "Pretty slick. Everyone knew where to find us."

"Exactly," said Harlow, pressing the key fob in her hand and opening the Land Cruiser. "Well, we need to think of that as the lite version of what APEX can pull off."

"Then it's a good thing we have this baby," said Decker. "Who's driving?"

"I am," said Pam, headed for the driver's side. "But this *baby* won't do us much good if they block the exit!"

"We have a secret weapon. Garza," said Decker, as if he'd just solved all their problems.

Harlow didn't know what to say, and judging by everyone else's reaction, she wasn't alone.

CHAPTER NINETEEN

Dave Garcia, a.k.a. "Garza," took another peek at the stretch of road connected to the SunBell Towers parking garage. Expensive cars and SUVs lined the two-lane street, packed tightly together. Showing up late had finally paid off, thanks to a few too many shots of tequila after far too many cervezas at one of his favorite watering holes. A small, sloppy miracle given the circumstances. But there he stood, peeking through a dense palm bush at the edge of a church parking lot. The only thing standing between his friends and what looked like a guaranteed firing squad.

He'd already identified three of the four hostile vehicles described to him by Joshua. The fourth was out of sight on Hancock Avenue, a street that ran perpendicular to Holloway Drive, directly in front of the parking garage exit. Joshua had somehow run the license plate of one of the vehicles and determined it was a rental, which strongly suggested it was unarmored. The same assumption had been extended to the rest of the SUVs. He didn't want to think about what would most assuredly happen if that hypothesis proved false.

Garza studied the men positioned around the exit. They moved like professionals, and according to Joshua, they packed some serious firepower. They'd be armored up, too, so Garza was looking at headshots. Not a problem if he could get close enough, which would be the biggest challenge, from what he could tell.

That and the simultaneous response from the three cars presumably filled with heavily armed, well-trained APEX operators. But if he moved quickly and shot accurately, Garza figured they had a reasonable chance of pulling this off. Reasonable relative to the prescribed situation. Objectively, their probability of success still fell somewhere between shitty and bad. Not exactly his preferred odds but the best he could wrangle under the circumstances.

Garza removed one of his noise-canceling AirPods and pushed the other as snugly into place as possible, letting his ears adjust to the dual input. Police sirens wailed in one ear—muted but still present in the other.

"You ready?" said Garza.

"We're all set," said Decker. "You?"

"Yeah. I just updated my will," said Garza. "Should be enough to cover the funerals."

"Dude. You're on speakerphone," said Decker.

"Oh. Shit. Sorry about that," said Garza. "We should be fine."

"Great pep talk," said Pam.

"It is what it is," said Garza. "I'm ready to kick this off when— hold on."

A police cruiser screeched onto Holloway Drive, a block to the east, and sped in his direction with the full siren and light show.

"I have a police car headed westbound down Holloway," said Garza. "Looks like he didn't get the APEX memo."

"This should be interesting," said Decker.

"Sure. If a dead cop qualifies as interesting," said Garza.

"We can't let them do that," said Harlow.

Garza ran a quick analysis around her statement, coming up with no solution that solved both problems. The only guaranteed way to save the police officer was to take immediate, drastic action to keep him from interfering with the APEX operation. A move that would almost assuredly get himself killed or locked away for years.

"Guys. It's either escape or warn the cop," he said, readying his pistol. "I need to know right away."

He edged through the bushes during the long pause that ensued.

"Warn him off and get out of here," said Decker. "We'll ride this out."

"Warn him," said Pam, followed by a chorus of agreement.

"This is what I get for being late," he said, stepping into the open, his pistol hidden behind his leg.

"Hold up! Hold up!" said Joshua. "Their jackets say DEA!"

Garza glanced from the oncoming police cruiser to the parking garage exit. Sure enough, two of the windbreakers now displayed bright-yellow letters: DEA. One of the operatives unzipped a panel on the remaining unmarked jacket, exposing the same letters.

"I need a decision in the next two seconds," said Garza. "These aren't DEA agents."

"Understood. Stand down," said Decker. "They wouldn't go through the trouble if they planned on killing a cop."

"Plans change," said Garza.

"Stand down and recalibrate yourself for the original plan," said Decker.

The cruiser tore past, leaving Garza in a trail of dust from the bone-dry street. He quickly retreated into the bushes to watch the exchange unfold.

"It's out of my hands now."

The cruiser skidded to a halt about thirty feet from the parking garage exit ramp, at the end of a designated bus stop zone. A lone police officer quickly got out and crouched behind the vehicle's hood with his pistol drawn. One of the fake DEA agents took off running in his direction, a badge held high. He waved his other hand in a frantic gesture to get the cop to leave. Garza had a bad feeling about this. Even from this distance, he could see that the guy carried some kind of mean-looking piece of hardware under his jacket.

"This isn't looking good," said Garza.

"The police officer hasn't raised his weapon. They're just talking," said Decker. "It's under control. This is how they managed to keep the police out of the building and off Holloway Drive. They must be impersonating federal agents to seal off the area."

Garza ignored the comment and focused on the police officer's tenuous situation. The guy had no idea what he'd stumbled into. Remaining mostly concealed by the palm fronds, Garza raised his pistol and aligned its sights with the APEX operative. A little payback was the least he could offer the dead cop's family. He'd taken all the slack out of the trigger, ready to fire the moment this went sideways, when the officer got back in the cruiser and sped away.

"Told you it was under control," said Decker.

"'Under control,' my ass," said Garza. "I'm on the move. Time to get this over with."

"Copy that. We'll time your approach," said Decker.

Garza returned the pistol to its concealed holster on his right hip and tucked the flap of his shirt behind the holster so he'd have immediate access. He picked up the tray of froufrou coffees he'd grabbed at one of Harlow's favorite coffee shops as a peace offering for stumbling in late, along with his backpack, which he positioned over the exposed pistol.

Satisfied that he looked innocuous enough under the circumstances, Garza stepped onto the sidewalk and started walking toward the parking garage, bopping his head as though he were lost in music—*and somehow couldn't hear the three hundred cop sirens blaring through the neighborhood.* Not entirely implausible. He'd seen people walk into honking cars while staring at their phones.

The team seated in the dark-green Range Rover directly across from the bus stop zone must have debated what to do with him. Garza had closed over two-thirds of the distance to the parking garage exit ramp before one of the fake DEA agents responded.

The man waved his hands above his head a few times before pointing at the letters emblazoned in yellow across the front of his jacket.

Garza nodded, pretending not to hear him. The guy started repeatedly screaming, "This is a DEA operation. Get out of here." Garza walked directly at him, pretending to remove an AirPod from his empty ear.

"What's going on?" said Garza, glancing around like he'd just heard the sirens for the first time.

"DEA operation! I need you out of here. Now," the man said.

"Holy shit. I'm on the sixth floor," said Garza, holding out the tray of coffee like it counted for something.

Tires squealed inside the parking garage, and the two men behind him stacked up against the salmon-colored brick wall next to the exit ramp, their stubby, compact rifles no longer concealed. The operative closest to the exit had a grenade launcher attached to his rifle. *Shit.* He hadn't expected that. Regular grenades—yes. Rifle grenades on the streets of LA—no. If APEX brought more than one of those to this show, their shitty-to-bad odds just dropped to fat chance.

"Should I, like, wait across the street or something?" said Garza, easing the backpack's strap off his shoulder and into his hand.

"Just get the hell out of here," said the operative, his attention oddly torn between the APEX firing squad crouched next to the wall and Garza's terrible performance.

"How far is safe?" said Garza, kneeling to lay the coffee tray and backpack on the grass.

The driver-only vehicle, parked on the other side of Holloway Drive, roared to life, headed exactly where he had predicted. Moments after that, the exit ramp's orange-and-white-striped security gate lifted. The operative suddenly turned his back on Garza, barking at him as he rushed toward his colleagues. This was almost too easy.

"I don't care how far—"

Garza's first bullet punched through the nape of the man's neck, permanently ending the conversation. Before the operative's knees had even buckled, Garza took two quick shots at grenade-launcher guy's head. The grenade dropped from his hand the moment his brains splattered the wall. Garza justifiably focused too much attention on the condition of the grenade, which mercifully appeared unarmed, allowing the second operative to snap off a shot—before another dark-red stain decorated the wall.

He muttered a few choice words at the agonizingly sharp pain in his left shin and shifted his aim to the BMW X7 that had just blocked the street in front of the parking garage exit. He fired a tight three-bullet pattern through the open driver's-side window, relieved that he didn't have to put their theory about unarmored SUVs to the test. Garza took off for the BMW, pushing through the pain in his leg as much as the bullet's damage would physically allow.

"Four hostiles down. The ramp is clear," said Garza. "One of these guys had a grenade launcher. Just in case you're curious."

"That's not good," said Decker.

"No. It's not," said Garza. "I recommend a dynamic shoot and scoot. Emphasis on the shoot."

"Got it," said Decker. "Did you get hit?"

"I'm fine," said Garza, grunting through every step.

"You don't sound fine."

"You do your job; I'll do mine," he said, raising his pistol.

Firing on the move, Garza emptied his magazine at the green Range Rover in a desperate attempt to buy back some of that time the leg wound had cost him.

The jacketed hollow-point bullets shattered the side windows and punched through metal, momentarily convincing its occupants to seek cover inside the SUV. The hastily fired volley bought him enough time to yank the dead driver out and get behind the wheel before the APEX operators got their shit together.

He ducked below the dashboard as several bullets struck the windshield and bloodied passenger window, spraying glass dust and fragments through the cabin. Raising his head just enough to see through the spiderweb-cracked windshield, Garza shifted the vehicle into drive and floored the accelerator—barreling straight for the green Range Rover.

Chapter Twenty

The BMW vanished from Decker's peripheral vision, Garza finally on the move.

"Here we go!" said Pam.

Decker braced the business end of the rifle against the top of the SUV's door. He had to make quick work of the two remaining vehicles, or they might not make it out of the neighborhood. The armored Land Cruiser could take a beating, but it was primarily designed to protect its occupants from gunfire, shrapnel, and the near-blast effects of an improvised explosive device. A rifle grenade hit against the side armor would be survivable. A hit to one of the windows would likely kill or injure everyone inside.

"Slow turn," said Decker. "Then gun it."

"I heard you the first three times," she said.

The Land Cruiser eased forward, Pam immediately starting a lazy turn through the intersection. By the time he had a full view of Holloway Drive, the silver Nissan Armada originally parked about seventy-five yards down the street had traversed half of that distance, headed toward them at full speed. Decker tracked the driver's head with the rifle's illuminated reticle while the Land Cruiser turned, stitching several holes in its windshield—until the Armada abruptly veered into a parked car.

Before he could even think about the next threat, Pam violently accelerated the Land Cruiser. "What the—" he started, his expletive-laced rant cut short by a black SUV that momentarily blocked his entire view as it rocketed past, missing them by inches. Decker glanced over his shoulder just in time to see the massive SUV pile into the concrete barrier protecting the parking garage ramp.

Garza's SUV plowed through the green Range Rover's open driver's-side doors like they were cardboard flaps and smeared a slow-reacting APEX operative between the two vehicles' frames. Garza slammed on the brakes and reversed direction before grabbing the MPX submachine gun he'd just noticed in the front passenger footwell.

After double-parking next to the Range Rover, he flipped the MPX's selector switch to "Automatic" and fired a few short bursts into the green SUV with one hand. When no immediate return fire lashed back at him, Garza twisted in the seat and shouldered the weapon, expending the bulk of the MPX's thirty-round magazine directly and methodically into the passenger cabin.

The Land Cruiser pulled parallel to the BMW as he fired the last burst, its wide-open rear passenger door calling Garza's name. Actually, everyone inside was calling his name. Frantically. He ditched the MPX and slid out of the BMW, building up a little momentum before diving across a sea of laps in the back seat. Bullets smacked into the SUV's armored shell and bullet-resistant windows as they sped away from the scene.

Chapter Twenty-One

Pam executed a full-speed right turn onto Westmount Drive—and the incoming gunfire abruptly stopped. They'd done it. Against all odds, they actually escaped the building and made it out of the neighborhood. Now for his next magic trick. More like a miracle. Decker flipped the rifle's selector switch to "Safe" and placed it between his leg and the door before checking his phone. No new messages from his daughter, Brooklyn, or his parents.

"They'll be fine," said Pam, a little too matter-of-factly.

Decker reluctantly nodded, placing the phone in one of the cup holders. He understood what she meant with her tone. Focus on what he could control right here and now. Expand outward from there. His first job. Keep everyone in this vehicle alive. They'd been on the road for about thirty seconds, having traveled maybe an eighth of a mile. Not exactly a safe distance—by any measure.

"Mazzie. Anything we should be worried about?"

Her drone now hovered about two hundred feet above the parking garage exit, giving them a bird's-eye view of the scene.

"Nothing. They're licking their wounds," said Mazzie.

"What does that mean, exactly?" asked Decker.

"The survivors are consolidating into the BMW and the Armada."

"Damn. I should have taken the keys," said Garza.

Decker turned to check on Garza, immediately focusing on his bloodied leg.

"Yeah. It's bad," said Garza, lying faceup across Harlow's, Sandra's, and Katie's laps.

"The body odor and tequila smell is worse," said Katie.

"I forgot to shower this morning. And yesterday, come to think of it. All related to the tequila," said Garza.

"Just turn your head or something," said Katie.

"I'm fine, everyone. Thank you for asking," said Garza.

"We have a stitch-and-fix kit in back somewhere," said Decker.

"That'll work for now," said Garza. "But this is going to take more than the hemostatic gauze trick. I'm still not entirely sure how I managed to get to the Beemer."

"Maybe the tequila numbed the pain," said Katie.

"Brutal crowd," said Garza.

"Just a little tough love," said Harlow.

"Speak for yourself," said Sandra from the middle seat. "I'm bearing his full body weight—and body odor."

Everyone got a quick laugh out of Sandra's joke, except for Pam, who slowed the Land Cruiser to navigate a roundabout. Decker sensed her tension.

"Sophie. Dig around behind you for the kit. It's stuffed behind the third row. Let's get Garza patched up for now," he said. "The rest of you watch your sectors. Or screens. We're still deep in enemy territory."

"Santa Monica Boulevard is about a block south of here," said Pam. "What are you thinking?"

They needed to disappear. Fast. In order to pull that off, he needed to call in the favor promised to him by the Sinaloa Cartel. Right now.

"I need to make *that* call," he said. "As much as I hate the idea."

His phone buzzed, lighting up the cup holder. He could read the contact name upside down. A moment later, the word DAD appeared on the SUV's touch screen. He jabbed the green button.

"Dad! Are you okay? Is everyone okay? Where's Riley?" he said, finally shutting up to let his dad answer.

"Riley is with us. Mom is fine," said Steven. "I don't know if I should tell you where we are right now. Can they listen in on us?"

His eyes teared up, the lump in his throat delaying his answer.

"Ryan. Are you guys okay?"

"We're all fine, Dad. Harlow. Everyone at the firm. We barely made it out," said Decker. "Don't tell me your location. That'll just make it easier for them."

"Do you want us to drive to you?"

"Are you still anywhere near the school?" said Decker. "Yes or no answer."

"Yes."

He had a better idea.

"Ditch all of your phones and drive south. Tell Riley to turn on the burner she keeps in her backpack. She's going to receive a call from someone that can help you."

"I'm driving us out of here right now," said his dad.

"Is that gunfire?" whispered Pam.

"Sounds like gunfire," confirmed Harlow.

They were right. Distant gunfire crackled on his dad's side of the call. Decker had been so absorbed in the conversation that he hadn't noticed it.

"Is Brooklyn with you?"

A long silence followed. "We don't know what happened to her. She held them off long enough for Riley to escape."

"I hear gunfire," said Decker.

"It's been going on for about five minutes. LAPD responded right away."

"Have you tried to get in touch with her?" asked Decker.

"She's not answering," said his dad.

He didn't know what to say, so he hit the default button. Back to controlling what he could.

"All right. Ditch the phones," said Decker. "You should get a call in a few minutes."

"We love you, Ryan," said his mom.

"Love you guys, too," said Decker, ending the call.

Harlow squeezed his arm. "They'll be fine. And Brooklyn has proven to be shockingly survivable in the past."

"I know," said Decker, grabbing his phone from the cup holder.

Pam glanced at him. "Are you really going to send a drug cartel to help them?"

Decker scrolled through his contacts until he found what he needed.

"No. I barely trust the Sinaloans not to sell us out to APEX," said Decker, pressing "Send."

The Land Cruiser's Bluetooth system took over, the touch screen displaying FBI GUY.

CHAPTER
TWENTY-TWO

Supervisory Special Agent Joseph Reeves stared beyond his office window into the deep-green fields of the Los Angeles National Cemetery, trying to process the call he'd just received from Ryan Decker. It wasn't that he didn't believe Decker. Given everything that had transpired between Reeves, Decker, and Senator Steele over the past few years, nothing Decker had said sounded implausible. Reeves simply didn't want to believe it. He didn't want confirmation that the system was entirely broken. And that gave him just enough sand to consider burying his head in. To doubt Decker.

"Dammit," he muttered, before calling Senator Steele.

He certainly couldn't ignore Decker's plea, but he sure as hell wasn't putting the lives of his agents at risk if Decker had somehow stepped in a new, unrelated pile of shit.

"Joe? Is everything okay?" asked Steele.

"Is there any reason it wouldn't be?"

"No. Not for you," said Steele.

"For Decker?" said Reeves.

The long pause answered his question.

"I just got an interesting call from him," said Reeves. "And I'm not exactly sure how I should proceed."

"He's well aware of the newly developed situation. I warned him as soon as I knew there was a problem—not even an hour ago," said Steele. "Sorry. I should have given you a heads-up. I didn't think he'd call you."

She had no idea.

"Senator. Ryan Decker was attacked in his office just minutes ago," said Reeves. "And they tried to grab his daughter from her school."

"What? That fast?" said Steele. "Oh God. Please tell me they're okay."

"Everyone is fine, for now," said Reeves. "How serious is this? Decker asked for some very specific help. The kind that puts me in an awkward spot. But most importantly, it puts my agents at risk."

"Joe. Nobody expects you to put yourself or your agents at risk," said Steele.

"Are you certain this is APEX?" said Reeves.

"I'm afraid so. I've had one of their top people under surveillance for several months. They uncovered something big about a week ago," she said. "I didn't tell you because I didn't—"

"Did Decker know?"

"Know what?"

"About you continuing to look into APEX?" said Reeves.

"No. He had . . . no idea," said Steele, her voice trailing away.

She'd obviously come to the same realization that had just hit him over the head like a frying pan. His family might be in danger.

"I need to hang up now," said Reeves. "I highly suggest you get somewhere safe—surrounded by people you trust. They're cleaning house."

He ended the call and dashed out of his office, drawing stares from the half dozen or so task force agents not assigned to field duty that morning.

"Where's Kincaid?" asked Reeves.

"Break room," said Special Agent Vale. "Simonetti brought in Dunkin'. I was just about to grab you before the doughnuts disappeared."

Reeves absently nodded at Vale before taking off again. He found Kincaid, Simonetti, and Gaines each holding a Styrofoam cup and a partially eaten doughnut.

"Shit. Sorry. I should have grabbed you," said Kincaid. "There's still a few left. Glazed, but—"

"Simonetti. Gaines. Grab a car and meet me at the edge of the parking lot, directly across from the mailboxes—in ten minutes," said Reeves. "I'll explain on the road."

He could tell by the looks on their faces that they understood the gravity of the situation. The absolute silence and speed of their departure confirmed it.

"What's going on?" said Kincaid, setting down his coffee and doughnut.

"How many vehicles do we have in the field—right now—carrying a tactical kit?" said Reeves.

Given the fluid, quick-to-escalate tempo of the Russian organized-crime division's investigations and the violence-prone nature of their targets, Reeves had fought tooth and nail with agency bureaucrats to proactively and properly equip his field agents for the high-risk work they faced on a daily basis. At any given time, a quarter of the division's vehicles carried the kind of tactical firearms and gear that gave them a fighting chance against the Bratva soldiers who would rather die in a blaze of glory than face a jail sentence.

"Eight," said Kincaid. "We can double that number in about thirty minutes, but it'll raise some eyebrows."

Reeves did the math. Each kit equipped two agents with an M4 rifle, several rifle magazines, body armor, ballistic helmets, communications gear, flash bang grenades, a hand portable door-breaching ram, and plenty of zip-tie restraints. He could put sixteen agents into action right now, which should be enough to dissuade APEX from making a costly mistake.

"Have the agents in the field gear up right now, wherever they are—and then send half to my house and half to your house," said Reeves.

"What the hell?"

"It's just a precaution."

"Sounds like more than a precaution," said Kincaid.

"Just get it done," said Reeves, already headed for the door.

"Do you want me to put together more teams?"

Reeves shook his head. "We shouldn't need more than that. This is mainly for show."

"Is my family in danger?" said Kincaid.

"No more than mine," said Reeves. "I'm pretty sure I'm just being paranoid."

Kincaid followed him out of the break room. "I'll get everything rolling and coordinate the rest from the car."

Reeves stopped. "I need you to handle something else for me, discreetly, while I run a separate related errand."

"You're not headed home?" asked Kincaid.

"No. Eight agents are more than enough. Have them escort our families back to the secure parking garage across the street. Park on the roof and sit tight," said Reeves. "I need you to run that as quietly as you can."

Kincaid nodded. "Got it. What's the other thing?"

"There's an ongoing shootout at Crossmount High School, just north of UCLA—"

"I know where it is," said Kincaid. "How do you know this? We haven't received an active-shooter alert."

"Just happened five minutes ago," said Reeves.

"How could you know that?"

"I promise I'll explain later," said Reeves. "A young woman named Nava Cohen has most likely been shot at the school. She's Riley Decker's bodyguard."

"Ryan Decker's daughter?"

"Yes. Riley is headed in this general direction with her grandparents right now. I'm going to bring them to the secure garage," said Reeves. "I need you to grab a carload of agents and head up to the high school to find out what happened to Ms. Cohen. If she's KIA, end of story. I'll meet you back at the parking garage. If she's still alive—do whatever you need to do to establish federal protective custody. She's not out of danger."

"We'll stay with her," said Kincaid.

"Smooth things out with LAPD and leave your agents with her," said Reeves. "This is going to scare the hell out of your family—and mine. You should get back here to see them as soon as possible."

"Right," said Kincaid, heading for his office.

"And Matt?"

"Yeah?"

"If there's a tactical car near the school, divert those agents to meet you at the school," said Reeves. "Six should be more than enough at my house."

"I'll keep you posted," said Kincaid, disappearing.

When Reeves turned, five agents stood waiting at the division's exit. They'd clearly overheard enough to know that the office had just been turned upside down by something that required an all-hands response. Special Agent Sarah Vale, who had been in the division from day one, shrugged.

"Where we headed?" she asked.

"You're coming with me," said Reeves. "The rest of you are headed out with Kincaid."

On the way to the elevator, Vale pulled him aside. "We should stop by my car on the way out."

"What?" said Reeves, peevishly. "Whatever it is can wait. We don't have the time."

"'Whatever' happens to be a California-compliant AR-15 and several noncompliant magazines," said Vale. "Just in case. Not that I was eavesdropping on your conversation."

"Just in case sounds good right about now."

CHAPTER
TWENTY-THREE

Brad Pierce sped away from his daughter's high school, headed south toward the agreed-upon rendezvous point. His daughter grunted in the passenger seat.

"Dad. I thought these days were behind us?" said Nicki.

"So did I. This is just a precaution," he said, not wanting to entirely freak her out.

"You literally pulled me out of a trigonometry test," she said. "And kind of made a scene. You don't do that if it's just a precaution. What's really going on, Dad?"

"I honestly don't know," he said, which was terrifying. "All I do know is that Uncle Ryan sent me a code about twenty minutes ago that he would only send if he thought there was a possibility that we were in immediate danger. Actually, the code was for everyone. Not just us. Something scared him that bad. That's why I made a scene. Your mother did the same thing at Tommy's school."

"Where are they?"

"On their way to the Arapahoe County Sheriff's Office," he said. "We'll meet them there."

The public parking area sat close enough to the main sheriff's office building to provide a deterrent and was far enough away from East Broncos Parkway to give them plenty of warning if APEX wasn't deterred. They'd transfer the gear he'd grabbed from the office vault into his wife's SUV and take a few moments to collect themselves before fleeing town. Their emergency evacuation plan had gone smoothly so far.

Anna, his wife, had driven away from the house in just under five minutes, after stuffing her vehicle with the prestaged bugout packs they kept in the garage, the travel packets locked away in their bedroom safe, and all the weapons in their gun vault. She'd practiced the drill several times since they'd moved into the house until she could do it by herself within that short time frame. Her diligence had paid off. The time between Decker's warning and their departure would clock in under thirty minutes. The only way they could have done it faster was if everyone had been home at the same time—a rare event these days in the Pierce household.

"I mean after that," said Nicki. "Unless that's it."

"No. That's not it," he said. "We're going back to Aguilar."

"For how long?"

"Until the coast is clear," said Pierce. "Who knows. This could be a false alarm."

His phone rang, and he grabbed it from the center console.

"That's odd," he muttered, answering the call. "Hey, Gunny," said Pierce. "I was just about to call you about taking an unplanned trip out your way."

"Then this ain't no coincidence," said retired Gunnery Sergeant Fowler. "Three ginormous SUVs just burned past my place. Something going on up there?"

"When we hang up, you and Denise need to get out of there," said Pierce. "And not to your hunting cabin a few miles away."

"I guessed as much," said Gunny. "Though I wouldn't mind doing a little recon up that way."

"Probably not a great idea," said Pierce. "My presence up in Denver isn't a secret. If they wanted to kill me, they could have shot me getting out of my car at the office. They're setting up some kind of ambush down there to grab us for leverage."

"Sounds about right," said Gunny.

"Go visit your grandkids. Between the five million cameras you have set up around your house and the one I have hidden up in the hills, we can figure out when it's safe for you to return."

"Copy that, sailor," said Gunny.

Pierce shook his head. "Stay safe. And pass on my apologies to Denise. And my best, of course."

"She'll be cursing your name all the way to Albuquerque."

"If it makes you feel any better, everyone's going to be doing the same in my car—all the way to wherever we're going," said Pierce.

"You know, it actually does make me feel a little better," said Gunny. "Give those kids a hug for Denise. And give Anna a big ol'—"

"You're breaking up, Gunny," said Pierce, talking over him.

"Probably for the better," said Gunny. "Watch your six, sailor. Out."

Pierce checked his messages while he had the phone in his hand. Still nothing from Decker.

"How did they find our place in Aguilar?" asked Nicki.

"They followed us back at some point," said Pierce.

"But we were careful, and Gunny was always watching," she said. "They couldn't follow us there without us knowing."

"All they really had to do was verify that the Aguilar area was our true destination," said Pierce. "After that it was just a matter of spending a lot of money on aerial surveillance. And these people apparently have all the money in the world."

Nicki just sat there, blankly staring through the windshield for several seconds.

"How do we make all of them die?" she asked.

He was shocked by the question. But not by the fact that his daughter had just casually suggested killing as a solution to a problem. Pierce felt the same way. What took him by surprise was its sheer elegance and simplicity. It was a question he'd never asked before—but he fully intended to pursue the answer with a new sense of clarity and purpose.

"I don't know, Nicki," he said. "But I'm going to find out. And your uncle Ryan and I are going to make them all die."

Or die trying.

CHAPTER TWENTY-FOUR

Decker was now convinced they were being tracked. A few blocks past West Martin Luther King Jr. Drive, the same metallic-green, two-door sedan appeared every time they passed a connecting street. The car's presence meant progress with the Sinaloans—or whichever gang they paid to do their dirty work up here. Until the car showed up, he'd thought negotiations with the cartel had ended, and they'd just wasted close to an hour driving through some of the city's roughest neighborhoods—with APEX closing in.

"Green car to the right," said Decker. "It's been ghosting us for a few minutes."

As they cruised past the next street, the little car appeared, matching their speed. He decided to give his contact another try. The direct line he'd been assured would be answered twenty-four hours a day turned out to be anything but direct. Or maybe this was all part of the process. The cartels were notoriously suspicious of anyone outside of their tight circle, especially north of the border. Decker couldn't blame them for taking caution to the next level under the circumstances, but he was running out of time.

The Los Angeles Police Department had issued a citywide all-points bulletin for their Land Cruiser about three minutes ago. He had APEX to thank for that. In addition to providing the heavily armed dead bodies that undoubtedly scared the hell out of every responding officer, the trick they'd pulled with the video surveillance system had likely delayed matters.

An eyewitness from the building, with a view of Holloway Drive, probably filled in enough blanks for police to find them on a nearby business's closed-circuit camera feed. The bullet dents and spiderweb-cracked windows kind of stood out.

Just another reason he had hoped to be off the streets thirty minutes ago. He redialed the number that had hung up on him a few minutes ago.

"Hello?" said the same Hispanic voice.

"Can we stop playing games?" said Decker. "You know exactly who this is. I need to get off the streets immediately. That was the deal."

"One million dollars. I'll text you the routing instructions."

"Seriously? I seem to remember us striking an agreement that more or less saved your organization hundreds of billions of dollars a few years ago. *Sí?*" said Decker. "Actually, that agreement probably netted you another hundred billion a year. Does any of this ring a bell?"

"I'm well aware of those particulars, but I'm not bound by the agreement—if my judgment dictates otherwise."

"And your judgment says you should squeeze some money out of me—because you can?" said Decker.

"No. But my judgment says I should get something in return for the twenty-million-dollar bounty I'm passing up. And the shitstorm my operation is likely to endure from a group that can afford to post such a bounty."

Harlow tapped him on the shoulder and whispered, "It's Steele's money. Pay the million." He nodded.

"I assume you don't expect a suitcase full of cash?" said Decker.

"Not unless you have one."

"I wish. Go ahead and send the bank transfer instructions," said Decker.

"Just like that?" said the man. "No counteroffer?"

"I don't have time for that," said Decker. "Just get us off the street."

"As soon as I have the money," he said, and a text appeared on Decker's phone.

He opened the text to find the requested financial instructions.

"I'll call you when the money goes through," said Decker.

"When the money goes through, you'll receive directions," said the voice. "Do not deviate from the directions. Failure to comply voids our deal."

"And makes you twenty million dollars richer?"

"Goodbye, Mr. Decker."

He passed the phone back to Sandra, who tossed it to Joshua.

"How long will it take?" asked Decker.

"Not long. I'm already in the account," said Joshua. "Assuming we don't have a transaction limit. We've never moved this much before."

"Don't even say that," said Decker. "The only option left is to pull up to one of these beat-down repair shops and try to buy a few hours of their time and discretion."

"Be a lot less expensive," said Pam. "That's for sure."

"I don't think any of these places accept bank transfers," said Katie.

"I grabbed the cash pouch from the vault," said Sophie. "That's about forty-five hundred."

"That should buy us about five minutes," said Katie.

He was too nervous to join the banter or even fake a laugh. His eyes darted back and forth along the road ahead of them. All it would take is one police cruiser with a half-awake officer behind the wheel to derail everything. They needed the cartel's help to pull this off.

"Get us off Normandie," said Decker. "We're pushing our luck on this road. We should be ducking and weaving through the neighborhoods. Like before."

"Your cartel contact very specifically said to drive south on Normandie," said Pam.

"That was before the APB," said Decker.

"They're watching us," said Harlow. "You heard what that guy said."

The traffic light at the West Slauson Avenue intersection turned yellow, and Pam slowed the Land Cruiser.

"We need to keep moving."

"You want to drive?" said Pam, easing them to a stop in front of the crosswalk.

"No. I'd probably get us killed right now," said Decker, before glancing over his shoulder. "How are we doing on the transfer?"

"Almost there," said Joshua. "I didn't hit a block on the amount, so we should be good to go."

"Decker," said Pam.

Her tone told him they were in trouble. He turned his head and immediately spotted the problem. A black-and-white Ford Interceptor approached from the east.

"Shit," said Katie, clueing in on their dilemma.

"What's our move?" said Pam, flexing her grip on the steering wheel.

Sitting first in line at the intersection, the officer couldn't possibly miss them. And a high-speed escape through the streets of South Los Angeles was pretty much out of the question with Garza lying unsecured across three laps.

"We sit here and hope the officer is legally blind," said Decker.

"We're home free. The money went through," said Joshua, blissfully unaware.

"We just bought a whole lot of nada," said Decker.

"Maybe not!" said Pam.

A black pickup truck flashed by her window and careened through the intersection, just barely avoiding a collision with the cross traffic. The Interceptor lit instantly, its siren wailing away as it weaved through the stopped cars in the intersection to pursue the pickup. Harlow handed Decker his phone, which displayed a text message.

Ur welcome. Continue south. Left on 59th. Right on Raymond. Left on Florence. Just past Vermont turn left into Quickstop Car Wash. Transfer inside automatic wash. Do exactly what is asked of you!

"Sounds like we're going to get a little wet," said Decker.

He guided Pam through the directions, which wisely took them off Normandie Avenue immediately after driving through the intersection. No fewer than three police vehicles zipped past Fifty-Ninth Street in Decker's side mirror. The same attention to detail had been given to the choice of taking them east on Florence. Two pursuing units raced by, headed in the opposite direction, the Land Cruiser's bullet-scarred back half mostly concealed.

When they turned into the car wash parking lot, a squat, serious-looking Latino gentleman walked them through the rightmost gate and motioned for Pam to lower her window. The guy's attitude matched his appearance.

"When everything stops, you get out and get into the white van in the lane next to you. Leave all of your shit behind. And I mean everything. Phones. Wallets. Watches. Nothing but the clothes on your back. *Comprende?*"

"*Sí,*" said Decker. "Will we get anything back?"

"Don't talk. Don't ask questions. Just do exactly as you're told. Get moving," he said, before pounding the hood.

Pam raised the window, her eyes squinted and lips pursed shut, until the glass stopped—when she broke out into a mouthful of expletives.

"Yep," said Decker. "That's pretty much how we all feel."

When her justified minitirade ended, she drove them into the wash while everyone frantically removed their tactical vests and emptied their pockets. Decker shook his head as he placed his wallet, pistol, and spare magazines on the dashboard. They'd be lucky to see any of this stuff again, especially the electronics equipment, weapons, and tactical gear. As much as he hated the thought of giving any of that stuff up, they wouldn't need any of it where they were headed. When it was time to return, they could always buy more.

The wash operated like any other automatic car wash he'd been through, until they reached the spinning brushes. Once the Land Cruiser had been fully enveloped, the brushes stopped rotating and started to retract. A man knocked on Pam's window after the mechanical spinners were clear of the vehicle. Decker assumed that was the signal to switch vehicles.

"Remember. Do exactly what they say. If something feels off, communicate that before acting," said Decker.

"This whole thing feels off," croaked Garza.

"I meant *really* off," said Decker.

"So did I."

"We're well past the point of no return," said Decker. "Let's go. Everyone out."

The moment Decker stepped down from the Land Cruiser he was unnecessarily manhandled and prodded with a rifle toward the white, windowless cargo van. It felt like these thugs sensed a cut of the twenty-million-dollar bounty—if they could get him to snap without going entirely overboard. He managed to grab Harlow's hand before the cargo door slammed shut, casting them into pitch-black darkness. That warm touch was his only form of reassurance right now.

"Everyone sound off!" said Decker, needing to be sure no one had been separated.

The entire group answered in quick succession. Once everyone had been accounted for, Pam and Sandra scooted to the back, followed by Mazzie and Joshua—making room for the rest of the team. The car wash brushes reactivated, thumping against the van's sides and top as the vehicle moved along the automated path.

A few minutes later, they were on the road. Decker tried to monitor their route, but he lost track within minutes. The van turned dozens of times, pulled into several driveways to reverse direction, and circled a few parking lots before finally coming to a stop for longer than a minute. Total elapsed time? He had no idea. They'd made him leave his watch in the Land Cruiser. He squeezed Harlow's hand, and she squeezed it back. Their fates were entirely in the hands of a gang of murderous criminals, and it didn't feel right in any sense of the word.

There was no way he'd put Riley and his parents through this. He'd hire a private jet to fly them wherever the Sinaloans ultimately took Decker and the crew. Jessica Arnay could arrange a safe, entirely anonymous place to stay somewhere between Los Angeles and San Diego until he made that happen. Fortunately, she'd been waiting inside the Edmund D. Edelman Children's Court lobby at the time of the attacks, deep inside the Los Angeles County Superior Court building—one of the most secure facilities in the city.

Reeves had graciously agreed to protect Jessica's and Decker's families until their final destination in Mexico had been arranged. He owed Reeves and his entire team one hell of a thank-you party when the dust settled from this mess. Not only had he managed to intercept and secure Decker's daughter and parents within minutes of his call, but he'd dispatched a team to locate Brooklyn, who had already been transported to the level one trauma center at the Ronald Reagan UCLA Medical Center less than a mile away.

A heavily armed four-agent detail watched over her while emergency surgeons fought to keep her alive. She'd been shot several times by the time the Los Angeles Police Department finally overwhelmed the APEX operatives sent to kidnap his daughter. According to the brief conversation he'd had with Riley, Brooklyn had sacrificed herself so Riley could safely escape. He owed Brooklyn everything for that and planned to make good on it.

CHAPTER
TWENTY-FIVE

The side cargo door abruptly slid open, filling the van with harsh fluorescent light. Harlow squinted and raised her hand to shield her eyes.

"We're here," said a man she recognized from the car wash. "Follow me and keep moving. I got you set up in back. We'll bring your stuff to you shortly."

She hopped down from the van, taking a quick look around before the man motioned for her to keep moving. A chop shop from the looks of it. Several luxury vehicles sat partially disassembled across an expansive, raised corrugated metal garage.

He led them to the back of the shop and a door that opened into a hallway belonging to a building attached to the garage. The man opened the second door on the right and invited them inside. Decker made his way to the front of the group, whispering in her ear as he passed.

"This is the guy I talked to on the phone."

He examined the room before any of them entered, quickly nodding his approval. As though they had a choice. The cartel thugs had dropped the pushing and prodding routine, but it was still crystal clear that this wasn't a social visit. The several neck- and face-tattooed, AK-47–toting gangbangers gently corralling them into the room didn't look like they would be breaking bread and swapping stories with them later.

Harlow followed her friends into what surprisingly resembled a small military barracks. Six metal bunk beds took up the entire left side of the room, spaced a few feet apart and topped with thin foam mattresses. Several folding chairs lay stacked in the far-right corner, next to two flattened card tables that leaned up against the wall. An empty watercooler sat in the corner closest to the door. Decker went back into the hallway to get Garza, helping him lie down on the closest lower bunk.

"It's not much, but you won't be here for very long," said their host. "I'll have someone bring a new water jug and some cups."

"And a doctor capable of taking care of our friend, please," said Decker.

The man studied Garza for a few moments. "I can bring someone in to stitch him up, but my guess is he's going to need more care than that if he wants to use his leg again."

"I do," said Garza.

"What are our options?" asked Decker.

"We can drop him off in front of an emergency room."

"He won't last long without protective custody. They'll be watching the ERs," said Decker. "I'd need to make some calls before you drop him off."

She could tell by the slight change in the man's posture and the tightening of his face that he had become very uncomfortable with Decker's suggestion. If Decker even hinted about their inside track with the FBI, this guy might think twice about the whole arrangement. Before Decker could sign their death warrants, Harlow intervened.

"Forget taking him to an ER. He's not exactly dying," said Harlow. "Give him twenty bucks and help him into a booth at any Denny's or IHOP in the city. Give us the location after you drop him off. We'll take care of the rest."

"I can do that," said the man.

"I'll need my phone," said Decker.

Harlow shot him a look. He was always pushing it at the wrong moment.

"I can't imagine our phones will ever show up in this building," said Harlow. "For security reasons."

"Your phones have already been destroyed. I'll provide you with a suitably encrypted and untraceable method of communication to be used at my discretion," said the man, nodding at her. "For security reasons."

"Given the circumstances, I think it's fair to say that we all appreciate your attention to detail," said Harlow.

A subtle, sly grin crossed his face. "That's my job. Paying the closest attention to all of the details."

"Would it be fair to assume you know the details of our departure?" asked Decker.

"You're departing in a few hours," he said. "The rest is up to you."

Decker displayed a puzzled look, which was reflected in all their faces.

"Is something wrong?" asked the man, looking back and forth between them.

Harlow took control again. Decker was on a hair trigger, and it couldn't be more obvious that the cartel had changed the deal again. A potentially explosive combination right now.

"Nothing's wrong," said Harlow. "I just don't think any of us expected to have a say in the matter. For security reasons."

"Security won't be a concern once you've reached your destination," said the man. "This is a delivery only."

Something was definitely off. Decker beat her to the next logical question.

"Are we still talking about the same arrangement? A safe haven in Mexico?"

"Mexico is no longer an option," said the man.

"Why the hell not?" said Decker.

The man shook his head. "You don't get it, do you?"

"All I'm getting is that your boss extorted a million dollars out of us, and now he's going back on the most important part of the agreement."

The man quickly yanked the door shut.

"You're either crazy," said the man, "or you're stupid. Or both. Because only a truly crazy or stupid person would yell out a number like that."

Holy shit. She just got it. Decker started to open his mouth, but she silenced him.

"The bounty," she said.

Now they all got it.

"For security reasons," said Decker.

"Precisely," said the man. "I knew you weren't stupid."

"Don't eliminate crazy," said Garza.

"I haven't," said the man, glancing in Garza's direction. "Your reputations preceded you."

"So. Where does that leave us?" said Decker.

"Mexico is out of the question," said the man. "Word gets around fast down there, and I can count the number of *paisanos* who would pass up twenty million dollars on one finger."

"El Jefe?" said Decker.

"*Sí.* He's a man of his word," said the man. "But he also understands the upper limits of loyalty. Keeping you out of Mexico is the only way for him to honor the arrangement."

"And your men here?" asked Decker.

"Word travels a little slower north of the border," he said. "Which is why I'd prefer to get you on the road as soon as possible. There's only so much I can control once word gets out. Some of your million-dollar fee will go to help with that."

"Sounds like we need to come up with plan B. Fast," said Decker. "What do we have to work with? How far can you take us?"

"Well, like I said. Word travels slower up here—but it eventually reaches its destination," he said. "So it all depends on your risk tolerance. There's no risk to getting you well clear of the greater Los Angeles area—say, Bakersfield or a similar distance up the coast. Barstow and Palm Springs to the east. Maybe San Bernardino National Forest. You could get lost up there for a while. Then there's San Diego. Though I'd recommend moving away from the border."

"I have an idea for plan B," said Harlow.

"Already?" said Decker.

"San Bernardino National Forest made me think of something."

"Then I'll leave you to it," said the man, glancing at Garza. "While I work on his situation. Shouldn't be long."

As soon as their host shut the door, Decker turned to the rest of the crew.

"You guys were awfully quiet."

"We didn't want to upset the perfect balance the two of you were striking between getting us killed and keeping us alive," said Pam.

"I was mostly just scared shitless," said Joshua, giving them all a quick laugh.

"I think we're fine," said Katie. "I don't trust that guy any farther than Joshua could throw him, but the whole Mexico angle makes sense in light of the twenty million. Hell. I might turn you in."

"Twenty million is an awful lot of money, Decker," said Garza. "I wouldn't trust any of these turds."

"Shit. He'll be on the phone with APEX before he finishes breakfast," said Pam.

"Uh. I'll borrow one of those gangbangers' phones on the way to breakfast," said Garza, even getting a laugh out of Decker.

Harlow wanted to join in on the fun, but the thought of a twenty-million-dollar bounty made her head spin. Then she thought of something they'd all apparently missed.

"What's up, Harlow?" said Pam. "You're usually the first to laugh at Decker."

Katie gave her a high five.

"Our new cartel friend never said the twenty million was for Decker."

"I knew she was going to kill the little fun we were having," said Pam.

"We can all laugh it up later. Right now I'd like to hear Harlow's idea," said Decker. "Because I can guarantee you that at least eighteen of that twenty million is for my head."

"Probably nineteen," said Pam, before glancing at Harlow. "I hope your plan involves selling Decker."

"That's plan C," said Harlow.

PART THREE

CHAPTER TWENTY-SIX

Sheriff Harvey Long excused himself from the conference room, where he'd been stuck for the past hour with county supervisors and their staff, going over the latest numbers in the entirely futile effort to halt the flow of unregulated cannabis from Humboldt County's share of the Emerald Triangle. He could have started and ended the meeting with one sentence: *Nothing's changed or is ever going to change, folks. Have a nice day.* Actually, that was two sentences.

"Sorry. I need to take this. Be right back," he said, before ducking out of the room.

Sherry Grover, the department's administrative manager, waited for him outside his office.

"Line two," she said. "I refreshed the mug on your desk. Figured you might want to take your time."

"I'd like to arrange my own kidnapping," he said. "You're the best, Sherry."

"Remember that at the end of the year," she said, nodding back toward the conference room. "When they're talking in circles about pay raises."

"You shall never be forgotten." Long paused in his doorway. "Did Decker say what was up?"

"No. Just that it was an emergency," she said. "He basically begged me to drag you out of that meeting."

"He didn't have to beg," said Long. "If I'm not back out in ten, why don't you offer them some water. Keep them from revolting."

"And break long-standing tradition?" she said.

"I'm not suggesting you bring them water," said Long, smirking. "Just point out where they can find the watercooler."

She laughed. "You're terrible."

"They're lucky the conference room doesn't have its own thermostat, or I'd make sure it was on the fritz every time they rolled in," said Long, before ducking into his office.

He picked up the phone after enjoying a sip of Sherry's piping-hot coffee.

"Ryan Decker. A blast from the recent past," said Long. "I'm guessing this isn't a social call?"

"Your law enforcement instincts remain infallible," said the familiar voice.

"I was tipped off," said Long. "What's going on?"

"The same organization that we evicted from Alderpoint last year just tried to kill all of us this morning," said Decker.

"Who is *all of us?*" said Long.

"Me. Harlow. Brad Pierce. Everyone at the firm. My daughter. Probably sent someone to the house to kill my parents. All of us," said Decker.

"Not to sound uncaring at the moment, but should I be worried up here?" asked Long.

"No. It's hard to explain, but this was triggered by something entirely unrelated to us," said Decker.

"I find it hard to believe that destroying their billion-dollar enterprise is unrelated."

"Two billion, from what I recall," said Decker. "And yes, it's all related, but I actually have a long history of messing with this group's profit margins. I just didn't know the actual extent of it until after the Alderpoint thing."

"You're really not convincing me that my family is safe," said Long.

"What I'm trying to say is that the vendetta is directed at me and the core group that has been at their throat for the past few years. There's no evidence to suggest they're targeting anyone outside of that circle," said Decker.

"I appreciate your assessment, but I'll draw my own conclusions," said Long.

"Fair enough."

"Since you weren't calling to warn me, I'll rephrase my original question," said Long. "How can the Humboldt County Sheriff's Department be of assistance?"

"I need to hide about a dozen people indefinitely," said Decker. "I couldn't think of a better place to disappear than Humboldt County."

Long had to laugh at that. This Decker guy definitely had a sense of humor.

"Sounds like a bad travel ad for the Alderpoint area."

"Have you been to Alderpoint recently?" said Decker, and they both laughed.

"Well, owing to the favor you did the Alderpoint community last fall, and the ungodly amount of money they're going to make from it, I can't imagine I'd have any problem finding you a quiet little hideaway up in those hills."

"You left the operation standing?" asked Decker.

"Hell no! We chopped down whatever was left and got half the county high with the biggest controlled burn in years," said Long. "Which also happened to be the Humboldt County Sheriff's Department's biggest win in years, so you're more than welcome to hide out up here on more than one account. Just as long as you don't bring any trouble back with you."

"If the people in those hills can keep a secret, I don't see that happening," said Decker.

"I'm sure they have most of those razed fields back up and running, but I haven't heard a peep. These people can keep secrets. Especially if it's in their best interest—and not pissing me off fits that criteria. What's your time frame and what kind of a setup are you looking for?" asked Long.

"Somewhere isolated and accessible by a midsize RV. Access to fresh water would keep down the number of trips back and forth," said Decker.

"I don't think we'll have any trouble finding something like that," said Long. "When can we expect you?"

"At the very earliest, late tomorrow morning," said Decker. "That's all still up in the air. Tomorrow for sure, unless something significant changes."

"Then I better get moving on this," said Long.

"Thank you. I'm not sure where we could have turned next," said Decker.

"No problem," said Long. "Did you call this line on purpose, or did you lose my cell phone number?"

"I ditched my phone," said Decker. "We're kind of starting from scratch. One more thing, Sheriff. I just remembered."

"Yeah?"

"Is that same sergeant still running the satellite station in Garberville?" asked Decker. "The one that arrested me at the motel?"

"Sergeant Russell?"

"I honestly don't remember his name. Just that he said something that felt really off—especially with his gun pointed at my head. That's why I snuck in that call to nine-one-one. If he's still in Garberville, we might be better off hiding in a different part of the county."

"Craig Russell is in the Sacramento state prison."

"He changed jobs?"

"No. He's in a prison cell," said Long. "I recalled you raising these concerns with me when you were in the hospital. I was too busy to give it much thought at the time, but when the dust settled from last fall's mess, I had internal affairs do a little digging into that office, and they discovered some irregular bank activity. He jumped on a deal to avoid taking the rap for pretty much everything that went sideways up on the mountain. I think dialing nine-one-one might have saved your life."

He gave Decker his number and wished him luck before buzzing Sherry's line.

"Something tells me you're bailing on the supervisors," she said.

"Yep. Something a whole lot more interesting just came up," said Long.

"That's not saying much," she said. "Do you need me to break the bad news?"

"No. I'll do it myself. Maybe give them a very abbreviated version," said Long. "While I'm in there making stuff up, would you mind getting in touch with Luke? I could really use his help with something."

"You know how he feels about this kind of thing."

"I know. I know. But I need to find a tucked-away place to hide some folks up on the mountain. Sooner than later," said Long. "And I can't exactly drive up there myself and start knocking on doors. I wouldn't ask if I didn't need the help. Decker's in trouble, and I think we should do right by him."

"When do you want to meet up with him?" said Sherry.

"I knew you'd come through. Thank you," said Long. "I'll buy him lunch somewhere out this way. I'm sure he doesn't want to be seen with me anywhere near the mountain."

"He barely likes to be seen with me—here in town," said Sherry. "But I'll whip him into shape. Big-sister style."

"You're the best, Sherry. I'll be out to break the bad news after I finish up your coffee. Pay raise is guaranteed this year."

"And the check's in the mail," she said, ending the call.

Long sat back and gave this whole thing a once-through. Maybe he'd have Kayla pack up some camping gear and ask her to hide out with them for a few days, while he made sure Decker didn't drag any trouble into town.

CHAPTER TWENTY-SEVEN

Senator Steele hustled down the jet's staircase onto the Frederick Municipal Airport tarmac, where a fully tinted black SUV waited. Rich stood beside the vehicle with his hands folded across his waist. All business as usual. She was relieved to see him. He was the only member of the team she had met since hiring the group through a longtime CIA acquaintance.

Given the day's startling series of events and the unorthodox nature of this transfer, immediately spotting a familiar face when the jet pulled to a stop may have been the only thing that kept her from ordering the pilot back into the air. The ruggedly handsome, weathered mercenary met her halfway.

"Can I take your satchel, Senator?" he said.

"Thank you. But I'll hold on to it," she said, and they started walking back to the SUV. "I'm feeling awfully possessive of this bag right now."

"I know what it feels like to walk away from everything and think you'll never get it back, ma'am," he said. "I've done it more times than I'd care to admit."

"Has there ever been a time when you didn't get everything back?" she asked. "And don't lie to me. I'll know immediately."

He cracked a smile. The first since she'd started working with his team.

"A few. But that comes with the territory in my line of work," he said. "You'll be fine. You're a United States senator. We just need to give the situation some time to cool down. APEX overreacted."

"Overreacted? They tried to kill people that had nothing to do with my investigation into Dalton and SKYSTORM," said Steele.

"The escalation was inappropriate and misdirected," said Rich. "But look at it this way. They specifically chose to send you a message instead of attacking you directly. I'm not saying life goes back to normal anytime soon, but I think this is finished. My job is to make sure you stay safe until we're certain that's the case."

"What if it's not the case?"

"Then we'll explore some proactive options," said Rich, opening the rear driver's-side door for her.

A woman dressed in a black business suit and gray turtleneck scooted to the opposite side of the bench seat, taking a mean-looking compact rifle with her. The sight of a gun in the hands of someone she'd never met before had more of an impact on her than she'd anticipated. Steele balked at getting in.

"Senator Steele. This is Cassiopeia. One of the group's best," he said, before opening the driver's door.

The woman leaned over and offered Steele her hand.

"Caz, ma'am. Just Caz," she said, smiling warmly. "And he says that about all of our people."

"That's because I only hire the best," said Rich.

"Margaret. Same goes for you, Rich. I'm tired of being called ma'am," she said, shaking Caz's hand.

"As you wish, Senator," said Rich.

"I suppose *Senator* will work if *Margaret* goes against protocol," said Steele, before climbing inside the leather cabin.

"It's more of a consistency issue," said Rich. "I need everyone to refer to you by the same name, so there's no confusion on your part if we address you under more stressful circumstances—and I'm the boss, so I get to pick the name. Plus, I'm a little old school, hence the formality."

"A little old school?" said Caz.

"Let me know when you're buckled up," said Rich, easing the SUV forward.

She engaged the seat belt. "Ready. Is this thing armored?"

The SUV took off and built up a scary amount of speed.

"No. Renting an armored SUV, even in the DC area, felt like a red flag. When that jet lands in LA empty, about six hours from now, they're going to know you pulled a fast one on them. APEX is thorough. Someone will check armored SUV rentals and figure out how to hijack the tracking systems used by each company. The big-picture risk outweighed the short-term protection. Caz brought an extra ballistic vest, if you want it."

"I'll pass for now," said Steele. "How long is the drive?"

"Roughly three and a half hours with traffic."

"How far out of DC are we going?" she asked.

Not that it mattered. She was just a little surprised they would range so far away from the city. Then again, if they felt she'd be the safest in Maine, who was she to argue?

"Rockville. To a secure estate. Ms. Ragan and her family are on the way. Under protective escort."

"Good. I was just about to—" said Steele. "Wait. It shouldn't take us that long, even with traffic."

"We have to run a fairly thorough surveillance-detection route," said Rich, slowing for the gate ahead of them. "Day and night conditions."

"What he means is we'll be taking the back roads," said Caz. "To make sure nobody follows us. The scenic route, as my dad used to say."

"I see," said Steele.

"If you're hungry, we can grab something to go in Frederick," said Rich. "I'd rather not stop once we start the SDR."

"Might be a good idea to use the restroom, too," said Caz. "I'm not sure Rich goes to the bathroom. Ever."

"Since you put it that way, I suppose we should stop," said Steele.

"There's a Wendy's close to the airport," said Rich.

"I don't think I've ever eaten at a Wendy's," said Steele. "Are there any other choices?"

"Mickey D's, BK Lounge, Chickwich, Taco Hell," said Rich. "The usual."

"Wow. Hard to choose," said Steele, thinking she might just use the bathroom and pass on the food.

"Do you like hamburgers?" said Caz.

"Is that a trick question?"

Caz laughed. "Wendy's. That's what he was steering you to anyway."

"Wendy's it is," said Steele, chuckling to herself.

She went from a relaxed, outdoor-patio dinner with a river view to scarfing down fast food in the back of a strange car—fearful for her life. Steele shook her head, ashamed of the thought.

"No Wendy's?" said Caz.

"Sorry. I was just scolding myself internally," said Steele.

For good reason. She'd unintentionally, but very selfishly, unleashed hell on Ryan Decker's world today, in addition to turning her chief of staff's home life upside down. And here she was, throwing a pity party for herself because she wouldn't be dining on crab cakes with rémoulade sauce. Steele had to fix this. She just wasn't sure how, though she suspected it meant finishing what APEX had started. They'd been too quick to strike at Decker, which meant they wouldn't hesitate to do it again, for whatever reason Ezra Dalton saw fit. Decker would never know peace.

"Rich. Tell me about these proactive options."

"There's a wide range, depending on the desired outcome," said Rich.

"Let's start with the nuclear option, and step it back from there," said Steele.

CHAPTER

TWENTY-EIGHT

Decker lay flat in the rock-strewn dirt, uncomfortably wedged between two thick, prickly bushes. His position sat on a small rise adjacent to Stagecoach Road, where he could watch over the approaches to the rendezvous point. The rest of his group was hidden on the other side of the road, about a few hundred yards up a dry creek bed, where they'd made their home for most of the afternoon and early evening.

Instead of a rifle, he was armed with a satellite phone and a hand-held radio. When they'd reached the requested drop-off point, the cartel guy in charge of the trip had handed Decker a gym bag filled with bottled water and Joshua's backpack, which contained his laptop with the battery removed, the cash Sophie had removed from the firm's vault, a freshly charged Iridium 9555 satellite phone, a prepaid SIM card for the phone, and a set of radios.

Their IDs and watches had been returned just prior to embarking on the two-and-a-half-hour journey in the back of a different cargo van from the chop shop to the Hot Springs Tavern, an oddly tucked-away, old-fashioned saloon pretty much smack-dab in the middle of the Santa Ynez Mountains. They'd studied their escape options to the north and east of Los Angeles, picking the area for two competing features they could use to their advantage—remote and rugged enough for them to detect intruders and hide but easily accessible by their rescue convoy.

After grabbing enough takeout food for lunch and dinner, they'd walked about a mile north along Stagecoach Road, passing under the Cold Spring Canyon Arch Bridge and stopping in a spacious turnoff for a religious camp—the perfect place for their pickup. Since the gate leading into the camp area had been closed and locked, they'd decided to hike up a nearby creek bed until they were well out of sight. They'd settled down in the shade and waited for Jessica to make the necessary arrangements for the rendezvous.

Five hours later Decker had hiked back to the road by himself to ensure that the rendezvous point hadn't been compromised. The inbound convoy, led by Supervisory Special Agent Reeves, had been well protected, but Decker and the team had spent their time out of sight and earshot of the road to throw off any enterprising cartel punks looking to cash in on twenty million dollars.

Satisfied that their hideout hadn't drawn a deadly crowd, he'd climbed up the steep bank on the other side of the road and nestled in, where he'd remained for the past hour, watching the mountains turn from bright orange to a hazy purple, until they became shadows.

His satellite phone buzzed, its screen casting a muted, bluish glow into the dirt below it. He lifted the phone up, doing his best to cover the light.

Passed Hot Springs Tavern. No apparent tail.

He replied with K. RP clear.

The convoy had exited State Route 154 a few minutes ago, winding through the hills until it reached the restaurant. So far, so good. He focused his attention north for a few minutes. The next exit off 154 was about a mile and a half down. Nothing. Headlights appeared toward the south shortly after that, vanishing and reappearing along the twisty road. His phone lit up again.

On approach.

C ur lights. RP clear, he typed.

As planned, the SUV carrying members of Reeves's task force turned off the road first and circled the expansive, packed dirt lot in front of the camp gate once before disgorging its heavily armed team. As the four agents fanned out to form a hasty perimeter around the lot, three Class C mini–motor homes pulled into the lot and parked side by side.

The last vehicle in the convoy cruised to a stop halfway across the opening, just off the side of the road. The two agents got out and immediately took covered positions on the lot side of their SUV, one watching each approach along Stagecoach Road.

One of the agents started yelling his name. That had to be Reeves.

"Up here!" said Decker, waving the illuminated phone. "I'll be right down!"

He triggered his handheld radio, stating a previously agreed-upon gibberish code to establish that he hadn't been captured before telling the others to head down to the lot.

"We're on our way," said Harlow.

"Take your time. We don't need a turned ankle," said Decker.

"Do you ever stop worrying?" she asked.

"No," he said. "See you in a few minutes."

Decker slid down the dirt bank, hitting the road harder than he'd expected. He stumbled a few feet before regaining his balance. So much for being careful. Reeves met him in front of the roadside parked SUV, clapping.

"That was graceful," said Reeves.

"I figured you and your team could use a little entertainment to cap off the day," said Decker, moving right in for a dusty hug that Reeves reluctantly accepted.

He patted Reeves on the back and disengaged. "Thank you. I really don't know what to say beyond that. I'll think of something later."

"No need. I have a favor to ask of you," said Reeves. "We'll call it even after that."

"Nothing can even this out. Seriously. I owe you forever."

"We'll see," said Reeves, turning to the agent positioned next to the hood of the SUV. "The two of you haven't formally met. Ryan Decker. This is Special Agent Matt Kincaid. My right hand. You'll be hosting his wife and daughter, along with my wife and kids, wherever this crazy train is headed, until I'm convinced it's safe for them to come back."

Decker shook Kincaid's hand. "Absolutely. It's my pleasure. How old is your daughter?"

"Fourteen," said Kincaid, glancing at Reeves.

"Riley is sixteen. A little older, but she's a solid role model," said Decker. "They'll get along just fine."

"Ryan. Can I be blunt with you?" asked Reeves.

"Sure," said Decker.

"Claire doesn't want to jump into one big kumbaya moment with this," said Reeves. "Matt's family and mine are pretty tight. The kids are close in age. It's nothing personal. She's just not comfortable with it."

"My wife feels the same way," said Kincaid. "I'm really sorry."

"Guys. I understand," said Decker. "I'll let everyone know the deal. They'll totally respect that. If anything changes, there's zero hard feelings. Someone will check with them a few times a day to see if they need anything. It'll be fine."

"I feel bad hitting you with this under the circumstances," said Reeves.

"Joe. I already told you. There's nothing I can do to repay you. I meant that," said Decker. "The same goes for all of your agents and obviously extends to your families. We're good."

"All right. How far away is the rest of your—"

"Dad!"

Riley ran toward him from the RVs.

"Not far. A few minutes," he said, rushing to meet her.

She cried and hugged him tightly until Harlow and the rest of the crew appeared in the wall of light created by the RV's headlights.

"We're going to be fine, Riley. I promise," said Decker.

Between the sobbing, he heard "I can't do this anymore" over and over again. His parents made their way over, and he took turns hugging each of them while holding on to Riley. Decker could feel an unspoken tension. Almost like a low-level static electricity among all of them. The drive up to Humboldt County wasn't going to be what Reeves had very aptly described as a kumbaya moment for any of them.

Sooner than later, Decker would have to convince his parents, Riley, and most importantly himself that he could drive a stake through the heart of this seemingly unkillable monster that kept clawing its way out of the ground to terrorize them. He wasn't sure how it was even possible, but seeing Riley like this again—after everything she'd been through and lost—made him want to drive a dump truck full of high explosives through the APEX Institute. And if that was what it took to put an end to this cycle of fear, he'd gladly get behind the wheel.

"Hey. We're gonna get moving," said Reeves.

"Thank you again," said Steven. "You saved the day."

"More than saved the day," said Audrey.

"All I did was escort your car for five minutes," said Reeves. "Two grandparents driving into a gun battle to rescue their granddaughter?" He patted Decker on the shoulder. "The apple didn't fall far from the tree. I'll check in with you later. Might take a little vacation time if this stretches out longer than a week."

"I'm told there's plenty of room on the property," said Decker. "Drive safe, FBI guys."

While Reeves and Kincaid said goodbye to their families, Decker walked to the RVs with his family to check in with Harlow and Jessica, who were splitting the group up between the two remaining RVs. The process looked pretty straightforward. The women took the center RV, leaving Joshua to join Decker, his family, and Harlow. An even split, numerically.

"I'm not even going to ask how you managed to rent three RVs that fast," said Decker.

"Oh, I didn't rent them," said Jessica. "We're now the proud owners of three brand-new motor homes and several thousand dollars' worth of camping gear. Purchased through our cutout, of course. I assume that's untraceable."

"Shouldn't be an issue," said Decker. "We're not checking into a campground, though we might consider staggering our arrival in Alderpoint."

"And approaching from different routes," said Harlow.

"We'll need to grab food, toiletries, and other supplies before we arrive, but we can figure that out on the way. Sheriff Long said he'll arrange a vehicle, so we'll be able to make supply runs without drawing too much attention," said Decker.

"Weapons and surveillance gear?" said Harlow.

"I tried," said Jessica. "But Reeves wasn't having any of it."

"That's fine. We might be able to work something out with Sheriff Long's contact on the mountain. Plenty of weapons up in those hills," said Decker. "And the Pierces should arrive tomorrow evening. Anna emptied their home gun safe, and Brad grabbed some surveillance and tactical gear from the vault at his office."

"Don't forget your mother's Sig Sauer," said Jessica. "I had to sweet-talk Reeves out of confiscating it. She doesn't have a concealed carry permit."

Decker shook his head. "She couldn't pass the training requirements. The marksmanship gene passed through my father's side."

"Good luck getting it away from her," said Jessica.

Harlow looked past him and nodded. "Pam says everyone's set. We should get this show on the road."

"I'll be right back," he said, and gave her a quick kiss. "I'm just going to check on the FBI families."

"Not the friendliest folks," said Jessica.

"Reeves said they were pretty shaken up by all of this," said Decker.

"They looked more pissed off than anything," said Jessica.

"Can't say I blame them," said Harlow.

Decker ran into Reeves and Kincaid on the way down the line of RVs.

"Just letting them know we won't bother them," said Decker. "Figured they should hear it from me. Also, I wanted to make sure they were okay driving one of these things. I hadn't thought of that earlier."

"We rent an RV every year and take a trip up the coast," said Reeves. "Claire has put in her share of hours."

"All right. I guess I shouldn't bother them," said Decker.

"Get everyone ready to head out," said Reeves, slapping Kincaid's shoulder. "Let's make this quick, Decker."

He boarded the RV with Reeves, who quickly introduced him to both families. Decker read the audience as passively hostile and tense.

"I just wanted to apologize for the mess I got you in," he said. "If you need anything at any time, or have any questions, please don't hesitate to ask. You can text by sat phone. They have the sat phone, right?"

"We have it," said Claire.

"Just text anything you think of to one of the other numbers on the contact list. Or call. Whatever you're comfortable with. We'll text updates or call if it's too complicated for a text. Or if it's an emergency. The plan is to drive straight through."

"Okay," she said.

"Thank you," said Decker, not sure how to end the awkward moment.

"And off we go," said Reeves, motioning for him to disembark.

The FBI agent shut the door after hopping down from the RV. "I've never seen you at a loss for words before."

Decker laughed. "Yeah. I really didn't know what to say to them."

"*Sorry* was a good start," said Reeves.

"Probably should have just quit there."

"Baby steps, amigo," said Reeves. "You're dealing with two protective parents, with limited to no trust in anyone outside of their inner circle. You know the drill."

"Oh. I do," said Decker. *Better than most.*

CHAPTER TWENTY-NINE

Ezra Dalton adjusted the webcam until the lighting and angle were just right. She considered applying a little more concealer to hide the most obvious signs of this nightmarish day—the dark circles forming under her eyes. Fourteen hours since this shit started, and she looked like she'd been awake for a week. A quick glance at the time told her she still had two minutes.

"Screw it," she said, reaching into the handbag lying next to the webcam.

She finished applying the makeup with fifteen seconds to go. Not the best job, but now she only looked like she'd been up for two days straight. *May as well get used to the look.* Dalton didn't anticipate any rest until she cleaned up the mess created this morning, which could be a while. Decker and Steele had so far proven to be extremely slippery. The videoconference connected—seven faces appearing in a grid on her widescreen monitor.

Harold Abbott, seated in his bookshelf-packed study, squinted into the camera and adjusted his wire-rim glasses. A light somewhere nearby blazed a reflection off his shiny bald dome. He cleared his throat and began the inquisition.

"I trust everyone has taken the requisite precautions to be here, given the surprising breach in security discovered a few days ago?"

She refrained from shaking her head or rolling her eyes. Her head was on the chopping block, a position she'd carefully avoided since ascending to the board of directors. A vote to remove her could be initiated at any time, by any member—a unanimous vote essentially signing her death warrant.

Dalton wasn't aware of any long-standing grudges against her, but as one of the founding members of the Institute, she inherently held a disproportionate amount of power. With that power came a natural envy or inescapable fear. A newer board member looking to level the playing field could make a move against her. Or an older one seeking to consolidate power. She'd have to take this lashing without pushing back too strongly, which meant ignoring Abbott's obvious insinuation.

Samuel Quinn took the opportunity to drive a nail in her coffin, which was understandable given that, technically, he shared responsibility for this mess. SKYSTORM was his project. Senator Steele was hers. When those two worlds had potentially merged with the discovery of a security breach at her town house earlier in the week, SKYSTORM and the senator became both of their concerns. This morning, when they'd detected an aircraft running a surveillance pattern north of the SKYSTORM site, moving methodically south, she'd made a decision that turned out to be . . . regrettable in hindsight. He'd seek to put some distance between the two of them. She'd do the same in his situation.

"All of my locations have been thoroughly swept," said Quinn.

No shit. APEX had dispatched a small army of security technicians today to inspect every primary and secondary residence used by the directors and key group leaders. They'd be moving on to the rest of the locations over the course of the next week. That was how long it would take to clear the rest of the properties owned by the directors.

"Regardless of the measures taken, which will be enhanced in response to this breach, we should all refrain from viewing or discussing sensitive information outside of the Institute," said Abbott.

Which is why everyone, except for her, was about to discuss the most sensitive ongoing APEX project—from the comfort of their own homes. Hypocrisy noted. Time to move on. She kept her face neutral while screaming those words internally.

"Ezra. Would you mind bringing the board up to speed on any current developments?"

"Unfortunately, we don't have much to report," she said, making sure to emphasize the word *we*. "Traffic camera analysis hits a dead end with the camera at the intersection of West Slauson and Normandie, in South Los Angeles. The Land Cruiser can be seen turning left off Normandie onto Fifty-Ninth Street, and that's the last time the city's camera network detects that same license plate. Analysts scoured camera footage from surrounding cameras. No black Land Cruiser.

"Our teams have searched the immediate neighborhood by vehicle and drones, covering nearly a half-square-mile area. Most houses do not have a garage, so they were able to do a reasonably thorough job, but we still have several dozen garages that we can't access without risking more problems than we already have. It's a heavily gang-infested area. Our stakeout cars have been harassed all day."

"Couldn't they have driven out of there and avoided the camera network?" said Franklin.

"Yes. That's entirely possible. But the camera at Slauson caught something unusual," said Quinn, briefly explaining the pickup truck that had lured away the LAPD Interceptor. "We're looking into the possibility that the Sinaloa Cartel helped them disappear. Organized Crime Drug Enforcement Task Force intelligence reporting suggests a strong cartel presence in Los Angeles, and the traffic camera jamming trick is one of their signature moves."

"The last thing we need is a confrontation with the cartel that draws the LAPD's attention. As you can imagine, they're on full alert after today's events," said Dalton.

"The last thing we need is Ryan Decker and his people running around!" said Allan Kline. "You need to double or triple the resources allocated to this and quit worrying about breaking a few more eggs. You already cracked a carton this morning."

Kline was an Institute plank owner like herself, Vernon Franklin, and Abbott, but he was far from a coequal—mostly owing to a lack of spine when it came to making hard decisions or taking ownership of major Institute projects. Unless you counted deciding which million-dollar property to own next.

Quinn jumped in. Not to save her hide, but because he had the most experience when it came to Ryan Decker. In addition to shepherding EMERALD CITY—the billion-dollar-a-year marijuana-growing operation in Northern California that Decker had single-handedly destroyed last year—SOUTHERN CROSS had also been his idea. Fortunately for him, the board had insisted unanimously to sell SOUTHERN CROSS—a bold plan to destabilize the Sinaloan drug cartel and replace it with a more "business friendly" border cartel—to Harcourt for a percentage of the operation's projected earnings.

The plan had an insanely lucrative upside, but the potential for political backlash if exposed was too high to be handled directly by APEX. It didn't ultimately count against Quinn as a failure, because APEX had no immediate hand in the operation. SOUTHERN CROSS had failed because Harcourt had once again underestimated the damage Decker could inflict with Senator Steele's backing—a mistake the Institute couldn't afford to repeat.

"We could crack enough eggs to start an omelet buffet, and we'd still never find Decker," said Quinn. "He's gone. And so is his crew. They've honed this skill to perfection."

"And now Steele is gone," said Kline.

"Steele is a United States senator. She can't stay away for long," said Abbott. "She's lying low, thinking this will all blow over, and she can come back to the bargaining table."

"Can't she?" said Dalton. "What's the downside? SKYSTORM is intact, and now she knows for certain that we're not messing around. We bring her back to the bargaining table and tell her that the bargain is we own her."

"If any aspect of the Decker mission had succeeded, I'd say we could consider proceeding in that direction," said Vernon Franklin, his palms pressed together under his jowly chin, as though he was about to add *namaste* to his statement. "But we've tipped our hand and come up short. We're in no position to bargain. Quite the opposite, actually. Decker is a loaded weapon now, and we need to keep Steele's finger off the trigger."

"Steele doesn't need Decker. Her mercenary crew is just as crafty and lethal," said Quinn. "They ripped through some of our best people at Dalton's town house."

"Decker and his people tore the LA team apart in close combat," said Franklin. "Don't underestimate Decker. Especially now. You tried to kill his daughter."

"Kidnap," said Quinn. "For leverage."

"I guarantee there's no difference in his mind," said Franklin.

Kline shook his head. "What exactly went wrong this morning? I thought the two of you had this under control!"

Typical Allan. Easily shakable in the face of—pretty much anything. She couldn't remember the last time he'd offered the board anything more than his timid armchair quarterback skills or his twenty-twenty-hindsight vision. Maybe he'd always been this way, and they put up with it because of the money he'd invested in the Institute during its foundational years. She'd have to keep a close eye on Kline moving forward.

"We scrapped the original plan this morning, after shooting down the hostile surveillance aircraft," said Quinn.

She couldn't let Quinn fall on his own sword, even though she was pretty sure he planned to dodge the blade at the last moment.

"In retrospect, I jumped the gun this morning," said Dalton. "We should have waited to see how Steele would react. Instead, I assumed that the downing of the surveillance aircraft would scare Decker into hiding. To your point, Allan, I was very aware that he's the wild card in all of this. I thought our plan in Los Angeles was infallible, even when we pulled the trigger early."

"It should have been," said Quinn. "We drew a wild card."

"Don't we plan for wild cards anymore?" asked Kline.

"Two wild cards," said Quinn. "The bodyguard assigned to Riley Decker proved exceptionally skilled. One woman held off three carloads of mercenaries until LAPD arrived."

"One woman?" said Dalton.

"You know what I mean," said Quinn. "Former Israeli commando. We knew she was good, but not that good."

"What happened with Decker?" asked Sloane Pruitt. "Another woman?"

Quinn rolled his eyes. "No. One of Decker's mercenary buddies showed up unexpectedly—at the absolute worst time."

"I'm sure it wasn't a coincidence," said Pruitt.

"Maybe not. But he killed seven men in the span of thirty seconds. That came as a surprise to the on-scene leader," said Quinn.

Dalton tried not to smile. Pruitt had a tendency to get under Quinn's skin. This had the potential to get ugly fast.

"We didn't use our own people, right?" said Pruitt.

"It wouldn't have mattered," said Quinn.

"Who did you use?" asked Donovan Mayhew.

Donovan was another second-guesser—second only to Kline.

"I sourced a team from an Athena Corp offshoot," said Quinn. "In case it went sideways."

"The leftovers from EMERALD CITY," said Pruitt.

"Tier Two operators," said Quinn.

"Enough. We can play the blame game all night. Time to fix the problem," said Abbott. "I share Vernon's opinion that we get rid of Senator Steele now and deal with Decker later. With Steele gone, we might even be able to negotiate a truce with Decker, so he can keep his daughter alive."

"Maybe we could throw in college tuition to sweeten the deal," said Franklin. "Listen to me closely. Please. Steele lied to us once. She'll lie to us again. Simple as that. And Decker? He's smart enough to know there's only one way out of this for him—and his daughter. This is a two-headed snake. We have to cut off both heads the moment the opportunity arises."

"Good point. I agree," said Abbott. "I say we move on Steele and Decker at the first opportunity, in whatever order they appear."

"I second that," said Kline.

"I agree," said Mayhew.

And on down the line until it came to Dalton, who had no intention of rocking this tippy boat.

"We'll get it done," said Dalton. "Until then, I strongly suggest we increase our security posture. Personal details should be augmented. Asset security enhanced. Steele's new friends are gloves off, nasty. And we all know what Decker is capable of."

"I'll take care of those arrangements," said Kline.

She had forgotten Allan could be decisive when his own ass was on the line.

"Last order of business for tonight," said Abbott. "SKYSTORM. Where do we stand?"

"The surveillance aircraft didn't get close enough to the site to capture imagery," said Quinn. "But in light of the extreme and necessary measures taken, we have to assume that another attempt will be made—sooner than later. I recommend packing up and shipping the entire operation to site B."

"Which should have been site A from the start," said Kline. "I knew this would come back to bite us. SKYSTORM is the apex—pun intended—of illegality."

"We've been through this already," said Quinn. "Starting from the ground up in Bulgaria would have been a logistical nightmare on every level. We're far enough along to shift production with minimal hiccups."

Kline started to say something, but Abbott cut him off.

"How long will it take to clear the site?"

"A week, maybe five days, if we work nonstop," said Quinn. "Another week to load it on the ship in Houston."

"Start immediately," said Abbott. "I want that site clean when Senator Steele's cowboys ride in. SKYSTORM could bring the roof down on our heads."

Abbott wasn't kidding. Not only did SKYSTORM's heavily armed, civilian-converted aircraft violate just about every international and US State Department arms-trafficking law imaginable, the project's end user, the Russian Federation, planned to use the aircraft against Ukrainian forces in the Donbass region. If exposed, SKYSTORM could land them in front of a federal firing squad—for treason.

CHAPTER THIRTY

Decker reclined in a folding camp chair at the edge of a sparse tree line, taking in the pristine mountain air while casually scanning the farthest visible traces of the dirt road that weaved through the vast bush-strewn valley. The hard-packed jeep trail, which had been more than sufficient to convey their RVs, connected with Dyerville Loop Road about a mile away, just out of sight beyond a flattened rise.

Sheriff Long's contact, who wore a bandanna and sunglasses to conceal his identity, despite having driven up to meet them sans costume, had come through with a solid location that met most of their requirements. Decker would have preferred something a little more sheltered by the mountain, but "Cush" had convinced him otherwise.

He pointed out that the only route that could support the RVs took them straight through the middle of town before branching off and following the Eel River. Cush was afraid people "would talk," which was all Decker needed to hear. He knew their presence wouldn't be a secret, but he could sense a real apprehension about taking them "straight down Main Street," even if Alderpoint's Main Street consisted of a general store no bigger than a 7-Eleven, a bi-level converted into a church, and a dozen or so homes with more No Trespassing signs than windows.

Instead, Cush took them around the western side of the mountain, along "the loop," where he sold them on a less insulated but infinitely more private property along Steelhead Creek. He'd stopped their convoy after turning off the paved road, gesturing all around them, repeating "nobody" every time he changed direction. Decker still wasn't sure, especially with a wide-open road so close, but his opinion shifted toward approval the moment they entered these trees. A half mile later, when they reached a compact, protected meadow adjacent to a lively, rock-strewn creek, he was entirely sold.

Tucked out of sight, the field gave them plenty of room to spread out. Security was manageable with a single lookout and a radio. Even in the dead of night, they should be able to spot a vehicle running with its lights out from a quarter mile away. Far enough away to warn the camp and run the spike strip across the road, buying everyone more than enough time to slip across the creek and melt into the woods. Sheriff Long had graciously provided them with the spike strip.

He felt as secure as possible under the circumstances. Only a scoped, semiautomatic long rifle would make him feel safer, and a few of those would arrive tomorrow morning with the Pierce family. They'd decided against bringing the Pierces into the camp at night, not wanting to draw attention to their location with headlights. Brad and his family were tucked away at a motel that would take cash, somewhere in Red Bluff, about three hours away.

A faint, out-of-place sound told Decker to look over his shoulder. His dad trudged down the dirt road, carrying a backpack over his shoulder and a folded camp chair in one of his hands. He checked the time. Even if Steven had swapped duty with Pam, Decker still had another fifteen minutes to go. He nodded at his dad, happy to have the company.

"Senior citizens are exempt from sentry duty," he said, when Steven got close enough.

"Fine," he said, taking the backpack off his shoulder. "I'll just take these beers with me back to camp."

"I'm happy to make an exception," said Decker. "Just this one time."

"You're damn right," said Steven, before setting up his chair next to Decker's.

His dad removed two perspiring cans of some kind of California-brewed IPA, and they cracked them open at the same time.

"Cheers," said Steven, clinking his can.

"Cheers."

The beverage went down smoothly, leaving him with half a can before he lowered it. His dad finished a similarly long drink.

"That hit the spot."

"Dangerous," said Decker. "I could drink three of these without thinking."

"That's why I only brought out two for each of us. Pam said they were good. She was right."

"Did you take Pam's spot on the watch rotation?" asked Decker. "I'll keep you company if you did. It's starting to get dark."

"You think your old man is afraid of the dark?"

"Yep. That and your eyesight," said Decker. "Mom said you're nearly blind as a bat and still won't get checked out."

"I don't need glasses. I can see perfectly fine. Day or night."

"Uh-huh," said Decker, before taking another sip.

He already felt a little light-headed from the beer.

"Either way, I'll stick around," said Decker. "Might be a bear or two wandering around. Better two of us than one."

"Pam's still coming. I just wanted to talk to you about something without the audience," said Steven, finishing the rest of his beer.

"Yeah. I think I know what's on your mind," he said, crumpling his can. "Round two?"

"Pam won't be happy to find two half-drunk Marines out here."

"Pam won't be happy no matter what I do," said Decker.

"How about we save round two for the walk back."

"Wise decision. This is going straight to my head," said Decker, pausing. "I know this isn't fair to Riley, or to you and Mom."

"It's not exactly what we had in mind for retirement," said his dad. "Riley is an amazing young woman. We've cherished this time with her, despite the tragic circumstances, but we want a real life for her. I mean, her life will never be entirely normal."

"Don't say that," said Decker, tears welling up.

"It is what it is. Was what it was. Whatever. Nothing can change what happened or bring back what was taken away from her," he said. "But this whole situation is entirely different. We were leery of bringing her to Los Angeles but thought it was the right thing to do. Now? I'm glad we came, or frankly, we'd probably be dead, but I don't see a future for Riley in an environment where the only thing standing between her and a bullet is an Israeli commando."

"I know. That's not the future I want for her, either," said Decker. "I'll have to see this one through to the end. I don't see any other way."

Steven Decker, a decorated Marine and veteran of the later years of the Vietnam War, looked uncharacteristically distraught by his pronouncement. He hadn't broadcast it across his face. That wasn't his style. The small tells were what betrayed the weathered Marine's face.

"You don't have to embark on a suicide mission. But you can't have it both ways."

"What do you mean?"

"Which part?" said his dad.

"The 'both ways' part," said Decker, though he was pretty sure he understood.

"You certainly can't live in the open with an organization like APEX breathing down your neck," said Steven. "What happened yesterday was inevitable. I kick myself for not seeing it. I mean, I did. But I was in denial. Same with your mother. We wanted things to be normal for you and your daughter. I just don't see how that will ever be possible with this monkey on our backs."

"That's why I have to end this, one way or the other."

"Or we vanish. I'm not very big on retreating, but even if we couldn't stay hidden forever, it would show APEX that we're no longer a threat," said his dad. "A retired Ryan Decker should ease their concerns."

"I tried that. They had absolutely no tactical or strategic reason to go after us the way they did," said Decker. "Steele purposely kept me in the dark about her latest investigation. Right or wrong."

"I'd say it was wrong."

Decker shrugged. "I can't say I disagree. Knowing that she was still poking that hornet's nest would have changed things. Either way, APEX went after us because they had a score to settle, and Steele gave them a convenient excuse. It doesn't matter where we go or how high we fly the white flag. All they have to do is keep the twenty-million-dollar bounty on my head active, and we have the same problem. We'll be sleeping with one eye open. They could drop it to one million with the same result."

"We have to protect Riley. And your mother. I hate to say this, but we might have to go our separate ways until you straighten this out."

"That's my only mission right now. To straighten this out," said Decker.

"What about Harlow?"

"The same. I got all of you into this—it's my job to get you out."

His father's ensuing silence asked the million-dollar question: How?

"We've proven resourceful enough to defeat a few Goliaths," said Decker. "With Senator Steele's help, we have a good shot at toppling this colossus."

"Did the senator recently acquire an aircraft carrier?"

"Better, apparently," said Decker. "She found an infinitely lethal team, with zero moral hang-ups."

"More mercenaries," said Steven.

"She said they're working pro bono."

"Doesn't sound like mercenaries. Maybe they're working on a contingency fee of some sort."

"That's all she said," said Decker. "I guess we'll find out soon enough."

CHAPTER
THIRTY-ONE

James Guthrie rode the elevator to the second floor for his meeting with Ms. Dalton. Truth be told, he didn't have a good feeling about the outcome. His team had been blindsided yesterday, with disastrous results. Worse than the extensive casualty count was the fact that they had left three bodies behind for law enforcement to identify. At least one of the operatives would be immediately identified, raising some serious questions.

Jeff Donnelly, who had been tasked to grab the surveillance tech at Dalton's town house, was former FBI. He'd led the FBI's elite Hostage Rescue Team, right up until a whistleblower complaint led to an audit of the team's travel-expense budget. Donnelly had "lost" close to seventy thousand dollars over a two-year period.

They could never prove he stole the money, but the discrepancy, compounded by some interesting testimony regarding travel-expense practices, had resulted in his immediate dismissal. APEX had hired him to apply his specialized skill set to the exact opposite of his job in the FBI. He had become APEX's "kidnap guy," a decision they were all one fingerprint or facial-recognition hit away from possibly regretting.

Adding Donnelly's team to the operation had been his decision. What had looked like a no-brainer at the time.

Guthrie had assumed they were up against a sophisticated surveillance crew, protected by a solid security team. Nothing more than that. He certainly hadn't expected a sudden Tier One response at Dalton's town house and an explosives-rigged decoy. Nobody could have anticipated that. But none of that mattered in the end. The disaster had gone down on his watch, and he was prepared to pay the consequences. Part of him would be relieved to be done with APEX.

His pay and bonus structure was second to none in the security-mercenary world, but field leadership suffered from "high turnover," a euphemism for "significant casualty rate." The reward for surviving long enough in the rapid security force (RSF) was an upward move into an operational role, where you worked the big projects and reaped even bigger benefits. Given recent rumors about disastrous Institute setbacks and the unexpected disaster yesterday, he'd started to rethink that goal.

The elevator stopped, the door opening to the operations and analysis floor. A suit-clad security officer escorted him down a hallway that spanned the length of the building in both directions. The floor was silent aside from their footsteps, the sprawling operations hub hidden away behind a long, featureless wall.

They passed a sturdy-looking, polished steel door flanked by a biometric handprint scanner and inset camera lens on the way to a compact, tucked-away conference room at the end of the hallway, where Ezra Dalton, Samuel Quinn, and Allan Kline sat at the far end of a short table. The thought that he might be reinterviewing for his job crossed Guthrie's mind. Or begging for his life. He'd heard those rumors, too.

"James. Please take a seat," said Dalton, pointing toward a folder in front of him.

He eased into the seat, his hand brushing over the folder. Termination paperwork?

"Before we get started, James," said Dalton, "we need you to sign a new employment contract—assuming you're interested in the new position."

Guthrie glanced from face to face, trying to get a read on the situation. Kline was unreadable. His beady, penetrating eyes and expressionless look gave nothing away. Quinn looked like he always did. A little too laid-back for the situation. Dalton? Nothing new there. Pleasantly impatient.

"Promotion or demotion?" said Guthrie, hoping to get some kind of reaction from any of them.

Quinn softly chuckled, while Kline held the line.

"Were you expecting a demotion?" asked Dalton.

"After yesterday, I certainly don't expect a promotion."

"Yesterday was an outlier," said Quinn. "New information has cast some light on why the town house op went sideways. Unless you have precognition. If you have ESP, I have a completely different job in mind for you."

"I don't have ESP," said Guthrie.

"Then you couldn't have known what you were up against," said Quinn. "Which brings us to the new interim position we'd like to offer you—within operations. We have a singular project for you to shepherd. If you succeed, your transition to operations becomes permanent. Interested?"

Guthrie hesitated long enough for Dalton to jump in.

"If it sounds too good to be true, you have good instincts," said Dalton. "The job involves going up against the same group that kicked you in the teeth yesterday. It won't be a picnic, not that any of your work up until this point has been easy. But this will be different, and exceedingly difficult. That's all we can say until you sign the new contract."

He rubbed his chin and gave it as much thought as they would tolerate—a few seconds—before opening the folder and picking up the pen.

"Count me in," said Guthrie, flipping to the last page to sign.

"You're welcome to read through the contract," said Dalton. "We can adjourn for ten minutes to give you the time."

"Any surprises?" said Guthrie, before twisting the heavy pen to reveal the ink tip.

"No. The interim nature of the position is spelled out in detail, on top of the position in operations you will be offered upon successful completion of the project. Special Activities Division leadership trainee assignment. Pay remains the same until transfer to SAD," said Dalton.

He signed his name and dated the contract. "Sounds perfect. Thank you for the opportunity. When do I get started?"

"Immediately after you recommend a replacement for your current position," said Dalton.

He didn't hesitate.

"Laura Bachmann," said Guthrie. "She's the only reason we got out of there with most of the casualties before Metro PD arrived. Extensive section leader experience. Strong leadership skills. Levelheaded. My first pick would be Moreno, but I can't imagine he'll be back in business anytime soon."

Allan Kline got up. "Bachmann was at the top of my list. We'll go with her. I may require you to spend a few hours bringing her up to speed."

"Absolutely, sir," said Guthrie.

"He's all yours," said Kline, brushing past him without any further acknowledgment.

When the door closed behind Kline, Dalton leaned forward and laced her fingers. "Last chance to back out."

"I think I just gave my job away," said Guthrie.

"Mr. Kline would be happy to put you back on the job," she said.

"No. I'm in," he said, sliding the folder across to her.

"Very well," she said, glancing at Quinn before continuing. "Your project is to locate and kill Senator Margaret Steele."

Guthrie sat stunned for a moment, really wishing he had taken her up on the offer to back out. Nothing about this sounded like a good idea. For APEX or himself. Authorizing a hunter-killer mission against a high-ranking member of the government reeked of desperation. Maybe the rumors about recent operational setbacks at APEX had been understated.

"Sorry," he said. "I wasn't expecting such a focused mission."

Quinn laughed. "Focused. You're damn right about that. It's your only focus from now until the job is done."

"Do we have any leads?" said Guthrie.

"I like this. Straight to work," said Quinn.

"She chartered a private jet yesterday afternoon to fly her from Ronald Reagan National Airport to Hollywood Burbank Airport, but she wasn't on the plane when it landed," said Dalton. "Video surveillance at the airport confirms she took off with the plane, so obviously she diverted. The pilots were back in the air before we could question them, headed to George Bush Airport, where the plane sits right now. We expect to question the crew this morning—assuming they show up."

"How much latitude do I have with this project?"

"Unlimited," said Dalton. "Run your requests through me. At this point you ask, you get. Keep me apprised of all new developments, ongoing progress, changes to strategy. I don't expect an update every five minutes, but I do expect regular reporting. I'll let you know if I need more or less."

"Understood," said Guthrie.

"Any questions before I set you up with operations?" said Dalton.

"The team? How will that work?" said Guthrie. "Especially with me kind of jumping into operations."

"Special projects call-up roster. Operations will walk you through it. We should be able to pull in some completely intact sections, which are always preferable to piecing together groups, but overall it's a solid roster, with no hierarchy issues. You're the project leader."

The call-up roster sounded similar to the method he'd used to source Donnelly. He couldn't wait to see what would be at his fingertips now that he was part of operations. His menu of choices had been somewhat limited in security.

"All right," said Guthrie. "And Mr. Quinn mentioned some kind of information that explained how we got sideswiped yesterday?"

"That's going to be your biggest challenge, but it also gives you a little more to work with. You'll have access to that file through operations, but the bottom line is that we finally identified the man that entered my town house, which led to a hit on the shooter in the alley. It's not good. They're operatives formerly associated with a mercenary group we thought had disbanded. Ever hear of General Terrence Sanderson?"

He shook his head. "Doesn't ring a bell."

"No reason it would," said Dalton. "He ran an off-the-books black ops group for the military but ran into trouble and was forced to retire. A few years after that, he resurrected the group as a private mercenary entity. Rumor has it that the CIA used the group for some of its darkest projects."

"How dark?"

She looked at Quinn, who nodded.

"Direct-action missions on Russian soil. Elimination of domestic terror organizations. High-profile renditions in Europe. That kind of thing," she said.

"And we have a file on them?"

"Not the most extensive file, but a list of names, aliases, profiles, suspected contacts. Enough to get started," said Dalton. "Our hope is that this is just a few scraps from the past, working together on a specialized contract. If the original organization is still intact to any degree—and working for Senator Steele—that will undoubtedly change our approach."

"That bad?"

"We'll cross that bridge when we get to it," said Abbott. "First priority is finding Steele or anyone formerly associated with the two men we identified. We'll decide how to proceed from there."

"Can't wait to get started," said Guthrie, hoping the spoken words hadn't reflected the sarcasm on the inside.

Chapter Thirty-Two

Senator Steele sat in the front row of the mansion's sprawling home theater, a camera on a tripod situated before her, just below her view of the massive, elevated movie screen. Rich sat a few seats away, a separate camera pointing at his face. The rest of Rich's team sat in the seats next to and behind him.

The team's annoying and frenetic tech wizard, Anish Gupta, had explained to her that splitting them up into two groups would clearly delineate who was speaking during the videoconference. It had something to do with the microphone picking up noise and highlighting their icons.

She'd suggested doing this old school, as a teleconference or a videoconference with one camera, but even Anish's much-older colleague admitted the meeting would flow better, especially since none of their faces would be displayed for privacy and security reasons. Somehow they could "take turns" better—or something.

"Ready, ma'am?" said Anish. "The other participants are ready. I can invite them into the conference at any time."

"And we won't see any faces?" she asked.

"No faces. Just the four black squares with initials where the images normally would appear. A yellow frame will line the active square—when someone in that group is talking."

"It works better than he's making it sound," said Tim.

"Dude. She was getting it," said Anish.

"I wasn't getting it."

"You were getting it, right—"

"Enough bickering. It never ends with you two," said Rich. "Senator Steele?"

"I was sort of getting it," she said.

"Told you!" said Anish, pumping his fists high above his head.

Rich buried his head in his hands. "Sorry, Senator. I meant are you ready to start the conference?"

"I know what you meant," she said, breaking into a reserved laugh. "Just trying to lighten the mood."

"Rich doesn't like that, sucka!" said Anish, before going completely straight-faced. "I'm done. Ready, ma'am?"

"Yes."

He darted off to the side and sat on a stool at the bar, typing on his laptop. "We're live!"

"Hello. It's Senator Steele," she said, activating the square with the single initial S.

"Read you loud and clear, Senator," said a familiar voice, triggering the RD square. "It's Ryan Decker. And I'm here with the team. Everyone but the two in the hospital."

"How are they doing?" she asked.

"Garza is fine," said Decker. "Brooklyn is still in critical condition. She's awake and hanging in there, but she has a long way to go."

"She sounds like a tough customer," said Steele. "We'll take good care of her."

"Yes, ma'am," said Decker.

"I know you're familiar with HB," said Steele. "Care to guess who that is?"

"Can't be. I thought he was lying low for a while," said Decker.

"That's what I thought," said Bernie. "Serves me right. Good to hear you, your family, and the whole crew made it out okay. Couldn't believe they went after you. Total bullshit."

"Ryan. And everyone else on your end," she said. "Bernie lost a surveillance jet yesterday morning, along with two crew members. They were shot down running an errand for me, which basically kicked off the whole messy chain of events."

"Quincy?" said Decker.

"Still here," said Quincy Rohm. "Not exactly sure how, but I'm still around."

"She had to walk something like ten miles to the edge of whatever counts as civilization out there," said Bernie. "We lost a copilot and our best sensor array operator."

"Sorry to hear that," said Pierce. "This is Brad."

"Hey, buddy," said Bernie. "Heard you had a little scare, too."

"Not so bad. We're all buttoned up nice and tight here."

"That's good to hear," said Steele. "I can't apologize strongly enough for setting off this chain reaction and endangering your lives and the lives of your families. I underestimated and underappreciated the potential consequences of prying into APEX's affairs again. I was so enraged by their harassment of you and your families last fall and winter that I let it cloud my judgment. I'm truly sorry, and I'm going to make this right—which brings me to an introduction.

"When I decided to keep looking into APEX, a team of unique specialists was recommended to me by an old friend. I've been working with them for three months. Just a small team. We started with the surveillance of a senior board director and rather quickly stumbled onto something they very dearly wanted to conceal. They shot down a jet over the Texas Panhandle in broad daylight. Tried to assassinate my surveillance team. And went after the rest of you. We obviously hit a nerve."

"That's an understatement," said Harlow.

"Good to hear your voice, Harlow," said Steele.

"I wish I could say the same, ma'am, but we're back to square one here. With our backs against a wall."

Decker tried to interrupt, but she clearly wasn't having it—which Steele completely understood. She'd feel the same way if the roles were reversed. Frankly, she was surprised they weren't all yelling at her at once. For a group that she had nearly killed with her carelessness, they were a relatively sedate crowd.

"Hold on, Decker. I'm not done. We're living in RVs and tents up in Alderpoint, because that's the only place we thought might be safe for a while. Alderpoint of all places. Sixteen of us, including Reeves's and Kincaid's families. FBI agents afraid for their family's lives. So. You hit more than a nerve yesterday, and we're all paying for it. I mean, how the hell do we even fix this? There's a twenty-million-dollar bounty on our heads! This isn't going away with a phone call and an apology to APEX."

A very long pause followed Harlow's very justified reprimand.

"I'm finished," said Harlow. "Just needed to get that off my chest and let you know how we feel. Now that we've gotten that out of the way, back to my original question: How the hell do we make this go away? We've been tossing around ideas, but it's a little hard to take any of them seriously given our obviously degraded state of affairs."

"Harlow. I appreciate your honesty, and you're right. I created a mess for all of you," she said. "And I plan to throw every resource I can muster or buy at solving the problem, which brings me back to my original point. We struck a nerve at APEX. There was nothing subtle about their response, which is strikingly uncharacteristic for them. There's something going on over there."

"There's always something going on over there," said Decker, getting a few laughs.

"Very true, but this feels different to me. I'm starting to think that APEX's back is up against a wall, too. A financial wall. And whatever they're cooking up right now is their version of a financial rescue package. By my estimation, our little partnership has cost them billions of dollars over the past few years. I have reason to suspect APEX stood to make money from the whole Mexican drug cartel plot. Combine that with the two billion that literally went up in smoke, and I'm starting to wonder if they didn't put all of their rotten eggs in a basket somewhere in Texas. It could be their Achilles' heel."

Or just another opportunity for Steele and Decker's crew to dig a deeper hole for themselves. She'd let them decide if they wanted to proceed and fully support whatever course of action they chose—with every resource at her disposal. She owed them that.

Chapter Thirty-Three

Harlow wanted to scream at the laptop sitting on the RV's foldable table, but she'd resigned herself to more or less going with the flow after speaking her mind. What choice did they have, really? Her life had been reduced to sleeping on a four-inch-thick mattress in an RV, waking up what felt like every fifteen minutes to listen intently for the noise she thought had woken her up in the first place.

Decker barely slept at all. He spent most of the night either tossing and turning on the couch in the salon or walking the meadow's perimeter. He'd put Riley in the over-cab bunk with her so she'd "feel a little more insulated and safer." Harlow didn't have the heart to tell him she was smart enough, and now had the real-world gun battle experience, to understand how bullets worked. She was doing everything in her power to keep the peace under the circumstances. They'd barely been here longer than twenty-four hours—with no conceivable end in sight.

She'd listen to Senator Steele's proposal with an open mind. As open as possible crammed into an RV that looked to be her new home for the foreseeable future.

"Before we start down this path, I want to make it clear that I will support you with every resource at my disposal, no matter what you decide. That goes for everyone individually. If you choose to vanish and weather out this storm, you can count on me to stand behind that decision financially and with whatever else I can muster."

Harlow glanced around the RV. Many of the faces looked like they'd be happy to take Steele up on that offer before hearing whatever plan she'd concocted. Most of them would be crazy not to. APEX had no real grudge with anyone here beyond Decker, Brad, and maybe herself. She'd always be at risk because of her relationship with Decker. Same with Decker's family. The rest of them could take the money and run, risking very little—yet there were no immediate takers. *We'll see in a few minutes.*

"With that on the table, I'd like to review what we know and talk about possible solutions," said Steele. "I'll very briefly summarize what our FBI contact told us."

Harlow found it interesting that she didn't use Reeves's name. The still-silent entity on the conference, represented by the initials BF, was clearly not privy to that information. She also assumed that Steele had opted out of displaying video to protect BF's identity. Some of Steele's vast fortune and a one-way flight to Bali were sounding better by the minute.

"In Los Angeles, the FBI confirmed a number of identities, many of them former Athena Corp employees, the company the FBI connected to the Alderpoint operation. Athena Corp was never formally linked to APEX, but we all know that was the case."

"It's a nice deniability move," said Decker. "Use twice-removed assets in case something goes sideways. APEX knows we have our sources."

"Correct. But they made a mistake with the ambush at Ezra Dalton's town house. Dalton is the senior director at APEX I mentioned earlier. Not only did they similarly underestimate their targets, but they also left people behind. The big difference being that they desperately tried to clean up the scene. My associate's counterambush didn't give them the opportunity.

"The FBI identified one of the men almost immediately, because he was a former FBI agent. Jeff Donnelly. Hostage Rescue Team leader turned kidnapper. He was killed in the process of trying to grab one of our surveillance techs. Donnelly is an employee of Cerberus Global, which looks remarkably like Athena."

"And will disappear tomorrow," said Harlow. "Like Athena."

"Quite possibly, but they piled body on top of body to get their people out of there," said Steele. "Cerberus might bear fruit if we can get a look inside before they fold up their tents."

"I think you're barking up the wrong tree," said Decker. "They wouldn't have left this Donnelly guy if he could be linked to APEX. You should be looking as closely as possible at the group piling body on top of body into the vehicles."

"Interesting. That's what my associates said."

"Can we get an introduction to our mystery guests?" said Harlow, getting a cross look from Decker.

She shrugged at him.

"I was about to turn this over to them," said Steele.

The BF square activated.

"Hi. I apologize for the brevity of this introduction, but the clock is ticking. My name is Rich. The original team provided to the senator consisted of myself, another tactical operative, and two surveillance operatives. We've just added four tactical operatives to the team in light of the circumstances. I've worked closely with nearly everyone on this team for more than a decade. We're good at what we do. Surveillance. Countersurveillance. Counterterrorism. Direct action. Espionage. Counterespionage. We don't advertise. We don't draw attention to ourselves—usually. That's it."

Some muffled laughter erupted from Rich's audio.

"What? This isn't share-and-tell hour?" said Rich, and pretty much everyone else laughed.

"I like this guy. Doesn't run his mouth all day like someone I know," said Pam, looking over at Decker.

"Funny," said Decker.

"Shit. Sorry about that. I thought my colleague knew to mute me at that point. I should have known better after a decade," said Rich. "Anyway. Here's what I propose. Bernie can fill in the details as we go along. Is that good with you, Bernie?"

"Works for me. I don't have much to say."

"Once again, pardon the brevity. I think Senator Steele's assessment that something may have seismically shifted at APEX holds merit. I don't know if I'd call it desperation, but we triggered what I'd consider a disproportionate response under the circumstances. They had discovered our surveillance of Dalton's town house, a fact we did not know. They could have shot down Bernie's plane and waited to move on our decoy stakeout location. Admittedly, I didn't think twice about approaching Dalton's town house—even after learning that the flight had been taken out."

"Why wouldn't you have waited?" asked Harlow. "Give it some time to cool off?"

Decker looked like he wanted to answer but thought better of it.

"I probably should have, but at the time, the two events had no observable connection. Shooting down an aircraft on the verge of exposing APEX's latest multibillion-dollar scheme didn't strike me as unusual. In fact, it encouraged me to go ahead with a surveillance change at Dalton's town house. We had planned to move one of the cameras to better support intelligence collection."

"They were waiting for you?" asked Decker.

"Yes. But I believe the plan to kidnap our surveillance operative was in place well before they knew we'd be flying a plane over their heads that morning," said Rich. "Long story short, they decided to neutralize the entire stakeout instead. Just a few hours after the plane went down. They had no idea we were planning to move one of the cameras that morning. They were in a hurry to bury any evidence of SKYSTORM, which is their name for whatever operation they're running in Texas."

Bernie's square illuminated. "I think I know what they're up to. The aircraft that took down Quincy's bird—"

"Hold on. This wasn't a surface-to-air missile attack?" said Decker.

"No. Wait until you hear this," said Bernie. "Quincy was hit by either twenty- or twenty-three-millimeter gunfire. She described the plane as boxy looking with a single propeller."

"One of those converted Thrush planes?"

"Gun pods on the wings. Possibly a two-seater. Hard to tell, hanging from a parachute," said Quincy. "Definitely a Thrush."

"I thought that program was dead. As in the State Department shut it down."

"The program under Eric King ended rather unceremoniously. I know, because the people running it asked me to consult on the project. I politely declined. A private company refitting and arming civilian aircraft for the military without government permission didn't sound like the best career move at the time—or ever."

"How much money can be made on these?" asked Rich.

"I heard that King had arranged a deal with South Sudan President Kiir to provide two planes for three hundred million dollars. That included pilots, armaments, logistical support, and an airbase. Everything the president needed to swat away a growing rebel insurgency."

"And the deal fell apart?" asked Senator Steele.

"It was a total shit show from the beginning," said Bernie. "Every aspect of it was a mess. They had to water it down so far from the original concept that the final prototype couldn't do a quarter of what they had originally promised. And you needed a team of mechanics to nurse it twenty-four seven. King kept delaying delivery because the plane sucked."

"How did the State Department find out?" asked Steele.

"Nobody really knows, but rumor around the campfire is that President Kiir tipped off the State Department because King couldn't deliver on his promise. The whole program disappeared overnight."

"It doesn't sound like the aircraft that attacked Quincy suffered from any performance issues," said Decker.

"I didn't see any," said Quincy. "The whole engagement was sort of like shooting fish in a barrel, but the pilot fired two sustained bursts and hit us squarely with both."

"I guess that begs the question: Is the plane a one-off built to guard APEX's newest secret, or is the plane the secret?" said Rich.

"There's only one way to find out," said Bernie. "I'll be airborne in a few hours to conduct a thorough aerial reconnaissance of the original surveillance area. I should have what we need by noon tomorrow."

Harlow glanced at Decker, who beat her to the obvious.

"Are you sure that's a good idea?"

"What are you, my mother?" said Bernie.

"Quincy. Can you help me out here?" said Decker.

"It's fine. The Thrush's max operating altitude is around twelve thousand feet," said Quincy. "I was flying at six thousand when I was hit."

"I'll be up at around twenty. Untouchable by one of those abominations," said Bernie. "They may not even notice me. I won't be flying a back-and-forth search grid. We had no idea what we were looking for before, but now we do."

"A runway where there shouldn't be a runway," said Rich.

"Connected to God knows how many buildings and hangars that shouldn't be there, either," said Bernie. "Hey. I have some work to do before we take off, so if you don't mind, I'd like to sign off."

"Be careful, Bernie," said Steele. "If something feels off, get the hell out of there."

"Don't worry, Senator," said Bernie. "Decker still owes me some drinks, and I'm not planning on checking out until he's made good on that promise."

"I owe you a new aircraft, come to think of it," said Steele.

"The jet was insured. The FAA wouldn't let me fly without it," said Bernie.

"The least I can do is cover the premium hike you're looking at," said Steele.

"Damn. I hadn't thought of that. We can discuss it when we settle up."

"Deal," said the senator.

"Preferably over a stiff drink or two somewhere warm. Adios, amigos," said Bernie, disconnecting from the conference.

"I like that guy," said Rich. "I sure as hell hope APEX doesn't have surface-to-air-missile capability."

"Don't even say that," said Steele.

"Sorry, ma'am. It was a joke. At that altitude, APEX would need a Patriot Missile system to shoot him down," said Rich.

Harlow almost started laughing at how badly Rich had read the room. Not to mention his deadpan delivery of a morbidly inappropriate joke. Decker elbowed her and mouthed, "What?" She leaned into his ear and whispered, "That was some joke." He stifled a laugh, which caught on with the rest of the team. Within moments, everyone was locked up, unable to make a sound without laughing.

"Okay. Well, let's hope they don't have one of those," said Steele. "Could they have that kind of capability?"

Decker pulled himself together enough to answer. "I can't imagine any circumstance in which they'd have access to something like that. And if they do—it's time for all of us to strongly consider your original offer."

"Fair enough," said Steele. "I suppose we should reconvene when Bernie returns, in case he doesn't find anything."

"Senator. What are you and Rich thinking we can do if Bernie finds something?" asked Harlow. "I assume you've had time to throw some ideas back and forth. What are we looking at for options? What resources would we need? Timeline? Anything."

"I'll let Rich cover that," said Steele. "He's batted around some ideas with the team."

"You're probably tired of hearing me say this, but I'll keep it short. Mostly because all of this is so preliminary. Keep in mind that the mission is to deliver a kill strike against APEX. Are we all in agreement with that strategy?"

"Yes. Assuming it can be done," said Harlow.

"That's how I'm looking at it," said Pierce.

"I don't see any other choice," said Decker. "For me at least. For some of the people sitting with me, taking your original offer might make more sense."

"I completely agree, Ryan," said Steele. "And that offer will always stand."

"But are we all in agreement that anything less than attempting a kill strike is pointless?"

Everyone agreed, and Rich continued. "Okay. Bear with me here. I see two distinct scenarios. One assumes we find something worth going after in Texas. The other assumes we don't. The simplest, but arguably more difficult, scenario is the latter.

"Without a high-value target in Texas, we can focus all of our resources on tactical strikes against APEX targets here in DC. Board members, high-level group leaders, the APEX building itself, their rapid security force annex in Manassas."

"Sounds good to me," said Pierce. "Why don't we just go with door number one?"

"Because we're talking about a near-simultaneous strike against more than a few dozen highly protected, hard-to-access targets. Given a Ranger battalion, we could pull it off—"

"Not to spend the senator's money, but . . . ," said Harlow.

Steele had a quick laugh.

"Trust me, Harlow. I already asked. Unfortunately for us, APEX has consolidated most of the mercenary market under their subsidiary corporations around the world," said Steele. "Very few independent groups or individual contractors will be eager to square off against them."

"Or pass up a twenty-million-dollar bounty," said Decker.

"And there's that," said Steele.

"So back to scenario one," said Pierce. "My guess is you were about to say that we'd end up doing mostly cosmetic damage. We're not blowing up a four-story building in McLean, Virginia, which is the only conceivable way of taking out all of our targets at once, so even if we manage to kill most of the board, that still leaves them with the spoils of their big project in Texas, and they fill the seats with warm bodies and move on."

"That pretty much sums it up," said Rich. "If it's the only option, we'll do our best to strike a mortal blow, but the odds are heavily stacked against us."

"Scenario two splits our resources, but you think the Texas side of our operation might be a little easier," said Decker.

"Not easier, but definitely vulnerable to the kind of asymmetric attack your team has brought to the table recently," said Rich. "Senator Steele has briefed me on your team's impressive exploits from Jacob Harcourt's mansion to the Mexico raid, capped off by your most recent feat of magic outside of a warehouse in Nevada. If there's an airfield and a hangar complex housing twenty of those Thrush aircraft, in various states of assembly, waiting to be sold to the highest-bidding banana republic dictator—I can't think of a better-suited mission. Seriously."

"I'm still listening," said Pierce.

"Me too," said Harlow, glancing around at some doubtful faces.

She didn't expect them to agree or disagree with Rich's idea. With the exception of Pam, and maybe Katie, they weren't trained for this kind of work. Neither was she, truthfully. Harlow had never felt more out of place than the Nevada warehouse raid—to the point where she'd considered her presence more of a danger than a service.

With Brooklyn and Garza in the hospital, and the prospect of bringing mercenaries they'd worked with in the past dampened by the twenty-million-dollar bounty hanging over their heads, Pierce and Decker pretty much composed all they had to offer as a strike force. Rich continued with his pitch.

"I know it sounds intimidating—"

"More like suicidal," said Katie, giving Harlow a break from being the voice of reason.

"Fair enough. But the Texas side of the equation doesn't have to be a high-explosive-focused, direct-action raid," said Rich. "I think with Bernie's help you could pull that off, but your best choice might be to gather rock-solid evidence and use the senator's Beltway allies to convince the feds to take a field trip to the middle of the Texas Panhandle. Or a combination of both. Screw things up out there and send the feds in. Kind of like you did in Nevada."

"It's sounding more and more feasible," said Decker. "Still in long-shot territory, but under the right circumstances, I can see it."

Harlow liked that Decker hadn't jumped in feetfirst and that Rich had suggested an option that didn't involve pitting Decker and Pierce against a small army. The chance of the next target location offering them the same opportunities and advantages as the last had were slim.

"We'll know after Bernie's reconnaissance run," said Rich. "If we can neutralize the location without turning it into a suicide mission, I should be able to do enough damage to APEX here in the DC area to open a hole in the ground and permanently swallow them up. Send them straight back from whence they came."

"Operation CLEAN SWEEP," said Decker.

"I like the sound of that," said Steele.

You're not the only one.

CHAPTER THIRTY-FOUR

Ezra Dalton placed the palm of her right hand on the biometric scanner and stared at the inset camera lens directly in front of her. Entry to the operations and analysis hub required verifying all five fingerprints, along with a successful facial recognition scan. The door clicked a few seconds later, allowing her to push the pneumatically assisted, reinforced door inward to reveal a tight square room with two small, mirrored windows situated just above thin rectangular slats. Gun portals.

The tiny antechamber served as a last line of defense in the near statistically impossible event that a hostile team or individual got past layer after redundant layer of security to reach this point—the only way in or out of the hub. Overkill for a good reason. The right intruder, with the right set of skills and stolen permissions, could unlock all of APEX's past and present secrets from inside the hub. She repeated the biometric process on the next door, under the watchful eye of a heavily armed team, until she was granted access.

Once inside, she navigated the orderly grid of corridors to reach a featureless, numbered door with a palm scanner. The austere hallways had been empty, aside from a few unobtrusive guards tucked away in alcoves. Contrary to popular belief, outside of operations and analysis, the hub wasn't a stadium-style beehive of constant, frantic activity like counterterrorism or operations centers in popular movies and television shows.

APEX's success relied heavily on compartmentalization and secrecy; each project or stand-alone operation was run separately. Analysts and operations specialists worked on one project at a time until its completion or termination. Individuals were plucked from ongoing projects to temporarily staff stand-alone operations like Guthrie's, always returning to their original assignments.

The staffing system limited APEX's exposure in the unlikely event of a breach in trust and significantly cut down on office politics. One group had no idea how important their project was in the grand scheme of the Institute's undertakings. Overseers with no stake in any particular operation or project deconflicted any competing interests. APEX had operated like this for close to twenty years without an internal hiccup. No external hiccups, either—until they ran afoul of Senator Steele and Ryan Decker.

Dalton verified her identity one more time and entered the compact office. Guthrie stood up the moment he saw her, the other two seasoned operatives remaining in their seats.

"Mr. Guthrie. We're not that formal within operations. That's more of an RSF-imposed formality," said Dalton. "Any updates? I'm headed into a directors briefing. I'm sure the topic will come up."

"I was just about to call you," said Guthrie, who remained standing. "Still nothing on the vehicle. The team is looking into armored SUV rentals, but that will take a little time. We did match a known associate of Jared Hoffman and Anish Gupta to the driver that picked up Steele at the Frederick Municipal Airport, and we were able to track them, using traffic cam footage, to a Wendy's near the airport. The drive-through camera gave us a clear enough image to work with. Sean. Can you pop the profile up on the screen?"

"Absolutely," said the ops analyst, transferring the information to the massive widescreen monitor mounted to the wall behind Guthrie.

"Richard Farrington," said Guthrie.

She shook her head. Guthrie had just confirmed what she'd suspected. Senator Steele had somehow managed to engage the services of the one group with the skills and potential to do some serious, long-lasting damage to APEX—with General Sanderson's protégé, Richard Farrington, at the helm.

"Given Rich's presence, we have to assume that a large portion of the organization is involved, which changes things significantly," said Dalton. "You've read the file?"

"What there is of it," said Guthrie. "It's a particularly nasty crew."

"Nasty but somewhat principled, which we have to take into account," said Dalton. "This isn't your typical mercenary group. Killing Senator Steele may not solve the problem. If she builds a postdeath clause into her contract with them, we'll be living with this problem indefinitely, and she definitely has the resources to pull that off. They'll keep coming after us until the money runs out—which is never."

"Then we'll need to focus on killing the entire group," said Guthrie.

"It's not that simple with them. Killing off the group currently assigned to Senator Steele would only buy us a little time. They'd send more, and we'd end up fighting a very costly and inconvenient guerilla war here in the US and abroad. Picture never starting your car again without worrying about an explosive device planted under your seat," said Dalton. "We need to start thinking about capturing her, if possible. I'll brief the directors and see if they agree."

"I'll work that into our operational plans as a priority objective as soon as you confirm their decision," said Guthrie.

"Add it now," said Dalton. "I don't anticipate any pushback from the board."

Especially with the SKYSTORM evacuation running ahead of schedule. If they could get the planes loaded up and underway without incident, they might be able to get the senator to call off her attack dogs. Especially if they had Steele as a captive audience.

CHAPTER THIRTY-FIVE

"Do you want the good news or the bad news?" asked Bernie.

Decker knew from the moment Bernie started that none of them were going to like what he had to report. You only posed this question when the bad far outweighed the good. The hum of the C-123's powerful engines dominated the background of his audio connection.

"The good," said Decker. "Since it shouldn't take too long."

"You know me all too well, Decker," said Bernie. "Well, the good news is that we found the facility in question."

When Bernie didn't immediately continue, Decker muttered a few choice expletives. This promised to be worse than he thought.

"That bad?" said Senator Steele.

"I'm trying to remain objective until you can examine the imagery for yourselves," said Bernie.

"You're not doing a very good job," said Decker.

"Figured I wasn't," said Bernie. "Anyway. You're looking at a ten-thousand-foot, east-west-oriented runway wide enough to accommodate just about anything. Five sizable hangars line the north side of the runway across a decent-sized tarmac. A cluster of structures sit behind the hangars, comprised of everything from a few low-rise apartment buildings to a small factory and some warehouses. Solar panels on all of the rooftops. No transformers that I could see, so it's fair to assume there's a generator building to supplement the solar. Overall, it looks like a self-contained operation."

"And the bad news?" said Pierce.

"Assuming you don't have a flight of ground-attack-configured F-18 Super Hornets at your disposal, I don't see how you're going to do anything but annoy these folks," said Bernie. "The airfield complex is surrounded by prairie land, providing little to no consistent or significant cover for at least fifteen miles on each side. My guess is it's converted farmland. And it gets worse closer to the facility. Flatter than a football field for a mile or two in every direction. They picked this spot for a reason. To keep the lookie-loos out and their secret in."

"Sounds ideal for a tactical night jump," said Decker. "We could land on one of the roofs or—"

"Solar panels," said Harlow.

"Or somewhere inside the cluster of buildings," said Decker. "Three a.m. landing. Scoop up the chutes and hide them."

"Bernie could fly in and pick us up on the runway like the Mexico op," said Pierce. "In and out with the photographic evidence. It's almost a repeat."

"Sounds solid to me," said Rich.

"Let me walk you through the rest of the bad news and see if that changes any of your minds," said Bernie. "Thermal and daylight imagery showed a platoon-sized force on site, in perimeter guard towers or actively patrolling the complex."

"Could be people moving between buildings," said Decker.

"I knew you'd say that, so I made two runs spaced apart by four hours. One at four a.m. The other at eight. The personnel configuration looked the same," said Bernie. "On top of that, you're probably looking at another platoon off duty."

"And a separate quick-reaction force," said Rich. "A dozen or so available twenty-four seven."

"Yep. And did I mention the heavily armed vehicles?" said Bernie.

"Not yet," said Decker.

"I counted six armored tactical vehicles. Not Humvees, but similar. All with heavy machine guns. And at least a dozen of those desert-patrol-vehicle dune buggy things. Heavily armed," said Bernie. "Even if you somehow managed to land unobserved and get into the hangars to take pictures, there's no way I'm pulling the Mexico runway trick. We're dealing with trained professionals, not cartel guys holding AK-47s around corners and blindly firing."

"You're right. It's not a viable option," said Decker.

Bernie's aircraft looked like swiss cheese after the Mexico operation. Landing at this airfield sounded more like a melted-cheese result.

"Bernie. Did you manage to see any of the planes?" asked Steele. "If they're gone, there's no reason to rack our brains trying to solve a near-impossible problem."

"That's a mix of good and bad news," said Bernie. "We caught a glimpse into one of the hangars on the second trip. High angle, so we didn't see too deep, but we definitely spotted the same type of Thrush aircraft that shot down the jet."

"That's good news," said Steele. "Not that we can really do anything about it other than try to convince the authorities to investigate based on your pictures and Ms. Rohm's testimony."

"Plus the evidence from the wreckage," said Harlow. "I mean, how hard could it be for an FAA investigator to determine that the plane was brought down by gunfire?"

"Sounds good on paper, but I don't think we have the time. That's the bad news," said Bernie. "We spotted about four dozen shipping containers lined up to the west of the hangars, along with side-lifter semitrailers and a few of those massive forklift handlers. They're packing up and moving out. Two trailers sat half-in, half-out of one of the hangars on the first pass. They were gone on the second."

"Dammit. They're going to slip through our fingers," said Steele.

"Then we have to track the containers," said Rich. "This could actually work out better for us. They're obviously loading them up on a cargo ship. Most likely at a Gulf Coast port. We hit the ship and disable it. Maybe sink the damn thing."

"But we have to find the ship first," said Bernie. "And I can't follow one of those semis from the airfield to Galveston, or wherever it's headed. Contrary to the impression I may give everyone, I don't have free rein over the skies. Air traffic controllers tend to get nervous when aircraft circle over cities or change flight patterns every thirty minutes—especially one this size."

"What about running vehicle surveillance on one of the semis?" said Harlow. "Bernie could vector us to the semi when it reaches a highway. We take it from there."

"That could work," said Bernie. "Especially if you intercept on the interstate. No way you'd be able to pull that off on one of the state or county roads without tipping your hand. Unless you could stay five miles back."

"The problem with vehicle surveillance is that it wouldn't take much for an organization with APEX's resources and reach to spoof or even take out our tail car," said Pam. "I think we're about as good as it gets when it comes to tailing vehicles, but unless APEX has just completely written off security, this won't be as easy or safe as it sounds. And that's not me backing out. I'm still in."

"It sounds like the best option so far," said Pierce.

"The only option," said Steele.

"We could augment your vehicle security with some operatives," said Rich. "Just in case."

Joshua Keller, who had been fidgeting in his seat next to Mazzie for the past few minutes, finally spoke up.

"Why don't we use a drone to magnetically attach a tracking device?" he said. "We can easily acquire the components needed to put one together. The one we have back in LA is a slightly modified off-the-shelf model. It zips in, attaches the tracker, and zips out, with Bernie guiding the drone's approach from above."

"The problem is we can't get close enough. Even if we could safely slip within ten miles, which sounds like it might be pushing it given APEX's security posture, it doesn't give us the range," said Decker.

Mazzie shot up from her seat, nearly knocking Joshua over.

"Wait! Wait! We can drop it from the aircraft," she said. "Problem solved."

They all stared at her, everyone thinking the same thing. How the hell was that going to work?

"I'm not tracking you," said Rich.

"None of us are, but Mazzie races drones semiprofessionally—so I learned the other day. The floor is yours," said Decker.

"It sounds crazy, but I read about this Russian guy that flew an off-the-shelf drone with a few battery modifications up to thirty-three thousand feet and back. The whole flight took twenty-six minutes. Twenty to get up to altitude. Six to get back. You can watch the whole thing. He uploaded the entire trip's drone feed to YouTube. We won't even need to make the battery modifications, because he used most of the battery power to reach altitude. Drew like one amp coming back down in a controlled free-fall descent. I know I can do this."

"Doesn't sound crazy to me at all," said Rich. "I'm getting a nod from my resident drone expert."

"Then that's the plan," said Decker.

"There's only one problem," said Mazzie. "Launching the drone from the aircraft at twenty thousand feet—or any altitude. The drone might break apart. Unless you can significantly slow down the plane."

Decker glanced at Pierce, shaking his head. They both knew what this meant for whoever was on board that aircraft when they launched the drone. There was only one way to essentially stop an aircraft's forward motion in midflight, and it wasn't something you wanted to experience more than once in life. If that.

"Leave that to me," said Bernie. "But we should probably deploy two drones to improve the odds of getting at least one out intact."

"Looks like Mazzie and Josh are going on a field trip," said Harlow.

"How soon do you see this happening?" asked Steele.

The deep hum of the aircraft engines cut in. "It's a seven-and-a-half-hour trip to the same airfield we used before in Redding. I need to refuel somewhere sort of out of the way. This thing tends to attract a lot of attention. So I should be able to pick you up about ten hours from now."

"Perfect. That'll give us time to gather up what we need for the drone. One of us can accompany Josh and Mazzie on the flight to help with the launch," said Decker. "Since that's going to be so much fun."

"Why don't I like the sound of that?" asked Joshua.

Pierce chuckled.

"What did I miss?" asked Harlow.

"Nothing. But you'll see for yourself soon enough," said Bernie. "Given the rate at which they're moving those shipping containers, I strongly suggest that the entire team comes along. We'll head to my remote operating field in Oklahoma after attaching the tracker and get you geared up for whatever's next. My guess is they're headed to Houston or New Orleans, so we'll need to move fast."

"You're right," said Decker. "We'll bring everyone we might need."

He squeezed Harlow's hand. Neither of them had expected to separate this soon.

Unexpectedly, she leaned over and whispered, "You're not getting rid of me that easily. I want to know what you two were chuckling about."

She hated flying, which made this even more surprising.

He whispered back, "You do remember we're talking about flying, right? Not driving?"

"How much worse can it be than that last flight with Bernie?"

"Good point," he said, letting it go there.

She had no idea what was in store for them all. Just the thought of it made his palms sweat.

CHAPTER THIRTY-SIX

The moment the teleconference ended, they decided who would go and who would stay in Alderpoint. Some of the choices had been obvious. Sophia, Jessica, and Sandra immediately opted to remain behind and watch over the flock. Katie put up a fight to go but was ultimately convinced by Pam to stay at the campsite. Next to Pam, who had the most tactical expertise, she was the handiest with a firearm and improvised tactics. If things somehow went sideways in Alderpoint, Katie would be their best bet to organize and execute a defense—or direct their escape.

Harlow had made her wish clear, and Decker wasn't about to suggest she rethink it. She'd more than earned the right to be on the team that would try to strike a mortal blow against APEX. In all truth, Steele and Decker owed this moment to Harlow, who had risked everything to give him, a total stranger at the time, a second chance at redemption and a seminormal life. That and she could hold her own in a tight squeeze. Decker also needed her to keep him from making a bad decision. He tended to exercise far better judgment when she was around, offering him good advice.

With the team finalized, everyone headed off to pack the few things in their possession. They'd outfit themselves in Redding between shopping for drones and other personalized gear that Bernie couldn't provide.

He ran into his dad just outside the RV.

"Looks like something's up," Steven said.

"We found the site, but we can't access it. We're looking at a two-step process that could take a few days, so the entire operational team is headed out in less than an hour," said Decker. "I was on my way to talk to Riley."

"She's down by the creek with your mom," said his dad. "One of the prettiest spots I've seen in a while. Hard to believe this place is so troubled."

"I thought the same thing when I first drove up here last year. Just breathtaking everywhere," said Decker. "Until it literally tries to steal your breath."

"You'd never know driving through," said Steven. "Hey. I won't hold you up. We'll have plenty of time to talk when you get back."

"That's right," said Decker, hugging his dad. "All of us together with entirely too much time on our hands. Probably get sick of me."

"Sick of you?" said Steven. "Nah. I don't see that happening. Unless you're thinking about completely retiring. Then we might have to set some boundaries."

He laughed and squeezed his dad one more time before letting go. "I was thinking more along the lines of cutting back on the hours, but retirement sounds pretty good right about now."

"Just get your ass back in one piece," said Steven. "Don't do anything stupid. I've been thinking about what I said the other night, and it didn't come out right. Riley can't lose you, too. We can take Senator Steele's money and disappear. I have a feeling it would be a pretty comfortable life."

"Probably very comfortable, for me, you, and Mom. Harlow if she bought off on it," said Decker. "But not for Riley. I don't want her to spend the rest of her life on the run. If I get even the remotest shot at sinking APEX, I'm taking it."

"I figured as much. Just wanted you to know that you're the most important thing in her life. Our lives. Get back in one piece. That's an order."

"Yes, sir," said Decker, before heading toward Steelhead Creek.

A little over an hour later, after the hardest farewell of his life, they drove the beater Bronco Cush had loaned them out of the meadow toward the dirt road that would take them back into the fight.

Decker glanced in his side mirror, well aware that these might be the last glimpses he'd catch of his family. A part of him wanted to stop the SUV and put it in reverse, selfishly and literally taking the money and running. He knew Pierce felt the same way. They'd discussed the situation over a beer after everyone had gone to bed, bone tired from the stress of the past couple of days.

They both understood logically that they couldn't run forever, but the instant gratification and short-term relief appealed to both of them on a deep but irrational level. They were both tired of running, and the thought of a temporary reprieve purchased by Steele's fortune sang true. But like a game of musical chairs, the music always stopped—and eventually they'd find themselves without a chair.

On the way down the long jeep trail leading to the Dyerville Loop Road, he got a call from Sheriff Harvey Long, informing him that two Special Enforcement Team officers, Humboldt County's equivalent to SWAT (Special Weapons and Tactics), would be up to the campsite to help them with lookout duty. He'd let Special Agent Reeves know that he'd secured an arrangement with the sheriff. Reeves hadn't been very happy to learn that pretty much everyone with substantial tactical experience would be gone within the hour.

Not that they were some kind of elite commando team. More like a motley crew cobbled together by a tactician with a warped sense of humor. Two shooters. A drone operator. An electronics wizard. An angry bounty hunter masquerading as a private investigator. And an airsick-prone private investigator about to spend the next twelve hours of her life in the air. As bad as that all sounded, he couldn't think of a better team to take into battle.

They'd beaten the odds time and time again together, throwing everything they had into the fight. The eternal underdogs always coming out on top. Whatever lay ahead of them didn't stand a chance. Of course, Harlow might walk off the job after the maneuver Bernie would have to execute over Texas, but he'd smooth that over later. Man, was she going to be pissed at him. He almost felt bad not giving her more of a heads-up.

PART FOUR

CHAPTER THIRTY-SEVEN

Harlow stiffened from another light bump, her body still completely primed for panic after seven hours of a "relatively smooth flight," as everyone kept telling her at first. Relative to what? A kamikaze mission? Mercifully, Decker made the rounds after they'd been in the air for about an hour, discreetly explaining to everyone that the combination of words held no meaning for her and did nothing to ease her fear. She had no flying experience to compare this to, and last year's borderline-crash landing in the desert didn't count. In fact, thinking about that flight made things worse.

Bernie's new crew chief, a friendly, Georgia-accented gentleman named Randy, had made her as comfortable as possible by constantly checking on her, bringing her small cups of water, and adjusting her motion-sickness bracelets. It was all theater, but it made her feel a little better. Randy's happy-go-lucky demeanor had shifted to all business about thirty minutes ago, which meant they must be getting close to whatever surprise Bernie had alluded to. And Decker had stepped up the charm at almost the same time, adding to her suspicion.

She'd been too afraid to ask about it before takeoff, and there was no point in making things worse for herself during the flight. It was already bad enough. Randy climbed down the cockpit stairs and forced a smile as he approached her.

"Time to strap in tight. We're about five minutes from releasing the drones," he said.

Decker squeezed her hand and got up to help Randy.

"How bad is this going to be?" asked Harlow.

"It'll be over before you know it," said Randy, the two of them tugging on her harness straps.

Randy had rigged five-point racing harnesses to the bench structure about two hours ago, which had initially calmed her down a little. She'd felt a lot safer nestled into the padded harnesses, until she started to consider why they were necessary in the first place. The belt system they used for the Nevada landing had been a standard nylon harness.

"You should feel as snug as a bug," said Randy, before giving the harness a few yanks.

"Yeah. That's one way to describe it. I can barely breathe," said Harlow.

"That's exactly how you want it," said Randy. "I gotta make the rounds. You're gonna be just fine."

She feigned a smile and nodded before looking at Decker.

"Why don't you look worried?" she said.

"This is my extreme game face," said Decker, before sitting down next to her and slipping into his harness. "And like Randy said, it'll be over before you know it."

"I don't want to know what's going to happen, do I?" she said.

"Nope," he said. "But rest assured, it's going to suck for all of us on the same level—so you won't be alone."

"Very reassuring," said Harlow.

He kissed her cheek and held her hand.

"Just close your eyes and breathe into your stomach. Deep breaths," he said.

"Shouldn't I have a barf bag or something?"

"You won't need it," said Decker, before taking a deep breath and exhaling.

"Breathe deep, huh?"

"Yep."

She tried to take in a deep breath but came up short, her chest tightening instead.

"Keep at it," said Decker, squeezing her hand.

Harlow scanned the cargo compartment to find everyone dealing with this in their own way. Pierce sat with his eyes closed, his stomach expanding and contracting slowly like Decker's. Pam was breathing through her mouth, her eyes fixed on a point above Harlow. They made eye contact briefly, and Pam winked.

Mazzie bobbed her head to the music she was pumping through her over-ear headphones. She looked fine. Joshua was another story. He looked three shades greener than Harlow felt. Now she understood why they'd brought both drone operators. It wasn't to fly two drones. It was to have at least one capable operator after the release.

After checking all the harnesses, Randy spent a minute with the quadcopters, which lay in a staggered line, one several feet ahead of the other, just behind the top of the aircraft's ramp. The quadcopters were attached at the top to a fishing line that extended all the way forward to the stairs next to Randy's monitor-packed sensor array station. She still wasn't sure exactly how they would launch the drones but assumed they would slide down the ramp at some point. All part of the surprise she had no interest in learning about in advance.

When he'd finished with the drones, Randy made his way back, stopping briefly to speak with Mazzie and Josh, who nodded as he talked. Decker donned a pair of headphones, nudging her arm a few moments later.

"We're lowering the ramp now. Just close your eyes and count to a hundred. Keep breathing."

She didn't want to close her eyes yet, but as soon as the ramp started to move, she slammed them shut. Cold, turbulent air buffeted the compartment for several seconds before settling down to the point where she dared to open them. Everything looked the same except for the gaping black void where the ramp used to be. She immediately felt nauseated and dizzy.

"Thirty seconds!" yelled Randy, who had turned his chair to face the ramp.

He held a pair of compact scissors to cut a set of lines that would unspool through the hooks and release the drones. She closed her eyes again and started counting slowly to herself while breathing as deeply as her constricted chest and tightened stomach allowed.

"Ten seconds!"

Now she was counting down from ten. Probably not the best idea. Decker gripped her hand when she got to seven—a moment before her stomach sank and her entire body pulled hard against the right side of her harness. She ripped her hand away from Decker's and grabbed both shoulder straps tightly, her entire focus on not falling out of the back of the plane. The terrible sensation intensified for a few more seconds before melting away into nothingness.

CHAPTER THIRTY-EIGHT

Mazzie fought the urge to close her eyes. "Once in a lifetime" they had called it, and she had no intention of missing a single instant. The aircraft pitched upward, immediately pressing her against the side of her harness and forcing her head to the left, toward the ramp. She instinctively gripped her shoulder straps and pulled tight, while Joshua moaned and mumbled a continuous stream of expletives.

As the climb steepened to an angle she didn't think was possible for an aircraft this big, the lines connected to the drones pulled taut, suspending them in the middle of the cargo bay—directly over the nothingness beyond the ramp. The propellers activated a moment later, and one by one they disappeared into the night, leaving nothing but fluttering fishing lines behind.

It all made sense. Bernie had effectively eliminated any aircraft-induced turbulence during the launch by reducing their horizontal speed to nearly zero. They were flying almost vertically when the drones hit the atmosphere's natural airstreams at ten thousand feet.

The aircraft pitched forward slowly, giving her the fleeting impression of weightlessness as it started to level out of its extreme climb. Over the next several seconds, the pressure against her harness eased to nothing, until she became convinced that they had steadied on their new altitude. A quick glance around the compartment revealed the casualties of the maneuver.

Harlow's head lolled forward, Decker trying to revive her by prodding her shoulder. Joshua groaned in the seat next to her, his head turned away from her. He didn't sound good at all. Pam breathed shallowly on the other side of her, looking pale but otherwise fine. Pierce just rubbed his temples, catching her glance and smirking.

"I have two drones waiting for operators. Solid line-of-sight data connection," said Randy.

She gave him a thumbs-up, and he turned his chair to face the two high-resolution video controllers Velcroed to the desk built into his station. Decker was already up and headed in her direction.

"Looks like you're it," said Decker, checking on Joshua, who muttered a few barely coherent words.

Mazzie released the locking mechanism and slipped out of her harness. She nodded at Harlow.

"How's she doing?"

"Out cold," said Decker, before helping her up.

Randy gave up his seat when they reached the command and control station, where Mazzie had her choice of two seemingly healthy drones. She pulled the one on the right from the Velcro tape and placed it in her lap. Her first step was to lock the drone onto the preassigned GPS waypoint directly over the container area. Now for the fun part.

Working with the flight instrument display on the screen, she brought the drone down to one thousand feet above the target site, fighting a stiff westerly wind most of the way down. At most the wind issue added a couple of minutes to her estimated flight time.

"I'm at one thousand feet," she said.

Randy patted her shoulder.

"All right. Put her in a hover, and let's get some eyes on the target before you give it a go," he said, before transmitting over the internal comms net. "Bernie. Can you bring us right one hundred and twenty degrees to a heading of three-zero-zero?"

The aircraft lumbered right in a long, lazy circle before settling on its new course. Randy had already pulled up a folding chair next to her, in front of a widescreen monitor. A distant grayscale image of the site appeared after a few clicks of a joystick-like controller. He centered the image on the middle of the container farm and zoomed in until they had a high-resolution, multispectral picture of the western half of the site. The aircraft's sensor array combined both thermal and traditional image-intensification night-vision technologies to create a highly useful hybrid view.

"There's your drone," said Randy, pointing at a bright green X floating in the foreground of the image.

They had attached infrared tape in the form of an X to the top of the drone so they could track it more easily.

"And there's your obstacle course."

She studied the football field–size container farm, noting the hot spots that indicated sentries. Approaching from the west and tagging one of the containers that would be loaded next wasn't an option. Two heat signatures sat along the western edge.

The more she studied the image, the more of a challenge it appeared. Moving at high speed, her drone could be heard several hundred feet away in the kind of quiet environment at the site. Cruising cut the noise in half, which drastically reduced the detection range, but the sentries' spacing still left her concerned. If Mazzie sneaked the drone along at slow speed from the south, crossing the runway, the sentries probably wouldn't hear it over the ambient noise created by the wind, but they might see it lazily drifting in from the distance. And dropping it slowly down on top of the containers posed the same problem but exposed all the sentries to the sound. She didn't have a good option.

"You seem stymied," said Randy.

"Did they change their sentry configuration?" asked Mazzie.

"Looks like they added a few more," he said.

"Is that going to be a problem?" asked Decker.

"Yeah. We're looking at a gamble here," said Mazzie, before pointing at the image. "I can approach this larger gap low and slow from the south, but there's a chance they'll hear it or see it. That's about it."

"If they hear a drone near the containers, they'll search those things from top to bottom," said Decker.

Pierce joined the discussion. "What if you pulled a few of the sentries away with the other drone and crashed it while trying to get a look in the hangar. That would create a bit of a distraction."

"That could work," said Mazzie.

Decker didn't seem convinced. "But if they find the tracker on the decoy drone, they'll know something is up. Why try to get pictures and risk detection when you can just drop a tracker on one of the containers, especially if the drones are that loud?"

"What if I do the low-and-slow approach thing on one of the containers they're loading and make a real attempt to attach the second drone's tracker?" said Mazzie. "If they detect it, we get a distraction that might give me a better opening around the containers. If they don't, bingo. Mission complete."

"I like it," said Pierce.

"Me too," said Decker.

"Can you pull this off by yourself?" said Randy, casting a glance in Joshua's direction. "Your friend doesn't look like he'd be much help."

"Shouldn't be a problem."

Mazzie grabbed the second controller and repeated the same flight for the decoy drone, bringing it into a hover a few hundred feet away from the first drone. A few more minutes of alternating between controllers brought both drones into position several hundred feet south of the facility. One centered on the current gap between sentries. The other on one of the containers sticking out of the rightmost hangar.

"I'm going to send drone one forward at a crawl on autopilot while I work the decoy," said Mazzie. "If it gets to the far side of the runway before the sentries react to the decoy, I need to know immediately. We don't want it getting too close."

"I'll watch that," said Randy.

"You got this, Mazz," said Decker.

"I'm closing my eyes," said Pierce.

"Ha! This is worse than that maneuver Bernie pulled," said Mazzie.

"Near vertical climb," said Randy. "Not recommended for a Vietnam-era aircraft."

"Glad I didn't know it was that old," she said, beginning her maneuver.

She had just reached the edge of the container when all hell broke loose from the hangar. The video feed showed at least two people firing automatic weapons as she tried to land the drone.

"Put it in hover and switch to drone one," said Randy. "One of the sentries just left his post."

"And the gunfire will drown out the sound of the drone," said Decker.

She put the decoy in hover a few feet over the container and took control of the first drone, moving it toward the container farm.

"How much room do you think I have?" she said.

"Aim for a point one-third of the way down from the western edge of the container field. The middle sentry has shifted east in response to the gunfire," said Randy. "The gap is twice as large as before."

"The decoy is down," said Decker.

She bumped up the speed a little, bringing the drone five and a half feet above the ground to keep it as quiet as possible.

"Looking good, Mazzie. You're almost there," said Randy. "Can you tuck it between containers?"

"What's the estimated distance between them?" she said, keeping her flight path steady.

"Five feet."

"That doesn't give me much room. I'd rather not risk it," she said.

"No problem. Still looking good," said Randy.

"Can we give the decoy some juice?" asked Decker. "Maybe draw the sentry's attention away at the last minute?"

"If it's still alive at all," said Mazzie. "Start playing with the controls. I can't think about that right now."

Decker grabbed the controller from the desk while she concentrated on the approaching wall of containers. Almost there.

"Ha! I got it flying again. Sort of," said Decker.

"They're shooting again, too," said Randy.

Mazzie stayed focused, gradually increasing the drone's speed until she was ten feet away, when she quickly maneuvered it up and over the containers. She drifted a few containers to the west before landing.

"The tracker should be in place," said Mazzie. "How are we looking?"

"You're clear to extract using the same route," said Randy.

She brought the drone up and over a few feet so she could verify that the tracker had successfully deployed. The compact black rectangular device sat between the container's metal ridges.

"Tracker is deployed," said Mazzie.

A few minutes later, they confirmed that her drone hadn't attracted any attention. Mission complete. She expertly flew the drone away from the field until it had passed the far side of the runway, when she programmed it to climb to five hundred feet and fly in a straight line until it ran out of battery power.

Randy handed them all ice-cold cans of beer he'd quietly produced from a cooler hidden inside a nearby storage compartment.

"Don't tell the boss," said Randy.

A voice over the intercom boomed throughout the compartment.

"I see all and hear all," said Bernie.

"So I was told," said Randy.

Quincy leaned her head between the cockpit seats. "Told you. He actually doesn't trust us."

"Trust but verify," said Bernie. "Just make sure there's one left over for me. Nice job, everyone."

Nice job indeed, Mazzie thought, prouder than ever of her work with the team.

CHAPTER THIRTY-NINE

Senator Steele could tell by Rich's face that he didn't bear good news. She'd convinced Karl Berg, the same longtime friend who'd connected her with Rich's team, to call in a favor from one of his contacts at the National Security Agency. Karl claimed he'd used up all his favors by the time he left the Central Intelligence Agency, but he always seemed to have one last trick up his sleeve.

Less than an hour later, while they were cleaning up from lunch, Rich received a call from an anonymous gentleman who agreed to engage in a discussion. Nothing more than that. He stepped out with Tim, returning in under five minutes. Neither of them looked pleased when they rejoined her and the rest of the team in the kitchen.

"Do I need to call Karl again?" asked Steele.

Rich shook his head. "Why don't we grab a seat and clean up later. This might take a while."

Definitely not good.

"Do I need a stiff drink for this?" asked Steele.

"That's entirely up to you," said Rich. "But I wouldn't say it falls outside of any parameters we've set or expected."

"Sounds like sobering news, so I'll skip the drink," she said.

Rich was stoic, while the rest of the team smiled or softly chuckled at her wordplay.

"It's like trying to get a public smile from the Queen's Guard," she said to a few more laughs. "Shall we adjourn to the living room? Or is that too casual?"

He caved in and grinned. "The living room is fine."

Once they'd all settled into the sunken, window-enclosed sitting area, Rich broke the bad news.

"Berg's contact came through in an unexpected way," said Rich, nodding at Tim, who took over.

"I cut right to the chase with him and asked him if they could run a cyber-vulnerabilities check on the APEX Institute, knowing full well he would never agree to it. I just wanted him to understand from the start where the conversation was headed," said Tim. "He immediately told me that wouldn't be necessary, because APEX requests these several times a year—and their network security was one of the best they'd ever seen outside of their own networks."

"But where there's a will and a checkbook, there's a way," said Steele. "We're all living proof of that."

Even Rich laughed at that one.

"Normally, I'd agree, but he told me that they've managed to breach APEX network security twice, and it yielded surprisingly little. Administrative stuff mostly. Nowhere near the amount of data you would expect them to be hoarding. He strongly suspected that the real data gold mine at APEX was air gapped."

"Air gapped?" she said.

"The ultimate in network security," said Tim. "The network is physically isolated from any connection to the internet or an unsecured network. They could run their own server network, with no connection to the internet, and hardwire all of their computers to that network. For the computers you remove USB ports, Wi-Fi cards, or anything that could connect one of them to the internet. Air gapped. It's impenetrable, unless we can physically sit at one of their computers."

"And there's no way we're getting far enough into the building to pull this off, without a prolonged, very loud fight. And I suspect we'd need to penetrate deep into the building to tap into the air-gapped network. Those offices and computers will be behind a second and third layer of security," said Rich. "We'd find ourselves stuck inside, sandwiched between the APEX security force and Metro PD within a few minutes."

"Well, shit," said Steele. "Where does that leave us?"

"Maybe it'll be enough to torpedo their SKYSTORM plans and rattle the shit out of them here in DC," said Rich.

"I don't believe it will be enough to bring them to the bargaining table. Certainly not in good faith," said Steele. "And I don't mean that to reflect on your capabilities."

"None of us take it that way, Senator," said Jared. "This is one of the most difficult operations we've run in years. A tough nut to crack. But we'll crack it."

"Jared's our optimist," said Rich. "But short of hitting the building with a precision-guided bomb or somehow driving an explosives-laden truck into the parking lot underneath it, we're not taking APEX down physically. Electronically, we can't touch them. We're kind of stuck with the original plan. Deliver the biggest blow we can and hope for the best."

"It's not a bad plan," said Steele. "APEX won't go down, but whoever fills in the smoking gaps left behind will think twice about continuing this war."

"We can always wage a war of attrition," said Jared. "Pick off the survivors one by one as the opportunity arises, until all of the directors are gone."

"They'll get to me first before they run out of people to fill those shoes," said Steele.

Anish jumped into the conversation out of nowhere, as always. "Why do they have that many satellite dishes on their roof?"

Tim answered before Rich could jump down his throat.

"Satellite calls. An organization like APEX communicates primarily via encrypted satellite phones. It's their securest option," said Tim. "They'll have a fixed repeater system throughout the building to route calls from individual phones through the dishes."

"How many are there?" said Anish.

"You know how many, and we already discussed the air-gap issue . . . ," said Tim, his voice trailing off in thought.

"Twenty. Which is enough satellite bandwidth to place eight thousand calls from that building, assuming four megs per dish. And that's just a number I remember from looking into Inmarsat dishes. Those could be eight or sixteen megs."

"It's a lot of data bandwidth for a satellite phone network," said Tim.

"Exactly," said Anish.

"It would be pretty amateur of them to connect that to their air-gapped network," said Rich.

"It would," said Jess. "And the NSA would have probed the dishes. Anish is right, though. For once. Something doesn't add up."

"I just don't see how we can exploit it," said Anish.

"How do they connect to the internet to do research?" said Rich. "Even just basic stuff like if someone wanted to know the population of South Sudan for some kind of strategic assessment."

"They probably maintain a massive air-gapped database with that kind of information. It could be updated daily by a research group on a less-secure network inside APEX, which puts together a package that is physically uploaded to the air-gapped network," said Anish. "And if they want something right away that's not in their archives, they could have stand-alone computer stations inside the air-gapped zone connected to the internet. It's a simple arrangement."

"So theoretically we could slip a virus into their update data stream," said Jared.

"That sounds promising," said Steele.

"Theoretically. Yes," said Tim. "But then we're left with the same problem. There's no way to get the data out, and I sincerely doubt we'd be able to design a virus that could both evade detection and wipe out their network. They'll have top-shelf virus protection protocols in place for any data headed into the air-gapped sector."

"I hadn't thought of wiping out their data," said Rich. "Wiping out the people is more my style."

"It certainly makes more of a statement," said Tim. "But with that more or less off the table, and no way to steal the information we could use against them, this is the only other play I see. Try to take out their server and deprive them of the data they've collected. If we can't steal their secrets and expose them, maybe erasing everything would be the tipping point we need to push them over the edge."

"Interesting," said Steele. "They must have thousands of unique files on people and companies. Government representatives and authorities worldwide. All of their research and planning. It could force them to start from scratch. Whoever steps in to fill the positions we open will face a daunting task. I think it's worth a try."

"We'll start working on it," said Tim.

"Then that's our plan going forward," said Rich. "Put the final touches on the Beltway strike and figure out how to drive that stake deep enough to put them out of business."

"Let me know what you need and if I can pull any other strings," said Steele. "I'll spend every dollar available to me and call in every favor I've collected over the past few decades to bring APEX down."

CHAPTER FORTY

Decker huddled around Randy's sensor array station with the rest of the team, eyes fixed on the big screen. Bernie stood above them in the cockpit door, sipping a whiskey from a thick glass tumbler.

"Did I miss the open bar?" asked Decker.

"Yeah. We had happy hour while you and Pierce were playing with the guns," said Bernie.

"Someone had to clean the two inches of dust off the gear you failed to properly store in the bunker," said Decker. "Not that I'm complaining."

And he truly wasn't. Bernie had flown them to an isolated airfield he maintained in northern Oklahoma for emergencies and the rare instance he accepted a job in the US or Canada.

By design, the airfield and hangar looked neglected from the outside, but the inside featured an air-conditioned, generator-powered double-wide trailer and several underground bunkers containing the spare parts for his various aircraft, top-off amounts of fuel, food and water stores, a respectable weapons stockpile, and apparently enough liquor to stock a bar.

They'd spent the bulk of the day cleaning the weapons and equipment they might use, which basically meant Decker had them ready everything.

"Sounds like it. All work and no play makes you ground pounders dull boys," said Bernie. "Find a plastic cup and I'd be happy to share a splash."

"I'm good drinking right from the bottle," said Pam.

"Not this bottle," said Bernie. "There's some Jameson in the hangar."

Pam and Joshua started to back out of the cluster.

"A little later," said Decker. "I'd like to do some preliminary planning once the tracker stops."

"I don't think the container is going anywhere for a while," said Pierce. "We know it's the Bayport Terminal. The truck is probably waiting to drop the container where all the trucks off-load. The terminal crews will move it onto the ship. Could take all night."

"I have a feeling this is going right onto the ship," said Harlow. "They appear to have picked up the pace after last night's drone incident."

"The plan looks simple enough," said Bernie. "You sink the ship."

"And that is why we'll wait until a little later to enjoy a drink or two," said Decker.

"What?" said Bernie.

"We can't just sink a ship like that," said Pierce.

"This isn't an environmental thing, is it?" said Bernie. "Because I'll program a flight pattern and crash this plane into that ship if that's what it takes to get this APEX monkey off my back. I don't care how much fuel leaks into the harbor."

"That's not the problem," started Pierce.

"How are you going to get off the plane?" asked Decker.

"Parachute. How else?"

"I'd actually like to see that," said Pierce, laughing. "Bernie skydiving. That's on my bucket list."

"Sounds like your bucket list could use an overhaul," said Bernie. "What else is on the list? Seeing Decker glide down the street on Rollerblades?"

Everyone broke out into a laugh.

"You'll never catch me on Rollerblades," said Decker.

"Back to sinking the ship, and more importantly, getting the terrible image of Decker in Rollerblades out of our heads," said Pierce, waiting a moment for everyone to settle down before continuing. "We don't have access to the kind of explosives required to actually put one of those things on the bottom of the harbor. It would require something on the order of what Al Qaeda did to the USS *Cole*, but bigger. We'd literally have to place a barge full of explosives next to the kind of ship they're most likely using. Even a medium- or smaller-sized container ship dwarfs a Navy warship like the *Cole*. And then there's the issue of the crew. They probably have no idea what they're transporting. We can't send them to the bottom of the channel."

"He's absolutely right," said Decker.

"Can't you blow it up from the inside? Set up some kind of chain reaction?" said Harlow.

"Same problem. We'd need to fill one of those containers with explosives and get it in the hold," said Pierce. "And that would require hijacking one of those trucks without APEX noticing and then getting all the way to the ship without raising any alarms."

"Sounds like a long shot," said Bernie.

"Very long shot," said Pierce. "I think our best course of action is to disable the ship or at least render it unseaworthy. A small explosion or two would give the feds a reason to board the ship and investigate. Steele can steer them in the right direction while they're on board."

"They'll just shuffle the containers to another ship with extra space or buy the other ship outright and make room," said Decker. "I guarantee they own this ship."

"Then we'll have to make enough noise to shut down the entire terminal and guarantee a thorough investigation," said Harlow.

"That's what I was thinking," said Decker, before poking himself in the head. "Like minds."

"I liked it better when she wasn't talking to you," said Pam. "Pretty soon you'll be holding hands again."

"I still can't believe Decker didn't give you any idea of what would happen last night," said Bernie.

"She wouldn't have come along if I told her, and we can't stand to be apart," said Decker, looking directly at Pam.

"Uh. Definitely liked it better with her mad at you," said Pam.

"The container is moving," said Randy, ending their banter.

They watched the signal move along a superimposed Google Maps image until it stopped in an off-loading area on the far western side of the three-quarter-mile-long concrete pier. The image was static, but the tracker's location put it right where it could be picked up by one of the massive cranes and loaded onto a ship. APEX wasn't wasting any time at all.

"I think it's fair to say they're loading it onto whichever ship is tied up on the western end of the pier," said Pierce.

"I guess the only question left is how do we disable the ship and create enough fireworks to bring every federal and local law enforcement agent within fifty miles to the terminal?"

Bernie cleared his throat intentionally.

"Yes?" said Decker.

"Aren't you forgetting something?" asked Bernie.

Decker shrugged.

"Damn ground pounders. How do you plan to magically get off the ship after creating that much noise? I assume you don't plan to drive a very visible boat up to the ship."

He gave it a quick back-and-forth in his head. Bernie was absolutely correct. Whatever stealthy method they used to board the ship wasn't going to be of much value on the way out. The Coast Guard would be there in minutes, along with the Houston Port Authority. They needed a way to put as much distance between themselves and the ship as possible in the shortest amount of time. Easy enough.

"Can you fly a helicopter like you fly this beauty?" asked Decker.

"No. I can't fly a helicopter at all," said Bernie.

"Shit. There goes that idea," said Decker.

"But Quincy flew SH-60s off carriers and small-deck warships. Did a few stints inserting and extracting SEALs during the Iraq War," said Bernie, before taking a sip of his drink. "And I can guarantee you she'd love the opportunity for some payback."

"Then the real question is, How do we get our hands on a helicopter?" said Decker.

Quincy poked her head through the cockpit door.

"We buy one. Aviation leasing companies tend to frown when you return aircraft with bullet holes."

"How quickly can we make that happen?"

"If we pay asking price in cash," said Bernie, "I'd say we'd be the proud owners of a ready-to-fly helicopter by noon tomorrow."

"Price range?" said Decker.

"One-point-two million will get you a Bell 206 JetRanger that can carry five. Nothing fancy, but it'll get the job done."

Decker looked to Quincy for a final approval.

"I've logged hundreds of hours in the 206," said Quincy.

"Then I'll call the senator," said Decker.

Chapter
Forty-One

Decker kicked methodically to keep up with Pierce, his fins propelling him forward at an agonizingly slow rate for the effort exerted. He had still been exhausted from a long, but fairly straightforward, surface swim when they'd pushed off on the final leg of their infiltration, a one-thousand-foot, near-pitch-dark underwater route to their target ship. Now he remembered why he hadn't been keen on pursuing a career in Naval Special Warfare out of the Academy. Swimming in open water at night scared the shit out of him. Kind of a deal breaker for a SEAL.

Putting aside every shark movie he'd ever watched, Decker followed the blue glow stick taped to the bottom of Pierce's left fin, never letting it pull farther than a few feet from his mask. He was fairly convinced that the visibility in this murky harbor water wasn't much more than that right now. He'd already experienced a few bursts of panic when the blue light inexplicably faded.

He checked his watch, noting that they had been underwater for thirteen minutes. Pierce had guessed the trip across the channel would take them fifteen minutes at a reasonable pace that wouldn't render them combat ineffective on the other side. Decker kept kicking, his mind a constant battle between focusing on the blue light and imagining what lurked in the darkness. He couldn't wait to get onto the ship and into what his mind irrationally determined to be a much safer situation.

The blue light unexpectedly drifted toward his mask, the bottom edge of Pierce's fin suddenly hitting his mask and breaking the seal. The mask filled halfway before he sealed it again, the salt water just below his eyes. *Great.* Now he was stuck like this. Pierce had expressly warned him against clearing his mask after the halfway point. An alert sentry could possibly see or hear the bubbles.

Pierce remained still in the water for several seconds, then continued at a much slower pace. They kicked leisurely for another few minutes before Pierce came to an abrupt stop, the blue light drifting down. Decker joined him, locking arms to stay together. It was almost impossible to tell, but he felt like the water was darker here.

They slowly ascended, Pierce kicking to set the pace, until their heads gently bumped the hull. A brief moment of panic seized Decker as he realized they had gone too far and now sat underneath a fourteen-thousand-ton hunk of buoyancy-defying metal. He got his breathing back to normal after Pierce held an oversize, illuminated wrist compass to his face and winked, indicating everything was under control.

He oriented them north, and they crept along the hull as it curved upward—until they broke the surface on the port side, about a hundred feet from the ship's stern. Decker was surprised by how much light the ship and pier cast across the water. Someone looking over the side would spot them immediately. Pierce pointed down, and they submerged a few feet to swim aft, where they could hide under the stern overhang and prepare for the next phase.

Once safely hidden underneath the stern, Pierce activated an auto-inflatable raft, which sprang to life, creating an uncomfortable amount of noise. They floated motionless until they were satisfied that the raft commotion hadn't attracted any attention.

Decker lifted his mask, rubbing his eyes, while Pierce started off-loading the gear bags attached to his suit into the one-person emergency life raft. This was the tricky part. Getting the gear into the raft without sending any of it to the bottom of the harbor. He waited for Pierce to finish instead of starting on his own bags, so he could enlist some help.

One near drowning later, Decker and Pierce had successfully transferred Decker's waterproof bags to the raft and removed his scuba gear. He clung to the side of the raft as Pierce prepped the magnetically attachable C-4 charges that would hopefully punch a few holes in the hull and cripple the rudder.

"What can I do?" whispered Decker.

"Don't drown?" said Pierce.

Pierce powered the cell phones attached to each two-and-a-half-pound charge and resealed their waterproof pouches before zipping them up inside one of the smaller waterproof bags. All he had to do was place each charge against the hull. They each carried a cell phone with the numbers on speed dial, with a backup cell phone on the helicopter.

"Be back in a few minutes," said Pierce, lifting the bag out of the raft.

He swam quietly along the portside hull, attaching the three charges just below the waterline at twenty-foot intervals. When he got back to the stern, he lowered his mask and pushed the regulator into his mouth before sinking below the surface. Decker took in the sounds of the harbor while he was alone, the mechanical grinding of the massive container crane dominant at one in the morning. APEX was working twenty-four hours a day to get SKYSTORM out of the United States.

Pierce surfaced less than a minute after he disappeared, ditching his scuba gear on the way back to the raft. Decker had forgotten just how comfortable Pierce was in the water.

"I attached the charges to the top of the rudder," said Pierce. "I'm a little worried, because they're about four to five feet below the surface. Getting a cell phone signal that deep might be an issue. The ship is sitting a little lower than I expected."

"APEX is loading it up fast," said Decker. "Either way, I can't imagine this ship will be going anywhere with a few holes punched through the side. Knocking out the rudder was the icing on the cake."

"I hope so," said Pierce, sifting through the bags in the raft. "You ready to get this over with?"

"I suppose we shouldn't keep everyone waiting," said Decker.

He unsealed the long bag and removed several three-foot lengths of one-inch-diameter PVC pipe, fitting them together by the connectors they'd already attached to each piece. Next he duct-taped a crude, oversize grappling hook to the top of the long makeshift pole, making sure the thick, knotted climbing rope coiled in the bag was tied securely to the hook.

"You sure this is long enough?" said Decker.

"We'll have to swim past the superstructure, where the hull dips closest to the waterline. Worst-case scenario, we have to kind of launch the pole up."

They slung the remaining two bags over their shoulders and swam with the raft to the lowest point along the side of the hull. Eyeballing the distance, Decker guessed they'd be fine. He nodded at Pierce, and they lifted the wobbly pole, placing it high against the hull. They slid it up slowly, the hook scraping against the painted metal before it finally plunked over the top edge, just under the lowest guardrail beam.

Before continuing, they waited a full minute and listened for any signs that the hook had drawn attention. Pierce tugged on the rope, gradually increasing the amount of weight until he could lift himself mostly out of the water.

"I think we're good," he said, before struggling up the rope.

If a sentry spotted them at this point, they were as good as dead. Shooting directly down at them, the APEX security team couldn't possibly miss. Pierce made it over the side faster than Decker thought possible, reappearing a few moments later to give him a thumbs-up. He grabbed the highest point within reach and heaved his body up, snagging the knot just above the waterline between his feet. He pressed up with his thighs and lifted his body out of the water, shifting his hands up the knots until he was ready to heave again.

His arms and legs burned by the time he reached the top, the combined weight of the water and gear making the climb far more difficult than it looked. Pierce leaned over the guardrail and helped him over, the two of them scurrying under the container stack structure.

"Now for the fun part," said Decker, before unsealing his bag.

CHAPTER FORTY-TWO

Brad Pierce hit the slide-release button on his suppressed, heavy-barrel HK416 rifle, chambering a round from the sixty-round drum he'd just inserted. Three more sat in the bulky pouch attached to the left side of his tactical vest. Once again, he'd play the machine-gunner role. He checked his gear one more time, making sure everything was snug.

They looked kind of ridiculous, wearing coyote tan combat boots, drop holsters, and unarmored tactical rigs over black full-body wet suits. Beggars couldn't be choosers when sifting through Bernie's bunker. The last thing he tightened was the strap holding a pair of PRIZM shooting glasses tightly against his face.

"Ready?" said Decker.

"Yep," said Pierce. "I suggest we take the external stairs as far up the superstructure as possible. Avoid contact until it's absolutely necessary."

"Sounds good," said Decker, pulling the hood of his balaclava mask over the top of his head.

Pierce did the same before following Decker out from under the thick metal platform. APEX would undoubtedly guess who did this, but there was no reason to further complicate their lives with a federal investigation. They walked swiftly toward the five-story superstructure,

Decker covering the front of their approach and Pierce watching the rear. To maintain the fast pace and keep his rifle focused on the deck behind them, Pierce employed a side step that allowed him to switch his view with minimal effort.

They'd made it most of the way when Decker's rifle cracked twice, the combination of subsonic bullets and a hefty suppressor reducing the gunshots to handclaps. Still noticeable if you knew what to listen for. He glanced past his right shoulder at Decker, seeing a figure slumped against the guardrail about twenty feet ahead.

Another figure stepped into view close to where they had climbed over the side, kneeling to examine the deck. He'd likely noticed the water they'd dragged on board. Pierce dropped to one knee and centered his holographic site reticle on the man's head, pressing the trigger twice in rapid succession. The shell casings rattled off the steel container next to him as the man pitched forward into the railing. His head went through the top two bars, suspending him from the guardrail when his body gave out.

He didn't need to look at Decker to know he'd taken off. Four suppressed shots would not go unnoticed. Radio checks would be going out to all sentries. They had a minute at most before the deck swarmed with security. He sprinted aft while Decker heaved the dead guard over the guardrail. Pierce reached him as the man's body hit the water. The splash almost sounded as loud as one of the gunshots.

Decker moved quickly but quietly up the exterior stairs leading to the first platform, while Pierce crouched at the foot of the stairwell, covering the deck.

"Clear," said Decker, and Pierce joined him.

They repeated the process again, reaching the second of four platforms, before the voices echoed from below. A quick look over the railing confirmed that security had seen the body in the water. Decker hadn't skipped a beat, continuing up the stairs to the next level. Pierce barely rounded the flight of stairs in time to catch a glimpse of Decker—headed for the final platform.

"Clear," said Decker, and Pierce barreled up the metal stairs in pursuit.

When he reached the platform Decker had just departed, the hatch swung open without warning, catching Pierce by surprise. Fortunately, he appeared to be the last person the body armor–clad security guard expected, providing Pierce with ample opportunity to drill a bullet hole through his unprotected face. A discordance of yelling inside the hatch convinced him they needed to take advantage of the confusion.

"On me. Flash bang," he said to Decker, before kneeling next to the hatch.

Decker mumbled on the way back down the stairs, but ultimately trusted his judgment, tossing a flash bang grenade inside the superstructure a few seconds later. The moment the grenade detonated, Pierce was on the move through the haze, firing short bursts at anything that didn't match the white bulkheads.

The security team inside never stood a chance. The one-million-candela "flash" combined with a one-hundred-and-eighty-decibel "bang" not only stunned them in place but also rendered them almost entirely blind and deaf. When he stopped shooting, the formerly pristine compartment looked like a Lubyanka execution chamber. Six bodies lay slumped on the deck below thick, bright-red splotches.

"Looks like the quick-reaction force," said Decker, passing him by on the way to the stairs.

Pierce kept staring at the gruesome massacre. *What the hell is all of this?*

"Keep moving. They'll be all over us in thirty seconds," said Decker, tugging at his vest.

He felt bizarrely stuck here for some reason. As though he'd finally crossed some kind of line.

"Hey!" said Decker, grabbing his arm and getting his attention. "This is the only way we keep our people safe. We didn't start this. They did. Don't ever forget that."

"I know. I know," said Pierce, the mental fog lifting. "I just—this is fucking brutal."

"Brutal but necessary," said Decker. "You good?"

He was far from good, but he had to push through it. Decker was right. This was the only way they got their lives back. And kept their families from the same ghastly fate.

"Yep. All good," said Pierce.

CHAPTER FORTY-THREE

Decker edged up the white-painted metal stairs, keeping the barrel of his rifle pointed at the closed hatch on the bridge landing. Anyone on the other side of that door was well aware at this point that all hell had broken loose a few decks below. He waited for Pierce to take his place watching the door before starting his ascent to the bridge, where they had spotted at least one guard from the other side of the channel.

He signaled for Pierce to join him next to the windowless door leading onto the bridge, where they removed the suppressors attached to their rifles. They wanted to make as much noise as possible from this point onward.

"This is going to be tricky," said Decker.

"Yep. Two flash bangs? One in each direction?" said Pierce.

The door opened almost directly into the center of the bridge.

"After clearing the area immediately around the door from cover," said Decker, "we're giving up any element of surprise, but I think that ship has sailed already."

"The guard will be on one of the bridge wings, just outside of the bridge," said Pierce. "That's where I'd be. The flash bangs won't do much for us."

"They get us on the bridge," said Decker.

"I have a better idea," said Pierce. "Toss them in without pulling the pins. Buys us an extra second or two."

Yelling echoed up the stairwell. It was now or never.

"We'll need it," said Decker, grabbing the door lever and waiting for Pierce to get into position with his rifle.

When Pierce nodded, he yanked the door open most of the way and braced his rifle against the edge, scanning his limited view of the right side of the brightly lit bridge. Pierce remained in place, his rifle aiming left. Nothing. The guard on the bridge had played it smart, forcing them to move into his preplanned kill zone. Or so he thought.

"Guess we do this the hard way," said Decker.

Pierce removed two flash bang grenades from his bag, one in each hand, and simultaneously tossed them onto the bridge. When they clattered against the steel deck, Decker rushed inside, centering his red dot sight on the open starboard-side bridge wing door. Pierce slid past him to cover the portside door. A short burst of suppressed fire from Pierce's rifle solved their problem.

"Target down," said Pierce. "I'll secure the door."

Decker moved forward through the starboard side of the bridge in case another sentry joined the first after they had set off to cross the channel. He reached the opening that led to the exterior bridge wing and checked outside.

"Clear," said Decker. "How are we doing on the door?"

"Locked. It's a pretty solid pirate-deterrent door," he said. "But this won't hold up forever."

"Set the Claymore facing the door, wired to blow if they open it," said Decker. "That'll buy us the time we need if they breach."

"As long as we're not on the bridge when they set it off," said Pierce.

"Swap rifles," said Decker. "I'm going to start the show. And get the helicopter moving. This won't last very long."

"Bossy tonight," said Pierce, digging through his bag.

Decker took the modified light machine gun, modeled off the Marine Corps Infantry Automatic Rifle, and leaned his lighter version against the bulkhead next to Pierce.

"Trade back when you're done," said Decker, taking off.

He drew fire the moment he stepped onto the exposed bridge wing, bullets sparking off the steel wall next to him and punching small holes through the thick glass windows. Decker dropped prone and crawled to the end of the platform before carefully scanning the ship and pier below him. A few guards fired from positions along the starboard side of the ship, concealed among and below the stacks.

Bursts of gunfire from a lone shooter crouched on top of a portside container snapped overhead, some of the bullets striking the guardrail posts and ricocheting close. A little too close. Decker steadied the rifle on the thick metal lip of the platform and sighted in on the guy, sending a sustained volley back at him. The man tumbled off the container and disappeared.

Tires squealed on the pier, a convoy of three large SUVs racing toward the ship. APEX reinforcements most likely. He slid his body north to face the approaching threat and centered the green illuminated reticle on the hood of the first SUV. Two long bursts sent the vehicle careening toward a tall stack of containers, ending with a sickening crunch.

He repeated the drill against the second SUV, which slowed to a steady roll after several bullets peppered the windshield. The guards in the back seat bailed out and made a run for it. Decker's next two bursts dropped one of them to the concrete. The third SUV abruptly turned and vanished behind a sea of shipping containers. He searched for the surviving shooter, unable to locate him. The guy had probably seen enough.

Pierce slid into position next to him. "What did I miss?"

"All the fun. Three SUVs just tried to deliver reinforcements. I took two of them out. The third ducked out of sight behind the stacks," said Decker, swapping rifles.

Pierce reloaded the rifle while a concentrated barrage of bullets pinged off the thick steel around them and cracked by their heads.

"Time to make some real noise," said Pierce, pulling the pin on a grenade and tossing it over the side.

Decker removed a grenade from one of the pouches on his vest and did the same, the first grenade detonating as soon as he heaved it. The two successive explosions quieted the gunfire long enough for the two of them to start picking out targets.

Pierce didn't hold back, sweeping the deck with automatic fire, pausing only long enough to pick out a specific target for a concentrated burst. Decker focused on the guards sniping away at them from concealed positions among the semitrailers parked in a long row on the pier. He could have used more magnification at these distances than the 4X ACOG rifle scope provided, but he was still able to get the job done.

One by one over the next several seconds, he either permanently silenced or temporarily suppressed the half dozen shooters who had been sending bullets their way. The cell phone he'd crammed into the wet suit's thigh pocket buzzed. It was time to wrap this up. He elbowed Pierce.

"The helicopter should be one minute out," said Decker, rising into a crouch and taking off.

A small explosion tore through the stairwell door inside the bridge, and Decker veered left, away from the opening.

"Fire in the hole!" he yelled back at Pierce, who had already hit the deck and rolled to the side.

A devastating explosion ripped through the bridge, instantly blowing out its windows and ejecting debris through the open doorway. Decker lay covered in glass, taking a few moments to regain his senses from the detonation. He could barely hear the bullets chasing him as he dashed onto the smoke-filled, blast-charred bridge.

Once inside, he tossed a high-explosive grenade through the missing stairwell door and backed into Pierce, nearly knocking them both over. The smaller explosion felt like a firecracker compared to the antipersonnel mine. He risked a peek, seeing nothing but body parts and gore.

They moved to the port bridge wing, staying low and as far back from the front edge as possible to keep from being spotted. Decker nestled into a location next to the bridge wing door, where he could watch the bridge interior, just in case the carnage didn't serve as enough of a deterrent for the next round of security that showed up.

Decker removed the cell phone from the suit's stash pocket and dialed Harlow, who picked up immediately. With his ears still ringing, he could barely hear her over the helicopter's rotor noise.

"We're in position!" she said.

"Start your run now!" said Decker. "Tell Quincy and Pam that this is a hot pickup."

"We're moving! Coming up the channel!"

He ended the call and stashed the phone in his bag, where he could get to it quickly in the helicopter. A quick glance east toward the entrance to the Bayport Terminal channel revealed a fast-moving, darkened object superimposed against the Port of Houston's industrial yellow-orange glow.

"They're on final approach!" said Decker.

Pierce crawled forward into a position where he could mark targets for the helicopter gunner and provide suppressive fire while Quincy maneuvered to pick them up. No matter how much gunfire they unleashed beforehand, the helicopter would be vulnerable alongside the bridge wing. There was simply no way around that.

CHAPTER FORTY-FOUR

Harlow took a deep breath and exhaled. She checked the safety line connecting the back of her flight harness to the thick metal ring bolted to the floor for the fiftieth time since the helicopter had taken off and hesitantly moved into the leather seat next to the open door. She'd tested the rig over and over again before takeoff and found that she could securely stand on the skids at its full extension, putting her entire weight forward safely.

Quincy had insisted that she do this until she had convinced herself logically that the rig would hold her. The theory being that, with enough repetition, Harlow's logical brain and fear-based brain should balance each other out enough to get her out on the skid—if the gap between the bridge wing and skids was too far for Decker and Pierce to negotiate without help. Quincy obviously had no idea how paralyzing fear worked.

Even on the ground, the mere thought of what might be required of her during the mission induced a near panic attack. Up here? Harlow had no idea how she was still functional. Unfortunately, there had been no other option.

Mazzie seemed unfazed by fast-moving aircraft, but her thin, five-foot-three frame and spindly arms didn't inspire confidence in her ability to pull two hundred pounds of muscle and gear into the helicopter. Pam could toss them inside without breaking a sweat, but she'd proven a hundred times more adept at the other critical job necessary to complete the mission. And Joshua? His name never came up. The job fell on Harlow's shoulders, whether she liked it or not.

Pam sat directly across from her, turned halfway in her seat to face out of the helicopter. She held some kind of Serbian-made light machine gun with a wooden stock across her lap. A large, rigid canvas bag had been attached to the side of the machine gun facing Harlow, its purpose to catch the ejected brass that would otherwise fly into Harlow's face and over her shoulder into the cockpit. Gunfire mixed in with the mechanical whine of the helicopter's engine. As if the experience weren't already bad enough.

"Pam. Stand by to engage," said Quincy over her headset. "Ten seconds out."

Pam lowered her night-vision goggles, which allowed her to see the IR lasers Pierce and Decker would use to point out priority targets. Pam shouldered the machine gun and aimed it at a shallow downward angle out of the helicopter door, bracing it on top of her closed knees. She'd already charged the weapon a few minutes ago over Galveston Bay.

"Engaging targets," said Pam, the machine gun thundering a moment later.

No wonder Decker had been so happy. The thing sounded like a cannon compared to their rifles. Pam fired a longer burst, the gunfire rattling Harlow's headset. She'd reluctantly turned in her seat to prepare for her role in the extraction when Pam sent another downpour of bullets toward the ship. Harlow followed the stream of green tracers to the bottom of a container stack, where they ricocheted off the deck and upper hull, some flying skyward as from a roman candle. The pyrotechnic show somewhat distracted her from the terror at hand.

"Five seconds," said Quincy.

It was almost time. Quincy's announcement was immediately followed by a series of sharp thunks that rattled through the cabin.

"Shit. Shit. Shit," she muttered.

"Taking fire. Taking fire. Multiple targets. Two platforms up on superstructure," said Quincy.

"On it!" said Pam, shifting the machine gun in her lap and firing three short bursts.

The tracers raced toward the superstructure in three distinctly separate, slightly arcing lines before they struck the platform and bounced in every direction. Harlow caught a glimpse of Decker and Pierce three levels higher and even with the helicopter. Pam fired again, hammering the platform with what felt like an excessive number of bullets.

"Pam. Cease fire. Cease fire. Cover the bridge wing door," said Quincy. "Harlow. You're up."

The helicopter slowed significantly as Quincy finessed their approach. Harlow continued muttering expletives as she willed herself to stand up. Once out of the seat, she locked her hands in a death grip around the horizontal bar next to the door and leaned her head out of the helicopter. Decker and Pierce crouched at the end of the bridge, their rifles already slung across their chests. Quincy eased the left skid into position next to the top of the guardrail, and Harlow stretched her hand out to grab Pierce. With a firm grip on both his hand and the safety bar, she pulled him into the helicopter. *That wasn't so bad.*

Decker was already perched on the bridge wing guardrail by the time Harlow got back in position at the door. She'd reached for his hand, which was just inches away, when a string of bullets punched through the aircraft, one of them slicing her left forearm and thudding into the ceiling above her. She instantly retracted her arm, and the helicopter shifted a few feet away from Decker's outstretched hand. Another burst of gunfire pounded the fuselage.

"It's now or never!" said Quincy. "We can't stay here much longer!"

Harlow looked to Decker, who winked at her before stretching his hand as far as possible without falling off the railing. Without thinking, she let go of the handle and stepped onto the skid with both feet. Putting all of her trust in the harness, she leaned forward and grabbed Decker's wrist using both hands.

He leaped for the helicopter, landing one foot on the skid, which gave Harlow enough leverage to yank him up and into Pam's waiting hands. She tossed Decker deep inside the cabin before snagging Harlow by the vest and pulling her inside. She landed next to Decker, who held her tight.

"All souls on board," said Pam.

The helicopter dropped from the sky—at least that was how it felt. As they picked up speed, Harlow understood that Quincy had ducked behind the ship's stern to keep them from taking any additional fire. The helicopter raced across the harbor for a few seconds before banking right and gaining altitude.

"I'm bringing us back around, outside of small-arms range," said Quincy. "So we can enjoy the show."

When the flight leveled off, Pam reached and pulled the left-side door shut, quieting the cabin. They removed their balaclava masks and gathered along the right side, staring out of the Bell 206 JetRanger's expansive window at the terminal complex as it moved into view.

"Cell phones," said Decker. "We'll take out the rudder first. Pierce on speed dial number five. Harlow number four. Like we rehearsed."

"Ready," said Pierce.

It took Harlow a little longer with the phone shaking in her hand. "Ready."

"Stand by to detonate charges four and five," said Decker, then started the countdown. "Three. Two. One. Boom."

She hit "Send" and turned to look out the window. Two near-simultaneous underwater flashes threw a massive geyser of water over the stern, erasing it from sight.

"Set up for the hull charges. Harlow number one. Pierce number two. I got three."

A few seconds later, Decker started his countdown again. Three flashes lit up the channel, sending up separate columns of water higher than the top of the superstructure.

"I'd say your underwater demolition training certainly didn't go to waste," said Decker. "Looks like the Battle of Midway down there."

"It's a thing of beauty, isn't it?" said Pierce.

Harlow swayed, suddenly feeling very nauseated. Decker grabbed her before she hit the deck, moving her onto one of the seats.

"You okay?" he said, immediately seeing the bullet wound. "I need the med kit. Harlow's hit."

A flurry of activity erupted in the cabin as everyone jumped in response to Decker's vague injury declaration.

"It's not that," said Harlow, hugging him tightly. "I'm afraid of flying, in case you forgot."

"Could have fooled me," he said. "I thought you were out of your mind stepping out on the skid."

"That wasn't a very smart thing to do."

"Not at all. But it sure beat having to swim back," said Decker, before kissing her.

She held on to him for a few more seconds before letting go.

"Time to call Senator Steele and give her the good news," said Harlow.

"Let's get you patched up first," said Decker.

"It's really not that bad," she said.

"That's my Harlow!" said Pam. "Took her a few years, but she's finally an official member of the *I got shot because of Decker, and all I got was this lousy T-shirt* club."

"Is there an actual T-shirt?" said Harlow, weakly, her hands clutching the seat and handle again.

"There will be when we get back."

Decker smirked. "Can I have the sat phone. Please."

"You said the magic word," said Pam, digging the phone out of one of the seat compartments.

He dialed the senator and put the call on speakerphone. Steele answered almost immediately.

"Is everyone safe?" asked Steele.

"Everyone is safe, and you're on speakerphone," said Decker. "We're flying toward the Gulf. Mission accomplished. That ship isn't going anywhere."

"That's fantastic news. On both accounts," said Steele. "I'll make a bunch of calls first thing in the morning, pressing every law enforcement and investigative agency to take a close look at the ship's cargo. I'm so glad everyone is okay. This didn't sound like an easy job."

"It wasn't, but Brad made it look easy," said Decker. "Bernie should be on the ground in an hour to pick us up. We're about forty minutes from the airfield. We can be in the DC area seven to eight hours after that."

"Don't you people ever rest?" she said, getting a laugh out of everyone.

"We can sleep on the plane," said Decker.

Steele's long pause told Harlow that something had changed. Her instinct was validated a moment later.

"As much as we could use your help here, I need you somewhere else. Two places, actually. First at the SKYSTORM airfield. I managed to pull a few strings and pique some law enforcement interest up there. It's an opportunity we can't pass up," said Steele. "I'll explain the second mission when you're airborne on Bernie's plane. It's a little more complicated."

"I'll let him know our plans have changed," said Decker.

"He knows," said Steele. "I've already sent him the information. I didn't want to distract any of you from the mission at hand."

Decker looked disappointed. Or possibly slighted? She couldn't tell, but he definitely didn't look happy about the news. He'd clammed up, which was a tell that he was frustrated.

"Okay. We'll review the missions when we get on board and coordinate from there," said Decker.

Steele must have sensed it, too.

"Ryan. You're not being sidelined," said Steele. "Rich warned me you might feel this way. We think we've figured out an endgame for all of this. It's a bit of a long shot, and we might be wrong—but we have to give it a try. The mission is almost tailor-made for you and Brad. You'll see what I mean when you read through the packet. If we're right, tomorrow's events should put an end to APEX."

Harlow hijacked the conversation, turning the lights off on Decker's pity party.

"We're ready to bury APEX," said Harlow. "You should have seen the charges go up on that ship. Sweet justice. And I lost my fear of flying for about a minute. But it all came back, so I'm hoping our next flight is shorter than seven hours. Two would be nice."

Steele laughed. "I wish I had better news, but you're looking at about nine to ten hours."

"Can't catch a break," said Harlow.

She nudged Decker, who took her hint. He needed to pick himself up off the ground and end this on a positive note.

"Do we at least get to do something cool?" asked Decker.

"Rich just nodded yes," said Steele, "if that helps. I think everything you guys do is cool."

Decker laughed. "It does."

"And Harlow, it's much lower risk than what we have planned in DC," said Steele.

"Sold," said Harlow.

CHAPTER
FORTY-FIVE

Ezra Dalton jolted out of a deep slumber, momentarily unsure where she was or what had woken her. A persistent, repetitive chime from her nightstand brought it all back. She was in her Mason Neck home. It was the middle of the night. And the specific ringtone meant nothing but bad news. She'd assigned it to a single number on her contact list—Samuel Quinn. Dalton reached over and grabbed the phone, steeling herself for whatever report he felt necessary to pass along at three in the morning.

"What happened?" she asked, skipping right to the point.

"SKYSTORM is dead in the water," said Quinn. "Literally and figuratively. Decker and his crew nearly sank our ship in Houston. They blew up the rudder and put three holes in the port side at the waterline."

Dammit. They should have killed Decker months ago. Along with Senator Steele. It had been a mistake to assume the two sides had reached a truce.

"Just transfer the cargo off the ship. The terminal and port authority should be doing that anyway if the ship is in danger of sinking," said Dalton. "We can put it on another one. They took their one shot. Decker can't keep blowing up ships. I assume the cargo is intact?"

"The cargo is fine, but it's not going anywhere anytime soon," said Quinn. "The police have evacuated and closed off the terminal, and it sounds like every SWAT team in the greater Houston area is on the scene. Port authority and Coast Guard fast boats are in the channel."

"The authorities will sort this out soon enough. Once EOD sweeps the ship and hull, we'll be able to move the cargo," said Dalton.

"I wish it were that simple," said Quinn. "But before they detonated the charges, Decker and his SEAL buddy, Brad Pierce, killed at least twenty members of our security detachment. I emphasize the words *at least* because the most senior surviving member of the detachment could only take a rough guess based on a sweep through the superstructure and a quick scan of the pier."

"Please tell me he's not still on the ship," said Dalton.

"He managed to gather up whoever he could find and flee the harbor in the detachment's fast boat. Eight that could walk out of a forty-strong detachment. From what he told me, it sounded like a war zone at the pier—even before the explosions woke up Houston. And ready for this?"

"Not really," she said, still trying to process the unmitigated disaster he'd just described.

"Decker escaped in a helicopter, after the helicopter machine-gunned the hell out of the ship and its team. So I think it's fair to say that the ship and pier are now a high-priority crime scene, and the SKYSTORM cargo will be in federal hands within a few days. I'm going to recommend that we cut all ties to the program. Turn our back on it completely."

She took a moment to compose her thoughts.

"Have you notified Harold?"

"He's up next. I wanted to give you a heads-up, because you'll be his next call," said Quinn. "Decker will go to ground again, but Senator Steele can't stay away from her job forever. Be prepared to authorize and execute a very public killing the moment she surfaces. Right on the Capitol steps or inside her office if that's the only option. Whatever it takes."

"We have her house covered," said Dalton. "I'll start working on public scenarios. Hitting Steele at her office might be the best option. We can hire independents and pay them a fortune."

"Like I said, whatever it takes," said Quinn. "Now if you'll excuse me, I have some calls to make."

"Good luck."

"Save it for yourself," said Quinn. "Mine ran out about forty minutes ago."

She lay there for a few minutes, staring through the floor-to-ceiling windows next to the bed and wishing the whole thing had been a bad dream. Her phone buzzed, killing the silly fantasy.

IMMEDIATE TIER 1 AND 2 RECALL. THREATCON DELTA.

Within moments, she heard a knock at her bedroom door.

"Ms. Dalton?"

"I saw the message. I'll be ready in ten minutes," she said.

"Can I make you a cappuccino to go?" said the rapid security team leader assigned to her personal protective detail.

"Thank you, John. That would be great," she said, before getting up to pack.

Dalton pulled a carry-on-size suitcase out of a compartment in her walk-in closet and placed it on the wide cushioned bench. She stared at it for a moment, deciding to swap it for a larger bag. There was no telling how long the Institute would stay at THREATCON DELTA, which required all directors and division leaders to remain onsite in temporary living quarters until the threat against APEX was neutralized or downgraded.

The thought of spending any more time than absolutely necessary with the rest of the board was incentive enough to find and kill Senator Steele.

Chapter
Forty-Six

"One minute!" said Randy, never looking away from the glowing screens in front of him.

Their crew chief's southern-accented voice barely betrayed the sense of anticipation felt by everyone in the cargo hold.

They were sixty very short seconds away from landing another blow against the APEX Institute. Nowhere nearly as damaging as the container ship mission, but it would drive a final nail into SKYSTORM's coffin and amplify the message that they were through playing games. Of course, this night's festivities were just the beginning. Tomorrow would prove to be an extremely long and trying day for APEX.

Harlow dry heaved into the dangerously full plastic bag provided by Randy—right before Bernie dropped the aircraft from twenty thousand feet to four hundred feet AGL (above ground level) to spoof local air traffic control radars. Nap-of-the-earth (NOE) flying required Bernie to maintain a constant altitude, which meant frequent adjustments to match the terrain. The aircraft had pitched up and down nonstop for forty-five minutes. Harlow's face had been attached to the bag the entire time.

Decker squeezed her knee and kissed the side of her head. She lowered the bag and tried to speak, unable to form a word before the bag came up again. He owed her a long, relaxing vacation after the hell he'd put her through on this trip. Nearly all their time had been spent in the air—Harlow's Achilles' heel. *Brave* didn't even begin to describe how she had leaned into the past forty-eight hours. *Fearless* came close. Tenacious and fearless. Even closer. More like *indomitable.*

"Thirty seconds!" said Randy. "Remember! Do not disengage your harness until you see the green light! We're looking at a hard stop on the runway and a possible full-throttle departure if things look too hairy around the hangars."

Decker gave the crew chief a thumbs-up, which was repeated by everyone else directly involved in the airfield raid—Pierce, Pam, and Mazzie. The rear cargo ramp lowered a few seconds later, instantly flooding the aircraft with crisp, early-morning high plains air. Decker tightened his grip on the bulky grenade launcher between his legs. Pam did the same with the light machine gun lying across her lap. She looked entirely at ease with the Serbian weapon. The aircraft suddenly pitched downward, feeling like it had slowed significantly.

"This is almost over," he said to Harlow, who just shook her head and groaned.

The unmarked runway rose to meet them, biting into the C-123's landing gear with a punishing jolt that slammed his bottom side into the stretched canvas bench seat and whipped his head forward. Before he could straighten his neck, the aircraft's powerful twin engines thundered, their propellers reversed to bring the thirty-ton beast to a rapid stop near the target hangar. The sudden deceleration pinned him against Harlow, who had lost her grip on the bag when they hit the runway, emptying its contents onto her lap.

Quincy Rohm's voice boomed over the loudspeakers a moment later. Harlow was on her own for the next minute or two.

"Primary target confirmed inside the first hangar. Secondary targets at last hangar," she said. "One armed vehicle guarding each target, along with visible security team. Make this quick. Green light in three . . . two . . . one."

The aircraft lurched to a stop, and the green light next to the ramp illuminated.

"Go!" said Quincy.

Decker released his harness and raced for the open ramp, Pierce's automatic rifle already pounding away from one of the fuselage windows before he set foot on the runway. He sprinted a good fifteen feet past the bottom of the ramp to make room for Pam, who ran down the ramp a second later. While he sighted in on the machine gun–equipped dune buggy parked next to the open hangar door, Pam dropped to the asphalt just beyond the ramp and extended her machine gun's bipod.

His first shot landed several feet short but close enough to momentarily disrupt the vehicle's machine gunner. Decker mentally applied a quick adjustment to the sight picture and fired again. The second forty-millimeter high-explosive grenade detonated inside the front seating area, erasing the driver and tossing the gunner's mangled body onto the tarmac.

Pam's machine gun boomed simultaneously, ripping into a group of heavily armed mercenaries who had made the unfortunate mistake of barreling out of the dark hangar—into the open. While a stream of green tracers stitched through the four-man team, Decker shifted his aim to the boxy Thrush aircraft deep inside the hangar and applied pressure to the trigger. A burst of gunfire snapped past his head, throwing him off. His third shot went high and wide, striking the back of the hangar. A bullet cracked off the runway a few feet from where he had knelt, followed immediately by another—just inches away. Both strong indicators that he was running out of time.

He reacquired the Thrush through the launcher's red dot sight and fired. The moment the grenade left the barrel, he knew it would strike dead center. While the projectile sailed into the hangar, Decker fired the remaining two rounds. The three grenades exploded in rapid succession, two detonating against the fuselage and one slamming into the right wing.

Decker didn't wait around to assess the damage. Despite Pam and Pierce's best efforts, the incoming gunfire had become too intense. They'd have to settle for whatever damage the three grenades had inflicted. He took off, sidestepping Pam when he reached the ramp.

"Let's go!" he said.

Pam fired a long, sustained burst into the hangar, dozens of green tracers creating a light show inside as they ricocheted off the walls and concrete deck. The C-123's engines roared as soon as they piled into the cargo compartment, the behemoth rapidly accelerating for takeoff. Decker raced to reload the grenade launcher, desperately hoping to do some damage to the secondary targets before they took off.

"Decker. Move!" said Pam, before nearly yanking him off his feet.

A quadcopter drone buzzed past, disappearing into the darkness beyond the cargo compartment's muted red glow. *Shit.* In all of the excitement, he'd forgotten about the drone. Mazzie would deliver the coup de grâce to the airfield from her seat at Randy's crew chief station.

He went back to work on the grenade launcher, replacing four of the grenades before Pierce stopped firing his automatic rifle long enough to shout a warning.

"We're coming up on the semis!" he said, before resuming his barrage of suppressive fire through the window.

Return fire started to punch through the starboard-side fuselage, a long string of bullets passing a few feet over his head and continuing toward the front of the aircraft. He instantly turned his head, relieved to see that Harlow had already released her harness and was helping Joshua take cover on the deck. If either of them had still been upright in their seats, he would have abandoned the final grenade salvo.

"Help me out with this," said Decker, lying flat at the top of the ramp. "Just make sure I don't fall out. I'm going to crawl down about halfway."

"This isn't a good idea," said Pam, taking a knee behind him and grabbing his ankles.

"What else is new?" he said. "Nice shooting, by the way. You're a natural with that thing."

"I was just getting warmed up," said Pam.

Decker crawled down the ramp until he had a clear view of the hangar doors, the abrasive nonskid surface scraping the skin off his elbows the entire way. He nestled the grenade launcher's stock into his shoulder, just as the first semitruck face appeared in his peripheral vision. The front of a second semitrailer, parked immediately adjacent to the first, materialized a moment later. Followed by a third. Decker did some very rough trajectory math in his head, taking the C-123's forward motion into account—and fired the four grenades as fast as the launcher's cylinder would cycle.

The first grenade missed, exploding against the edge of the hangar door just to the right of the first semitruck. The rest hit home, destroying the three tractor trailers and effectively stranding the last three APEX containers at the airfield. Pam helped him up the ramp as the aircraft picked up speed. Decker sat against the side of the aircraft next to Pam, staring into the darkness beyond the ramp. The C-123 lifted off from the runway after several more seconds of rapid acceleration, Bernie putting them into an immediate steep climb to get as far away from the airfield as possible before the climax.

"Good hits!" said Pierce, securing the window he'd used as a firing port. "We left them a big enough mess without the finale."

"Mazzie! How long until the fireworks?" said Decker.

"Not long!" she said. "I'm almost there!"

Senator Steele's mercenary friends had sent Joshua and Mazzie the necessary instructions to equip a quadcopter drone with remote detonatable explosives. They had identified a sizable fuel tank behind one of the hangars, which they assumed had been the primary source of fuel for test flights. The drone carried a half-pound block of C-4, the largest charge Mazzie felt comfortable attaching to the quadcopter. Pierce figured it would be enough to detonate the fuel used by the Thrush's turboprop engines, if she could land it directly on the tank. No problem for a semiprofessional drone racer.

"Five seconds!" said Mazzie.

Pierce joined Pam and Decker at the top of the ramp.

"Harlow's out cold, by the way," said Pierce. "You owe her big-time."

Decker glanced over his shoulder. She lay flat on the deck next to Joshua.

"Yeah. I don't know how I'm going to make this up to her," said Decker, turning his head back in time for the grand finale.

"Three. Two. One!" said Mazzie.

Night turned into day for a moment, close to a thousand gallons of aviation fuel exploding roughly a half mile behind them. His face warmed from the burst of radiant heat created by the blast, a single thunderous clap reaching them a few seconds later. He really hoped they hadn't just erased the evidence Senator Steele had arranged to fall into the hands of a combined Texas Ranger–state trooper SWAT unit staged about fifteen miles south, along the only road in or out of the airfield.

Not that the Department of Homeland Security, Federal Bureau of Investigation, and about a dozen other federal and local law enforcement agencies would have any trouble gathering plenty of evidence at the Port of Houston, where the bulk of SKYSTORM sat stranded by their earlier attack. The trick would be linking it all to APEX—a feat Steele was confident and determined that she could make happen.

Decker watched the distant scene for a few more moments, the blinding fireball quickly replaced by hundreds of small dancing fires in the darkness below.

"How long until the Nevada jump?" he asked.

"About nine hours," said Pam. "With a stop for fuel somewhere on the way."

"Long enough to get some well-needed sleep," said Pierce.

"That sounds heavenly," said Decker, forcing himself onto his feet. "After I get Harlow cleaned up and settled in."

"I tried to convince her not to come," said Pam. "But there's no talking her out of anything when it comes to you."

"There's no talking her out of anything—regardless of the subject," said Decker.

"Good point," said Pam. "But that doesn't mean you don't owe her big-time. Like Pierce said."

"Don't worry. I plan to make this up to her," said Decker. "And all of you. I haven't forgotten that I got everyone into this. From the very beginning."

"You've definitely made the past few years interesting," said Pam.

"I guess you could say that," said Pierce. "If you consider almost getting killed several times interesting."

"Get some rest. There's still one more opportunity to get killed ahead of us," said Decker, before heading forward to take care of Harlow.

PART FIVE

CHAPTER
FORTY-SEVEN

James Guthrie studied Senator Steele's boat dock from the house across Weems Creek through a pair of binoculars, confirming what his sniper team had reported. He hadn't driven down here because he doubted their judgment. The mission was simply too important for him not to double-check everything within his control. The assault team's primary staging area was seven minutes away. Dalton would expect him to make the trip to see for himself.

As conveyed by the team, Steele's sailboat indeed looked as though it had been prepped for an afternoon or evening on the water. The mainsail cover was gone, the jib line and mainsheets had been wound around their winches, and the cockpit seat cushions were in place. Was it possible that she would actually show up? Something big had happened last night. That was for certain.

He'd received a call from Dalton at four in the morning, changing her original order from capturing the senator to a kill on sight. That was enough to tell him that something had gone wrong. Big-picture wrong. Killing a US senator at her house would send shock waves throughout the Beltway and the country, guaranteeing a massive, thorough murder investigation. Whatever had occurred between his last check-in with

Dalton late yesterday evening and the call he'd received early this morning had convinced APEX that the fallout was worth the risk.

He shifted his view to a group of four people carrying two huge coolers across her expansive backyard. Guthrie studied them, looking for any signs that they could be a covert team. Three high school- or college-aged kids led by a portly middle-aged guy with long hair. All of them wore navy-blue polos with some kind of emblem and tan shorts. Definitely a boat service crew.

Now he truly wondered what had transpired last night. What would give Steele the confidence to brazenly reemerge like this? The coolers looked large enough to carry drinks for a dozen or more people. Just like that, she was taking friends out for a sunset sail on the Chesapeake Bay? Mind blowing. He sat in the plush leather couch facing Steele's house, the midday sun dancing on the water below. A thick suppressor floated in his peripheral vision.

"How far to the boathouse?" he asked.

"Five hundred feet," said one of the men behind him.

He glanced over his shoulder at the sniper team, who sat side by side at a desk they had moved from one of the bedrooms. The desk lined up with the top of the couch, providing a stable platform for the rifle and a fairly concealed location if Steele's security team took a hard look at possible threat locations within line of sight of her estate.

"How about the house?"

"Six hundred and fifty to the deck," said the sniper. "Easy shot."

Guthrie nodded. He had no doubt in their ability to reach out and touch the senator. They were one of APEX's best sniper teams.

"And you think it's okay to keep the sliding door open? Doesn't look suspicious?" asked Guthrie.

"There's a nice breeze. This is the day to have your screen door open," he said.

"Sounds good," said Guthrie, getting up. "Same ROE. If you get a solid opportunity—take it. You don't need my clearance. Don't even waste the time reporting it. Shoot and let me know on the way out."

"Easy enough," said the sniper.

"Any bonus for her security detachment?" asked the spotter.

"Actually, no," said Guthrie.

"Seriously?" said the spotter.

"Yes. But they've increased the overall bonus for the primary target," said Guthrie. "Trust me when I say you'll be very pleased with the amount."

"Right on."

"The target is special," said Guthrie. "Very important."

"That's one way of putting it," said the sniper.

"Looks like the two of you have this well under control," said Guthrie, handing him the binoculars. "I'm heading back to the staging area. I'll let you know when the senator is inbound."

"We'll be here," said the sniper, setting the binoculars on the table next to the sniper rifle and spare ammunition magazines.

The spotter looked up from his tripod-mounted range-finding scope and gave him a mock salute.

"Lunch is in the kitchen. Crab cake sandwiches and fries," said Guthrie. "Still warm."

The sniper gave him a thumbs-up without looking back. Guthrie locked the door behind him on the way out and got back in the vehicle. Part of him really didn't want to leave these two alone to decide his fate, or more importantly, APEX's. But picking competent operatives and delegating responsibility was exactly what set apart a leadership position in the security force from one as an operations project head. As a security team leader, he rode in the first car of the convoy or kicked in the first door. In operations, he was expected to plan the mission, then step back and let the pieces he'd assembled do the work.

He supposed it didn't matter. He couldn't be in two places at once. If he was forced to raid Steele's house and root her out, his tactical expertise and leadership experience would be far more useful during a direct attack. The sniper would succeed or fail regardless of his presence. The assault team was a different story.

Guthrie started the SUV and backed out of the driveway, dialing Dalton on his satellite phone.

"If you're calling to tell me she's dead, there's a one hundred-thousand-dollar bonus with your name on it," said Dalton.

"No. But she should be dead within a few hours," said Guthrie. "I just confirmed, with my own eyes, that her sailboat has been prepped for immediate use. I watched a boat service crew carry two oversized coolers down to the boat. It looks like she's throwing a party."

"I bet she is," said Dalton. "The nerve of that woman."

"That's what I was thinking," he said.

"I'm tempted to drive out and watch," said Dalton.

Whatever Steele had pulled last night must have been bigger than he thought. Dalton made it sound almost personal.

"The sniper team is set up with a clear shot to the pier and the house. If she steps outside, they'll take the shot," said Guthrie. "If a shot isn't practical, I have a full urban assault team staged seven minutes away. We'll kill her inside her own house."

"Can you hit her before she gets to the house? A preemptive strike?" asked Dalton. "I don't like the thought of Steele getting into her safe room. I want her dead. Today. If she gets in that room, we're back to square one. And the hundred-thousand-dollar bonus I got approved for you this morning is off the table."

"There's no way for us to prestage a hit-and-run team in her neighborhood without drawing immediate police attention. It's a very exclusive, well-patrolled area. I'd have to position multiple vehicles along three different approaches just to detect her arrival, significantly diluting the assault team."

"I'll send you more people," said Dalton. "It's that important."

"It won't be necessary. I have the code to open the safe room door," said Guthrie.

"What?"

"The company that designed and built the senator's safe room programmed the keypad system with a unique reset code she can access by contacting the company's chief security officer directly in the event that she forgets the original," said Guthrie. "I spent most of the operation's remaining discretionary budget to acquire those sixteen digits. That code opens the door so she can reset it from the inside control panel."

"Are you serious?" said Dalton.

"Very serious," said Guthrie. "I still intend to keep her from reaching the safe room, but even if she somehow gets inside, it'll be her last resting place. The woman I paid for the reset code deleted it from their system. I'll punch in my own code after we kill her and shut the door. They'll have to cut the room open with a thermite torch to get her body out. That's assuming they somehow figure out she's inside. It could be weeks before they decide to open it up to check."

"Couldn't you make that happen anyway?" asked Dalton.

"I suppose I could," said Guthrie. "If that's what you want."

"I most definitely want the senator's next public appearance to be in the form of a rotting corpse," said Dalton.

"Consider it done," said Guthrie, making a mental note to stay on Dalton's good side.

CHAPTER FORTY-EIGHT

Senator Steele fidgeted in the seat, her mind racing with fear, as Klink, one of the last operatives to arrive, turned the SUV onto Claude Street. They were less than a minute from her house.

"I really don't think this is a good idea," said Steele. "It feels like they could hit us at any time."

Rich spoke from the front passenger seat without turning his head away from the street in front of them.

"The roads are clear. One of our teams drove through a minute ago, and our eye in the sky is keeping a close watch over us. You'll be safe inside the house before you know it."

She understood this to be true on nearly every level. A team she had never met had installed an array of concealed sensors on her property and inside her house, then monitored them for months, looking for evidence of intrusion or irregularities. Steele just couldn't stop focusing on the one remaining irrational level, where APEX was all-powerful and all-knowing—capable of anything.

"I know. It's just nerve-racking," said Steele. "I keep thinking they could have drilled a hole underneath my house, from one of the neighbors' homes, and planted a bomb. Or they could drop some kind of massive homemade bomb on the house from a helicopter the minute we stepped in the door. They have the resources and the kind of sick imagination to pull something like that off. The scenarios are endless."

"They are, and there's always the very outside possibility that APEX has taken an entirely extreme and unexpected course of action. But there's nothing we can do about that."

"Except stay away from the house," said Steele.

"We can take a right instead of a left up ahead and get out of here," said Rich. "It's entirely up to you."

The plan to take down APEX required the kind of momentum they might not be able to build again if she turned them around. Depriving them of SKYSTORM, less than a year after literally burning down their two-billion-dollar cannabis operation, put APEX in a uniquely vulnerable and desperate position—the kind of position where people tended to make bad decisions under pressure. Steele knew it was either now or possibly never. She couldn't realistically expect Rich's team to keep her alive long enough to reach this point again.

"No. Stick with the plan. This ends today," said Steele. "I hope."

"I have a good feeling about it," said Rich.

"He's never said that in the ten-plus years I've worked with him," said Jared, who lay across the third row, out of sight. "Never even hinted at it."

"Is that good or bad?" asked Steele. "I really have a hard time reading any of you, except for Anish and Caz."

"Caz is still a work in progress," said Rich. "Anish is Anish. There's no hope for him."

The entrance to her estate came into view as the SUV pulled up to the stop sign at the end of Claude Street. Two thick redbrick pillars flanked a black dual-swing gate.

Rich turned in his seat to face her. "Last chance to turn back."

"This isn't just about me," said Steele, thinking about Decker, Pierce, and everyone else she'd inadvertently dragged into APEX's crosshairs. "Let's get this over with."

The SUV turned left onto Simms Drive, Rich pointing a paperback book–shaped device at the gate about halfway down the street. The gates swung inward and had cleared the brick driveway by the time they pulled up, allowing them to continue to the house without stopping. Steele squeezed the door rest handle the entire ride, only easing up when the SUV pulled directly into the garage bay farthest from the house. Caz was out of the vehicle before the garage door started on its way back down, presumably making sure nobody slipped inside. She knocked on the window when the door stopped.

"That's our cue," said Rich, the locks clicking open.

Caz opened Steele's door and helped her down from the oversize vehicle.

"Stay close behind me," Caz said, drawing her pistol. "We'll get you inside the safe room and do our thing."

She followed Caz through the garage to the door leading into the house while Rich and the others gathered near the back of the SUV. Caz punched in the code to open the door, turned the dead bolt when the keypad flashed green, and slipped inside the house. She ushered Steele into a small walk-in closet on the right and examined the home security system touch screen.

"Everything looks good," said Caz, before disabling the system.

It was almost like they knew the house better than she did. That alarm had given her enough trouble over the past few years that she often didn't set it when leaving the house. She didn't like the time pressure of having to enter the code within a minute after gaining entry.

"We're going to keep you clear of any windows facing the water until we're set up and ready," said Caz. "So we'll take a right at the end of the hallway and make our way through the guest area to reach the safe room. Sound good?"

"Lead the way," she said.

Steele paused when they reached the end of the hallway and looked over her shoulder. Rich and Jared slid a long, jam-packed green duffel bag inside the house.

"Let's go. We may not have a lot of time," said Rich, before the two of them headed back into the garage.

"Let's keep moving, Senator," said Caz.

Steele nodded and started to move but stopped again, convinced her eyes had been playing tricks on her. She could have sworn she'd just seen Klink carrying some kind of fully dressed mannequin or life-size doll.

"Sorry," she said, following Caz toward the safe room.

When they reached the safe room door at the end of the hallway in the bedroom wing of the house, Steele couldn't resist asking about what she'd seen.

"Caz? Did I see Klink carrying a mannequin?"

The operative smiled. "Something like that."

"You're really not going to tell me any more, are you?"

"Trust me, Senator. You really don't want to know what they have planned. Just stick to me like glue and you'll be fine," said Caz, punching in the safe room code.

"What about them?" asked Steele.

"Don't worry about those three," said Caz.

All she'd really been told about the plan was that she'd never be directly exposed to any danger and that she had to do exactly what she was told at all times—without hesitation. Unsatisfied by the lack of details, she'd pushed Rich until he'd casually stated that "the house would require extensive repair work when it was all said and done."

After hearing that, Steele quit asking questions. She stepped into the safe room, convinced she was better off not knowing any details of their plan.

CHAPTER FORTY-NINE

Ezra Dalton needed to be in this meeting right now like she needed a ruptured appendix. Steele had returned to her house in Annapolis nearly an hour ago with three mercenaries, two of whom had been directly linked to the early days of retired General Terrence Sanderson's Black Flag program—Richard Farrington and Robert Klinkman. The third, a still-unidentified woman, appeared to be the senator's primary personal protective agent. The few glimpses the sniper team had so far managed to catch of Steele indicated the woman never left her side.

The SKYSTORM fallout was Quinn's job to clean up. Senator Steele was hers. But instead of sitting in the hub's war room, directly monitoring Guthrie's communication and video feeds during a moment pivotal to the Institute's survival, she was stuck listening to little more than feeble rants about past mistakes and generic prattle about the path forward.

"Sorry if this bores you, Ezra," said Kline, clearly sensing her detachment from the proceedings. "But we wouldn't be sitting here if you hadn't insisted you could control Senator Steele."

"Finger-pointing tends to get boring," said Dalton. "Particularly from someone who hasn't initiated or run a single significant project for close to a decade. When this setback is behind us, maybe it'll be time for you to consider a more risk-averse retirement than your current one."

"Setback? You call this a setback?" said Kline. "We should have booted your ass out of here years ago, before you could do too much damage. I predicted all of this."

"Poor Allan. I hate to think you might have to sell one of your dozen mansions to stay afloat," said Dalton. "Mansions you bought with the money the rest of us fought tooth and nail to bring in while you jetted around the world with wife number four, five, six . . . Who can keep track?"

"This isn't about me or money," said Kline.

"Really? Because you get like this when the big payouts don't pan out," said Dalton. "I remember your epic meltdown after EMERALD CITY."

"For shit's sake, Ezra, we're looking at real exposure with this SKYSTORM mess. The feds have the terminal locked down and are going container by container with explosive ordnance disposal teams, thanks to some strategically placed anonymous tips. I wonder how they'll react when they start opening our containers. And then there's the airfield mess. The Texas Rangers have our entire SKYSTORM production facility locked down—soon to be put under the microscope."

"The program can't be linked back to us. Samuel has been careful— like always," said Dalton. "Something you wouldn't know anything about at this point in your semiretirement."

"It doesn't matter how careful we've been!" said Kline, standing up. "With Senator Steele connecting the dots—"

"Senator Steele will be out of the picture very shortly," said Dalton.

"Why very shortly? Why not right now?" said Kline.

Dalton considered reexplaining the reasons for giving the sniper option some time to develop, which all boiled down to minimizing APEX's potential exposure during the inevitably thorough investigation of the senator's assassination, but decided to skip it. If Kline wasn't convinced that a single suppressed gunshot from an untraceable house was worth waiting a few hours for—to avoid turning one of the most exclusive waterfront neighborhoods in Annapolis into a war zone—maybe he wasn't the only one. Perhaps everyone's patience had worn thin.

"Is anyone here opposed to me giving the order to hit the senator's house right now?" said Dalton.

Nobody actively indicated any opposition. Samuel Quinn, who arguably had the most experience running this kind of sensitive operation, didn't look enthusiastic about the idea but remained silent. He had very smartly recused himself from sticking his neck out any further than necessary given his precarious situation.

"Then it's settled," said Dalton, picking up her phone to dial Guthrie. "In less than thirty minutes, Senator Steele will no longer represent a threat to APEX."

"Don't count your chickens, Ezra," said Kline, before sitting back down. "General Sanderson's protégé burned you pretty badly before."

When the dust settled from all this, she would look into getting rid of Allan Kline, through a directors' vote or an assisted fall down the winding marble stairs in his favorite Tuscany villa.

CHAPTER FIFTY

Guthrie tucked the satellite phone into a side pouch on his plate carrier vest and triggered his radio.

"All assault teams. This is ZULU. We've been ordered to breach the estate," he said. "Stagger departure by twenty seconds. Form up at the rally point for the final approach."

The other four vehicle team leaders acknowledged the order as his driver started across the half-empty lot toward the stop sign at the business park's exit.

"SIERRA. This is ZULU," said Guthrie, reaching out to the sniper team individually. "Has anything changed at the estate?"

"Negative. Farrington is inside patrolling the western half of the house. Klinkman is on the deck," said the spotter. "I caught another glimpse of Steele and her guardian angel, but not enough to risk a shot."

Steele's security detail was playing it safe until the guests showed up—mistakenly thinking APEX wouldn't kill her right in front of everyone.

"If you get a shot at the primary target anytime prior to or after our arrival, you are cleared to take it. The senator takes priority," said Guthrie.

"Understood."

"Set up on Farrington. I'll let you know when we turn onto Claude Street. That's about thirty seconds out. We'll time your shot with our turn into the estate. Farrington first. Klinkman second."

"Copy that. Shifting to Farrington as the first target," said the spotter.

The whole operation would be over in under fifteen minutes. Guthrie was about to simultaneously throw twenty battle-hardened mercenaries and a sniper team at a fairly straightforward assault. Overkill for sure under the circumstances but absolutely necessary against the legendary covert operatives who had nearly wiped out his rapid security force team in Georgetown. He wouldn't make the same mistake again.

The sniper team would at least kill one of the biggest threats before they arrived at the house. Hopefully both. Even if Klinkman somehow managed to get back into the house, the two remaining operatives didn't stand a chance against the overwhelming odds and firepower Guthrie would direct against them.

Within moments of the teams breaching the house, Klinkman and his colleague would be forced by the relentless gunfire and aggressive tactics to retreat to the safe room, where a flash bang grenade or two in that confined metal box would rattle their brains to the point of delirium. A few point-blank gunshots to each of their heads shortly after that would put a quick end to APEX's Senator Steele problem—and earn him a tidy bonus to go with his promotion.

"Hold tight and keep me apprised of any changes," said Guthrie. "Ground assault ETA is seven minutes."

CHAPTER FIFTY-ONE

Jared Hoffman listened carefully to the exchange, noting the obvious and reading between the lines. He could hear only the spotter's side of the conversation, but it should be enough. And if he detected any disparity between what he saw through his rifle scope and what he interpreted from the spotter's words, Jared would immediately take the shot.

Rich's and Klink's lives hung in a delicate balance specifically designed to lure APEX deep into a trap, and Jared's spot judgment was the only fail-safe built into the system. If he misread the situation, at least one of his two friends would die. *No pressure at all.* The radio exchange between the spotter and whoever ran their show drifted to a natural conclusion.

Jared was hooked into two different communication feeds, one in each ear. The sniper team conversation had been piped through a listen-only frequency, compliments of a tactically placed, satellite-enabled listening device. The team net was a standard P25 encrypted radio setup.

"They took the bait," said Jared. "We have about seven minutes until the ground assault reaches the estate. The sniper team has been ordered to take out Rich first. Sounds like they were originally targeting Klink."

"That's a relief," said Klink.

"For who?" asked Rich.

"You guys don't trust me?" asked Jared. "That kind of hurts after all these years."

"It's not that I don't trust you," said Klink. "I just don't like knowing I'm in the crosshairs. Next time you can stand out here."

"With you shooting? I'll pass," said Jared.

"Me too," said Rich. "How's the senator holding up, Caz?"

"She's fine," said Caz. "We're both ready to go."

"That's what I like to hear," said Rich. "Jared. I'm not going to say another word until the convoy turns onto Simms Drive. It's apparently in my best interest to keep you laser focused."

"What was that? I was just checking Facebook," said Jared.

"That's not even funny," said Klink.

"I kind of thought it was funny," said Caz.

"You would. You're sitting in a bomb-proof vault."

"Scott. How are you doing?" asked Rich.

"Ready to pounce," said the former Navy SEAL, who was hidden directly adjacent to the sniper house. "And sweating my ass off. I forgot how humid Annapolis is in the summer."

"Are you a Boat School graduate?" said Rich.

Scott Daly, a twelve-year veteran of the team, waited on the other side of the creek to finish his critical role in the trap they had set. An hour earlier, he had placed the window listening device Jared would soon rely on to seal the plan.

"Funny how you can't seem to retain that information," said Scott. "Must have something to do with your own faulty education."

"How long ago did you graduate, Scott?" asked Jared, who was a West Pointer like Rich.

"Can we postpone the interservice rivalry shit-talking for later?" said Klink. "I'd really like to keep Jared focused for the next seven minutes or so."

"Fine. Everyone leave me alone," said Jared. "T-minus six minutes."

Throughout all the playful chatter, Jared never took his eye off the target. In fact, his scope's crosshairs had remained centered and steady on the opposing sniper's face for the past forty minutes. He'd studied the shooter's facial expressions and ticks. The way he adjusted his grip on the rifle when the spotter passed along information. How his face reacted to the information. What did he do to ease the discomfort of sitting in one position for hours on end? Did he ever look bored or distracted?

Based on the time he'd spent observing the sniper, Jared assessed him to be a pro. As in the guy could kill both Rich and Klinkman at the drop of a hat, if given the opportunity, which is why Jared had no intention of taking any chances. Given the confirmed timeline, he took the opportunity to make a few final adjustments to his own position prior to the insanity that would shortly ensue. All microchanges to his body's main points of contact with the ground. Elbows. Knees. Hips. Why not? He was perfectly concealed.

Jared had slowly worked his way under the deck and into the middle of a fully bloomed rhododendron bush, the tip of his rifle's suppressor just barely breaking through the thick lavender-purple flowers. He'd carefully snipped a few branches to clear a line of sight between his scope and the target house. Lying on his stomach, with the rifle nestled securely in the crook of one of the bush's thick core branches, he'd easily reached the state of semicomfortable equilibrium sought by trained snipers.

With the final adjustments made, Jared maintained his silent, motionless vigil as the clock ran down. In the far-right edge of the rifle scope's field of view, the spotter alternated his attention between his range-finding scope and watch. Ticktock.

When Jared's watch indicated one minute to go, the spotter turned to the deadpan sniper and said, "It's about to go down. No change to ballistic variables." A few seconds later, Rich broke the team's silence.

"A five-vehicle convoy just turned left onto Simms from Claude. You're up, Jared."

He took a slow, deep breath before starting a measured exhale through pressed lips. His final-moment breathing trick steadied the scope's crosshair drift across the sniper's face.

"Green light," said the spotter.

The rifle bit into Jared's shoulder, the customized MK12 Special Purpose Rifle's recoil manageable enough for him to instantly shift to the adjacent target. The shooter pitched backward from the impact of the first shot, just as he settled the crosshairs and pressed the trigger. Jared's second shot punched through the spotter's jaw, knocking him out of sight.

"Sniper team down," he said.

A moment later, Scott appeared behind the sniper team, tossing a handheld battering ram to the kitchen floor. He rushed toward the downed sniper team with a suppressed pistol, disappearing behind the couch. When he reappeared, Scott held a headset microphone up to his mouth.

"Rich and Klinkman are down hard. Head shots," he said, before winking at Jared. "No sign of the primary. Standing by to engage targets of opportunity."

Scott listened to the headset's earpiece for a few seconds, taking in APEX's reaction to his erroneous report, before tossing the set on the couch. He picked up the sniper's rifle and aimed toward the house before snapping off a quick shot. A window shattered, the broken glass cascading across the deck above Jared's head.

"You got me," said Rich. "How are we looking?"

"Sounds like they bought it hook, line, and sinker," said Scott. "Nice shooting, Jared."

"Nothing but a thing," said Jared, grabbing his rifle and crawling out of the bush.

He had coolers to move and a boat to start.

CHAPTER FIFTY-TWO

Guthrie tightened his grip on the overhead handle as the SUV rammed the gate leading into Senator Steele's estate, the vehicle's reinforced bumper knocking the wrought-iron obstacle aside like it was made of plyboard. Losing no speed, his vehicle hurtled down the brick driveway toward the senator's house.

"SIERRA confirms that our two major threats have been neutralized. We're up against one operative," said Guthrie over the radio. "Same plan."

His SUV skidded to a halt a few feet in front of an expansive brick porch. The three-man breach team seated behind him already on their way to the mansion's stained-glass double-door entrance before he even unbuckled his seat belt. Guthrie started to press the transmit button on the shoulder microphone attached to his tactical vest before he remembered his role in the grand scheme of things. Like a good coach, an operations project leader put together the right team and let them play the game.

Guthrie hopped down from the SUV and strode confidently toward the ordered mass of operatives stacked up beside the door, waiting for the primary breach team to clear the way. A second, smaller team went to work on the garage-bay door closest to the house with a pair of crowbars—to no avail. The door didn't budge an inch.

"Forget the garage!" he said, scattering the second team.

"Breaching!" yelled ALPHA team leader, quickly backing up from the front entrance.

Guthrie ducked to the left as several small explosive charges simultaneously detonated with a harsh crack, momentarily obscuring the front entrance. A second member of the breach team slid into place in front of the door with a handheld battering ram, quickly landing a blow against the demolished door and knocking it out of the way. Ram still in hand, he turned to the breach team leader and nodded—a red mist exploding from his head an instant later.

"Contact. Foyer—" started the breach team leader before a bullet punctured his throat.

The third member of ALPHA team pulled the team leader back as a sustained burst of unsuppressed gunfire punched through the still-standing half of the entrance—one of the bullets catching him in the face. The two men toppled off the patio, landing in the bushes next to the blasted doorway. Something was off. Either the third operative was far more skilled than they had anticipated, or a fourth had stayed out of sight on the ride up to the house. Jared, most likely. Guthrie quickly backtracked to his SUV to personally direct the two teams lined up along the unexposed side of the convoy.

"BRAVO up!" yelled the next team leader in line, the four members of his team stacking up at the entrance. "Flash bangs!"

Guthrie wanted to press the pause button on the attack but was afraid the entire assault force would fall apart if he broke their tempo. He decided to let this play out a little longer before making a decision. He crouched behind the hood of the vehicle, CHARLIE team lining up behind him as BRAVO team prepared to toss flash bang grenades into the house. He turned to CHARLIE team leader that had just settled in next to him.

"Take your team up to the door," said Guthrie. "Follow BRAVO in."

"Got it," said the team leader, urging his operatives forward.

Three of the four BRAVO operatives clustered near the entrance tossed grenades through the open doorway as CHARLIE team rushed forward to join them. Both teams, eight operatives, vanished inside the house after the flash bangs detonated. Several furious exchanges of gunfire erupted after a long pause.

"This is BRAVO. We have one man down. Headshot. A second with a leg wound. I'm sending him back out. There's only one hostile as far as we can tell. Giving us a hell of a time."

"Copy that," said Guthrie. "CHARLIE team. What's your status?"

"Inside. Covering the west side of the house," said the team leader. "All team members up."

"Can you confirm the status of Klinkman and Rich?" asked Guthrie.

"Affirmative. Klinkman is down hard on the deck. Bleeding out. I don't have a solid view of Rich. He's sprawled on the floor, partially concealed by two chairs. The window above his body is sprayed with blood and brain matter," said CHARLIE team leader.

"It's possible we're looking at two remaining shooters. They may have snuck a fourth in with the SUV," said Guthrie. "I'm moving in with DELTA and ECHO to reinforce."

The remaining two teams took their cue from his last radio transmission and formed up next to the SUV as the wounded man from BRAVO limped out of the house.

"You good?" asked Guthrie.

The man gave him a thumbs-up and hobbled down the porch steps to get out of the way.

"Hang in there. We'll be right back," said Guthrie, before heading inside.

He moved carefully through the spacious foyer and adjacent formal dining room before quickly locating BRAVO team leader, who was bunched up with a second mercenary, both of them aiming down a short hallway. The third lay collapsed in an expanding pool of blood in the middle of the hallway, a single hole drilled through his forehead.

"Hold up, sir," said BRAVO team leader over the radio. "We took fire from the hallway directly in front of us. I don't think there's a second shooter. Bruce was hit with a burst of fire from the end of the hallway. We exchanged gunfire a few times until the shooter went quiet. We haven't taken fire from two locations at once."

"That tracks with what we saw on the video feeds," said Guthrie. "But we'll assume there's a fourth shooter until we know for sure."

"How do you want to proceed?"

He peeked around the corner with his rifle, spotting what looked like blood splatter on the wall at the end of the bullet-riddled hallway. He triggered his rifle light and gave it a closer look through the magnified ACOG scope. The concentrated bloodstain on the wall connected with a smear on the floor by the corner.

"Tony. Did one of you land a shot on target? I'm seeing blood on the wall and floor just beyond the corner leading into the bedroom hallway."

"It's possible," he said. "The last exchange was pretty fierce."

"Stand by to move down the hallway with DELTA team," said Guthrie, leaning around the corner to cover the end of the hallway with his rifle. "I think you tagged the senator's last hope. They're probably locked up in the safe room calling for help, which means we need to pick up the pace."

"Moving out," said BRAVO team leader, stepping into the hallway with the other mercenary, their rifles locked on the corner.

"CHARLIE. Clear the rest of the great room. ECHO. You have the kitchen area. Make sure nobody comes up behind us," said Guthrie, before turning to the DELTA team leader. "Let's go."

He led the four men into the hallway, quickly catching up with BRAVO team. Guthrie moved in front of BRAVO as they approached the corner leading to the senator's bedroom, where the safe room was hidden.

He signaled for everyone to hold up, crouching a few feet back from the corner and removing a tactical mirror from one of his cargo pockets. Adding the mirror to his loadout had been an afterthought that morning. From this point forward, he'd make it a mandatory item for all his team leaders.

Guthrie extended the mirror toward the blood-smeared floor and angled it to give him a view around the corner. Clear. He moved up and aimed his rifle down the hallway. Thick splotches of blood on the floor led to the master bedroom door, which had been left open, giving him a partial view into the room. Thin, semitransparent white curtains muddled the view through the expansive sliding glass doors, which opened onto the wraparound deck. All he could see with any certainty beyond them were the leaves of a nearby tree swaying with the bay breeze.

"Blood trail leads into the master bedroom. DELTA clears the room. BRAVO peels right and clears the master bathroom and walk-in closet. I'll cover the doors we pass," said Guthrie, moving back against a black lacquered decorative cabinet to let the teams by.

He followed the six operatives down the bedroom hallway, walking backward at the same pace so he could watch the four additional bedroom doors. They stopped briefly outside the master bedroom, the two teams sliding inside a few moments later. Guthrie remained in the doorway; his rifle pointed back the way they had just come.

"Bedroom is clear," said DELTA team leader. "Blood leads right to the safe room door."

When BRAVO reported the same, he grabbed the nearest operative from DELTA team and set him up to watch the hallway and doors, then walked over to the safe room door just beyond the master bathroom. BRAVO team emerged from their sweep at the same time.

"Whoever's still around is behind that door, and I have the code that opens it," said Guthrie, before putting a hand on BRAVO team leader's shoulder. "When it's open, you'll toss in a flash bang. As soon as the grenade goes off, I want your team inside."

The team leader crouched next to the reinforced metal door and removed a grenade from his vest, pulling the pin while Guthrie slid a note card from one of his pants pockets. He entered the sixteen-digit code into the touch screen above the team leader's head and stepped back to make room for the second operative. The locking mechanisms activated the moment he pressed the last number, the reset code instantly bypassing the screen's menu. The door immediately swung inward, the team leader backhanding the flash bang deep into the safe room.

The grenade blast temporarily deafened him. Guthrie had underestimated the grenade's sensory impact just outside the vault. Having only one direction to escape, the thick metal walls sent all the sound waves toward the opening, giving the team a slightly dampened taste of their own medicine. The team leader took a few seconds to recover his senses before rushing inside with the remaining Bravo operative.

The team leader yelled something back to him, but Guthrie caught only the words "wrong" and "nobody." His hearing was severely degraded by the flash bang miscalculation.

"Say again, Bravo," he said over the radio net.

"Nobody's here!"

Impossible. He stepped in front of the opening to see for himself. *What the hell?* The space was entirely empty except for a bookshelf set against the far wall.

"Search for hidden compartments," he said, before stepping out and activating his radio. "All teams. Stay alert. The safe room—"

A long string of unsuppressed gunshots from the other side of the house interrupted his transmission, followed by pandemonium on the radio net. He demanded information, but the two team leaders kept talking over him. A few seconds later, he finally got through.

"Klinkman just started firing at us," said one of the team leaders. "I have one KIA."

"Is Klinkman still there?" said Guthrie.

"Negative. He's gone."

More suppressed fire erupted from the house.

Guthrie swiveled to face the wall-to-wall bank of sliding doors with his rifle. "Klinkman's on the deck!"

DELTA's team leader reacted swiftly, grabbing a handful of the curtain and running it halfway across the room before the leftmost slider shattered—one of the crouched operatives stumbling backward into the hallway. Everyone scrambled as a second bullet punched through the center glass pane, dropping it to the carpeted floor.

"Shut the fucking curtain!" said Guthrie, taking cover inside the bathroom doorway.

A third bullet thunked into the doorframe a few inches above his head. He dropped to the marble floor and rolled left as the curtain raced back across the slider. Somehow the team leader made it all the way. Guthrie rose to a crouch and peeked into the room to check the status of his men. The three remaining members of DELTA team lay pressed against the wall on the far left, rifles pointing toward the billowing curtain. BRAVO team leader poked his head out of the safe room.

"Anything?" said Guthrie.

"I can't find—"

The man vanished from sight in a cloud of black smoke, his body ripped to pieces by an explosion inside the safe room that sprayed human spaghetti and steel fragments across the room directly in front of the vault door—splintering the canopy bed and blowing the glass slider and curtain onto the deck. Guthrie stumbled backward and fell onto his back, unsure what he'd just witnessed. The safe room had basically torn the two men apart and ejected them like a tree shredder. He'd never seen anything like it.

DELTA's team leader knelt next to him, yelling into his ear. He could barely hear him over the ringing.

"It's a trap!" he yelled, the words coming out muffled.

Guthrie nodded. "Get your team out of the house! I'll coordinate the withdrawal."

The mercenary helped him to his feet before leading his team down the bedroom hallway. Guthrie tried to follow but faltered, his sense of balance disrupted by the blast's overpressure effects on his ears. He grabbed the doorframe and steadied himself as DELTA reached the end of the long corridor—and disappeared in a blast that knocked Guthrie flat on his back.

He lay there for a minute, covered in drywall chunks, splinters, and blood, before pulling himself together enough to stagger down the smoke-filled, debris-littered hallway. A small fire danced on top of what looked like a charred corpse. DELTA team had been ripped to shreds. A third explosion rattled the house, stopping him in his tracks. He cleared his voice and pressed the radio button.

"CHARLIE. ECHO. Report."

Nothing. Guthrie tried again, with no success. He felt for his headset, discovering that it had been torn from his vest by the explosion. Stepping over the crumpled, dismembered bodies that had once been DELTA team, he reached the turn in the hallway that led to the kitchen and living areas of the house. The black lacquered cabinet was gone, replaced by a smoldering crater in the wall. Judging by the fragmentation pattern along the hallway walls, he now understood what had happened.

Rich had lured him into the house under a false sense of security—strategically detonating hidden Claymore mines to cut his team down to a manageable size. He raised his rifle and turned the corner, expecting a counterattack at any moment. A figure dashed across the hallway leading out of the kitchen. Guthrie snapped off a quick burst and retreated behind the blast-shredded wall. A frenzy of return fire kept him in place for several seconds, finally dying down to a slow trickle.

He crouched low and peeked with his rifle, catching a quick glimpse of one of the shooters before they vanished through the opening that led to the dining room. *Shit.* That was ECHO team. Not wanting to take a bullet to the face or chest from a member of his own assault team, Guthrie gave them time to move on before stepping into the hallway. A fourth explosion shook the walls, a billowing cloud of dust and smoke filling the house ahead of him. ECHO was gone. So was CHARLIE, given the silence that had overtaken the house.

Instead of trying to navigate the house of horrors his tormentors had constructed, Guthrie returned to the master bedroom and stepped through the curtains onto the deck, hoping for a bullet. There was zero point to continuing. Even if he managed to somehow escape the estate, he couldn't return to APEX. Two mission failures in a row, making essentially the same mistake, meant one thing: termination. And not the kind where you sign a noncompete agreement. The kind that ended with a boiling lye bath in the back of a nondescript warehouse two states away—the resulting slurry poured down an industrial drain. He wasn't going out like that.

When a bullet didn't come, he removed the satellite phone from the pouch on his vest and called Dalton, who answered before he heard any indication of a ringtone.

"Everything went to shit on the radio," she said. "What the hell happened?"

"It was a setup. The whole thing," said Guthrie. "Everyone's gone."

"What do you mean 'everyone's gone'?"

"I mean I'm the only one left alive. I think. I don't know. Maybe a few survived. I really can't say," he said. "It's that bad over here."

"I'm sorry to hear that, James. We underestimated Sanderson's people."

"Yeah. Just slightly," said Guthrie. "And if I had to guess, I'd say they weren't finished with APEX. Not by a long shot."

"I'm going to let you go now," said Dalton, ending the call.

And just like that, APEX was done with him. He put his back against the brick wall next to the open slider and slid down to the glass-covered deck, taking a few moments to enjoy the blue sky and fluttering leaves before unsnapping his pistol.

CHAPTER
FIFTY-THREE

Senator Steele sat in the dirt against the concrete foundation of her house, the deck a few feet above her head. Caz and Rich knelt next to her, one on each side, their weapons ready. Whatever they had done to her house seemed to be over. The shooting stopped after four distinct explosions had shaken the ground and foundation, raining dust down on her head.

When Rich had said the house would require extensive repair work when this was finished, he hadn't been kidding. From the sound of things inside the house, she wouldn't be surprised if it had to be demolished. Maybe that was for the better. Sitting under the deck had triggered a painful flood of memories.

Her husband had taken his life not too far from here, the kidnapping and murder of their daughter, Meghan, kicking him into the dark hole he'd circled for years. She could feel his presence in the cool, musty darkness under the deck. It would be hard to say goodbye to this house.

"What's the holdup, Scott?" asked Rich, waiting for a reply over the radio net.

She couldn't hear Scott's answer, but it clearly annoyed him.

"This guy's taking forever. Ten more seconds and you put him out of his misery. I hear sirens."

When Steele arrived at the house, she had no idea how much thought had been put into what had transpired over the last several minutes. The more she learned, the more she understood why Karl had recommended this group. For a small, inconspicuous team, they packed an oversize punch—and they were thorough to a fault. About ten minutes ago, while waiting inside the safe room, she'd been told that a sniper team had been watching her house for the past two days. Thermal-imaging cameras installed months ago by Rich's people had identified an odd pattern of use at the house across Weems Creek over the past several weeks. They'd been watching it closely ever since.

Meanwhile, Rich identified the safe room's reset code from the very beginning as a possible vulnerability, taking measures to ensure it couldn't be used against her. He had taken a trip to meet with the security company that constructed and installed the room, convincing their chief security officer that no amount of money was worth betraying the senator and that she should notify Rich immediately if any attempt was made to acquire the code. A call from the company a few days ago had set this entire plan in motion, Rich and his team building onto it as other developments unfolded.

The plan had been solidified well in advance of Steele's arrival at the house. While she and Caz hid in the safe room, Jared had "taken care of" the sniper team. Afterward, the women had slipped out of the room and under the deck, where Scott, one of the operatives she'd met in Rockville, watched over them from the house.

"What are we waiting for?" she said quietly.

A single gunshot somewhere above them caused her to flinch.

"That," said Rich. "We're clear to move."

He nodded at Caz, who waded into the seemingly impenetrable wall of rhododendrons directly in front of them, Steele catching a glimpse of the shimmering water as she pushed through.

"Follow closely behind Caz, and don't look behind you," said Rich.

"Because you don't want me to see what you did to my house?" said Steele.

"No. Because you might take a bad step and sprain an ankle," said Rich. "You'll see what we did from the boat. There's really no way to hide it."

"I'm not opening my eyes until we're on the Severn," she said, before fighting her way through the fragrant bushes.

Halfway to the long pier, the Hinckley picnic boat's engine started with a deep thrum, Jared seated at the helm in the covered cockpit. When they reached the boat, Caz helped her on board, while Rich loosened the docking lines. He tossed the bowline on board and worked his way aft to the stern line.

After a few seconds of making no progress on the line, he glanced across the creek and yelled, "You want to swim back?"

Steele got up and leaned over the side, quickly loosening the line from the cleat and giving Rich a hand into the boat.

"First time on a boat?" she said.

"Now I got you busting my chops, too," said Rich, grinning. "Get us out of here, Jared."

"Are we picking up the squid?" asked Jared.

"I suppose we don't have a choice," said Rich.

The luxury yacht roared to life, speeding dangerously fast across the narrow stretch of water. Jared immediately put it into reverse, nearly throwing Steele out of her seat.

"Have you driven a boat like this before, Jared?" she said, already on her way toward the cockpit.

"I have, but it's been a while," he said, sharing a knowing look with Rich.

"Do you mind if I take over?" she asked. "I know these waters better than anyone."

Jared hopped down from the captain's chair and slid into the seat next to it. Steele settled into the cushioned seat and eased the throttle forward, bringing them alongside the short pier. Scott grabbed one of the cockpit roof handrails and jumped onto the portside deck, quickly swinging into the salon. When he was seated, she backed the boat just past the pier and cut the wheel left, pointing them toward the Severn.

"You make this look easy," said Jared.

"I grew up on the water," she said, pushing the throttle forward. "Tough life. I know."

The bow rose with the sudden influx of power, the thirty-seven-foot luxury boat rapidly picking up speed.

"Someone has to live it," said Jared.

"I guess so," she said, before taking a quick look across the water at her house.

Wisps of black smoke exhaled from the missing master bedroom and kitchen sliders, drifting over the roof and dissipating above the house. Compared to what she'd heard while hiding under the deck, the damage didn't look that bad from here. She was sure that wasn't the case.

"It's way worse than it looks," said Rich, as though he were reading her mind.

"That's what I figured," said Steele. "What's in the coolers?"

"Drinks. Shrimp cocktail. Cheese plate. More drinks," said Rich. "I figured we may as well enjoy the remainder of the afternoon. The rest is out of our hands, anyway."

"When will we know if it worked?" said Steele.

"A few hours from now. Maybe sooner," said Rich. "If the upload hasn't happened by then, it probably won't happen."

"It'll happen. I have a good feeling about this," said Steele as she eased the boat into a lazy starboard turn, headed for the open water of the Chesapeake Bay.

CHAPTER
FIFTY-FOUR

Ryan Decker stood side by side with Pierce near the top of the C-123's short ramp, steeling himself for the jump. At twelve thousand feet, the landscape almost looked stationary, creating the illusion that the aircraft was barely moving. Only the occasional turbulence-induced rattle reminded him they were in fact humming along at a brisk one hundred seventy miles per hour.

He scanned the monochromatic high-desert panorama of tan and beige. Classic Nevada landscape. The only distinguishable topographic feature in sight was a distant mountain range. The target site was about as isolated as it gets—for a good reason. If Senator Steele's new friends were right, APEX would want to keep this place as far from prying eyes and electronic snooping as possible.

Under a unique set of circumstances, which the team in DC intended to compel, the site represented a potentially lethal vulnerability to the organization. If they succeeded, Decker and Pierce would be in place to pound the final nail in APEX's coffin. At the very least it would severely cripple the Institute, forcing them to reconstruct the very foundation APEX had been built on—information.

The aircraft slowed and the jump light above the ramp turned red. They were a minute out, with Bernie bringing the airspeed down for the jump. Decker turned to check on Harlow, who sat in the farthest seat away from the ramp with her eyes closed. Pam tapped her knee and pointed in his direction. Tightening her death grip on her harness, Harlow glanced up at him and forced a smile. He winked at her and mouthed, "I love you." She briefly nodded and closed her eyes again.

Harlow had been through the wringer on this trip, spending more time in the air than on the ground—the back-to-back, gut-wrenching experiences probably cementing her fear of flying. He'd have to make up for this by driving her down to Cabo San Lucas for a few weeks of vacation.

The aircraft's crew chief swiveled his seat to face Decker and Pierce. He gave them a quick hand signal. *Thirty seconds.* He gave Randy a thumbs-up before facing the ramp. Decker gave himself a once-over, more a nervous habit than anything. Pierce and Decker had spent thirty minutes checking and rechecking themselves and each other, under Randy's close supervision. The explosives, electronics gear, and weapons were cinched tight in firmly attached bags specifically designed for military skydiving.

The light switched from red to green.

"See you on the ground!" said Decker over engine noise and wind.

"Not if I see you first!" said Pierce, before walking down the ramp and diving headfirst out the back of the aircraft.

Decker stole one more look at Harlow before diving after Brad. She surprisingly met his glance and gave him a thumbs-up. He kept that image in his head as he hurtled toward the ground at two hundred feet per second.

CHAPTER FIFTY-FIVE

Tim shut his laptop, closing the book on the gruesome affair they'd undertaken at Senator Steele's house. He typed a quick text message on his satellite phone and sent it to Rich.

Police stormed house. Captured three.

Rich responded with a picture taken from the boat. It looked like they were drinking beers.

Wish u were here.

Seriously? Another text quickly followed.

That was Scott. Nobody drinking beers. Yet. Any word from Nevada?

He typed a reply.

They're all set.

Decker had called him a few minutes ago to report that they had arrived at their target and assembled the electronics gear required to detect the incoming satellite signal.

Advise when drone mission complete.

He swiveled his chair to face Anish, who was fiddling with one of the drone's remote controllers. Just the sight of him with the controller in his hands made Tim nervous. Each drone was fitted with a one-pound, remote-detonated C-4 charge.

"Please don't blow us up," said Tim. "How are we looking?"

"Ready in a few minutes," said Anish.

Good. He wasn't sure how much longer they could stay parked here. Their windowless cargo van sat tucked away in the corner of a Safeway parking lot, a quarter of a mile from the APEX Institute's four-story glass-and-metal headquarters. The grocery store hadn't been busy when they'd arrived a few hours ago, but as the afternoon wore on, employees from the dozens of major corporations based in Tyson's Corner had started to trickle in to do a little last-minute shopping before heading home.

Six drones zooming out of the back of a windowless van fitted with an unusually powerful antenna—less than a mile from the Office of the Director of National Intelligence—was bound to attract the wrong kind of attention. He gave them three minutes from launch to pull off the attack. Any longer than that was pushing it, which didn't give them much leeway. At least thirty seconds would be taken up by the drones' preprogrammed flight to the building.

"I think I'm ready," said Anish, placing the drone he'd just finished inspecting on top of the folding table set up directly behind the van's rear doors.

"Think?"

"I'm ready," he said. "Just paying respect to Murphy's Law. Anything that can go wrong will go wrong."

"Just make sure the six pounds of C-4 doesn't go wrong inside this van," said Tim, "while I'm sitting in it."

"The bombs have not been armed," said Anish. "I may be crazy, but I'm not cray cray."

"Let's get this over with," said Tim.

He got out of the seat and made his way back to the makeshift launching pad. His job was simple for now. When Anish maneuvered a drone out of the back of the van, he placed the next one in the stack on the table. Rinse and repeat until all six drones were headed toward the APEX building along their preprogrammed flight paths. Things got a little complicated after that.

"Ready?" asked Anish.

"Do it," said Tim, switching the display on his watch.

Anish pushed the dual rear doors wide open, exposing their drone-launching operation to the general public. Tim started the stopwatch the moment the quadcopter rose from the table, setting the phone aside. By the time he had returned his attention to the table, the drone hovered just outside the van.

Tim grabbed the next quadcopter off the stack beside him and set it on the table, just as the drone behind the van zipped skyward with a high-pitched buzz. A few heads turned in the parking lot, and he revised the timeline. They'd drive out of here in two and a half minutes.

Wasting no time, Anish attached the controller to its assigned Velcro patch on a long two-by-four board mounted to the van wall behind him and took down the controller labeled #2. He repeated the process, launching the second drone a little quicker than the first. By the time they cycled the drones out of the van and shut the door, forty-five seconds had elapsed.

Anish shut the doors and retrieved controller #1, taking control of a drone hovering directly over the APEX building. He quickly landed it between two massive rooftop HVAC units before taking control of drone #2 and setting it down between a second grouping of HVAC enclosures. One minute and fifteen seconds down. Now for the hard part. Or fun part, depending on how you looked at it.

"I'm maneuvering drone number three toward the underground parking garage entrance," said Anish.

Tim slid into the driver's seat and grabbed the cell phone in the cup holder, placing his finger over the number three button. Each drone's cell phone trigger was linked to a speed-dial number on this phone.

"Are you in?" asked Tim.

"Yep. I'm just looking for—no freakin' way," said Anish.

"What? What's wrong?"

"Nothing's wrong, but I do have an open elevator door," said Anish.

"With nobody inside, I hope?"

"It's empty," said Anish. "Aaaaannnnd now it's out of order. Detonate drone three."

Tim pressed and held the button.

CHAPTER

FIFTY-SIX

The floor shuddered under Ezra Dalton's feet, instantly killing the heated discussion between directors. The war room went quiet, interrupted a few seconds later by a phone call at Allan Kline's workstation. He picked up the handset and listened, shaking his head.

"Security thinks a bomb exploded in the executive parking garage," said Kline. "The guards at the entrance said a drone flew past them, disappearing inside just before the explosion."

"A drone?" asked Vernon Franklin.

"Do we need to evacuate?" asked Donovan Mayhew, getting up from his seat.

Samuel Quinn spun his chair away from the screen at the front of the room to face them.

"What kind of drone?" asked Quinn.

"Does it matter?" asked Kline.

"It kind of does," said Quinn, sharing an annoyed look with Dalton.

Kline requested information and listened to the answer. "It was about two feet across and had a bunch of propellers."

"Sounds like a quadcopter," said Quinn. "They can't do much more than cosmetic damage to the building. Especially at that size. We're talking one, maybe two pounds of explosives."

Two successive thumps rattled the room, the lights briefly flickering.

"Are you sure about that?" asked Kline. "That sounded like more than cosmetic damage."

Dalton picked up the phone at her station and dialed the building's security commander directly. She started speaking the moment he picked up the call.

"Krueger. What the hell is going on?"

"Ma'am. We just had two explosions on the roof," he said.

"What hit us?"

"We're reviewing the camera footage. Hold on."

"I need to know what we're up against right now," said Dalton.

"I understand, ma'am. There it is," said Krueger. "Shit. It was another drone. Quadcopter."

A fourth explosion shook the room, sounding like it had detonated right outside the operations hub.

"Dammit, Ezra," said Kline, finally snapping. "What the hell is happening?"

"They're just trying to rattle us," said Quinn.

"After the boat and the massacre at the senator's house, I'd say they're doing a good job," said Abbott.

"Krueger. I think another one hit the third floor," said Dalton.

"I'll send—" started Krueger, his words cut off by another explosion, this one just slightly vibrating the floor.

"Krueger? Krueger?" she said.

The security commander answered after an uncomfortably long delay. "They flew one of those things right into the revolving door in the lobby! Blew all of the door's glass out! I just sent RST to make sure nothing gets through."

She stiffened at the thought of an explosive-laden drone flying around the Institute's hallways.

"What?" said Abbott.

"The last explosion blasted the glass out of the revolving door," said Dalton.

Quinn finally stood up, the typically collected expression on his face replaced with one of genuine fear.

"Does he have people in place?" asked Quinn.

"RST is handling it," she said.

"Would one of you kindly let us in on your little side conversation?" said Kline.

"Krueger thinks the drones could fit through the missing glass of the revolving door," said Dalton.

"Wonderful," said Kline. "We're basically trapped in this room is what they're saying, unless you can outrun an explosive drone."

A brief tremor passed through the room. The sixth explosion within a minute.

"Krueger?" she said, waiting a few seconds for a reply.

"They blew a small hole in the underground parking security door," he said. "The team lowered it right after the first one exploded."

"Can a drone fit through that hole?" said Dalton.

"Hold on. Let me ask," said Krueger.

"Another breach? How big?" said Quinn, before heading toward her station.

"Garage security door," she said. "They're checking the size of the hole."

Krueger finally responded. "They're pretty sure a drone could not fit through."

She didn't like the sound of *pretty sure*.

"Send some of your shooters down to the parking garage to make sure nothing gets through," said Dalton.

Quinn asked her for the phone, which she reluctantly handed over. Dalton had a feeling he was about to overcomplicate the situation.

"How many RST and regular security officers do we have in the building?" Quinn asked Krueger.

After hearing Krueger's reply, Quinn said, "That's not enough. Scramble the Manassas Annex. Get everyone over here immediately."

"In rush hour traffic?" said Kline.

Quinn shot him a look before yelling into the phone. "I understand it's rush hour. I said immediately. Spool up the helicopters and get them over here now!"

He slammed the phone into the receiver, muttering a string of expletives. She'd never seen him like this in the fifteen years he'd been with the Institute.

"Samuel. We don't have clearance to fly those helicopters into Tyson's Corner," said Dalton. "And even if we did, I don't think it would be a good idea with explosive drones flying around the building."

"I really don't give a shit what you think, Ezra," said Quinn.

Quinn had either snapped or he had decided to try to salvage his seat on the board by turning the group against her—which wouldn't be a difficult maneuver under these circumstances. A few more drone attacks and he could probably call for a panicked vote right now to dismiss her, though it would most likely serve him no ostensible purpose.

Once the dust settled over the next few weeks, a comprehensive review of the past week's debacle would lay a scathing indictment at his feet. He'd somehow allowed the SKYSTORM shipment to be tracked back to the ship in Houston, a small oversight that had cost APEX several billion dollars and landed an army of federal investigators at their doorstep.

Instead of giving him the moment he wanted, and engaging in an unwinnable and certainly futile argument, she shrugged. Quinn wanted to play games? *Fine. Let's see how this all works out for him when the two helicopters fall out of the sky onto rush hour traffic, setting half of Tyson's Corner on fire.*

"I guess we sit tight and wait for the cavalry," said Dalton, taking immense pleasure in watching him partially deflate right in front of her.

Chapter Fifty-Seven

Jeffrey Munoz watched the busy hangar through his light machine gun's reflex sight with little interest beyond finishing the job and getting on the road. He didn't feel like sitting in traffic for three hours to get to Annapolis, and their window of opportunity for missing the worst of it was rapidly fading.

They'd been on the road most of the day already, having driven from the senator's safe house to the team's base of operations in the Allegheny Mountains—a seven-hour round trip to retrieve the weapons they would soon put to use. The "bucket list" crab-eating experience touted by Rich and the senator had better be worth the added time in the car.

The tail rotor on the first helicopter that had been rolled out of the hangar started to spin, picking up speed, as the main rotors engaged. The second Blackhawk's rotors began moving a few seconds later. Behind the dark-gray war machines, about twenty heavily armed and armored operators gathered for a briefing.

"I'm ready when you are," said Enrique Melendez from a position thirty feet away to his right. "What are you thinking?"

Melendez had been his partner in crime on the team for more than a decade, extending back to General Sanderson's reboot of the Black Flag program. The combination of Melendez's unrivaled long-range shooting skills with his more direct, close-up approach yielded a formidable team. The fact that they had worked together so closely for so long made them nearly unstoppable.

"The primary mission is to disable the helicopters," said Munoz.

"Rich didn't send us back to retrieve these just to ground the helicopters," said Melendez. "I could have done that with one of the rifles back at the safe house."

"Thirty seconds," said Munoz. "Then we're out of here. No exceptions."

"Thirty should be long enough to put this operation out of business permanently," said Melendez. "I'll hit the one giving the pep talk first, then work on the helicopters."

"As long as you're done in thirty seconds," said Munoz, before placing the gunsight reticle center mass on an operative kneeling to the left of the group leader.

"On my shot," said Melendez. "Two. One."

His fifty-caliber sniper rifle boomed; the overpressure created by the muzzle wasn't so bad this time. Placing him thirty feet away had been the right call. The last time they'd worked side by side like this, using similar weapons, he couldn't hear a damn thing for a week.

Munoz checked the second hand on his watch and pressed the M249 Squad Automatic Weapon's trigger, unleashing a short burst at the assembly. The bullets struck the concrete several feet in front of the group, a few skipping into the security team and knocking them backward. He adjusted his aim and fired a longer burst, which dropped at least three more—as the entire group scattered.

Melendez's cannon pounded away at the helicopters, while Munoz chased the rest of the security team back into the hangar, leaving about half of them dead or wounded on the tarmac. A quick look at his watch told him they had about ten more seconds to inflict as much damage as possible. Bullets snapped through the bushes and thunked into the tree trunks around him as he fired a sustained burst at a small group that had started to return fire from the corner of the hangar, momentarily quieting their rifles.

"You almost done?" he yelled at Melendez, who was in the process of swapping out the fifty-caliber rifle's outrageously sized ammunition magazine.

"One more magazine. Just to be sure!"

Munoz shifted his aim to the leftmost helicopter, finding that its main rotor had come to a stop, but its tail rotor was still spinning. For all he knew, the pilots had shut down the main rotor before taking cover. There was only one way to be sure the helicopter couldn't take off. He sighted in on the helicopter's tail and fired several short bursts until the rotor assembly broke apart, shredding the horizontal stabilizer underneath it.

"I was working on that!" said Melendez.

"Work faster next time," said Munoz, sweeping the hangar from left to right with the rest of the machine gun's two-hundred-round box.

The fifty-caliber rifle boomed, Melendez firing projectile after projectile into the remaining helicopter—which felt like overkill under the circumstances.

"You having fun?" asked Munoz.

Melendez ignored him and continued firing, entirely focused on something other than disabling the helicopter. He could have done that with two more well-placed shots.

"Booya!" said Melendez, followed by a loud metal-on-metal screech.

Munoz turned in time to see the rightmost Blackhawk roll onto its left side, the fully engaged main rotor blades slamming into the concrete and exploding into dozens of thick metal splinters that tore through the other helicopter.

Munoz rose to a crouch and took off, leaving the machine gun behind. Melendez did the same. The weapons had been taken from a Wyoming militia group's arsenal, in the wake of a search-and-destroy raid they had undertaken a few years ago. Forensically, they were a dead end for any investigator.

Sporadic gunfire chased him deeper into the forest until it tapered off to nothing. Melendez had caught up to him a few hundred yards later, at the edge of a recently tilled field—where their pickup truck waited on a jeep trail in the late afternoon sun. Munoz tapped a quick text message to Rich on his satellite phone after hopping in the frying-pan-hot passenger seat.

Helicopters and half of annex detachment OOC.

Rich replied in seconds.

BZ. Dinner at 8.

Five minutes later they were driving through light traffic on Prince William Parkway, headed for Interstate 66 and their unavoidable rendezvous with the Beltway's notorious showstopping traffic. They'd be lucky to reach Annapolis by eight o'clock.

Chapter

Fifty-Eight

Samuel Quinn's face went pale after he picked up the phone, his expression going from partially deflated to flat within seconds. It was way too soon for the helicopters to have reached the building and come to a fiery end, so Dalton assumed the security team had discovered another breach. It turned out to be a combination of both, but not at all what she'd expected.

"The annex was attacked, right before they loaded the teams onto the helicopters," said Quinn. "Both helicopters were destroyed, and half of the rapid response team is gone. Laura Bachmann among them."

"More drones?" asked Abbott.

Quinn shook his head slowly. "Machine-gun and heavy-caliber fire. One of the helicopters somehow rolled over."

"Maybe we should reconsider our position regarding Senator Steele," said Donovan Mayhew. "In light of the damage she's inflicted in the past twenty-four hours alone, a truce might be our best option. What else does she have planned?"

Dalton considered offering her advice, which leaned toward staying calm and letting this storm pass without making any spurious decisions, but Quinn looked like he was on the brink of self-defeat—so she decided to hold back for now. He'd flipped on her without the slightest hesitation or warning. If he was about to pound another nail in his own coffin, who was she to stand in his way?

"I think I've figured out her endgame. If you can call it that," said Quinn.

"Just like that you've figured it out?" said Kline. "I'm all ears."

Dalton allowed herself one quick indulgence.

"Me too," she said, receiving a venomous glare in return.

"The rooftop explosions took two-thirds of the building's HVAC capacity off-line. It's late in the afternoon, when this building is always naturally warmer from a full day of sun. That's why we're cooking in here right now."

"Can you speed this up?" asked Kline.

"Facilities is worried that the server farm will overheat," said Quinn.

"Then we shut them down until we can either reroute the rest of the building's capacity to the server farm or rent temporary portable air-conditioning units to tie into the system. You think this is her endgame?" said Dalton.

"It doesn't sound like much of an endgame," said Donovan Mayhew. "I say we pursue the options Ezra just highlighted."

"And shut down the servers? For how long?" asked Quinn. "We're talking a global disruption to our operations, which might be exactly what Senator Steele wants. She's been one step ahead of us the entire time."

"More like two steps . . . ahead of you," said Kline. "What do we have in progress internationally that could be more damaging than SKYSTORM?"

Vernon Franklin emerged from his shell long enough to lob a bomb at Quinn.

"Nothing we've undertaken since the founding of the Institute has carried this much risk," he said. "SKYSTORM makes the rest of our ongoing operations look like back-of-the-trunk gun deals."

"And the end user can't be identified," said Quinn. "The Texas site has been sterilized. Even if the cargo containers are somehow tracked back to APEX, there's no way to link the planes to the Russians."

"Unless the Russians decide to dribble the information into the public sphere themselves," said Franklin.

"Why would they do that?" asked Quinn.

"To get ahead of the story while we're still dusting ourselves off from a total ass-whooping," said Franklin. "Spin the narrative against us to deliver a kill shot. Let's be honest. The Institute hasn't exactly been aligned with their interests in the past. Quite the opposite, actually. This was a one-time opportunity that fell apart rather spectacularly. We've basically teed ourselves up for them to take a swing."

"The Russians can't afford to burn bridges with us," said Quinn. "Eventually, they'll need us again. It's not like their little proxy war strategy in Europe is going away anytime soon. We just need to come up with another proposal. They'll be nibbling right out of—"

Abbott cut him off. "We can discuss this later, when our servers aren't melting. Do we shut them down or not?"

"I'm of the opinion that shutting us down for a day or two isn't Senator Steele's endgame," said Franklin. "She could have blown up the satellite array if that was her goal. I say we shut them down. There's no way we're playing into her hands by doing that. We'd be denying her the only thing left that she could use to hurt us."

"What if there is no endgame, so to speak? Maybe her goal was to send us the same warning we tried to deliver in Los Angeles," said Sloane Pruitt. "The drone attacks have stopped, and she never targeted one of us personally. I'm inclined to believe that the people she hired to massacre Guthrie's operatives, cut our rapid response team in half, and launch a coordinated, explosive drone attack against a fortified building would have been entirely capable of killing at least half of us before we went into lockdown. We could be looking at an opportunity to negotiate a truce, like Donovan suggested."

"Sloane. You're more than welcome to test that theory by taking a stroll outside," said Quinn. "We'll watch from here."

"Enough," said Abbott. "Why would Steele have targeted the air-conditioning when she could hit the satellite dishes? We're missing something directly related to the servers, which makes me extremely nervous."

"The server farm is air gapped. The data isn't going anywhere," said Quinn. "But if it makes everyone feel better, we can shut the servers down."

"Even if we shut them down," said Mayhew, "we're still left with the very distinct possibility that Steele isn't finished."

Quinn's eyes narrowed. "Donovan. The data can't be accessed without someone physically interacting with the system. That's what *air gapped* means."

"What if this is a diversion?" said Pruitt. "And someone's down there right now stealing the SKYSTORM data. Among other things."

"Have you ever been down in the server room?" said Quinn, not waiting for an answer. "It's a bunch of servers. There's no way to search for data. There's no interface."

"Actually, that's not true," said Mayhew. "With the right equipment and technical knowledge, you can access the database direct from the server room."

"Yes. Technically, you could do that, but you'd need the end-user encryption from one of the operations hub computers. The only vulnerable interface point on the server level streams encrypted data, unless you somehow knew exactly which server contained the information you were after. And we spoof that by constantly data-hopping servers, like frequency-hopping radio encryption, but a thousand times more secure. Shall I continue?"

"You made your point," said Mayhew.

Pruitt started to speak, but Quinn stopped her.

"And we restricted access to SKYSTORM to the directors after the Houston terminal attack," said Quinn. "Unless someone is sitting in one of our hub offices with a pad and paper, or a camera, the project's information is safe. Did I answer your question?"

"Yes," said Pruitt. "And you can kill that smug tone. You're in no position to lecture anyone."

Despite having started the day in a hole over his head, he couldn't stop digging. Something had glitched the normally unflappable Samuel Quinn, and Dalton was pretty sure she knew exactly what it had been—fear. And not the intangible kind, like fear of failure or embarrassment. The fear of immediate physical harm had transformed him into a condescending, thin-skinned bully. Quinn was nothing more than a coward at heart, and judging by the looks on a number of the directors' faces, they had come to the same conclusion.

"Shit," said Kline, in what seemed to be a random, unrelated outburst, until he repeated the word.

"Allan?" said Abbott.

Kline shook his head before starting. "What if she wants us to shut down the servers for a few days to buy time for her FBI and State Department friends to open up and dig through all of our cargo containers?"

"The containers don't have APEX stenciled on the side," said Quinn. "Neither do the aircraft parts."

"Given everything that's happened over the past twenty-four hours, are you really willing to bet against her?" said Kline. "The feds have a lot of bodies to work with—in Los Angeles, Houston, and Annapolis. You don't think a few of those backgrounds are going to intersect with APEX? How about the three men captured at Steele's house this morning in a blatant assassination attempt? Or the wounded men taken into custody at the Houston terminal? Not to mention the dozen or so that surrendered to the Texas Rangers at the SKYSTORM facility. All it takes is for someone who knows more than they should to talk."

"We've never had a problem with that in the past," said Quinn. "We're insulated from Cerberus Corp. Just like Athena."

"No amount of insulation is perfect," said Kline. "Not with someone like Senator Steele out for blood. Of every scenario we've discussed tonight, this one makes the most sense to me. She took the HVAC systems out for a reason."

"The more I think about it, the less I like the idea of keeping that data around until we know Steele's endgame," said Abbott. "And I'm not just talking about SKYSTORM. I'm talking about everything. The operations archives. Intelligence archives. Decades of irreplaceable information."

"Are you suggesting we trigger SHELL GAME?" asked Quinn, not sounding entirely opposed to the idea.

"I am," said Abbott.

"I second that motion," said Kline.

"If we're going to shut down the servers anyway for a day or two," said Mayhew, "we may as well take the extra precaution until we know what we're up against. And global operations will still be able to access the time-sensitive information they need. I can't see any downside."

Dalton couldn't argue with the logic. SHELL GAME protocols had been designed exactly for this purpose. When initiated, a copy of the APEX Institute's basement server-farm database would be uploaded via satellite to their secure data complex in northern Nevada. Once the upload had been confirmed by the team stationed at the remote site, the IT security team here would scrub the basement server farm, deleting the data—and a similarly structured, sanitized copy would be sent back.

A version that matched their publicly advertised mission as a think tank, not their true role as a quasi–intelligence agency and paramilitary power broker. The treasure trove of information they had collected, legally and illegally, over the years—and continued to collect on a daily, if not hourly, basis—would remain safe at their entirely secure data center in the middle of nowhere. In the wrong hands, particularly the

FBI's, the vast extent and scandalous substance of the files would destroy APEX overnight. Nobody would trust or do business with them again.

"I concur with executing SHELL GAME," said Dalton. "Better safe than sorry."

"And the rest of us?" asked Quinn.

Vernon Franklin and Sloane Pruitt agreed, leaving Quinn to cast the final vote. Dalton really wanted him to dissent, to have it on record if Steele still had a trick up her sleeve. It wouldn't alter the decision to safeguard the data, but it would definitely drive one more nail into his coffin. True to his newly unveiled nature, Quinn took the easy way out.

"For the record, I think we're overreacting," he said. "But I accept the suggestion to move forward with SHELL GAME."

"How decisive of you," said Pruitt.

Ezra Dalton sat down and leaned back in the chair, savoring her small victory over Quinn, which in the grand scheme of everything that had transpired over the past week was all that would truly matter when the dust settled. From what she could tell by watching the other directors' reactions, they didn't appear to appreciate Quinn's new persona. Dalton may have avoided a career catastrophe by simply standing aside while Quinn self-destructed. Only time would tell, but she felt good about her continuing prospects at APEX.

CHAPTER

FIFTY-NINE

Decker and Pierce lounged against a shed-size stairwell enclosure, hiding in a slim band of shade from the relentlessly hot midday sun. A laptop propped up on the equipment bag lay between them. Beyond Decker's folded knees was a flat, football field–size roof, a quarter of it packed with arm-span-diameter satellite dishes. They'd landed on the roof close to an hour and a half ago, stowing their parachutes and immediately going to work on the daisy chain of explosive microcharges that would disable the entire rooftop satellite array.

With the charges ready, they unpacked and assembled the satellite snooping kit, setting up a portable satellite dish in the middle of the array. Joshua assured them the placement didn't need to be precise, as long as the dish had an unobstructed view of the sky when set to the same azimuth and elevation as the array. Once they were satisfied that the dish would intercept an incoming signal, they ran a coaxial cable to the shade and connected the cable to Joshua's laptop through a USB adapter.

As rehearsed a half dozen times on board the aircraft, Pierce successfully launched the software programs that would detect and roughly decipher the download signal. A basic diagnostic test created by Joshua verified that the laptop and satellite dish could talk to each other. *Foolproof,* he had called it—for good reason.

They'd been sitting here ever since, sipping water and watching the laptop screen for signs of activity. Decker inched his boot to the right, back into the shade. In about thirty minutes, the sun would creep all the way around the northwest corner of the enclosure and cook them alive. He checked his watch. Thirty-five minutes had passed since the annex attack.

"You're gonna drive yourself crazy doing that," said Pierce.

"I can't help it," said Decker. "The longer this drags out, the less likely it'll happen."

"Says who?" said Pierce. "This entire mission is one big scientific wild-ass guess. I don't need to win both showcases to walk off this show feeling like a winner."

"What are you talking about?" asked Decker.

"*The Price Is Right?* Final showcase?"

Decker shrugged.

"You really didn't watch TV as a kid, did you?" said Pierce.

"I really didn't," said Decker. "I barely watch it now."

"I always thought that was something you kind of made up," said Pierce. "Maybe like partially true and you decided to turn that into your thing."

"My thing?" said Decker.

"I don't know," said Pierce. "Everyone has a thing. It makes them more interesting."

"What's your thing?" asked Decker.

"I don't think I have a thing," said Pierce.

"I agree," said Decker. "Which explains a lot."

Pierce chuckled.

Several green lines spiked in the sniffing program's diagnostic window, rapidly moving across the digital chart and disappearing. Decker sat up and edged closer to the screen to get a better look.

"Data spike," said Pierce.

"Nothing big, though," said Decker, relaxing a little.

A second sequence of spikes started across the screen, the chart quickly turning green. When the data transfer rate didn't drop after a minute, he started to laugh.

"What?" asked Pierce.

"I can't believe this worked," he said, standing up and dusting off the thin layer of sand that had already accumulated during their short stay.

"We'll never really know if Steele's idea worked," said Pierce. "Even after we destroy this place. It's all based on a hunch."

"Their hunch found this place," said Decker. "And you have to admit that the timing of the data dump is spot-on."

"My money is still on this being a data backup in response to the coordinated attacks," said Pierce.

"Like you said, one showcase is enough," said Decker.

"I thought you'd never watched *The Price Is Right*?"

"Your analogy wasn't that complicated," said Decker.

By the time the download started to show signs of slowing, the sun had been beating down on them for nearly forty minutes—the off-white, semireflective roof coating broiling them from below. They sat side by side now, their backs turned to the sun to keep the laptop from overheating. The green spikes on the screen dipped several times before disappearing entirely.

"I think that's it," said Pierce. "Let's pop the array and get this show on the road."

He closed the laptop and stuffed it into his rucksack, heaving the bag onto his back. Decker helped him to his feet, and they stretched their legs for a few seconds. Pierce connected the explosive chain's firing wire to the electrical firing device and disengaged its safety bail.

"Ready?" asked Pierce.

"Do it," said Decker, before covering his ears.

Pierce squeezed the firing-device handle, simultaneously detonating the thumb-size "popper" charges they'd attached to each satellite dish's feed horn. Individually, the explosions were no louder than a gunshot, but twenty at once sounded like a small cannon. Decker grabbed the sniper rifle leaning against the wall and slung it over his shoulder.

They moved around the corner to the western side of the enclosure and positioned themselves just past the inset, windowless metal door. Since the door opened inward, they would be visible the moment anyone stepped outside. If the responding technician's attention wasn't fully focused on the satellite array in the other direction immediately upon emerging, Decker and Pierce would have to move fast.

Roughly five minutes after detonating the charges, the door opened without warning, and a man dressed in pressed khaki pants and a tucked Oxford shirt stepped onto the roof—his focus entirely on checking the array. As he walked toward the obviously damaged satellite dishes, Decker moved swiftly into place behind him and pressed his pistol against the man's head.

"Arms out sideways. Like a T," said Decker.

The man instantly complied.

"There's two of us, so don't get any crazy ideas," he said, before patting the man down. He took the radio off the man's belt and attached it to his own. "Anything I missed?"

The man shook his head.

"Hands behind your head. Fingers laced," said Decker. "How many people are in the building, not including yourself?"

The man hesitated, and Decker returned the pistol to the back of his head.

"I'm trying to get a sense of what I'm up against here so I can adjust the level of force necessary to accomplish the mission," said Decker. "My default when faced with zero information is to use the maximum amount. Basically, to kill my way through the problem. How many people are in the building?"

"Four."

"Any security types?" asked Decker. "Or are they all IT types like yourself?"

"Two security guards. The other two work with me," said the man.

"Are these rent-a-cop types, or *Call of Duty* operators?"

"*Call of Duty* operators."

"Serious or laid-back?"

"Serious," he said. "They killed and buried a couple that hiked too close to the facility four months ago."

"Is there a larger detachment nearby?"

He nodded. "Five miles away at the support station. The team here monitors the sensor arrays guarding the approaches to the building. You must have parachuted in. There's no other way."

"Good assumption," said Decker. "What's your first name?"

"Ron."

"Ron. Is it fair to assume you're not willing to die for whoever owns this facility?"

"Yes."

"What about your IT friends downstairs?"

"They would not want that, either," said Ron.

The man's handheld radio squawked. "Ron. Did you find anything? The guys are getting a little nervous down here."

"What are they nervous about?" asked Decker.

"We have a very high-priority upload that needs to go out immediately," said Ron. "It's like a DEFCON One situation."

"All right. Listen to me, Ron," said Decker. "Be very careful what you say. The best thing you can do for yourself and your friends right now is to get everyone up here to take a look at the satellite array. We will not kill any of you unless it becomes necessary. Let's keep it from becoming necessary. Understood?"

He nodded, and Decker put the radio up to his right wrist. "You can take the radio."

Ron very slowly took the radio.

"Mark. You are absolutely not going to believe this," said Ron. "The array is gone."

"What? What do you mean 'gone'? Destroyed?" said the voice over the radio.

"No. I mean it's no longer here," said Ron, shrugging. "It's like it was never here."

"What the hell are you talking about?" asked Mark, voices in the background expressing similar sentiments.

"Just get everyone up here now. Security, too. This is really freaking me out," said Ron. "I feel like we've been punked. When was the last time you actually laid eyes on the array?"

"I don't know. Why would I—hold on, we're coming up!"

Decker took the radio back. "That was impressive. Let's head around the corner where they won't see us."

He nodded at Pierce while moving Ron out of sight. Pierce crouched and pressed himself as flat against the wall as possible. When they rounded the corner, Decker instructed Ron to sit down against the wall in more or less the same spot he and Pierce had occupied minutes earlier.

"Ron? Look at me."

The man hesitated but finally looked up at him.

"I'm not going to kill you or your coworkers," said Decker, before nodding at the array over his shoulder. "This business has nothing to do with any of you."

Ron swallowed hard and nodded, not looking a bit relieved.

Yelling erupted from the side of the building, Pierce ordering everyone onto their knees. Decker sidestepped to the right, keeping his pistol aimed at Ron, until Pierce and four men with their hands on their heads came into view. The two security guards definitely looked like *Call of Duty* types. Serious assault-style rifles and magazine pouch–laden ballistic plate carriers.

"It definitely worked," said Decker.

He was about to coordinate disarming the guards with Pierce when one of the security guards whirled and put the closest technician in a headlock to create a human shield. Pierce didn't skip a beat, shooting the other guard in the head before he could do the same. Decker instantly shifted his aim toward the struggle between the technician and guard. He applied pressure to the trigger and sighted in on the guard's face, waiting for a clear shot.

He didn't have to wait long. The guard eased his grip on the man in an attempt to grab the rifle hanging at his side, which allowed the hostage to break free. Decker fired three times, snapping the security officer's head back and dropping him to the rooftop. He glanced back at Ron, who hadn't moved an inch.

"Your friends are still alive," said Decker.

After reuniting the two technicians with Ron, Decker set his rucksack down and removed a five-pound block of C-4, prompting one of the techs to mutter an obscenity and Ron to start praying.

"Good. Some of you recognize this," said Decker. "I only have eight of these—"

Another round of prayers and cursing.

"And I really need to destroy the server farm below us. So, if you have any suggestions, I'm all ears," said Decker. "Given the fact that your own security tried to use one of you as a human shield, I can't imagine you're feeling much loyalty to the company running this place right about now. But if you are, we can just tie you to the satellite dishes and figure this out for ourselves. Maybe the building comes down, taking you with it. Maybe it doesn't."

"What happens to us if we help?" said Ron.

"Worst-case scenario. You walk five miles in this miserable heat to reach the security station," said Decker. "But I have a feeling you won't have to walk very far. They'll be over here pretty quick once the fireworks start."

"The server racks are fragile," said Ron. "Eight of those should do the trick."

"Without a doubt," said the guy who had been taken hostage. "Might even be overkill."

"The word *overkill* is not in our vocabulary," said Decker.

About a half hour later, in the low hills west of the isolated data center, Decker and Pierce sat side by side in the cargo compartment of the IT team's SUV, legs hanging over the rear bumper. The liftgate shaded them from the sun while they waited for the stark-white building to explode. A quarter of a mile south of the building, the three IT guys walked briskly down the road leading toward the support station.

"Ten seconds," said Pierce.

They counted the remaining seconds out loud until the structure rippled from one end to the other—in a rapid series of ground-shuddering internal explosions—remaining almost entirely intact.

"Huh," said Decker, hopping down onto the ground. "That was a bit of a letdown."

Pierce jumped down and slapped him on the shoulder. "The servers are in a million pieces right now. That's all that matters. We got to twist the knife in APEX's back. That's pretty satisfying."

"I know. It just feels a little anticlimactic for my last op," said Decker.

"Last op?" asked Pierce. "You retiring and forgot to tell me?"

"I'm not sure what to call it yet," said Decker. "But it's definitely going to look different than this."

He truly had no idea how this new life might look day to day, but it was time for a change. The current trajectory wasn't sustainable. Realistically, it never had been. The loss of his wife and son, followed by the mayhem of the past two years, had painfully proved that now-indisputable fact. It was time to walk away from the adrenaline-fueled life he had always known and start a new one.

CHAPTER SIXTY

Senator Steele's picnic boat lay at anchor in a shady creek just north of the Upper Chester River Sanctuary. One of a thousand tucked-away anchorages dotting the rivers feeding the Chesapeake Bay. They'd pulled into the quiet haven an hour before kicking off the drone attack, to better coordinate all of the operation's moving parts. Once Rich's team crippled APEX's security annex, there had been little to do beyond waiting and enjoying the occasional cool breeze off the bay. Steele had been staring on and off at the satellite phone in front of her for the better part of the last hour.

"Decker should have called by now," she said, instantly losing the well-played patience game Rich and his team appeared to have mastered.

"Give it some time," said Rich, looking somewhat relaxed for the first time since she'd hired him. "The data off-loading theory is a long shot based on something Tim had heard about a Wall Street trading firm a few years ago. They very unsuccessfully tried to make a copy of their database server network and replace it with a clean version for the SEC investigators looking into reports of fraudulent activity. They ended up scrubbing everything permanently, creating a bigger problem than they had in the first place."

Logically, she understood the odds against Tim's theory, but discovering the Nevada site had significantly boosted her hope that they might actually topple APEX. Karl Berg had very generously delivered the data center tip, presumably after expending another closely held favor on their behalf. Berg certainly didn't owe her any favors. The first call to his NSA contact had been more than she'd expected from him. She sensed a deeper link between Berg and Rich than either of them had initially divulged.

"I know. I'd just hate to come this far and not deliver the coup de grâce," said Steele.

"Destroying a multimillion-dollar data facility is a nice kick in the side while they're down," said Rich.

"Kick in the head if they lose some archived data," said Jared.

"More like a kick in the—" started Caz.

"Yeah. We get it," said Klink.

"I guess that'll have to do," said Steele. "What I wouldn't give to be a fly on the wall inside APEX right now."

"Next time we'll have to fly one of those microdrones into the building before we start the real show," said Klink. "And give you that fly-on-the-wall experience."

"Do those exist?" asked Steele.

"Not like you see in the movies—or in Klink's imagination, apparently," said Rich. "The smallest camera-and-microphone-equipped drone we've experimented with can fit in the palm of your hand, but it has serious battery power limitations. Five minutes in the air, which is significantly reduced when moving. No more than fifty yards."

"Doesn't sound very useful," said Steele.

"They're mostly recreational, but I guarantee the Department of Defense and some of our intelligence agencies are working on a more viable version," said Rich. "Next time we'll be able to offer fly-on-the-wall capability."

"Hopefully, there won't be a next time," said Steele. "With APEX at least."

The satellite phone chimed, and Steele abandoned all pretext of decorum. She swiped the phone from the varnished teak table, knocking a full glass of water into Jared's lap. Rich and Klink broke out laughing.

"Oh my God, I'm so sorry," she said, before answering the call. "Are you and Brad safe?"

"We're a little roasted from the sun, but other than that we can't complain. Thank you for asking," said Decker.

"Ryan. I feel like you're holding me in suspense," said Steele.

"We are driving toward the extraction point with a destroyed data center in the rearview mirror," said Decker.

"That's fantastic news. We really kicked them in the stomach, the head—and below—while they were down," she said, nodding at Caz.

"Oh, I think we did more than that," said Decker. "We registered a massive, encrypted data download prior to destroying the satellite array. I don't know how many giga-tera-dog bytes were downloaded, but it lasted a little over an hour."

"Oh wow," said Steele. "Can I put you on speaker? Rich and his team will be able to make more sense of this."

"Sure."

She activated the speakerphone function and set the phone on the table, standing up.

"Okay," she said. "Decker just told me that they registered a huge satellite download that lasted over an hour."

"Holy mother," said Jared. "That's a big download."

"This is very good news," said Rich. "Hitting them out of the blue at a top-secret site will unglue a few of the bigwigs at APEX."

"Our thoughts exactly," said Decker. "But it gets better. The IT team at the site confirmed that they were minutes away from uploading a similarly large data package to the same satellite."

"Hot damn," said Jared, high-fiving Klink.

Senator Steele didn't know what to say. The download and immediate upload attempt fit the pattern. If APEX had deleted their Tyson's Corner database while uploading it to the data center, Decker and Brad may have permanently destroyed the data. APEX would be ruined.

Decker continued, "They didn't know the upload destination, and I believe them, but I think it's fair to say they were sending something back to DC like you thought. On a somewhat separate note, the site is run by Ares Corp. Maybe you should look into them. Sounds very similar to what we saw with Athena Corp and Cerberus."

"I think we will. After I get some rest. Or I'll just let Rich and his crew handle it. They don't seem to sleep," said Steele, tearing up. "I wish you could be here with us, Ryan. We're actually headed to Cantler's later. Crab season is in full swing."

"Ah. Very jealous. I can taste the Old Bay seasoning and ice-cold beer right now," said Decker.

"Cantler's?" said Pierce in the background.

"Yep," said Decker. "We might have to check with Bernie about a new flight plan. Shouldn't take us more than twenty hours—maybe twenty-four with a refueling or two—to get there."

"I hope we can all get together soon," said Steele. "I'd love to have both of you and your families out. Just as soon as I either repair my current house or buy a new one. Rich and his crew set off four Claymores inside—so I'm told."

"Okayyyyy. Remind me not to offer up my home as one of Rich's ambush sites in the future," said Decker.

Rich and the crew had a good laugh at Decker's comment. Steele wished the two groups could have met in person. Though they were cut from a different cloth, she could tell they would get along. She saw so many similarities in the personalities on each side. Ideally, there would be no reason at all for them to meet in the future, but part of her felt it was a shame that they hadn't. An opportunity missed, perhaps. She may never know.

"My very solid assumption is that we're all past the days of ambushes, parachute operations, and Claymore mines," said Steele.

"Speak for yourself," said Klink.

"That's called Tuesday," said Jared.

"Sorry you had to hear that bravado, Decker," said Rich. "It was a pleasure working with you and your crew. Best of luck to you."

"Same to you guys," said Decker. "Take care of the senator."

"She's in good hands moving forward," said Rich.

"Am I sensing a longer-term relationship?" asked Decker. "Am I being replaced?"

"Do you not want to be replaced?" asked Steele.

"Senator. I'll always be there if you need me. I feel pretty confident saying the same for Harlow, and Brad is nodding in agreement," said Decker.

"That means a lot to me, Ryan. Seriously. And no offense intended for the very capable group here, but you and your friends are irreplaceable," said Steele. "Whether you are in a position to lend a hand or not, it's been a pleasure tearing down a few multibillion-dollar schemes with you."

"I'm thinking maybe you call us for the couple-hundred-thousand-dollar-level schemes," said Decker. "Let Rich take care of the small armies and drug cartels that get in your way."

Steele broke out laughing along with everyone else.

"Ryan. I'm going to let you go," said Steele. "I have one more call to make."

"Tell Ezra Dalton I said hello, and that if I even catch a whiff of APEX in our lives, I will personally duct-tape a Claymore mine to her head and set it off," said Decker.

"I'll pass that along. I like the way you put it better than what I had planned to say," said Steele. "I'll be in touch."

She ended the call, sat down, and leaned back against the plush boat cushions, feeling absolutely certain about the path forward. A strange feeling that had mostly eluded her since she'd lost her family.

"Time to send Decker's message," she said, producing the business card Ezra Dalton had left on Steele's desk after her most unpleasant visit last fall.

CHAPTER

SIXTY-ONE

Ezra Dalton's vision wavered a few times, to the point where she had to take a seat. She'd never experienced anything close to a panic attack before in her life—had always been in complete control of herself—until a few minutes ago. Racing heartbeat, shortness of breath, and muscle spasms in her back, all starting the moment Abbott took the call from Nevada.

The muscle spasms spread to her chest, just twinges here and there in the lower rib cage, triggering a tightness that continued to intensify. For a few moments, she wondered if she was somehow having a heart attack at age fifty-five and in perfect health. Dalton quickly dismissed that ironic thought when the tension dominated the right side of her chest. Wrong part of the chest for a heart attack.

No. She was in the throes of her first anxiety attack. And the timing couldn't possibly have been worse. The data center had been destroyed, taking the only copy of APEX's data archive with it. They'd scrubbed the basement server farm after uploading the most up-to-date copy to Nevada to make room for the sanitized, FBI-friendly version, which failed to follow.

Calls to the team on duty at the server building had gone unanswered for twenty minutes, until Abbott contacted the support station and had security dispatch a crew to check on the facility. They'd found the team walking down the middle of the service road in the direction of the support station—shortly after hearing what sounded like a series of explosions. Abbott had been in the process of describing what the security team found when she felt like she might black out. In all reality, passing out right now would be a mercy.

"Ezra. You're looking a little pale," said Quinn.

"I just need a drink of water," she said, trying to take deep breaths without making it obvious. "I think I'll grab a bottle from the kitchen."

"Right now?" asked Abbott.

"Yeah. I haven't kept myself hydrated today," said Ezra, successfully standing up again. "I'll be right back."

"It's true," said Quinn. "She fills that rubber-coated glass bottle at least twenty times a day."

Ezra feigned a smile, wondering what they'd do if she walked out of the hub and went home. She had to stop thinking like that. It hadn't been her idea to initiate SHELL GAME. They couldn't pin the crowning failure on her head, though Quinn would undoubtedly try to make the case that all of the past week's disasters should be laid directly at her feet.

It all depended on how he behaved. If he came out swinging at the rest of the directors, parading the fact that he had been the only one opposed to SHELL GAME—he was finished at APEX. On the flip side, if he walked them through the chain of events, convincing them that she had left the board no choice but to pull the server trick, Ezra's time at the Institute would come to an unceremonious conclusion.

Or maybe she was overthinking all this, and they'd rally together and figure out a way to salvage the situation. The look on Quinn's face suggested he wasn't finished with whatever power play his bruised ego had conjured during the drone attack. Her cell phone rang before she got more than a few feet from the desk. She stopped, hesitating too long to start walking away again.

She reached for her satchel to retrieve her phone, painfully aware that everyone was watching her. Not because she had a phone in the hub. Directors were authorized to carry them anywhere in the building. But because the sound of a ringtone stood out, particularly since nobody else had made or received a call since they'd convened over three hours ago. Not to mention the fact that the timing of the call felt suspicious—even to her.

"Ezra Dalton," she said, not having recognized the number.

"Ezra. This is Senator Margaret Steele."

Shit. This was the absolute last thing she needed right now. She hesitated too long, and Quinn must have sensed something was wrong.

"Speakerphone, please," said Quinn. "Unless it's a private call."

"Is it private?" asked Allan Kline. "Or does it concern all of us?"

There was no way to back out of this nightmarish scenario, so she leaned into it instead.

"Senator. I'm placing you on speakerphone," she said, setting the phone down on her desk.

"By all means," said Steele, her voice broadcast across the room. "What's the saying? Better to kill two birds with one stone. Or however many there are of you."

"Senator Steele, this is Harold Abbott. I think we can all agree—"

"Save it, Harold," said Steele. "This isn't a negotiation. You have zero power in the equation. Within the last twenty-four hours, I put SKYSTORM permanently out of business, nearly sinking your ship in Houston and knocking the airfield facility in northern Texas out of commission. I also landed state and federal investigators at your doorstep. What else? I launched a drone attack on your building that could have been ten times worse. I swatted your elite security teams at my house and your Manassas outpost like flies. I destroyed your data center in Nevada, taking your archives with it. And I'm ready and willing to keep up the momentum. The only problem is that I've run out of high-value targets. The only targets of any value that remain at APEX are the board of directors. So here's what I propose—"

"Margaret. There's no need to threaten—"

"I'm not threatening, Harold. I'm promising. If I catch even the slightest whiff of APEX near me or any of my associates in Los Angeles, I will have my people duct-tape a Claymore mine to your head and explode you inside that fancy building of yours. That goes for the rest of you—and your families."

"That's crossing a line you don't want to—" began Quinn.

"What? That I don't want to cross? Interesting that one of you might say that, given that you tried to kidnap Mr. Decker's daughter a few days ago. Not to mention the fact that APEX had its fingerprints all over the murder of my daughter, Mr. Decker's wife and son, and countless others slain by Jacob Harcourt a few years ago. All to divert my attention away from his plan to privatize the war in Afghanistan. Or should I say—your plan."

"We had nothing to do with any of those murders," said Abbott.

"The Afghanistan conspiracy, like the cartel border war plan, may have been executed by Jacob Harcourt, but it reeks of APEX. Directly or indirectly, I don't care," said Steele. "And you can actually thank Ms. Dalton for connecting those dots for me. The files she left in my office last year, with the full intention of scaring me off, were just a little too detailed for an organization supposedly just watching Harcourt from a distance."

Dalton had to sit down again. Her vision narrowed dangerously close to full blackout. Steele had just killed her career—if she hadn't killed her literally.

"We keep close tabs on everyone in our sphere of influence. You know that," said Abbott, shooting her a deadly glare. "I guarantee you that the information in those files was routine work for us."

"I don't really care. Here's how this works moving forward. I've already paid my new associates, in advance, to kill each and every one of you, so get any thoughts of a preemptive strike out of your heads right now. And I'm dead serious about killing all of your families. If you don't believe me, I can email you the detailed file I've compiled over the past month on each of you. And you can rest assured, I put together those files with one purpose in mind."

"We believe you," said Harold. "APEX will not pursue you or any of your friends and associates from this moment forward."

"I'd like to hear that in the form of a board vote," said Steele.

Dalton barely mustered the voice to vote in favor of Harold's immediate resolution to cease and desist all hostilities toward Steele.

"Now that we have that behind us," said Steele, "let me make one more thing clear. I don't know if your institute will survive. I sincerely hope it doesn't, but that's out of my hands now, unless you violate the terms we just discussed. If you do somehow survive, you don't get a free pass to run amok in the Beltway. We'll be watching you very closely, and don't forget the ten terabytes of data we managed to collect. It's encrypted, but that shouldn't pose much of a problem given the resources I have to throw at it."

The call ended, and the room went deathly still for several moments—until Samuel Quinn stood up. Dalton knew what was coming but couldn't muster the strength to oppose it. She was locked into a full anxiety attack, her vision blurry and dulled.

"I move to immediately remove Ezra Dalton from the board of directors and to terminate her employment at APEX," said Quinn.

She heard Allan Kline second the motion before it all went dark.

CHAPTER
SIXTY-TWO

Harlow stood on the hard-packed desert floor, searching the hills with binoculars for Decker and Brad's SUV. Bernie's venerable C-123 roared a few hundred feet behind her, its propellers generating a small sandstorm that had obscured her view from the bottom of the ramp. He'd insisted on keeping the plane ready to take off at a moment's notice.

Decker hadn't spotted anyone trailing them from the data center, but Bernie wasn't taking any chances. If the support station had access to a helicopter, APEX could follow the SUV from a distance and pounce on their desert rendezvous at the absolute worst moment.

As much as Harlow didn't want to get back on that thing, she was glad to know it could lift her to safety in a matter of seconds if things went sour. And truth be told, a part of her felt comforted by Bernie's plane, when it wasn't maneuvering radically or landing in the middle of a desert. It gave her a feeling of protection, like nothing bad could happen to her inside it. She could see why he placed so much trust in the forty-five-year-old aircraft. It didn't feel capable of letting anyone down.

She glimpsed something distinctly out of place in the distance, but it quickly disappeared. Harlow trained her binoculars where it had briefly appeared, a dust cloud rising in its place. It had to be them. Her radio crackled.

"Harlow. I just got a text from Decker. They spotted Bernie's aircraft from a hilltop. ETA five minutes," said Pam.

"I'm pretty sure I just saw them," said Harlow. "I'm going to keep an eye out behind them. Make sure they haven't brought friends."

"Good idea," said Pam. "I'll keep your seat warm."

Harlow scanned the skies beyond the hills, looking for anything out of place. A glint of sun. Another dust cloud. Any sign of trouble. The horizon and landscape looked clear. A few minutes later, a white SUV crested one of the hills, speeding toward them. She kept her vigil with the binoculars until the vehicle skidded to a halt next to her.

"Need a ride?" asked Pierce.

"Yeah. Back to Los Angeles. Preferably not in that thing," she said, pointing her thumb at Bernie's plane.

"No can do, lady," said Decker. "This car is fresh from a crime scene. And probably has a tracker installed. We need to get out of here ASAP."

She hopped in the back seat, and Decker took off.

"I spoke with everyone back in California," said Harlow. "They don't seem to be in any hurry to leave Alderpoint. Anna especially. I guess it's turned into one big camping trip for the whole crew."

"I don't blame them. It's a gorgeous spot," said Pierce. "I plan on sitting around the campfire drinking beer for a few days before we even think about what's next."

"I like that plan," said Decker. "How is Riley holding up?"

"She's hanging out with Nicki and Tommy, and the FBI kids," said Harlow.

"That's great to hear," said Decker.

"The FBI folks finally came around, huh?" said Pierce.

"Sounds like tensions have mellowed on that front, but Reeves and Kincaid will be there in a few hours. They're headed up the coast with one of the RVs. Kind of an impromptu vacation."

"Good for them. They deserve it. Are they going to stick around for the night?" asked Decker.

"I don't think so."

"I kind of hope they don't," said Brad. "I just want to chill with the crew."

"Me too," said Decker. "And to be really honest, the FBI-safe versions of our war stories won't be nearly as fun."

"That's probably why they're heading out," said Harlow, laughing.

Decker stopped the SUV directly behind the ramp and got out, opening her door, while Pierce hauled their rucksacks and rifles into the waiting aircraft. Sand and bits of debris gusted into the back seat, washing over her face. She coughed a few times and squinted from the dust in her eyes. Decker helped Harlow down from the SUV and pulled her close the moment she was clear, kissing her briefly but passionately.

Harlow had never felt more relieved to see him than she had a few minutes ago. Back in Los Angeles, working the streets day in and day out, they faced the danger and uncertainty together. Even when they worked different cases, she knew what he was up against out there. The danger was real, but it was entirely manageable. And the job was the same for both of them, despite his affinity for seeking out trouble.

But every time Decker flew off in Bernie's plane or drove away with Pierce, the stakes skyrocketed, and she wasn't sure she'd ever see him again. He disappeared into a world infinitely more lethal and unforgiving, where pure chance all too often spelled the difference between life and death.

She'd gotten a taste of it enough times to know that both Decker and Pierce shouldn't be alive. They hadn't just defied the odds—they'd cheated the house. And the house always won if you played long enough. Harlow wanted him out before they collected on his overdue debt.

"I really think we did it," he said. "I spoke with Senator Steele on the way back from the data center. She was about to call APEX and deliver an ultimatum. More like a threat, backed by her considerable resources—and her new team."

"New team, huh?" she said.

"I can always call Steele back and let her know we don't mind scrambling for our lives once or twice a year," said Decker.

"Don't you dare," said Harlow. "We. Need. A. Break."

"That's exactly what I told her," said Decker, and he kissed her again.

"You two lovebirds planning on driving back?" yelled Pam from the top of the ramp. "We're kind of on a schedule here."

"Missed you, too, Pam!" said Decker, before taking Harlow's hand. "You ready for this?"

"As long as you promise this is the last time you take me on an airplane, I suppose one more ride on Bernie's relic won't kill me," she said.

"What if I wanted to take you to Paris or Amsterdam?" said Decker. "Or Hawaii?"

"There'd have to be a really good reason for me to get on a plane for that long," said Harlow.

Like a marriage proposal, she thought—and almost blurted out.

"Then I'll have to come up with one," said Decker. "I already have an idea in mind."

Buoyed by Decker's surprising hint about their future, Harlow stepped onto the ramp and pulled him into the aircraft—entirely fearless.

CHAPTER SIXTY-THREE

Ryan Decker hustled a bucket of ice-cold beers to the patio, where Pam was holding court with his parents and Garza. He could have kicked himself for not hiring a drink service along with the caterer. It wasn't that he didn't want to spend the money. He'd just assumed it wouldn't be necessary for a beer-and-wine party. Bad assumption. Next time he'd listen to Harlow, which was what he'd said the last time. And the time before that.

"There he is!" said Pam. "Thought you got lost!"

"No. Just taking a nap again," said Decker, placing the steel bucket between them. "Is my dad still making stuff up?"

"No. We've moved on to more interesting stories about you growing up," said Pam. "I never figured you for a Dungeons and Dragons type, Decker."

"Or a theater guy," said Garza, fishing a bottle out of the bucket and handing it to Decker's dad. "We got to hear all about your moving performance as Sonny in *Grease*."

"Jesus, Dad," said Decker.

"Don't look at me. Your mom's the one with the loose lips over here," said Steven. "They've been plying her with wine."

"I've already hit my limit," said Audrey, tapping the empty glass on the side table next to her. "So your secrets are safe for now."

"For now?" said Decker. "I'm going to have to keep an eye on this group."

He caught a glimpse of Brooklyn in the great room, looking stuck on the wide sectional couch that faced the valley behind their house. Seven months and at least that many major surgeries after the attack at the school, she still couldn't walk without the use of a cane. After ensuring that his daughter had escaped, she'd continued to engage the APEX mercenaries until they'd pinned her down on the school's front sidewalk.

Unable to reach cover, she'd lain flat on her back with her feet facing the attackers, firing her pistol until she'd run out of ammunition, which very fortunately coincided with the arrival of the first LAPD units. By the time police officers had dragged her to safety behind a nearby parked car, she'd been hit eight times—seven bullets ripping through her feet and legs. He owed Brooklyn everything for what she'd done that morning.

"Need a hand?" asked Decker, stepping into the spacious, airy room.

"Was it that obvious?" said Brooklyn, trying to push herself up again and gently easing back down into the couch. "It's really the shoulder more than anything. I can't get the leverage to push myself far enough up. And this couch is huge. Sorry to drag you away from everything."

Decker helped her up. "This couch is like the deck of an aircraft carrier. And please don't ever apologize for anything, or I'll be forced to retell that little story about—you know—how you saved my daughter. Seriously. There's no such thing as an inconvenience when it comes to you."

"Thank you," she said, holding back tears.

"Where would you like to sit?" said Decker.

"Somewhere outside, please," she said. "But not by Pam. She tends to get loud and a little obnoxious after she's had a few drinks."

"I don't think that has anything to do with the alcohol, to be completely honest, but it certainly aggravates the situation," said Decker. "How about I set you up with Katie and Sandra? Sophie will naturally gravitate that way when she's done making the rounds. Same with Jessica. That's an easygoing group, and I know they like you."

"Sounds perfect," she said.

After relocating Brooklyn, he searched for Harlow, who was in the kitchen with the catering crew.

"Everything running smoothly?" he asked, before giving her a kiss on the cheek.

"I think so. They're going to set up on the dining room table. We'll open the sliders so everyone can get to the food from the backyard, where the tables are set up. Everything will be ready in an hour."

"Awesome," said Decker. "What else?"

"They have an extra person who can serve drinks, unless you're fine running back and forth to the coolers all night."

"Sold," said Decker. "I will never doubt your wisdom again."

"Yes you will," she said, squeezing his hand. "I'll be right out. Everything should be on autopilot from this point forward. Nothing to do but relax and celebrate a birthday. And speaking of that, Riley was adamant that you do not give a long speech."

"So she's fine with a speech?" asked Decker.

"A short one," said Harlow. "She wasn't kidding."

"I believe you," said Decker.

The doorbell rang, which could mean only one thing—the Pierces had arrived. Within a month of the APEX finale, Brad and Anna had moved into a gated community in Calabasas, nestled into the Santa Monica Mountains about thirty minutes northwest of here. The decision to pick up and leave Denver had been an easy one.

Their kids had fallen right back into place with Riley on the Alderpoint camping trip, enjoying themselves more than Anna had seen since they'd been forced into exile. On top of that, Harlow's partners had convinced Anna that the Pierces' security consulting business would thrive in Los Angeles, especially if it was directly affiliated with the firm. They had no shortage of ready clients and client leads.

Decker sealed the deal when he convinced the Crossmount School directors to extend a full scholarship to Tommy and Nicki Pierce, in exchange for him not holding the school liable for the treachery committed by their chief security officer. The Pierces put Colorado behind them by selling their house outside Denver and giving their valley hideaway to Gunny. Having the Pierces back in their lives had helped bridge a little more of the gap that still existed between Decker and his daughter. Decker had finally returned something beyond himself that had been taken from Riley. He opened the door to welcome them.

"First things first," said Decker. "Riley is out on the patio flying a drone over the valley with Mazzie. They're looking for coyotes. We hear them all night but have yet to see one."

"Even with fourth-generation night vision?" said Brad.

"They're crafty. Mazzie has a few drones set up, so have fun. Just don't bother the neighbors," said Decker, getting out of the kids' way.

Anna gave him a hug and presented him with a bottle of champagne.

"For mimosas tomorrow morning," she said.

"Always two steps ahead," said Decker.

"Three. But who's counting?" said Brad, handing him an envelope. "For the birthday girl."

"I'll add this to her loot crate," said Decker. "Everyone's here, so make yourselves comfortable. Pam's plying my parents with alcohol for stories from my youth, so avoid her at all costs."

"I have some choice Annapolis tales I could tell—in exchange for a drink or two," said Brad.

"I seem to remember a few stories myself," said Anna.

Brad and Anna had met during their junior year at the Naval Academy, and Decker had spent many wild weekends partying with Anna's friends at Georgetown University.

"Yeah. Those stories should remain classified," said Decker. "I don't need Harlow second-guessing her decision."

"Mum's the word," said Pierce, before giving him a big hug. "She could do a lot worse."

"Thanks," said Decker, shutting the door behind them.

He'd successfully launched the Pierces into the backyard fray and returned to the kitchen to look for Harlow—when the doorbell rang again. As far as he remembered, they weren't expecting anyone else. Harlow emerged from the bedroom hallway, looking like she'd refreshed her hair and makeup.

"Are we missing anyone?" she asked.

"Not that I know of," said Decker, extending a hand to her. "Want to see who it is?"

"Probably Special Agent Reeves," said Harlow. "He has a knack for showing up at odd times."

"I like Joe, but his presence might be a bit of a buzzkill for this group," said Decker.

"Just slightly," said Harlow.

Decker opened the door to see Senator Margaret Steele holding a bottle of wine in one hand and a set of car key fobs attached to a colorful array of curly ribbons in the other.

"There's no way I would miss this," said Steele, stepping in to give him a hug. "Sorry for the surprise, but Harlow made me promise I wouldn't say anything."

"This is a very pleasant surprise," said Decker, taking the bottle of wine so she could hug Harlow more easily.

Across the street, he spotted a serious-looking woman standing next to the senator's black town car with her arms folded.

"Your security officer is more than welcome as well. She looks like she'd fit right in with the crowd inside."

"Oh. I'm not going to stay for too long," said Steele. "I'm pretty much crashing your party."

"You were invited," said Decker.

"I know. But I want everyone to be able to relax," said Steele. "People have a hard time unwinding around me sometimes."

"You stay as long as you'd like, Senator. Everyone in here will be thrilled to have you," said Harlow, before nodding toward Steele's car. "And get her inside, too. I won't be able to relax knowing she's standing around by herself. Unless she'd rather not for professional reasons."

"Caz isn't like that. For a stone-cold field operator, she's about as down to earth as anyone I've ever met," said Steele, motioning for her to join them.

"And those keys you're conveniently not talking about?" said Decker.

"These," said Steele, dangling them in front of him. "Riley's birthday present."

Decker raised an eyebrow. "She already has a driver."

"Oh, for crying out loud, Ryan. When Harlow told me that you drive Riley back and forth from school every day, I knew someone had to intervene. She's seventeen years old and a junior in high school."

"Given everything she's been through—" started Decker.

"She needs to feel normal. Period," said Steele. "Normal kids her age might not get BMW convertibles for their seventeenth birthday, but she needs some space."

"Pretty much every kid that lives up here gets something like that for their birthday," said Harlow.

"See. Normal. Her new car is parked on the street. I had it dropped off," said Steele. "Trust me on this. The past will always be there, but the more the two of you look forward, the better chance you'll have of escaping its very dense gravity. I've embraced the future, which has eased the past's grip over me."

Decker gave her another hug, fighting back tears. When he'd finally composed himself, he showed her to the living room. A few steps down the hallway, Steele turned to him.

"And speaking of the future," she said, "congratulations on your engagement. That's a big part of why I'm here. I couldn't imagine not passing that along in person. If you're in the market for a used helicopter, consider that your engagement gift. If not, have Bernie make me a below-market offer, and I'll send you whatever we settle on. I have no foreseeable use for a helicopter. Right, Caz?"

"APEX seems to be toeing the line," Caz said, cracking a smile.

"More like standing several feet back from it," said Steele.

The APEX Institute had disappeared from the scene immediately after the events of last June, resurfacing a few months later with little of its original Beltway clout. While the damage they had inflicted on APEX had been catastrophic, the Institute hadn't completely imploded as they had hoped. Instead, it had returned to its roots as a formidable think tank—with the rot carved out and new leadership at the helm.

Samuel Quinn had died a week after Steele delivered her ultimatum, his fifty-four-year-old, seemingly healthy heart expiring without explanation while he slept in his Georgetown home. Ezra Dalton had broken her neck three days after that while getting out of bed at night to use the bathroom, in the psychiatric hospital she had been taken to the night of the drone attack on APEX.

Harold Abbott and Allan Kline had retired, or gone into hiding, depending on who you asked. The Institute's failure to deliver on that fiscal year's "dark budget" funding had put them at the top of the Beltway's persona non grata list. Steele had learned all these details from Vernon Franklin, APEX's new senior board director, who had promised her in person that the past was truly behind them.

"I'll reach out to Bernie on Monday," said Decker. "That's very generous of you. And completely unnecessary."

"Too generous," said Harlow.

"There's no such thing as unnecessary or too generous when it comes to the two of you," said Steele. "So. Where's the birthday girl?"

A half hour later, Decker stood just inside the open slider, sipping a beer and taking in the bustling party. No deep thoughts or big observations. Just enjoying it for exactly what it was—entirely normal. Harlow sneaked up behind him from the kitchen and took his arm without saying a word. She put her head on his shoulder and quietly watched with him. Their journey to arrive in this backyard at this point in time had been an epic struggle against the odds, but here they stood, surrounded by the only things that truly mattered. Family and friends.

Nothing would ever take this from him again.

ACKNOWLEDGMENTS

I'll try to keep this short, not that there was any shortage of help creating the fourth and final book in the Ryan Decker series. Final for now. You never know when Ryan, Harlow, and their motley crew may show up again.

Thank you to my family for putting up with "deadline Steve" again. I had the best intention of starting *Skystorm* full throttle in January—then a little news story out of China caught my eye. And kept my attention for a little too long. I told them it would be different for the next book, and they believed it. Seriously. I couldn't do this without their support, with or without a pandemic.

An even bigger thank-you to my wife, who read the first draft on a compressed schedule due to the pandemic and not my time mismanagement. See what I did there? She reads along and nudges me in the right direction before I get too far off track, which has pulled me from the brink of character and plotline disaster more times than I can remember. Somehow, she remembers all of them, twenty novels later.

To the editorial team at Thomas & Mercer for the incredible success of the Ryan Decker series. They've put an incredible amount of talent and energy behind this author's career. Megha. A huge thank-you for steering each book, and the entire series, in the absolute right direction. I'm beyond excited about our next project!

Kevin. It was a pleasure working with you on the series. I especially appreciate you giving me the green light to write a few more action-oriented scenes for *Skystorm*. I had left some room for "breather" chapters for readers, and Kevin talked me out of it. You can blame him if this keeps you up all night. Look forward to working with you again.

To the Mountainside crew for the camaraderie, insightful observations, and invaluable guidance. BoJack in particular. Can't wait to get together post-pandemic.

To my advance reader team. I've enjoyed sharing sneak peeks, cover reveals, and advance copies with you. Thank you for the candid feedback and getting the word out!

Finally, to the readers. I know I say this every time, but without you—none of this would be possible.

ABOUT THE AUTHOR

Steven Konkoly is a *Wall Street Journal* and *USA Today* bestselling author, a graduate of the US Naval Academy, and a veteran of several regular and elite US Navy and Marine Corps units. He has brought his in-depth military experience to bear in his fiction, which includes *The Rescue*, *The Raid*, and *The Mountain* in the Ryan Decker series; the speculative postapocalyptic thrillers *The Jakarta Pandemic* and *The Perseid Collapse*; the Fractured State series; and the Zulu Virus Chronicles. Konkoly lives in central Indiana with his family. For more information, visit www.stevenkonkoly.com.